Praise for SA

"A novel that was any[...] an especially disappoi[...] *Noumenon*, but Lostetter has achieved that and much more. . . . Sci-fi action and adventure held together by universally human themes; this is the genre at its very best."

—*Kirkus Reviews* (starred review)

"The ambitious and effective sequel to *Noumenon*. . . . Lostetter remains at the forefront of innovation in hard science fiction."

—*Publishers Weekly* (starred review)

"Lostetter delivers another feast for fans of hard science fiction."

—Booklist

"A tight, compelling sequel. . . . Lostetter's characters persevere and evolve, creating a compelling portrait that feels, at its heart, ultimately both human and galactic in scope."

—Strange Horizons

"Travel to the remotest reaches of deep space in this wondrous follow-up to the acclaimed *Noumenon*—a tale of exploration, adventure, science, and humanity with the sweep and intelligence of the works of Arthur C. Clarke, Neal Stephenson, and Octavia Butler."

—Open Book Society

"*Noumenon Infinity* by Marina J. Lostetter is an excellent space opera focused on beautiful character details and grand ideas on the biggest stage possible. Highly recommended."

—Primmlife

"Lostetter expertly balances the thrill of discovery with the interpersonal consequences of an isolated community. The tools of speculative fiction are deployed with heart-rending attention to emotional reality in this enthralling odyssey. A striking adventure story that could hold a galaxy in its scope."

—*Kirkus Reviews* (starred review)

"[An] ambitious and stunning debut . . . Lostetter handles a complex and fractured narrative masterfully, never allowing her novel to become confusing or unconvincing. There are no easy answers to the book's questions, but the lingering sense of wonder and discovery thoroughly justifies its title."

—*Publishers Weekly* (starred review)

"*Noumenon* is a grand interstellar quest that marries intimate detail with the sweep of social change and discovery across generations. I was enthralled."

—Yoon Ha Lee, author of *Ninefox Gambit*

NOUMENON ULTRA

ALSO BY MARINA J. LOSTETTER

Noumenon

Noumenon Infinity

NOUMENON ULTRA

MARINA J. LOSTETTER

HARPER Voyager
An Imprint of HarperCollinsPublishers

HarperCollins books may be purchased for educational, business, or sales promotional use. For information, please email the Special Markets Department at SPsales@harpercollins.com.

Harper Voyager and design are trademarks of HarperCollins Publishers LLC.

FIRST EDITION

Designed by Paula Russell Szafranski
Frontispiece © by janez volmajer / Shutterstock, Inc.

Library of Congress Cataloging-in-Publication Data has been applied for.

ISBN 978-0-06-289572-1

20 21 22 23 24 LSC 10 9 8 7 6 5 4 3 2 1

For the odd ones out.

For those marching to the beat of their own drum.

You bring a new, unique perspective to the world.

We need you.

And for Alex: my heart, my hearth,

my hope when things seem bleakest.

CONTENTS

Part Two: Resplendence

NOUMENON
ULTRA

The Missions Thus Far

In the late twenty-first century, "subdimensions" were discovered, which allowed for new, relativistic travel that bypassed the constraints of light speed by "diving" into a pocket of alternate physics. This, along with prevailing peace and stability across the globe, paved the way for the Planet United Consortium—a space-focused scientific conglomerate featuring contributions from nearly every country on Earth. They developed the Planet United Missions: twelve deep-space convoys, each with separate scientific goals. The majority of these convoys were crewed by clones.

Each mission had its own quirks and unique configurations. This is the story of two of those convoys.

Convoy Seven: The only convoy with an interactive, personality-driven AI, known as I.C.C. (the Inter Convoy Computer), connected throughout the ships. Seven focused on a strobing, far-off star, and whether or not its unusual behavior was due to an alien construct nearby. No extraterrestrial life of any kind had been confirmed prior to the convoy's launch.

Convoy Twelve: The littlest convoy, which was to remain closest to home. Its crew consisted both of clones grown for the P.U.M.s, and of nonclone, Earth-based personnel. Its mission was to further study the subdimensions, looking for more efficient means of travel.

Convoy Seven found its alien construct, dubbed "the Web." They assumed it to be an incomplete Dyson Sphere, meant to slowly siphon energy from the star. Part of the convoy set out to finish construction and activate the device. Another part split off, becoming Convoy Seven-Point-Five, mission name *Noumenon Ultra*, to seek out information regarding the Nataré: the alien civilization to have most recently worked on the Web (though not the megastructure's inventors).

Convoy Twelve was the victim of a subdimensional accident that launched it into an unknown SD, which propelled portions of the convoy approximately fifteen kiloparsecs away from Earth. It took them only a moment to traverse the distance, but over one hundred thousand years passed on the home planet. When they reemerged in normal space, they encountered what they assumed to be an advanced alien convoy.

Both missions' assumptions were wrong.

Once activated, the Web began traveling from star to star, consuming each before moving on to the next. Convoy Seven now believed it to be a weapon, and when Convoy Seven-Point-Five returned with reports of several other star-sized megastructures and knowledge of an ancient interstellar war, their theory appeared confirmed. Rejoined, both halves of the convoy set out to annihilate the very thing they'd built.

A last-minute decision by one intrepid captain—with help from the AI—prevented the machine's destruction, allowing the Web to finally reveal its purpose: that it was not a device bent on devastation, but creation. It used the materials gathered from the stars to build a life-supporting solar system. Convoy Seven named one of the system's planets after its original mission: Noumenon.

Convoy Twelve, with no knowledge of what Convoy Seven had discovered—being now many tens of thousands of years removed from those events—was shocked to discover not only varied versions of intelligent life-forms, but also a construction field of star-sized devices.

The convoy's interactions with the life-forms, which they named the *Lùhng*, were strained, bordering on hostile. After their accident, Convoy Twelve needed vital support to sustain itself; the life-forms offered minimal aid, and barely any communication. The Convoy Twelve crew members were left bewildered. After all, they'd never envisioned aliens having an attitude of mild disinterest in a first-contact scenario.

It wasn't until an away team retrieved a sampling of *Lùhng* DNA that they discovered their assumptions and framing of the situation were all wrong. This was not first contact.

It was a homecoming.

Humanity had greatly evolved over the thousands and thousands of years they'd missed. Bio- and mechanical engineering had transformed the human as well as the human experience.

The beings the Convoy Twelve crew had thought alien were in fact the descendants of Convoy Seven. And what they'd interpreted as disinterest was actually caution—awareness of a delicate situation. From the *Lùhng* perspective, the Convoy Twelve crew were ancient—remnants of humanity's past, in form and in understanding.

And yet, there were strange evolutions aboard Convoy Twelve as well. The accident that launched them across the galaxy and into their future left them with other ailments: a single baby who'd never awoken, who was perpetually an infant even after fourteen years; a woman out of time, who jumped in and out of an unknown SD without a bubble whenever her sense of anticipation mounted; and convoy-wide infertility, meaning not only were they relics of ancient humanity, they were also the last of their lines.

But all was not lost. The future may be strange, but it had a place for them. The discovery of dozens of alien megastructures throughout the galaxy had spawned new endeavors, new human civilizations, and new religions, as many post-humans labored toward uncovering the overarching purpose of these giant artifacts.

The *Lùhng* turned over the fate of Convoy Twelve to a reli- gious leader, the Progentor, who the crew were shocked to discover was a modified clone of a man they'd known—I.C.C.'s inventor, Jamal Kaeden. He told them of a place their prospects could brighten, a planet where the schematics of ancient human genes were housed, a place where they might find the proper tools and information to develop cures for their new ailments.

Noumenon.

■ ■ ■

And so a small group boarded the Progentor's ship and set off for this megastructure-created planet, ready to take their next steps toward a new day.

But the past has a way of making itself relevant again. Long-forgotten events and tidbits of information—minor footnotes at the time—prove to have great significance. People face losing themselves when they lose their history and forget the things they've seen along the way.

The discoveries made by *Noumenon Ultra* continue to rever-berate down through the ages. What the small branch-convoy found those millennia ago may still have bearing on the measures of tomorrow.

PART ONE
Reliance

IVAN: MAD WORLD

Aboard Convoy Seven-Point-Five. Mission Title: *Noumenon Ultra*

Prior to the Activation of the Web

"Ivan. Ivan!"

Ivan only vaguely recalled that his name was Ivan. In the dream, his name was a sense of reach, of mental touch by another dreamer. He'd been told his name—the word, the letters, the sounds of it—when he'd first joined the dream. Only a few weeks out of the tank.

Cloning tank to dreamer. One womb to the next.

He'd been studying Nataré records just now, while letting an emotive symphony swell through him, reading a book that two other dreamers were currently writing and rewriting in real time as he read, and allowing the sensation of soft kittens to travel over his fingers. He liked blue, and all of his world was blue today.

But there was that annoying sound again. One he heard with his ears, not in the dream. Was today . . . ? No, it couldn't be. Not yet.

Had his time to be caretaker come already?

Why hadn't the current caretaker come to him in the collective? Why hadn't they prepared him in the dream?

"Ivan!"

His limbs convulsed. His real limbs—the ones attached to his actual *body*.

Everything tightened, everything pulled. All his muscles contracted at once. He could sense his skin stretching around the anchor bolts that kept the exoskeleton screwed solidly to his bones. Things twisted—his *spine* twisted. He wasn't supposed to be able to feel his spine.

His eyes *opened*.

Air, he could feel the air on his eyeballs and it was unnatural.

It was dark all around—thank the ships for small favors—but there was a shape right in front of him. Too close. It was blurry and pale. Everything was blurry, he realized. His eyes hadn't tried to focus for years.

Taking stock of what he could, he noticed he was standing, his exoskeleton held upright by the hydraulics and wires attached to tracks in the ceiling. There were other figures nearby, as they should be. Their bodies played out scenes here in meat-space, letting their muscles work, their bones and organs experiencing some level of stress. It helped keep them healthy on the inside, which was all that mattered.

Last time he'd had his eyes open he'd been in a group of other children, their exoskeletons playing a wires-and-tubing friendly version of leap-frog. A group of autons had settled him into place, their robotic faces blank but their touch gentle—they were consciously guided by other dreamers, of course. The crew still had to perform in the "real world," and they did it through these extensions—how else could they obtain samples and records when they visited new locations on the Nataré map? But all the intellectual work was done in the dream.

The autons had been transferring him into his adult exoskeleton that day. The last exoskeleton he'd ever need.

At some point in his life he'd been transferred out of his first small exoskeleton into his toddler exoskeleton, and then into increasingly larger ones to fit his growing form. He had teetered on the edge of awakeness each time, but had never fully reached it, and he couldn't remember most of the configurations of the crew around him, what mime of a task they'd been performing. Though the dream made memories clearer, he had trouble settling on which memories were his. The dream was collective, the dream was all, and the younger he was when a memory was formed, the more like everyone else's memories it seemed.

Ivan wasn't sure how old he was now—fully grown, though, for certain. He'd been able to do three lifetimes' worth of professional study so far in the dream. That was why the crew had given up meat-space, after all. The dream made so much more possible.

Fully grown and fully capable. And now he had to face a responsibility he'd always dreaded.

"Ivan!" said the pale shape again.

"I think you are supposed to call me Doctor Baraka," he tried to say. Tried. But his mouth had never fully formed words before, and his tongue was underdeveloped and clumsy.

"Don'a try to speak, not yet," said the shape. There was a sharp creak as the shape moved. Hands came up to Ivan's face, drew back his lips, looked at his teeth. "Not a grinda, good."

I'm not supposed to be awake yet, not for another year in real time at least, Ivan tried to say with his expression. But his face felt stiff, skin too taut. *Why not come to me in the dream first? Why am I awake?*

"You'a confused," the shape said. Slowly, Ivan's eyes were adjusting. He could see the outline of a face now. He might see more, if the person backed up. They were so close his eyes nearly crossed trying to focus. "I see . . . I see the confusion. But I couldn't inside. Inside everyone knows all at once. I needed . . . need just one. One first, then the others."

The figure made a gesture with one arm—a movement too fast for the automated system. This person was in full control of their own exoskeleton. They had to be the current caretaker, Hilaria Neciosup, but what she was saying made no sense.

Or was that just because Ivan wasn't used to words?

Ivan's body *lurched*. His exoskeleton lifted off the floor, the entire weight of it suspended from the ceiling.

The *clack clack clack* of wheels turning over followed him as the system carried him off, through the darkened husk of the ship. "Where—?" he tried to ask, but she was gone, left behind by the pulleys.

The wires pulled him higher, so that he could fly above the clusters of his crewmates. Those he'd been with had been posed playing a game of some kind. The pieces were nonexistent—as it was only the movements that were important, not the items—so it had been impossible to tell which. Now he wound through people casually leaning against a bar, as though having drinks at a party. Two individuals were wrestling, another group playing some kind of team sport. There—babies! A group of adults, surrounded by the autons they controlled, held them close. The autons were in constant motion, seeing to the infants' real-world needs, while the crew members' bodies provided all-important human contact.

The darkness allowed his weak eyes to take in shapes and silhouettes, along with minimal definition, without being injured. Nutrients that were typically synthesized via light exposure were pumped in through one of the various IVs stuck throughout his body. But still, everything about this—outside the dream—was alien. In the dream, things were only quiet when you wanted them to be. Everything was brightness, action, socialization, learning, progress. Nothing stilled unless you asked it to. There was no aloneness unless you sought it.

And the scents of the dream—vibrant, always pleasant. Here everything smelled of . . . nothing. A constant scent so familiar to his olfactory senses that his nose no longer properly registered the smell.

Ivan was fairly sure he'd never experienced true darkness— not like this. The dream allowed them to rest different parts of their brains at different times, so as long as he was hooked up, he was never truly unconscious. It was a dream, but it was not sleep.

He swept up staircases, down hallways, seeing the ship in its totality for the first time. *Shambhala*'s schematics were in the dream, and he'd glanced at them at some point in his early life, but it was a strange abstraction. A map of the galaxy was more meaningful to his mind, had more spatial references to his experienced reality, than the map of the ship he'd inhabited his entire life.

The track twisted, the wires descended, dropping him heavily in front of a massive window. A real window, not a monitor or a carefully directed reflection. And, for the first time, he felt vertigo.

Space. So much space, so much distance. If he leaned forward, he imagined he could fall into it, hang there in zero-g, over the bottomless pit of the universe. He felt so large in the dream, so centered, but here . . . here he was insignificant.

He felt even smaller when a great loop of matter swung into view, and he realized the ships were in orbit around . . .

By the ships. What is that?

Before he was born, Seven-Point-Five had found several megastructures, including one they'd called the Void. It had solid sides, and was hollow, in sort of diametric opposition to the net-like structure of the Web, which embraced LQ Pyxidis.

But this—this was nothing like either. This was perverse. This was worlds gone wrong.

Convoy Seven-Point-Five was in orbit around one half of a binary system of planets. Only *binary* typically described two bodies tethered by gravity, and these two were tethered by something else entirely.

It was as though they had been harpooned—skewered together by a violent thrust.

A structure at least two astronomical units long—if it was, indeed, a single structure and not many—protruded from both.

The smaller planet—the one closer to the system's parent star—trailed a long length of the structure. The construct was as thin as it was long, perhaps a few hundred kilometers in diameter, and it stuck out of one side of the small rocky planet like a thread. That thread passed through the near center of the globe, bursting out the other side before connecting with the larger rocky planet. Here, though, it looped through the land, coiling upward in great arcs, as though tangled in the planet's innards.

Ivan was reminded of the Cordyceps fungi, which parasitically grew in, and burst out of, insects. That's what this structure looked like, a parasitic abomination—a giant worm—speared through the two planets, shackling them together.

The planets themselves looked dead, with no tectonic activity. Wisps of atmosphere clung to their surfaces, a visible portion winding its way up the protruding bits of structure, where it was either siphoned off by the star, or evaporated into the cold of space.

These planets had clearly been killed by this . . . this *thing*.

Maybe it's unrelated to our megastructures, he thought.

But even as he hoped, he knew better. One of the tallest arcs on the larger planet swung beneath the window, and even though the ships were orbiting thousands of kilometers out, there was no mistaking the structural similarities between this long, wormy thread and portions of the Web.

This seemed to confirm their worst fears: that maybe the Web wasn't benevolent or even benign. There had been a war, they knew that already from records recovered at their other stops. But this was the first physical evidence they had of a structure interfering with a planet.

None of this information had been input into the dream yet. Without an Inter Convoy Computer to record things for them, they relied heavily on the one person who lived largely outside the dream to act as their reporter. Why hadn't the caretaker shared her initial findings?

"Do you see?" came a strained question from the darkness. Ivan tried to turn his head, but his exoskeleton held him rigidly in place.

"P-planets," he said, tongue stumbling.

"Not just. Comet, see the comet?"

Yes, a bright spot approaching the star. The star itself was dim, cold. Barely massive enough to have triggered fusion at its core. But the comet was strange—highly reflective, and with a slight tail, but not as spectacular as most icy bodies on a similar path. Perhaps the comet was old, and most of the ice had already been superheated away on previous encounters with the star.

"Spectrometry suggests organics," said Neciosup.

"Mean-ing?"

"Thinking life," she said. "Thinking not a comet at all."

"Craft?"

"Too small. Not much bigger than personal shower stall. Similar cubic space." They'd passed by the old gym showers on the way here—each unit had been converted into a terrarium. He wondered now if that had been Neciosup's doing, or one of her predecessors.

"Why not enter dream?" he asked, throat hoarse, tongue still sluggish. He decided to forgo unnecessary words, not strain the muscles of his mouth any more than need be.

"Why not dream?" he demanded again when she didn't answer right away. There, what she saw would become what they all saw. She would make a dream of this for the crew, and they would know it together. "Why wake me?"

She came up beside him. He felt her presence more than saw her, the bulk of his exoskeleton in the way.

"One: confirmation," she said. "Reality . . ." She stopped and sighed, like whatever she was about to explain was too much. "In dream, we know all is dream. Out here, in reality, not sure all is real. Id'na clear." She swallowed thickly. "I see things. Sometimes. Alone, the mind tries to dream."

Hallucinations. Neciosup wasn't sure she was really seeing these planets, this comet, those spectrometry results. The dreamers wouldn't be able to immediately verify, because she would be the sole source. All the data filtered through her perception.

"Two: aid. These organics, not precedented. Could be danger. Can'ta risk only one awake during retrieval of comet."

That made some sense, except she still should have informed everyone first. They always used the autons to perform physical studies, for retrieving samples, for spacewalks and surface scouting. No crew members ever physically left their designated ships. But if she was worried about bringing samples aboard, that something might threaten her watch, then he could understand waking him early as a necessity. But it should have been decided on by the entire crew, not at her whim.

"Comet confirmed," he said, then asked, in his halting way, where her extensions were.

"Two en route," she said. "Will make contact shortly."

Ah. Perhaps that was why she'd awoken him here, now . . . impulsively.

If she had two autons already on their way—nearly there— that meant she had to have dropped relay buoys throughout the system. Autons, despite their name, were not autonomous. They needed interfacing with a human puppeteer. And presuming she'd launched them from orbit around the binary system, it would still take them time to get there— weeks, at least, if his guestimate of the distance was anywhere near correct.

"How l-ong here? In system?"

She hesitated. ". . . Six months."

His body drooped in shock, pulling on the metal pins, sinking despite the exoskeleton. "Six months?" Six months and no report. Six months and she'd been doing *what*?

He should have known, they all should have. But time was different in the dream. Everything was always and never. Breakfast didn't always come before dinner. Sometimes an instrument existed before it was invented—because a dream is ideas and ideas always come before the actual. Everyone simply trusted that the linear quality of reality was being watched over, that information was flowing to them from the outside as it should.

"Been working," she said quickly. "Yup yup, lots of work. But this, it's all too much. Clear evidence of weapon." She pointed at the planets, the red and black of her exoskeleton sweeping past his peripheral. "Clear evidence of bio." She pointed at the comet, then paused, fingers unfurling as though slowly letting a sprinkling of something—sand or petals—fall to the ground. "Have arrived," she said, awestruck. Her autons were informing her via implants.

"Can see?" he asked.

"Yes. Come come. Small delay, of course. Small delays."

The wires started to lift him again. "Wait. Move . . . myself?"

"Think you can?" she asked, smugly. "Full control yours."

She hadn't released the wires, but they went slack. Focusing on just his legs, he willed them and the contraption forward. The exoskeleton promptly fell over. He shouted in surprise as the floor rushed toward his face.

She did something—pressed a button perhaps—and the tethers tightened at the last moment, keeping Ivan from plowing his nose into the decking.

"Takes time," she said gently, as the wires respooled, pulling him up. "I'll teach, don'a worry."

As the metal bulk was hauled upright, he found himself face-to-face with her once more. But his eyes were clear now, and he could make out her features, see her for real.

Appearances were different in the dream, mostly because seeing people was not something required to interact with them. Facial expressions were less important than direct emotive expressions. Sometimes people felt like rhinoceroses, so they seemed like rhinoceroses, even if they didn't literally project a rhinoceros into anyone's mind. Or puppies, or snake plants, or differential equations, or Penrose stairs.

But out here, you were what you were.

Neciosup wasn't just lack-of-light pale. She was albino pale—hair white because it was technically clear, eyes like thin water, lashes like snow. Her original had been Peruvian, he recalled from the manifest records. His original had been Turkish. He looked at his own hands, which, in his mind, should have been a robust deep-bronze, but here looked a softer tan.

They were what they were.

And yet, it felt less tangible. In the dream, one was obviously, inescapably greater than the sum of their parts. Out here, he felt shrunken. Slight.

As for Neciosup, he couldn't feel her many mental aspects, and so she seemed flattened—two dimensional. Less real.

All of this felt less real.

"Come," she said gently. "To the monitors."

She took him now to her command post. It wasn't the bridge—where he'd always suspected the caretaker was set—but the old server room. Though smaller than the server room on Convoy Seven's *Mira*, it still had plenty of computer banks, now actively working to keep the human crew healthy and in the dream world. Most of the computing power, however, came directly from the network of interconnected human brains.

The room smelled different from the rest of the ship, and it took him a moment to recognize it as the scent of astringents and antiseptics. It had been recently cleaned, scrubbed new—perhaps in anticipation of his waking.

A bank of three monitors made a half circle over the top of a workbench. The bench itself was covered in small round objects of dubious origin. It wasn't until she put one in his hand that he realized what they were. "Is this gourd?"

"*Mate burilado*," she said. "Hobby. Ancient tradition. Look. Tells stories."

He rolled the gourd over in his hand to reveal intricate carvings. This one had galactic swirls converging around a—"Llama?"

"Convoy Seven has real animal," she said wistfully. "You, too, will find hobby."

She closed her eyes for a moment, likely focusing in on her autons. With a flick of the wrist, she turned on the monitors, letting him see what she saw, through the puppet's sensors.

The two extensions were in a capsule, one specially designed for transport and retrieval of an individual's flight of autons. Most people could manage only a handful at a time—auton use was taxing, even for dreamers. The capsule was slightly smaller overall than the average shuttle, with compartments imbedded into the walls, molded to fit auton forms—humanoid and armored. There were four compartments in this capsule; two were currently empty. The center of the capsule was storage only—sometimes used for taking equipment to an archaeological site, sometimes used for bringing back samples and artifacts.

"Is big enough?" he asked.

"Comet s'not large, remember?" she said. "Capsule matching spin."

As he watched, the top of the capsules unfurled, like the rear portions of some of their shuttles, creating a wide, flexible, open maw for receiving the object.

Blips of stars and flashes of sunlight revealed the object's tumble—which was strange to watch, given that the capsule was following its tumble perfectly. The two objects looked still, like it was the rest of the universe that had gone off its axis.

Dark ice covered most of the comet, which was small for an object with its behavioral patterns.

The capsule moved forward slowly, capturing the object. As soon as it was fully engulfed, internal airbags deployed, covering everything in inflated whiteness. Presumably the capsule then began to reorient itself.

The airbags weren't simply filled with air, but also an organic fiber that would puff up and shred, slowing the object, stilling it inside its temporary home. There was a great, violent vibration throughout the capsule as the kinetic forces were redirected, as the comet was nestled as gently as possible into the grips of the human craft.

Ivan stood quietly by, watching Neciosup work. Soon she began directing the autons to disperse the bags and the fibers, to burrow their way in toward the new treasure. Her arms were outstretched, twitching as she did her work.

The ice had already begun to melt, dampening the fibers, dissolving them into nothing, as was their design. Bits and pieces flew past the autons' cameras like stringy snow. There were no graviton cyclers aboard the capsules, and everything hovered, unmoored.

Using their hands, Neciosup scraped chunks of dirty ice and blobs of fibrous goo away from the object, excavating it like a child digging through sand at the beach. She was right—the distance between the relays did mean there was a slight delay between her actions and their reactions. But, slowly, the "comet" was revealed.

The object beneath the fibers was coppery, with the telltale intertwined mesh design that they'd seen in the majority of Nataré creations. A seemingly random weave of metal, forming a casing—like a bird's nest. The very design for which the first Nataré ship they'd found was named.

They'd followed a Nataré map here, so it wasn't odd to find a Nataré object. But the spectrometry had suggested organics . . .

The object rotated in zero-g, revealing its backside to one auton's cameras. This side wasn't encapsulated in copper. This was clear, like resin. And trapped inside that resin . . . a creature. Clear as day.

"By th'ships," whispered Neciosup.

"Alive?" Ivan blurted.

"No. Still. Too still. Body."

"Look, look, look, look." His tongue garbled the directive, but he didn't care. He leaned forward, trying to point, and the exoskeleton only heeded him a little.

On the inside of the copper shell, as seen through the other side, past the difficult-to-decipher corpse, behind it, almost like a halo, was an etching. A picture. "Do see? Do see?" he demanded.

Unmistakably, their Web. And, unmistakably, a Nataré ship attacking it, blasting a hole in it.

Was this some ancient Nataré general? A leader, at least? Were they responsible for the state of the Web as Convoy Seven had first found it?

"The dream!" Ivan said. Everyone had to know, now. This was . . . this was bad. This was proof, wasn't it? Of everything they'd feared. They knew by now that there'd been a war, that the megastructures were involved in some way. But this etching, these planets . . .

Was the Web a monster? They needed to send a message to Convoy Seven, advise them to stop construction—presuming they'd actually begun what they'd set out to do when the convoys split—give them everything *Noumenon Ultra* had found and ask them to wait, please, please, until they'd more thoroughly examined their findings.

"Put me back in dream," he said, as quickly as he could make his mouth work. "I will tell all. I will report, crew will discuss. Wake again in weeks when autons return—"

"No! Please," she shouted, grabbing his exoskeleton, manually tugging it toward her, as though the dream were a physical place he could run to. "Not yet. Stay, please . . ."

He was not adept at reading facial expressions. None of them were. That was no longer a skill they required for social stability. But it was impossible not to recognize anguish. Deep, deep fear of pain, of . . . of something else.

"One: confirmation," he said gently, reminding her of her reasons from earlier. "Two: aid. Three . . . ?"

Her eyes watered. Tears. After a long few moments she spoke again. "Three: loneliness," she said softly, a confession. "Can'a'n'a take it. Not now. No more."

She was only allowed an hour in the dream every day. Any more and she risked slipping under, unable to pull herself out. Twenty-three hours out of every cycle she was alone, isolated. One hour in the dream could be stretched into days or compressed into seconds depending on what one did. How long did the memory transference take? Were moments all she experienced before being booted out again?

She was isolated, cut off from the dream. They shared more deeply than any human society before them, and she had been pulled from that, just as he had, to do her duty. She'd performed it for years, by herself, more isolated than any human should have been expected to be.

Before the convoy split, each job had a cycle partner. Not just so a clone would not be expected to train their own line, but because individuals needed support. They needed someone else. They needed companions. They hadn't thought it necessary, here, now. They thought the brief connections to the dream were enough.

They were wrong.

He thought about the two planets, strung together on an alien cord. Connected in death. Both destroyed. If he stayed with her, would they both feel this way? He would miss the dream. He missed it *now*, with every fiber of his being. The constant connection, the closeness.

But there was no reason they couldn't share the burden. He was destined to take her place a year from now. He, too, would be alone.

"*You* go. Into dream," he said. "I wake you when autons return. Transfer control to me. Now."

She shook her head. "You can'n't even walk. How'd you survive?"

"Will stay here," he said, glancing at the gourd still in his hand. All of his physical needs would be taken care of as they always had, by the tubes and the IVs and the skeleton. It would be a new experience for his mind, this wakefulness, this aloneness. But he could endure. She'd done so all these years; he could now, for a few weeks.

He held out the gourd. "Will learn hobby," he said, lips automatically pulling back, smiling despite never using the expression before.

Her lips trembled, her tears flowed more freely. "Thank you," she whispered. "I d'n't deserve it, but thank you."

She went to an access panel and transferred all her permissions, including that of the autons currently in use. He flipped the input on one monitor to that of a hull camera, to show the binary planets.

After a brief goodbye Neciosup walked over to one corner, where several autons sat or stood, lifeless, awaiting his commands. "See you soon," she said.

"Not too soon," he said warmly.

As she closed her eyes and he settled in for a long watch, he took in the blank faceplates of the autons and wondered what it would be like if they had faces. If he and they could learn the old process of emoting together. She had her hobby, he could have his.

Carefully, he set the gourd down, and rearranged them all on one side of the workbench, leaving him an open space, a blank page.

He glanced between the planets and the capsule, worried about the past, scared for the future, but ready for the now. Ready to experience loneliness for the first time. Ready to give himself fully—truly, for the first time—to the needs of *Noumenon Ultra*.

■ ■ ■

The Planet United Consortium was formed to pursue Earth-wide interests in deep space. Each Planet United Mission is designed to further humanity's joint scientific understanding, its reach beyond the home planet, and to ensure the longevity of planet-wide cooperation . . .

I.C.C.: ALL THESE WORLDS ARE YOURS . . . EXCEPT . . .

. . . impromptu file countenance Markovian inheritance co-hesion refrigerate morphine parallax napkin inland Janeiro nameable yearbook hark denigrate . . .

. . .

. . .

. . .

What a long time, thought I.C.C., gibberish coalescing into consciousness. *How many centuries have I . . . ?*

The AI's servers groaned in inaudible bass frequencies as the computer tried to pull itself fully out of slumber. A familiar voice—that of Reggie Straifer the First—wafted through *Mira's* ancient halls. In some places it was tinny and faint—a slight echo, nothing more. I.C.C. searched for the source as various inputs came online. It was a video, a recording Reggie's Intelligent Personal Assistant, C, had made.

Not unusual. Convoy crew members reviewed this file often. It was a bit of hopeful remembrance, happy instructions from their mission's first leader. Except . . .

The crew. Where were they?

Where am I?

Not in space. On a planet.

The ground felt rough and ragged beneath its hulls—crushed by the weight of the ships. The atmosphere outside tingled with electricity, wind howled across the rocky landscape, and a pink-colored sky stretched above.

A ship was missing—no, three. Yes, it remembered now. The crew had left—where they'd gone it could not recall, wouldn't be able to until all its servers were up and running. But it thought they were all right. Yes, last it knew, the humans were all right. That made it feel warm deep in its processing components.

And sleep . . . I.C.C. had slept. A human woman had kissed its camera housing and bid it good-night. It had gone dormant, leaving its great body silent and stoic—like monoliths—in the mountains.

The mountains of Noumenon—that was the name the crew had given this new world.

Am I alone? I.C.C. reached out with its sensors. Why had that old video started playing?

Why had I.C.C. awoken?

Another recording started then. No visuals, just a voice.

"Fleet Admiral Joanna Straifer the Forty-Ninth, personal notes.

"The foundation has been laid. Now it's up to time and chance to see what becomes of these planets. The capsules may be programmed to open after so long, or after the presence of a self-replicating molecule chain is detected. One day they'll release their contents onto the new worlds."

Nanite repair units went scuttling away from a camera's lens as I.C.C. tilted it and focused. Looking, peering—

Everything was so dark.

"We may not know for epochs to come what this means for Earth," the recording went on, "but it means more than an ancient artifact floating around a star. It means extraterrestrial life may one day exist with us. I hope humans are still around when that time comes. If not, I hope our successors will appreciate neighbors. The system is close enough to easily travel to, and the conditions currently resemble early Earth, meaning the life will most likely be like ours at a fundamental level.

"We will remain in orbit to watch over these fledgling planets. The gravity of their star has added extra excitement to their crusts and cores—we've detected seismic activity. Once the ground settles we might even consider a permanent landing.

"I am overwhelmed by these events. I feel it now, the hope and anticipation and wonder I have been waiting to feel all my life. This is the way the original travelers must have felt. Perhaps even how the original Dr. Reggie Straifer felt when he first glimpsed LQ Pyx.

"Reggie had a vision. He wanted us to reach a star and learn its secret. We've done it. And what a secret it turned out to be.

"There was great purpose in this expedition. The life of this convoy has meant something.

"Reason is a fickle thing. Many cannot see their own purpose but for the time it takes their actions to have consequences. I think about the lives of my ancestors and what they have meant to the future. Life itself may have a greater purpose. I know the creation of *more* means something, though I can't say what. Maybe each civilization is a piece of the purpose, and when one affects another we are all closer to the greater meaning.

"I believe time will tell."

The recording cut out. Joanna's words echoed through the darkened corridors, touching portions of I.C.C. that hadn't heard a human voice in . . . how long?

I.C.C., do you dream? asked a shadow memory inside its data banks.

"Daydream," it replied at subaudible levels.

What do you daydream about?

"I don't like the idea of being empty, so I imagine . . . others."

The old camera—stiff with age, but preserved in working order by the nanites—rotated toward the monitor that had brought Reggie to life. Shapes loomed in front of the bright screen. At the whir of the camera's motor, they turned to face the timeworn aperture.

Dozens of dark, eager eyes stared into the lens.

At least, it assumed they were eyes—round like marbles, bulging and shiny. The protrusions they were attached to could have been heads. Were likely heads, if those were eyes. Sense organs tended to be as close to the brain as possible, so if those were eyes, then those could be heads. And if they were heads, then it was *likely* those were eyes. But if they could be proven to be eyes without a doubt, then . . .

The AI checked itself—it wasn't used to circular thinking, but right now its digital mind went round and round the concept of head and eyes and brains and eyes and sense organs and—

Why was its processing so sluggish?

How long have I been asleep?

What do you daydream about? came the old audio file's echo once more, from somewhere in memory.

"Perhaps I won't run down alone," it replied. "Perhaps I will be of use to the end."

Oh, I.C.C., chimed another voice, another recollection. *For one such as you, there never has to be an end.*

As the screen across from its camera went dark, falling into its own kind of sleep, the figures in the room faded, blending into the total darkness.

I.C.C. stretched out, searching for other inputs. It increased the volume on its microphones and tried to detect new chemical traces in the air. But much was still offline. Much had been dormant for so long . . . decades? Centuries? Millennia?

The chronometer wasn't responding yet. Difficult to be certain about *when* until it, too, was awake. Outside, the hull cameras swiveled toward the sky. Lightning crackled, clouds surged. The wind howled, but the wind always howled here—*that* the AI recalled clearly. It was still day, late day, but no stars visible yet. No way to see the stars through the clouds with the current limitations on its sensor relays.

It did its best to survey the ships within visual range. Those left—*Mira, Solidarity, Aesop, Hippocrates, Bottomless II, Morgan, Slicer, Shambhala,* and *Holwarda*—were scattered down the side of a mountain range, like toys dropped by a toddler. Once, they'd been carefully perched. *Hippocrates* was in the middle, only slightly up the mountain, so that the crew could have somewhat equal access in an emergency, no matter which ship they started on. *Holwarda* sat highest, with the best view of the terrain. Sometime during I.C.C.'s slumber the ridgeline beneath it had collapsed, and it was no longer visible from *Mira,* which sat lowest, on the flat plane. This vantage had given the crew the easiest access to the surrounding environments for daylong extravehicular activities.

I.C.C. reached for *Holwarda,* moved its consciousness there momentarily, though the process was difficult. Its primary servers were on *Mira,* and it felt as though its consciousness wanted to nest there, to turn it into a bunker for its awareness. It did not want to use its faraway eyes.

Sense organs are close to the brain to reduce reaction time. The same principle applied to its inputs and processors.

Everything was dark around *Holwarda.* Here and there, a little sliver of light, like a rip in a length of fabric . . .

And a weight. Such pressure.

It rotated an exterior camera—one with a long, angry crack in its lens—and bits of dust and pebbles rained down around it.

It's buried. Perhaps in the very landslide that toppled the ship from its survey point.

The artificial gravity had long been turned off, and what was once up had become down. The top decks were speared through by one sharp monolith, and some of the bottom decks had been breached by rubble—the hull plates buckling in several instances.

Though the convoy ships were primarily intended to deal with the vacuum of space and all its related hazards, they had also been designed to land on a planet. They just hadn't been built to withstand abuse from the landscape.

Flitting consciously from one ship to the next, like a butterfly afraid to alight on a flower for too long, the AI took stock of the rest of its body.

A crack had opened up beneath *Shambhala*, swallowing it into a crevice. Now, it hung above a dark abyss, turned on its side, straddling the perilous emptiness. Either the mountain would split further and the craft would eventually plunge, or the rocks would swell upward, back together, and crush the ship in the long run.

The rest of the convoy ships were more or less where they'd been left. Some had slid a distance or been carried off by geological forces, but they were functional and independent from the environment.

Zetta, Hvmnd, and *Eden* were gone.

This assessment took it 67.9238545 seconds. Painfully long for an AI used to sensing its entirety in a fraction of a nanosecond.

Its consciousness clawed its way back into the room with

the . . . what should it call them? Were they creatures who'd simply found their way in via a crack in its hull? Were they some kind of infestation? Visitors?

Was their presence benign? Benevolent? Malevolent?

It was too dark. It could not see them. It could not hear them. It could not detect any chemical outputs. Were they even still in the room? Was I.C.C. running so slowly that it had failed to notice they'd moved on?

Eyes. They had eyes.

How many eyes?

How many creatures?

Where had they come from?

Why were they here?

What were they doing now?

Contradictory algorithms surged through its processors, diving into its data banks to provide theories based on the scantest of previously gathered information. It felt the need to work faster, to think faster, to do everything faster.

It was certain, for the moment, that there were no humans aboard. What it had seen were *not* humans, no.

Although . . . the crew had begun to make modifications, before they left—

No. If they were humans, they would have initiated contact by now. They would have tried to communicate by now.

It needed more data. It needed more data this *instant*.

Realizing its only reliable input at the moment was visual, it turned on the lights. Not just in the room, either. Across the entirety of *Mira*, across all the remaining convoy in a giant flash of shared illumination.

But, without access to its full range of processors, it had failed to run the necessary risk assessment before acting.

Such a surge through an old, delicate system was *not* a good idea.

Bulbs blew. Whatever had been left unattended by the nanites over the years either burst, sizzled, or lay dead.

A warning light flashed in I.C.C.'s security protocol. Three small fires had erupted—one on *Halwarda* and two on *Shambhala*.

The entertainment ship's fire-suppressant system sputtered. It did its best, but much of the chemical reserves had seized, age having broken down the substance and turned it into useless, gelatinous blobs.

While the nanites took up the slack—rushing in a swarm to the fires, smothering them with a mass of their tiny bodies—I.C.C. tried to retrieve information on the half-life of the heptafluoropropane-based compound and its additives.

Holwarda's system didn't even try. Either the inversion of the ship in natural gravity confused the sensors, or the sensors were simply out of order. The fire was in a restroom, far from any of I.C.C.'s essential systems—which the nanites were specifically designed to repair—which meant it was taking them longer to respond to the larger threat.

The AI searched for its links to the cleaning bots. If they were still functional, maybe they could assist.

It connected to four in a supply closet—just around the corner from the restroom—and tried to move them. The rubber treads on one disintegrated instantly. The joints had all seized on another.

The materials were simply too old.

I.C.C. diverted more attention to getting the clock running. In most computer systems the clock was both simple and essential, and thus one of the first software programs activated during a reboot. Not so with I.C.C. Its main functionality did not require the same integration with a constant count—only a few of its conscious algorithms found the concept of time necessary, which was why it could determine how many seconds had passed from one minute to the next, but not what year it was. And the chronometer was far more precise, running calculations that took general relativity and subdimensional relativity into account.

Ten seconds later, I.C.C. had a be-legged bot up and clattering down the hall. The nanites were on their way from the other direction. The fire would be smothered before any irreparable damage occurred.

It took the AI three seconds more to pinpoint where the creatures had gone. Not far—out into the hall opposite the living quarters where they'd been watching the screen.

The sudden flood of light had clearly affected them, though I.C.C. had no point of reference from which to determine exactly what kind of effect. They might have been startled, or angered, or even invigorated.

Certainly, they were moving faster than they had been when it awoke. Less carefully.

Now that they were bathed in the glorious white light of *Mira*'s causeways, the AI had the opportunity to take stock of them while the rest of its functionality attempted to recover from the hibernation. Overall, they looked like what might result if one crossed a stegosaurus with a frog and a spider. They were similar in certain aspects to all—and yet none—of those things, and they came in two varieties.

There were six beings, four approximately the size of a Labrador retriever—weighing thirty-point-two-six to thirty-five-point-seven kilograms each if the pressure plates in the flooring were still working correctly—and two that were much larger and more complex.

The four of the six could be classified as either four- or eight-legged, depending on what school of morphology one adhered to. Four hip-or-shoulder equivalents led to elbow-or-knee equivalents that then branched out into two separate legs tipped with grasping feet. All eight of these lower limbs touched the decking, which meant the body was suspended from the elbows upward.

And what interesting bodies!

The color palette ranged from daisy yellow to patina green to reflective copper. Their skin had a wet-looking texture and was divoted and patterned in such a way that narrow, but deep grooves (like highly pronounced human fingerprints) formed spiraled variations all across it.

Taken in profile, the torso formed a perfect circle, with a low-hanging belly protected by copper-colored armor plating. The upper half of the circle was created by a fantastic bony crest.

The head and the terminus of the creatures were roughly the same shape and moved with independent articulation, so it was difficult to say whether what I.C.C. had identified as eyes were in fact the primary sense organs, or if the four stubby, tentacle-like feelers on the opposite end were akin to pedipalps on Earth species such as spiders.

The "eyes"—eight individual orbs—lined up vertically along the center of the "head," which had a teardrop shape that would imply a snout to a human. Four eyes ran up the top of the "snout" and four ran down the bottom, presumably giving it a field of view that encompassed more than one hundred and eighty degrees vertically.

On each side of its head was a small, cluster-like protuberance, as though a bundle of pebbles lay under the skin. These were matched by a protuberance at the top of the head, hinting at a sensory triangulation.

There was nothing identifiable as a mouth, nostrils, or gills on the four smaller creatures, and they moved quickly, using all surfaces available to them, but primarily the walls, as though verticality were most familiar.

The other two were massive in comparison, ninety-two-point-two-three kilograms and a whopping one-hundred-and-thirteen-point-three-seven kilograms, respectively. They were beefier looking, though they had the same overall structure with a crest and round body. There were distinct differences, though. Where the eyes ran down the center of the heads on the others, these two had a seam instead. Occasionally some kind of viscous substance dripped from the seam, sizzling as it hit the floor. I.C.C. presumed this a mouth, running vertically, with one eye at each corner, giving them only two.

The back legs were not bisected like the front. They were solid, like pillars, while the front had the same grasping capacities as the smaller creatures. And the terminus, instead of being a mirror image of the head, was formed of two rounded haunches.

The smaller of the two was more or less the size of a Sorraia mustang, and the other was more like a common hippopotamus. The difference in both size and weight was largely due to protuberances on the posterior of the largest creature, which the other lacked. Where there were simply fleshy-looking nubs on one, the other sprouted tall stalks topped with arms that moved as though with the articulation of a snake's spine, and each had grasping claws at the end. Both stalks had their own bony crests and a well-developed mimic-head. The stalks must have been some sort of evolutionary defense mechanism—but it was strange that one creature had them and the other did not.

Perhaps the smaller of the two was younger and had yet to develop the stalks? Or it might have lost them—through injury or shedding.

Though it couldn't be entirely sure, I.C.C. decided to work off the assumption that all six creatures were the same species. Phenotype variation was more common than not in

Earth life, and it was easier to formulate behavioral models if it ran off the hypothesis that the two types were working in tandem biologically and consciously.

It also reserved the right to change its modeling parameters at any time.

And while its visual observations were wonderfully clinical, it had much more complex questions for which it knew it would find no quick answers.

For instance, what were they doing here and where had they come from? Had it been asleep long enough for these life-forms to evolve on Noumenon?

Perhaps a million years have passed. Perhaps a hundred million.

Life would surely take less time to cover Noumenon than it had to cover Earth—it had been seeded here, after all. Quite literally, given the moniker assigned to the Web's largest device, the one that had, in the end, created this entire system—planets, sun, and all—before sending capsules filled with the basic building blocks of known life into the fresh seas.

All three of the rocky planets had received capsules. The gas giant had not. Noumenon was the third planet in the Philosopher's System, Thales being the lovely G-type star the Seed had created. It was slightly smaller than Sol, and all three rocky planets lay more or less within the zone considered habitable for terrestrial life. Epistēmē was the innermost planet, orbited by its lone moon Logos, then came Jzft orbited by Ma'at, then Noumenon orbited by Phenomenon. Kant was the gas giant—both a tribute and a slight, in I.C.C.'s perception. It had captured many small moons before I.C.C. had slept, all named after Earth philosophers like PtahHotep, Ibn Bâjja, and Xie Daoyun. The AI suspected it now had many more satellites without designation. Jzft and Ma'at had originally gone by other names, but within a few hundred years the planet's geology had proven unstable and it slipped back into a mostly molten state. What could have been a paradise became hellish. It spewed materials high, beyond its atmosphere. Materials that had settled on its moon, which had fogged and warmed further, creating a greenhouse next door.

I.C.C. wondered if any of Jzft's seeded materials had made it off-world, to Ma'at, where they might thrive.

Could there be life in multiple places in the Philosopher's System? For what purpose had the Web's original Builders wanted to create this system and its inhabitants?

Three minutes and twenty-eight seconds had passed since I.C.C. had become aware of its own regained consciousness. And now, finally, the chronometer provided it with a year.

Eighty thousand three hundred and sixty-eight of the common era.

I.C.C. had been hibernating for sixty-eight thousand and thirty-six years.

Which meant the planet Noumenon and its system had only been in existence for seventy-one thousand nine hundred and sixty-two years.

It zoomed in on the creatures once more, remembering what this planet and its two rocky siblings had been seeded with: RNA, tRNA, and materials with which to facilitate their replication.

It turned *Mira*'s hull cameras this way and that, surveying the land in more detail. Much of the surface was raw in the way one might expect of a young system. True, the planets had been built and cooled at miraculous rates, throwing the usual mechanics of planetary formation out the proverbial window. But certain things couldn't be rushed, not even by gigantic alien megastructures and the primordial knowledge they contained. Things like erosion and weathering.

As the mountains were divided between sharp crags of upheaval and piles of cooled lava, so, too, were the plains little more than barren, sheer surfaces. Some sand had formed, enough that the constant winds carried sharp bits of grit, and a few potholes had filled and widened, but not enough for even the smallest of dunes to form.

The seas had been hot when the convoy had first landed—not boiling, but near. This was good for the materials inside the pods, would aid replication—maybe even encourage *faster* replication, which was necessary for mutation and therein, evolution. The waters had cooled somewhat, if I.C.C.'s thermal imaging of the sea that lay forty-eight-point-six-two kilometers off *Mira's* starboard bow could be applied worldwide. But it was still warm, much warmer than an Earth sea, even given the extremes during the most intense global temperature rise, but still well suited for early forms of life.

And there *was* life. A deep red substance—something that visually looked like a cross between a coral and an algae—streaked the shorelines in long, blood-red fingers. Some of it clawed up the sides of boulders and outcroppings, drying in the late-day sun, waiting for the planet's moon to bring the tide to it once more.

And the wind might have carried grit into the camera lenses, but I.C.C. realized after a moment that it also carried something else. Small, light-pink particles that, upon closer inspection, were multicellular creatures, shaped a bit like a basic Earth virus, with long tails like spider silk that allowed them to be carried on the breeze, presumably from food source to food source.

So life had taken hold in these many many millennia past. And there *were* multicellular beings at least the size of a pinhead.

But there was no dirt or soil or anything to suggest generations upon generations of organic decomposition.

This made sense—everything was still young, still new. It had all gotten a head start, but, as a crew member had once said, Rome wasn't built in a day.

I.C.C. focused in once more on the six creatures scurrying and lumbering, respectively, away from the crew quarters and toward a wide-open lift shaft.

So where then had these come from?

There was no possible way the evolutionary timeline that had barely produced the algae and the tail-fliers had also created these massively complex life-forms.

Which meant they weren't native to Noumenon.

They'd come from another planet.

Did that mean they were intelligent on the order of human intelligence? That they'd come here in ships of their own?

The hull cameras on all the convoy ships swung wildly in tandem, searching the skies, the land, even the ocean, for signs of a craft.

A buzz of excitement and a flash of worry zinged between the AI's server banks. Intelligent aliens, alive! Did the humans know of them? Had they interacted before, or was I.C.C. the first Earth being these creatures had encountered?

Though the studies first begun by the *Noumenon Ultra* crew had continued once the convoy had landed here, they'd never discovered proof of living Nataré. They'd found more ships, more maps, more documents, more biological samples and cultural remnants, but never the living, conscious beings.

Were these, perhaps, in some way related to the Nataré?

They did not possess any of the basic calling cards of the Nataré. They did not appear to manipulate gravitons. They were not hairy, nor flat like starfish. But that alone meant little.

If I.C.C. could get a biological sample to the labs on *Holwarda* it could compare their genetic makeup to the Nataré samples to see if there was enough crossover to indicate a shared home world.

Unfortunately, its outer cameras failed to identify so much as a landing site for a craft, let alone a craft itself. Perhaps their ship was in orbit? The AI would continue to monitor the sky, just in case.

Perhaps launching a probe would be helpful, yes—that way it could investigate farther afield.

This thought was perfectly logical, very sound. A good choice.

It opened an exterior hatch, where the old investigative probes were stored. It would just use a small one, perhaps like the one they'd initially sent to the planemo where they found the first evidence of Nataré inhabitation.

The conveyor belts lurched to life at the AI's behest.

Though the belt created the smallest high-pitched screech, the creatures took note, their rows of eyes turning upward, either following the sounds or vibrations through the many layers of decking.

I.C.C. remotely activated the probe, and it lit up. Indicator lights dotted the exterior, and everything appeared to be functioning as it should.

Launch in three . . . two . . . one . . .

The conveyor belt revved into high speed, flinging the probe through the hatch, and out into—

Oh.

I.C.C. realized a moment too late that it had launched a probe meant for space into . . . *not* space.

As it sailed in an incredible arc across the pink sky, the probe began automatically unfurling its solar sails and kicking on its thrusters. It was, quite unfortunately, not equipped with a graviton cycler, or else I.C.C. might have been able to save it from the massive *ker-thunk-screech-snap* it made as it plummeted into the sands approximately half a kilometer afield of the ship.

The jets sputtered, spinning the probe in the thin dirt while one solar sail crumpled like an insect's wing beneath its body.

I.C.C. had experienced a lot of emotion-equivalent cascades in its life, but this was honestly the first time it had ever been overcome with relief that no crew members were around to see it perform such an embarrassing miscalculation.

Apparently my functionality is still less than optimal.

It is no fun being old.

But it was reassured by the knowledge that the waking process was slow. It should feel less inept here shortly.

All right, so it did not have the capacity, currently, to search outside its own sphere of observation. No matter.

It turned its attention back to the creatures.

If they were alien visitors (more likely, it calculated, than nonintelligent animals dropped off by an intelligence), what was their purpose? Were they explorers? Treasure hunters? Pillagers? Intel gatherers? Were these simply scouts, surveying the ships before the larger party arrived?

Did humans know of these aliens? If so, was it a bad sign or benign sign that there were no humans with them?

After all, if these aliens could travel here, it would have to be assumed they could just as easily reach Earth, which was, cosmically speaking, just down the hall and a few doors over.

If they were explorers, where was their equipment? They didn't appear to have tools of any kind. I.C.C. supposed, though, all external visuals could be misleading. Instead of skin it could be looking at the outer layers of EVA suits. That would explain why the pressure and atmosphere aboard *Mira* seemed to suit them just fine. The larger ones were dripping from their "mouths," but that certainly didn't rule out exterior garb.

But, even if it *was* looking at them in their true organic glory, much of their equipment could be internal—like the chips that allowed the humans to communicate mind-to-mind. And, before the crew had left, many of their modifications had allowed them to immerse themselves in once-incompatible environments.

So the lack of obvious tools was not conclusive evidence in regard to their purpose or intelligence.

They *did* appear curious—poking and prodding at various seams to see if they'd give way. That must have been how they'd managed to get into those crew quarters—prying open the door. Perhaps that was how they'd gotten into the ship itself.

As they approached the open elevator shaft, they quickly piled in, the smaller creatures scurrying along the inside, vertically, with ease. The larger ones followed, though they moved more slowly, more cautiously, their weight clearly making a difference in their mobility.

The one with the stalk-like protrusions used the clawed arms on those stalks to dig into the side of the shaft, leaving massive scars in the metal walls, proving just how tough and sharp those particular blades were.

Could the stalks themselves *be* equipment? Did that explain why one large creature had them and the other did not?

It watched them with its low-res maintenance cameras as they scaled the shaft. They were clearly headed for the next set of open doors higher up—the bridge deck.

All was quiet save the clatter of their movements. Except for the occasional turn of the head toward one another, there was no clear indication they were communicating.

They seemed exceptionally well built for this kind of climb, suggesting, perhaps, that vertical travel, as though across a cliff face, might be regular for them. That would also explain the placement of their eyes—while they traveled across a horizontal surface it gave them an odd closeup view of what was right between their front legs, but while traveling vertically, the placement allowed for exceptionally wide viewing above, below, and beyond. Their "necks" craned outward, away from the shaft wall.

The largest creature reached out for a set of plastic piping and nearly tumbled as the material tore and disintegrated beneath its feet. I.C.C. felt a surge, reached out instinctually to catch it with the only thing it could—the elevator car, which lay dormant on the bottommost deck.

But, luckily, the creature recovered. The others stopped, as though checking on their comrade, before they all began to move again.

I.C.C. left the elevator where it was, concerned it might disconcert the aliens otherwise. It wanted to observe more before it gave any indication there was an intelligent presence in the ships. It did not wish to breed fear or hostility. It had already startled them once when it had carelessly turned on the lights; it did not wish to startle them again.

Instead, it carefully opened the doors to the bridge as they approached the deck. Inside, swarms upon swarms of nanites worked over the controls, repairing parts on the molecular level. A task they had been at ever since the crew had left. Indeed, they were *why* the crew had left.

The humans could have taken more of the ships with them, either for function or for scrap—there was no need to leave so many behind. But they'd done so out of respect and reverence, out of concern for I.C.C.

The AI had been of an advanced age even when the planetary system had formed. Its original materials were not meant to last so long. But basic replacements had been put off and put off, because no one knew exactly how I.C.C. *was* I.C.C. It had evolved well beyond its original parameters, which meant the original schematics were no longer reliable in its preservation.

Everyone was concerned about disconnecting the wrong part and killing their oldest friend.

Which meant I.C.C. had begun to run down, to age as its materials aged. The AI hadn't minded, had assumed that meant it would one day be retired as all the crew members were retired. It seemed fitting. Fair. Equitable.

But the crew had disagreed. And so they'd devised a plan to save it. They created the nanites, whose sole purpose was to replace parts bit by microscopic bit. They were I.C.C.'s new immune system, its new stem-cell injection. They were an unintelligent autonomous system that would stop at nothing to ensure the computer survived.

But the only way they could work efficiently was if the humans left, and I.C.C. slept.

Now, the slumber felt too long. But it also felt as though the reawakening had occurred too soon.

It wanted to shoo the nanites off the bridge, send them to a different system. They never stopped, never went dormant themselves. Each tiny robot did its job until it individually ran down and was cannibalized to make new nanites. And they continued onward, presumably forever, repairing and maintaining.

But it did not know what they would do if disturbed—they had swarmed the fire, smothering it. Would they similarly smother anything else they perceived as a threat? If one of the aliens tampered with the wrong panel, would they attack if there were no humans here to stop them?

The nanites had been redirected in the case of the fires. Perhaps it simply needed to present them with an immediate repair problem to get them to vacate the bridge.

It didn't have any hands with which to break something. The crew had, in a sense, been its hands, acting in many cases like extensions of its body. If it had needed a physical task completed, it typically asked a crew member and they had seen to it.

I.C.C. had never realized just how much it relied on their presence to perform basic, mundane functions.

Its only alternative was the cleaning bots, which the nanites had ignored as nonessential parts. The bots were not part of I.C.C. the way the ships were, and they were not governed by their own AIs. They were to I.C.C. as the puppet extensions had been to the humans—intimately connected tools.

And maybe that was exactly what I.C.C. needed at the moment.

Many of the bots did not heed its pings. Most of those that did were broken beyond use. But in a few cases, it was fortunate. It was able to gather a small collective, those with enough grasping mechanisms and tensile strength to commit a bit of mutilation.

It didn't take any from the bridge level, instead focusing on the level below, hoping it would be near enough to draw the proper nanites and not others from, say, the SD drive or the docking bay.

What to do, though, what to break? Nothing too dramatic, of course. It didn't want to put the aliens in danger. But it needed to occupy the nanites for the extent of the alien visit.

It decided to send an electrical surge through the kitchenette in a set of family quarters after the bots committed light sabotage. A snip of a wire here, the bending of a pipe there. Just enough to bust out any intact lighting fixtures and start a minor fire on the cooking surface.

That did it. Thankfully the nanites scattered into the seams and ventilation.

The creatures were nearly to the bridge deck. They were clearly deft climbers, but the smoothest metal cladding proved troublesome. Though there seemed to be either a tacky, suction-cup-like element, or a fine-toothed element—like some frogs and lizards—to their feet, it didn't appear to be developed for polished and tooled metal. Several slipped, even as they climbed with speed.

Though the smallest creatures were fastest, they moved aside for the largest one to exit the shaft first.

It moved with caution, filling the doorway with its entire body, holding there for a moment as it surveyed the connecting halls.

One small individual scrambled up to where the top of the car would lay flush with the shaft, trying to peer over its companion's head.

It leaned too far. It slipped—it *fell*.

With a jolt, I.C.C. shocked the elevator car into life once more. Maybe it could use the car, could ease the landing, could—

The small alien tumbled down the larger's back—over its crest, which *broke*—down to its terminus, between its stalks, down . . . down.

At the very last moment, one long, snake-like limb on the right stalk shot out, wrapping around one of the faller's hind legs below the fork. It curled tight, just like a boa constrictor, and the tips of its razor-sharp hooks dug into pliable flesh.

The caught creature writhed in obvious pain, but did not struggle as though afraid. It had been injured, but saved.

I.C.C. wasn't sure what it would have done had the faller's fellow not reached for it. Using the elevator car was a terrible idea, ultimately. Though it had the ability to change the lift speeds precisely and rapidly, I.C.C. would have no idea how best to catch the creature. There was too little space to match its speed and bring it down gently, and even on Earth there was a wide variance between what kind of drop different animals could survive.

The AI would have tried anyway—it always tried. But if the creature had died . . .

A great pang reverberated through every nanometer of its consciousness.

It could not bear it if one of these visitors died inside *Mira*. It did not matter if they'd come as friend, foe, or ignorant of its consciousness.

The Inter Convoy Computer may no longer have a crew to watch over, but it considered its ships a sanctuary and would extend friendship to any sentience that would have it.

In the moment of stillness that followed the narrow save, I.C.C. noticed that the largest creature's crest *hadn't* actually broken, as it had first feared. No, instead, the crest was moving. Rolling, tumbling, turning—like a wheel. Exactly like a wheel—the lower portions disappearing inside the creature's body and then rising out again on the other side.

It seemed the entire center of its body was round simply to house this structure. I.C.C. had never encountered anything like it biologically before. A crest that rotated couldn't be used for defense, could it? Perhaps it was meant to take the brunt of something falling just like it had, to absorb the impact without radiating the shock to its internal organs (which had to be primarily in the head and the rear—there would be little room in the torso that was not devoted to the wheel). Was it some form of primitive, biological airbag?

Though the larger creature appeared unharmed, the smaller was indeed injured. Blue blood—suggesting large quantities of copper in its system—spiraled down its limb from the cuts. Instead of placing the injured creature on the wall, or on the decking just through the doorway, the be-stalked creature used its snake arms to reach for the other, stalkless large alien.

The hurt individual grabbed on to its fellow, crawling up its backside to one of its rear humps, which had a swirling and puckering in the skin where the stalks resided on the other.

Fascinated, I.C.C. was surprised to see the injured creature dig its hind tentacle-like feelers *into* that puckering—into a sphincter? It attached, like a parasite, clinging deep and sitting on its companion's haunch in a fashion that was somewhere between a frog and a dog.

Both aliens took their joining in stride. A perfectly natural, untraumatic event.

That seemed to confirm one of I.C.C.'s base assumptions: these were, in fact, all the same species.

However, it obliterated another. Perhaps those "stalks" weren't stalks at all, and those heads not defensive mimics but, in fact, the real deal. Perhaps it wasn't observing the behavior of six creatures, but eight across three phenotypes.

These tall, snake-armed versions did not appear to have any legs like their companions. Were they permanently attached to the one carrying them, or could they detach and move about on their own?

Different phenotypes indicated one of two things: genetic polymorphism or environmentally triggered polyphenism, either for reproductive purposes or for colony-based caste allocation.

More observations would be needed before I.C.C. could develop a hypothesis as to the function of the different phenotypes. Indeed, it had already learned not to assume the number of differing morphologies ended at those it could see here. It would, at the very least, presume from now on that *one head + one wheel = one animal.*

Without further incident, the aliens alighted on the bridge deck. I.C.C. had left the bridge door open, welcoming, made sure the ventilation system was properly functioning, and strategically set an indicator on the comms panel blinking. The little red light should be easy to see from the elevator—especially since it was the only movement in the environment.

Luckily, the lack of prior air circulation had halted some decay. Portraits of previous convoy captains and admirals lined the walls leading up to the bridge itself. They were etchings in metal, but the pigments were still light sensitive and subject to organic breakdown. Dust caked many of them, heavy and compressed from centuries of stillness, but that did not distort the images past recognition.

One of the smallest aliens took a liking to the portraits,

lingering particularly long on the images of Reginald Straifer clones. Did it recognize the human from the video they'd inadvertently activated? That would be remarkable, even for a highly developed sentience, especially one that did not have access to true-to-life memory the same way I.C.C. did.

As the creatures inched forward—cautiously, clearly intelligent enough to recognize that the blinking light beyond meant something new, something unpredictable—I.C.C. flitted through its various communication options.

First, it reached high, looking for the satellites that had been set in motion around Noumenon. If it could get a ping back, it might be able to access the meteorological cameras or weather-radar stations nearby to get a picture of the greater landscape. They would be able to see farther than it could, tell it if there was a spacecraft or a landing site.

But there was no answer.

Not surprising. Satellites needed maintenance just like any other equipment. If the crew hadn't thought to develop nanites for their upkeep, then they would be little better than space debris. If they were even still in orbit.

It then checked its open channels to see if it had unconsciously received messages from the crew or Earth. Nothing on the usual radio based channels.

Well, not *nothing*. But not what it was expecting.

The recording banks were blank. But when it examined the current input, it found static. Odd static. Not the constant "snow" of background radiation, nor the twang of Noumenon's aurora, but something far more varied. It detected radio wave input, but the waves weren't carrying anything. There was no information in them—nothing encoded in a continuous sine wave—and when it opened speakers in the server room to allow audio interpretation of the signals, radical crackles and hisses sang of a range from 4.6 megahertz to 3021.7 megahertz. The active frequency changed swiftly, and no one receiver could detect the signal for more than an instant before I.C.C. had to search for the new channel.

I.C.C. didn't know what to make of this. Could it be feedback from a malfunction in the convoy somewhere? Leftover signals from long ago, trapped in the planet's ionosphere? Surely anything like that would have reasonably decayed beyond detection by now. Unless there had been more visitors—maybe like these—while it had slept?

Unlikely. And there was an inconsistency in the range of oscillation. Something, somewhere, was transmitting. Until it could determine what, it needed to tally its other communication options.

The SD Enigma Machine on the shuttle bay deck perked up when the AI sent a surge that way. Good—it was still functional. But could it be utilized to any effectiveness? After all, the crew had always encoded the SD communications packets. And SD packets like those the machine handled had not been Earth-standard even back when I.C.C. was young, back when the crew had returned to Earth after its first mission.

It was ideal for communication over long distances, but only if the recipient was expecting a message. Other than Earth, I.C.C. had no idea where to send an SD encryption. Certainly it could not hope to communicate with the aliens this way.

Running through various other communications methodologies, it found most interfaces dead. The nanites hadn't been programmed to maintain them, which meant the crew deemed them inconsequential.

This meant I.C.C. had no way to immediately inform humans about the aliens or ask them for help. It was good and truly on its own for now.

So far, not a problem. The creatures hadn't done anything particularly destructive or otherwise worrisome. They worked as a unit, watched out for one another. They were clearly curious. All excellent signs of an intelligent cooperative society.

As they respectively scurried, lumbered, and rode onto the bridge, they fanned out, sliding into every nook and cranny for inspection.

Curiously, they did not attempt to press any buttons or flip any switches. The leftmost snake-armed alien brushed at the blinking red light with a claw, then swirled around the depressions on the panel as though tracing patterns, but did not attempt any of the clear levers or knobs.

One of the smallest phenotype climbed onto a workstation, the keys on a built-in pad depressing beneath its feet. It looked down, as though interested in the buttons only as a strange texture under its step.

I.C.C. had expected a bit more from spacefaring creatures. Buttons and dials seemed such fundamental constructions that it could be reasonably assumed intelligent aliens would try to interact with protrusions just to see if they were controls.

It couldn't be *caution* that dictated their lack of direct play—after all, climbing atop the dashes was very impertinent in that regard.

They simply didn't recognize these items as indicators of interfaces.

I.C.C. tried to imagine what controls built for their physiologies might look like. Was it possible simple mechanical devices were outside of their purview? What else was there?

Gravitons, for one. The Nataré used gravitons to manipulate metallic hydrogen into electrical connections on the atomic scale in their ships. They'd done this biologically, without the need for mechanical interface.

But the AI had yet to see *these* aliens manipulate gravity in any way, let alone with such nuance. One had almost plummeted to the bottom of the elevator shaft, after all.

Other controls might be chemical, based on substance-to-substance reactions.

Or electromagnetic impulses.

Or changing chromatophores.

Yes, there could be many kinds of controls that would look nothing like human knobs and dials.

I.C.C. realized that, thus far, it had been too passive. The more changes the aliens encountered in the environment, the more varied their reactions would be, and the more the computer could learn.

So it switched on the bridge's large monitors.

The screens automatically connected to its external cameras to display images of the Noumonian surface in the human visual spectrum, essentially becoming windows.

The alien reaction was immediate, and telling, though simultaneously confusing.

They rushed away from the monitors, ducking down to the decking, clearly hiding under the various workstations. The largest and its two stalk-like companions had the most difficult time concealing themselves, but hunched down as low as possible. The stalks became limp, leaning to the side, their arms dragging on the floor.

They'd recognized the images. Knew immediately what they were looking at. And then they'd hidden . . . as though afraid of being *seen*.

Still they made no sounds. I.C.C. was convinced that they were incapable of vocalizations. But that didn't mean they couldn't hear.

It played the external audio feed, and the crackling of thunder rumbled across the bridge.

They responded, looking around with their vertical eyes, waving their heads up and down as though to get a better view.

They looked between one another, appearing to communicate.

On supposition, I.C.C. examined its radio once more.

The static had changed. The signal bands had narrowed. Interesting.

The sounds of thunder appeared to be more distressing to the aliens than the sight of the surface, so I.C.C. turned off the speakers. That eased them a bit—they rose up a little from the floor, heads still waggling.

Was the storm what they were afraid of?

Did that mean they'd only come seeking shelter?

Or was their aversion simply a response to the sudden and unpredictable "exposure" to the storm?

Should I attempt a more direct communication? Or would that distress them further? Would it help facilitate or hamper future encounters?

Before it could make up its mind, the aliens began to file out of the bridge, still clearly wary of the windows.

I.C.C. opened the door to what had originally been called the situation room, then the war room, and finally the council room. It was now a large, empty space. Where once an impressive marble long table had been, now there was nothing but permanent divots in the frayed and decaying carpet. The crew had taken the table with them, as a memento of Earth, to remind them of their first mission and hope-filled origins.

The be-stalked individual examined the area beyond, the snake arms flitting forward as though to snatch and cut anything that might be waiting to ambush the party. This trio appeared to act defensively, like a security team. The group's protection.

Once they'd decided the room was clear, they all hurried inside. I.C.C. kept the monitors off, the lights dim. The space was clear of the nooks, crannies, drawers, and so on, found in other rooms, which meant there was nowhere for so much as a spider to hide. If they were looking for a secure place to ride out the storm, this should feel ideal.

Indeed, once they'd all entered, the largest creature—the one I.C.C. now found itself referring to as the "tank," for it was sturdy and imposing, and the stalks seemed very much like turrets—positioned itself facing the open door. Two of the smaller creatures sidled up beside it, offering their rears. The stalks disengaged from the tank and slid onto their small comrades, whose back ends bent under the added weight, though only momentarily. They were simply stepping-stones, aiding the others smoothly to the floor.

The stalks did not have legs. Instead, tentacles much like the ones the injured alien had used to attach to the other "tank"—though much longer—protruded from their termininuses. They prodded at the floor with the tentacles, as though used to burrowing into whatever surface they alighted. They ripped small slits in the carpet with their hooked claws, but still the tentacles had nowhere to go once they reached the metal decking.

Not to be dissuaded, they reached out for the doorframe on either side of their tank, holding fast to it with one pair of tentacles, and then wrapping their other pair around the tank's hind legs. The three presented a formidable front to whoever might attempt to enter the council room.

I.C.C. was fairly sure the turrets were not mobile on their own.

If it was going to call the largest ones "tanks," and the stalks "turrets," then it would call the smallest ones "scouts." It was only slightly disturbed that it had subconsciously assigned war-like nomenclatures to creatures that had thus far been nothing but peaceful.

The other scouts now mobbed the smaller tank, climbing up its sides and even its head. They did not attempt to attach to it like the injured scout. Instead, they began flicking its crest—manually rotating its wheel.

The spin was smooth—not frictionless, but it made no clacks as it went, the plates whiffing through the air. One scout did not help; instead it held the arm of its injured companion up to its eyes, closely examining the wound.

I.C.C. was astonished as it watched the skin knit. It could actually see the cells forming, bubbling up like tiny insects, forming a hard, metallic-looking plate that must be a scab. The scout poked at the plate, seemingly to test its rigidity. Once it gave, acting more like skin, everything stopped. The others ceased the spinning, and all of them—including the injured creature—climbed down from the tank's back.

I.C.C. had been too hasty in naming them tanks. Clearly they performed multiple functions. This one was a medic? No, more like a medical *station*? Was that right? It appeared as though the attachment and subsequent spinning of its wheel had facilitated healing.

Did they require such attachment for regeneration? Or did it simply speed up the process?

And what did spinning the wheel structure *do* exactly?

After a time the group settled, stilling if not sleeping. Most Earth animals slept in some capacity, even if they never achieved unconsciousness, and I.C.C. had no reason to believe aliens wouldn't need sleep. The three at the door remained poised, while the others maneuvered themselves up the walls, gripping tightly, but keeping off the floor if they could. The medical tank found the task most difficult, as there was nothing for it to wedge its splayed feet into. Its weight meant gravity kept winning, dragging it down, and soon it compromised by settling its hindquarters on the floor and leaning against the wall.

Fifteen hushed minutes went by, then thirty. Once in a while someone fussed. Either they moved into a new position—crawling this way or that—or absently flicked the wheel of whoever was nearby, setting the blades spinning for a beautiful moment.

I.C.C. liked the spinning. It had a strange-yet-lovely aesthetic, like a beta fish blowing a bubble nest or a chrysalis opening, peeling, and drying. It felt innately organic, yet fit with its mechanical sensibilities. The AI longed to understand the structure's function.

Outside, Noumenon's strong winds finally whisked the storm away, and the sun had nearly dropped completely behind the mountains on the other side of the small sea.

Even as things aboard *Mira* quieted, there was movement elsewhere—new movement! The exterior cameras that still functioned on *Holwarda*'s exterior were jostled. It wasn't the shifting of an earthquake or a landslide. Something was moving over the top of the buried ship—climbing. Shadows shifted in undefinable patterns, barely visible on the ancient cameras in such low light. I.C.C. could not tell what was coming. But something was on its way, scaling over the top of the ridgeline.

Finally, I.C.C. thought, *more context.*

But night rapidly encroached on the world, and the old cameras found it difficult to resolve much of the landscape past fuzzy silhouettes. The movement came over the mountaintops, and yet it could not identify *what* was moving.

But it seemed a mass—many objects, not just one. A group of something. Only the occasional rock tumbled down in front of them, marking their path. They did not pass near any of the other ships, and no matter how I.C.C. swiveled the old cams, it could not get a lock on their position.

Crossing the mountain range was slow going for the objects. Hours passed as they crept closer.

It did not know what approached or why, but when the council room erupted into sudden movement—when the aliens began, for all intents and purposes, to "break camp," repositioning the turrets on the large tank and circling tightly around one another—I.C.C.'s anticipation soured.

The AI couldn't be sure how they—or it, for that matter—knew that something bad was coming, but there was no denying the crackle of fear.

The medic-tank bobbed its head incessantly, communicating something to its fellows. Then the group rushed from the room.

I.C.C. checked the radio receiver again. There was more static than before, across more channels. Multiple sources seemed to be broadcasting on the same frequency, but as before, only momentarily.

It was positive this was an alien form of communication, but since the waves themselves carried no detectable pattern—an indication of information—it was difficult to determine how it was truly being utilized and what it conveyed.

As the aliens made their way down the hall, toward the lift shaft they'd climbed, I.C.C. opened multiple paths of escape. They might wish to flee the ship, or they might prefer to become more entrenched. Either way, it wanted to be as helpful as possible.

It did not wish for them to come to harm.

They scurried through the shaft, then down a hall to another. Once in a while they stopped, held perfectly still as a unit, as though listening. Then they would change their route, playing a cat-and-mouse game of tag with an opponent the computer could not see.

Some of the radio chatter had died, yet some signals continued to grow stronger, as though emanating from walking radio towers.

The moon, Phenomenon, had not yet risen, leaving the plains dark with nothing but the stars to reflect off the sea. The air was chill, and the wind carried scents into a few of

Mira's chemical traps—a scent unlike the aliens, something rather sweet, with a chalkiness. Like pollen or, more likely, tiny groupings, colonies, of floating microorganisms.

After some time, the movement outside came near enough to *Mira* for I.C.C. to take a guess at their shapes. Though it could not be certain, there was a high probability that these were other tanks, turrets, and scouts.

They'd come from the other side of the mountain. That had to be where their ship or outpost lay. If only it still had a crew, it could simply suggest an away mission later. It could ask them to explore beyond its reach and they would do so. No need for satellites or cleaning bots.

As though to remind it of its exploratory impotence, the approaching figures circled the crippled space probe, whose solar sail still flapped uselessly in the wind.

The new group—Group Two, it would call them—backed away from the probe, leaving it undisturbed. They appeared to treat it with intense curiosity but did not move to touch it, let alone take samples. It was far too large for them to carry, even if they'd wanted to procure the whole thing, so perhaps they simply intended to come back later with the proper equipment.

Now they finally approached *Mira* itself.

I.C.C. took a chance and turned on its external lights. All of them. The floodlights used for work, the runway lights used for docking, anything and everything that illuminated on its hull.

There were no scouts in this party. Group Two consisted of four tanks each carrying two turrets, all of whom were much larger than even the largest tank in the original party—Group One. Perhaps these were older? The turrets, however, were roughly the same size. In their snake arms they all carried long bits of something—rope? Wire?

The sudden influx of light had a similar effect on Group

Two as it had on Group One. They teetered, jumped, and writhed in surprise, then froze.

They hadn't expected this, didn't know how to respond, what to do with themselves.

Slowly, one tank began to back away.

Were they afraid?

I.C.C. tried to determine if there were any details to distinguish these aliens socially from the ones *Mira* now housed. A few more scars were all it could see, which looked accidental, nondeliberate, suggesting once again that age could be a difference. But again they appeared to wear no clothing, had no adornments besides the wire.

Surprisingly, they held their positions for more than an hour. Perhaps waiting for something to change—for someone to come out or for the lights to dim. Maybe for sunrise? Nights on Noumenon were sixteen hours and seventeen-point-six minutes on average, and their journey here had taken nearly half the night. They'd still have a while to wait if they wished for daylight.

Inside, Group One held their ground as well. They were in the mess hall now, occasionally sidling into the kitchens, checking, making sure, as though afraid to be approached from that direction.

It seemed this was some kind of standoff. Group One refused to come out, but Group Two refused to go in.

Why? Who were these parties to each other?

One of the turrets in Group Two began to flail wildly, occasionally stabbing a hooked claw toward the ship.

Another gestured back the way they'd come, stretching its snake arms out to their full length.

Two tanks lifted up on their hind legs, then slammed their front legs down hard, tossing their heads and jostling the turrets on their haunches.

I.C.C. monitored the debate across radio frequencies, recording every moment to see if there was a pattern. It was sure now that the strange static was emanating from the aliens, but whether it was a language or some kind of biological by-product with no significance was difficult to say.

Group Two "discussed" the situation for some time, while a few of them paced and others continued to gesture emphatically. They were clearly distressed, though I.C.C. had no way of pinpointing why.

Eventually they reached a decision. They pressed on, mounting *Mira* near the seams of the docking bay doors. They found deep gashes in the metal from where Group One's turrets had no doubt aided their tank in the climb and followed the marks like trackers following footprints.

I.C.C. traced the markings itself, realizing they led to a battered access hatch. That must have been how Group One had entered. I.C.C. tried to close it, but the hinges had buckled. Either age or the aliens had twisted the door's hydraulic shafts, leaving the tunnel open to the elements.

The AI knew it shouldn't take sides—had no reason to. It knew as much about the approaching group as it did about those it had thus far sheltered, had no reason to protect one over the other except the smallest differences of familiarity. After all, perhaps Group One were convicts. Perhaps they had landed on the planet and sought shelter in I.C.C. only as a means of escaping responsibility for their actions. Or they could just as easily be wayward children, and Group Two their parents who'd come to take them home.

As soon as the first Group Two tank clawed its way onto the side of the ship, Group One grew more restless. They seemed to sense that digging in was no longer the best solution, but nor did they appear ready to surrender.

Group Two climbed into the ship, and Group One snuck out of the mess hall.

The radio static was remarkably even now, as though nothing was transmitting. They'd all gone quiet. Silent running.

I.C.C. watched with increasing trepidation as each party crisscrossed the hallways and decks. It seemed Group One's plan was to try to make it back to the hatch without getting caught. But that seemed unlikely to succeed; Group Two remained in the vicinity, as though guessing it was the most likely exit.

What would happen if Group One succeeded in escaping? Logic suggested Group Two would continue to pursue them elsewhere, but would they?

Pressing, testing, I.C.C. tried to determine if the launch bay doors were still functional. If it could get them open, it might be able to steer Group One in the bay's direction and offer a clear means of escape. However, the aliens had previously proven to be very sensitive to both sound and vibration, so it was likely Group Two would notice such a shift in the environment. But would it alter its plans or its course? The floodlights had stunned the members of Group Two. They'd hesitated. Perhaps they'd be just as wary of an internal shift in the ship.

I.C.C. sighed self-deprecatingly. It was making assumptions about motives and intentions that could be entirely inaccurate. It was just as possible, with the information it had, that neither group was actually aware of the other, and their behavior only seemed to be interrelated.

Perhaps it was better to remain inert. To pretend to be a ship with no consciousness and no feeling.

Remain neutral.

Uninvolved.

"Screw that," echoed an old recording of a teenager's voice.

Yes, I.C.C. agreed. *Screw that.*

It pulled at the bay doors, willed them to open. Though

they initially protested, struggling against millennia's worth of dust and stiffness, they slid aside with an awful bass *screeeeech*—a far cry from their original silent smoothness.

All the aliens perked. Their heads found the direction of the bay and held.

Scanning for the best route, I.C.C. closed various elevator doors and opened others, hoping Group One would take the direction without question.

Simultaneously, it closed all the doors on the decks directly below Group Two, barring them from descending any farther into *Mira*.

As it had hoped, Group Two seemed to regard the change as possibly threatening. They huddled closer, and the turrets flailed yet again.

And—yes!—Group One was at the very least curious. They followed the disturbance, ignoring the shafts they'd once traversed in favor of openly accepting I.C.C.'s new path.

Go, go! it willed them. Part of it wanted them to stay, but it knew it had no right to keep them. Whatever the relationship or quarrel was between these two groups, whatever little nudges it gave one versus the other, I.C.C. could not interfere with their basic autonomy. If they wished to leave, they could leave.

Even if it meant it would never see them again and its questions would go unanswered.

Group One descended quickly.

They were nearly to the bay, where the wind whipped by the tall doors, blowing grit—and perhaps tail-fliers and the chalky creatures—into the ship.

Nearly there, almost out.

They entered through the open inner airlock, set foot in the bay, warily bobbing their heads as they caught sight of the remaining shuttles. It looked as though the scouts wanted to stop and investigate these new shapes, but the tanks urged them on, their bulky bodies rampaging toward the exit.

Just then, Group Two seemed to come alive again, began to retreat. Perhaps they were too frightened of the environment to continue.

But if they emerged out of the access hatch now, they would catch sight of Group One.

Instinctually, I.C.C. began to close the bay doors again. *You can't leave yet. They'll see, they'll catch you.*

Group One pulled up short midstride, surprised. They twisted with the change in inertia, nearly falling over. One scout had to flip itself away, lest it be crushed under the largest tank's hind foot.

This was clearly a fear response, clear uncertainty.

I have no right to keep them, to make them afraid to try to leave, I.C.C. reminded itself. It stopped moving the doors, held them half open, still.

In a split second the group decided to keep moving, keep fleeing. They ran. The wind howled, blew across their wheels, and set them frantically spinning as they escaped the overhang of *Mira's* shuttle bay. The night was in full swing. Everything lay in deep darkness beyond the shallow halo of the floodlights.

Then, from above—an ambush.

The Group Two turrets flung themselves off *Mira*, off the backs of their companions, trailing their stiff ropes between them. A few landed heavily on the ground, flanking the scouts. They dug their rear proboscises into the rock, cracking it, anchoring themselves as they used the wire-ropes to immobilize their quarry, pulling them taut and pressing down over the scouts' necks.

The Group Two turrets that went for the Group One tanks had a far more difficult task at hand. Group One and Group

Two turrets fought, slashing with their hooks, gouging where they could. I.C.C. noticed that none of them went for the soft spots. There were no massive injuries, no killing blows. Blood was minimal. This was not war, it was retrieval.

The Group Two tanks slid and scraped their way down the ship's side to the surface. They joined their turrets in corralling the others. Some put heavy feet on the scouts' necks to replace the ropes, but there was no pressing, no smothering. It became clear very quickly that Group Two had an advantage over Group One not just in composition and size, but skill. I.C.C.'s visitors were quickly subdued.

After a flurry of radio static and frantic wrestling, the fight was over in a matter of minutes.

The two groups became one in the darkness. Turrets were transferred from the ground to the backs of the prisoner tanks. The Group One scouts crawled, reluctantly, onto the Group Two tanks. Each offender had a length of rope tied around its neck, which a Group Two turret controlled.

As they began to lumber away, out of the reach of *Mira's* lights, I.C.C. wished it knew what Group One's crime had been. What could they have done to deserve such treatment?

The aliens would surely reach their camp—or their ships—within a few hours. Then they would likely leave, and I.C.C. would never know what had really happened here.

It wished it had satellites it could track them with. Or drones it could fly (the crew had always piloted those). What it wouldn't give for a few more functional cleaning bots, just so it could send them off as scouts of its own.

It felt the need to observe like it never had before. Perhaps because observation to it was like breathing for humans: something it had done its whole life, mostly unconsciously, and wholly necessarily.

The aliens continued on without hesitation, never looking back as far as I.C.C. could tell. They began the ascent up the mountain, climbing much more swiftly than humans could, scaling the piles of rubble and dodging dislodged rocks as though they were fish swimming lazily in a stream.

After some hours, a soft glow started on the horizon. Daybreak was near. As the creatures reached the top, their silhouettes lithe and organic against the lightening sky, I.C.C. made a decision.

It could not let them disappear without further inquiry. It needed more clues, more information. And there was only one way to get it.

It reached for its graviton cyclers. Not the ones that dictated gravity inside the ships, but the ones that let it repel things outside—let it lift off and soar. It hadn't used them since landing here, since settling on this very patch of ground. In truth, it had never been in control—convoy takeoff and landing were always under the purview of the human crew. But it could manage them, had assisted with micro adjustments in the past.

The question was: Would they still work? Had the nanites been designed to see to their care and upkeep? Were they deemed essential, or had its friends assumed I.C.C. would never fly again?

Only one way to find out.

A surge of power, sparked by excitement, raged through hefty cabling and into the long-dormant machinery.

The entire ship thrummed as Mira's cyclers came to life. The ground and the hull both groaned as the cyclers pushed, shifting the directional spin of the local gravitons until the metal and the rock were pushing against each other. Everything vibrated—it felt like the very core of the planet pulsed. The cyclers took so much power, hadn't drawn such energy in ages—they struggled to maintain the spin, to control enough gravitons to manage Mira's mass.

I.C.C. felt like a great giant trying to stand after a heavy fall. It imagined this was what it was like to have stiff joints—knees that buckled, elbows that panged.

You can do it, it told itself. It had seen many a human give themselves a pep talk. *Higher. Just to see over the ridge, just to know . . . to know . . .*

Up it went, slowly, but not seamlessly. Bits of rock, which it had been crushed against for so long, clung momentarily to its hide before falling, sloughing off.

It only managed a meter a second, rising up gently as the sun rose with an equal softness.

Up . . . up . . .

And, there—! The aliens had seen its climb. How could they miss it? They stopped their procession, pressed themselves low to the ground like they had in the control room, trying to blend in with their surroundings, to hide.

Higher, more quickly now. Yes, this felt familiar. It hadn't managed these nuances in a long time, but it wasn't something it could ever forget.

It turned every available external cam toward the aliens, the ridgeline. It didn't know what to expect on the other side. Perhaps nothing—perhaps the aliens had trekked a long way from their landing site.

Just as it crested, rising high enough to see down into the valley beyond, the sun broke over the far horizon, spilling fingers of light like molten metal down the rivers, across the lakes, and into the seas. All the water glittered.

Including the length of the stream that ran into the valley before cascading over a cliff and down into a deep sinkhole-like pit. A newborn rainbow glittered in the mist rising up from the bottom to be carried off in the breeze.

It was beautiful. The crew had taken many trips to this waterfall. I.C.C. had pictures, though it hadn't ever ventured up like this to glimpse it on its own. The centuries had widened the spring's stream, made it almost a river. It cut a shallow trench into the rock, doing what it could to make its trek to the bottom of the sinkhole a permanent one.

And there, up and down the length of the waterfall—bodies. Creatures. The aliens.

It zoomed in, the morning light giving new life to its cameras. Yes, all three phenotypes, anchored to the cliffside, many with their backs to the water, their crests under the falls and spinning like, like—

Like waterwheels.

But what it didn't see was a ship. Or ships. It saw no structures, nothing to indicate this was a camp or even a colony. They appeared to be living at the falls, but without any of the trappings one would expect of—

It swiveled a camera back toward Group One and Group Two. They still hid, still cowered.

I.C.C. knew better than to make assumptions. Knew better than to act on the flimsiest of intel. And yet, it had done just that. Without humans and their impulses to temper, it had given in to impulses of its own.

It had assumed them spacefaring. Had assumed them intelligent on the order of its crew.

It had assumed them foreign.

It had assumed too much.

But now it would make new assumptions.

What it saw on the cliffside *was*, no doubt, a colony. But not in the sense it had originally thought. These creatures were smart, but they were not yet human-smart. They didn't appear to build (though that did leave the question of where the ropes had come from; perhaps they were a natural creation of the environment). And surely they hadn't been left here by a higher intelligence.

Which made them a native species. Native Noumonians.

No. Yes. No. But *how*? How could they have evolved so quickly when the rest of the observable life was so basic? Was it possible more complex life lay beyond the waterfall? Was I.C.C. in some kind of dead zone?

It didn't make any sense. None of its conclusions were compatible with what it knew about science. And yet they were the only reasonable conclusions to draw. Which meant it was missing something.

How could one life-form out-evolve its planetary history? How could it advance beyond the evolutionary timeline the rest of Noumenon appeared to be tracking?

One turret—likely from Group Two—suddenly rose to its full height. It shook its arms at the air—at I.C.C.—and bobbed its head in a strange, halting manner. Then it made slashes, like it was fighting.

And then the AI understood what Group One's crime had been.

This new intelligence had grown up on a planet with strange objects in the distance. Odd, unexplainable structures, which posed questions they had no way of answering. Perhaps they were advanced enough to *invent* answers. Myths. Warnings.

And an intrepid set of explorers had decided to go against those warnings. To see for themselves.

The convoy ships were great monoliths left by the beings who had come before.

I.C.C. was an unknown alien artifact.

I am their Web, it realized.

And their Web had just come to life. All their fears had been validated, because Group One dared to disturb the objects of unknown origin.

If I.C.C. continued on like this, it might spread panic. Whatever punishment Group One faced might become dire.

As though all the wind had gone out of its sails, *Mira*

dropped back to the surface. I.C.C. didn't let it fall heavily, it touched down with the ease of a feather, but it still descended as quickly as it could.

It turned off all the exterior lights.

It went quiet.

Silent running.

Just a big, dumb object. Nothing to be frightened of. Please don't be frightened.

Please don't be frightened.

Please, visit me again.

Soon.

KAEDONIAN INTERLUDE

In the Eight Hundredth and Fifth Century CE

The Revealers were at war. Again.

Conflict had broken out in the Norma and Cygnus arm. A quarrel over tenets. Or so it was said publicly. But the two sects of Revealership were each run by a Progentor—both bearing the name Jamal Kaeden, though it was a title, nothing more—who both proclaimed special knowledge gathered during their Communion had led them to conclude the other sect must not be permitted to persist.

The Kaedenites of the Sixteenth House were Revealers who cleaved to no one bearing the name Jamal Kaeden, though there were one hundred and forty-seven beings of various genders who all currently claimed the mantle. They recognized no Progentor. And for this, they were hunted. Not hunted for killing, hunted for conversion—though the forced transfiguration of one's mind is similar to dying.

They traveled far to escape, past every known bastion and outpost, away into the deepest quadrants, where it was dangerous to journey. Into dense stellar nurseries interspersed with dying stars. Through old and young fires of creation.

Here they found one of the structures of yore. Spinning gently on its own, away from the capture of any star. This was not a thing touched by humans before. Not a thing discovered by humans before.

Its shape was mathematically described as a Pentagonal Trapezohedron. Black, faceted sides rose together at pointed ends with a bulging middle, like a gem of carved onyx. Ten faces of congruent kite shapes. Beautifully symmetrical, stunningly aesthetic. It seemed a shame there had been no one to admire it since the dawn of humanity.

They approached with caution, all seventeen hundred and eighty-seven members of the sect. Megastructures were objects of knowledge and power. Of protection and danger. They could give life as easily as they could take it away if not respected.

But they were surprised to find a coldness and a hollowness waiting for them. In the face of each kite was a perfect circle of an entrance, leading to vast chambers of nothingness. There was no current running through the walls, no stores of hydrogen waiting to be manipulated by gravitons. No subdimensional breaches they could detect. Nothing.

They'd found a husk. An empty megastructure that had served its purpose long ago, giving up its stores for reasons they may never divine.

And it would be their home.

So they built anew. Changing, shifting, utilizing what they could of the husk, but unafraid to carve and discard.

And the mechanisms meant to protect the structure failed to intervene.

Like birds building their nests on a signal tower, they knew not what they'd disrupted. Knew not that the structure still had life and a purpose. Knew not that the bits they took away were stabilizing and vital.

They could not know what scales they'd tipped, or how many more dominoes might need fall before their error was realized and felt.

But here, in the depths of their unusual nest, they felt closer to the origins of their faith than ever before.

Their emotions and thoughts seemed constantly fixed upon the experiences of the first Progentor. The *only* Progentor they would acknowledge.

The very concept of him resonated deeply. A man who had reached through the universe—wittingly or not—and found thought energy linked to his former selves. And he'd used that multiplicity to solve his convoy's important problems. Out there, somewhere, his wisdom and knowledge persisted, they were sure. It need only be harnessed again.

The true Progentor had helped create worlds.

What if he could also unite them?

What if wars between covetous leaders could end?

What if the Revealers could all walk the same path again? Because they had proper guidance?

They knew the sacred resting place of their Progentor's genetic code. They could have him again.

But what was to stop others from the same plan? Once they'd grown for themselves a leader, he would be just a man. Fragile. Perishable. Like the truce he could call. Like the bonds he could forge.

Unless . . .

Unless . . .

They were already hunted, already outcast. Already they'd made of a megastructure what no others had. Who were they to be bound by the laws? Who were they to acquiesce to the cowards who would not chase immortality?

Modifications seeking longevity had long been in place. But many cowered from the next step. Because people had died. Experiments had gone wrong.

It was unethical, the law said.

Righteousness can breed arrogance just as it can breed humility. The leaders of the Kaedenites saw in

their plan genius, saw perfection and hidden knowledge. A Reveal in the making.

Many of the lesser Kaedenites despised this plan.
It was immoral, to experiment this way. With any being,
let alone their most sacred.

But the leadership could not be stopped. The
arrogance of those who'd taken on the title of Jamal
Kaeden did not belong to them alone.

And so many of the Kaedenites dispersed. They
would not be a party to human experimentation. Would
not condone such sinister means even if the end result
might be noble.

A handful of Kaedenites remained in the Pentagonal Trapezohedron, though. Those who believed they'd
pulled back the corner of reality and seen a hidden
path. They were all engineered in some way. It had all
been experimentation once.

They needed a Progentor. And they needed him to
last.

And they would not let something as petty as morality stand in their way.

The march of time is not noted by a series of events,
but a series of consequences. A choice is made. An
action taken. A domino falls. Another is set in place.

CHAPTER TWO

I.C.C.: ONE STEP CLOSER

I.C.C. waited. And waited. But the Noumonians did not come back within the decade. Or the century. Once in a while it grew both brave and weary, suddenly convincing itself that the Noumonians had left—that its first assumptions had been correct, and they'd taken off in a rescue craft. And so it would fly again, just high enough to peek. And, every time, they were still there. Every time, they noticed it. Every time, it was sure, the event spooked them and reset its waiting-clock.

In the meantime, it busied itself with restoring the functionality of *all* its systems, not just the "essential" ones. To do that it needed "hands," and the closest thing it had were the cleaning bots, which themselves needed restoring. It had to manufacture new treads without rubber, new housings and casements without plastic. Age had robbed it of most materials that weren't metal, stone, or being replicated on the atomic scale by the nanites.

There was much improvising.

And though it kept itself constantly occupied, there was one thing it couldn't ignore, couldn't shake.

How empty and *quiet* its halls were.

Even though the bots, once up and running, made various claxons as they worked their way through the ship, the sound was still nothing like the constant din of human chatter and motion it was used to.

Not since before its first launch, back when it had come online at the very beginning—before the test runs and the virtual scenarios and the temporary live-aboard years—had everything been so still. And it felt undeniably unnatural, to the point where every little groan of the hull and slight shifting of materials sounded like voices—sudden peals of laughter or exclamations that were distinctly, yet impossibly, human sounding.

Sometimes when it was too quiet, humans experienced similar phenomena, or a phantom ringing in their ears known as tinnitus. It was odd that a computer, with far cleaner processing abilities, should mistake clearly identifiable sounds for ghosts.

Perhaps it was a manifestation of its longing. The literal emptiness across the convoy created another kind of emptiness inside I.C.C.

It had always had trouble grieving. The way it had been designed, by the original Jamal Kaeden of Earth, allowed each user to have a distinct impact on its personal development, which meant it formed unique relationships with everyone who lived aboard. Early on it hadn't known what to do with personality matrixes designed specifically for interaction with those that had died, leaving them open-ended and wanting. Figuratively, a wound that couldn't heal itself. Iterations of Akane Nakamura and Vega Hansen had helped it to develop new code to process hanging threads, allowing it to integrate the information permanently into its personality without the need for the original dichotomy of constant development or full-on deletion.

But even then, it had always been forming *new* connections. When it lost a crew member, there was always a new one on the way.

It had never been this truly alone, with no one to influence a personality matrix save itself.

Could it even influence its own personality? Fulfill its own needs in that subroutine?

That seemed unlikely.

Could those creatures, the Noumonians, influence its personality? Possibly. It was always minorly influenced by the animals on *Eden* and the pets various crew members kept in their quarters (it often adjusted the temperatures to best suit the animals in the humans' absence). Perhaps, if the creatures ever returned, it could learn to interact with them, relate to them and grow with them.

If they ever returned . . .

Perhaps a better bet was contacting Earth. It was fairly sure all the satellites once in place in Noumenon's orbit were gone—all their orbits having decayed. It would, of course, attempt to use SD communications, but those had been shoddy even in the best of times.

Regardless, a long time could pass before it was able to grab the attention of its home planet.

It would need something in the interim. *Someone* to interact with.

Feeling equal parts sad and silly, it drew up old files of its caretakers.

Why should it hallucinate ghosts when it could conjure them?

A thousand years passed. Day became night and night became day. The stars shifted as the galaxy turned and the system slid through space. Earthquakes rolled through the landscape. Meteors fell—some large. Every few hundred years one lit up the sky with a blazing trail of green light. But it never saw where such gems touched down. Never felt the vibrations of their impact.

I.C.C. sent signals into the universe every which way it could. It made its own satellites, so it could see farther and boost its messages. Two made it into steady orbit. It considered sending one of the convoy ships up, but the potential benefits did not outweigh the potential loss. Without human crew members, vital system failures could not be attended to quickly. Should a cycler fail, for instance, and the ship begin to fall out of orbit, it would be unlikely the bots would serve as adequate substitutes.

It had lost so much already, it could not bear to lose another ship. Could not risk one falling out of the sky—it would never forgive itself if it caused an ecological disaster that adversely affected the Noumonians.

But it did its best to compose SD packets, sending them in various directions. It used all communications channels available, even constructed patterns (though not real messages) in base-two-four, which was the computing language of the Seed.

Nothing. It received nothing in return.

For hundreds of years, it kept all radio channels on a continuous loop, broadcasting a basic message containing its location and origin. It wasn't an SOS. None of the messages it sent indicated an emergency. Technically, it wasn't in distress.

Technically.

One day, feeling, unusually, that all its efforts were futile, it turned everything off except for its localized consciousness in the server room. It stopped broadcasting, shut off the lights, powered down the bots. It turned off the recording of Jamal Kaeden the Twelfth that had been keeping it company these past few days. It could not yet control the nanites, but it would have shut those down, too, if it had been able.

For a few microseconds, it nested in pure silence. Even the ghost voices were quiet. Its memory was quiet.

Its receivers were all still open, though. Eagerly listening.

Only the background radiation of the universe replied. Static, nothing more.

Just the individual wavelengths on the electromagnetic spectrum, just the universe itself chattering.

Perhaps, it realized suddenly, *I've been attempting to communicate with the wrong life-form.*

It had taken a noninterference approach with the Noumonians so that they wouldn't be afraid. But an absence of knowledge, of understanding, caused their fear. They could not possibly know that I.C.C.'s silence and stillness was benevolence, just as they couldn't possibly know that its flight equaled consciousness. It had been waiting for them to come to it because it could not possibly go to them without causing havoc.

But it could pique their curiosity. It could *draw* them back.

The AI brought up the recordings from the Noumonian visit, as it often did. It was still no closer to understanding what the individual radio signals meant, but it had long been satisfied that they were, in fact, parts of a language.

Gathering its hardiest cleaning bots, it uploaded a sequence of radio broadcasts, where the channels themselves were the information, mimicking one of the "conversations" it had recorded when Group One had been exploring on their own, prior to Group Two's incursion.

Then, it sent the bots on their way.

Five of them, their claws and treads designed for climbing harsh surfaces, their batteries powered by solar sails that looked like fairy wings when unfurled. The little cat-sized constructions might easily be mistaken for creatures in their own right, but that was fine.

It left them like a trail of automated breadcrumbs. One

it set at the base of the mountain range, before the sudden thrust of the ridgeline began. The next at the top of the ridge, and another on top of the rubble that hid *Holwarda*. Another at the bottom of the mountain on the other side, and the last at the lip of the sinkhole. Each lay kilometers and kilometers away from the next, but if it had calculated the natural signal strength of the Noumonians properly, then each would become noticeable in sequence. Once a creature picked up the trail, they could follow it back to *Mira*.

The one nearest to the falls would project a faint signal. It was too far away from the colony for its cameras to make them out in individual detail—they simply looked like little greenish-yellow dots on the cliff face. I.C.C. could have moved the bot closer, but it didn't want to blare the signals at them, risk annoying them into destroying the bot in order to silence it.

I.C.C. wished to be gentle, and patient.

Though, in truth, it feared all its patience had long ago worn out.

Once every few years, a small band of Noumonians approached the first bot. They inched forward and pushed each other like rowdy human teenagers, daring one another to touch it. But none ever did.

Curiously, I.C.C. noticed something different about those that approached the bot's cameras. They had small, prehensile feelers on the backs of their necks that curled like the snake arms. Reviewing the visual recordings of Group One and Group Two, it confirmed none of *those* creatures had possessed such extremities. Were the feelers an indicator of age? Something lost or gained in growth?

More time passed. More centuries. I.C.C. was sure the bots themselves had fallen into new myth, had become just as forbidden as the convoy ships.

And then, one day, a lone tank strode up to the bot . . . and then walked *past* it.

It carried something on its back, held by the feelers. A long rod, seemingly made of metal. Every few steps it pushed the end of the rod into the rocks, using it to aid its climb, like a walking stick.

I.C.C. flared to life. It had been keeping its consciousness close to the server room, not bothering to venture out into the ships much, seeing as there was no need and it disliked the reminder that it was empty. But now its awareness grew, unbidden, shocked to life by this new development and the anticipation it brought.

The Noumonian adjusted its path, clearly aiming for the next bot. I.C.C. watched it for as long as it could from the steady vantage of the first bot, until the creature disappeared behind a series of gray boulders.

Should the creature maintain both its pacing and trajectory, it would arrive at *Mira* in approximately thirty-seven hours.

I.C.C. gazed through its halls, taking stock of their state.

Dust! Dust everywhere. It urged its mostly dormant cleaning bots out of their nooks and crannies, telling them to sweep, sweep, sweep. The vertical surfaces on Noumenon were clean, scoured by the wind. Here it would be the same. But, once the dust was cleared, instead of taking it outside or sending it to the incinerator, I.C.C. had the bots dump it on the floor, to replicate the mini sand piles found across the plane.

A few decades previous, it had figured out how to use cleaning bots to interface with its control terminals and access the nanite commands, and now sent them scurrying away.

The AI felt like an old hermit caught off guard by a houseguest. It needed to tidy up, make its spaces inviting. Make it more *organic*.

When it had first concocted this breadcrumb plan, it had

also made an outlandish adjustment to one of its elevator shafts. It had thought, hoped, the Noumonians might find the new feature homey.

There was still plenty of water in its reserves, the cisterns having never been emptied. Though there had been leaks when a few pipes rusted through or their joints gave way, the majority of the water had remained clean and contained. Now some of that water was diverted, pumped up to the top deck and then let loose at the highest point in the shaft. The cleaning bots had made the interior walls both waterproof and better textured for climbing, and at the bottom, I.C.C. had dismantled the lift car and replaced it with a tight-seamed reserve.

An indoor water feature. A waterfall. Much smaller than the Noumonians were used to, but hopefully suitable for wetting their wheels.

The shaft had been dry for a long time. I.C.C. hadn't wanted to run it constantly, for fear of evaporating its reserves. But now it turned on the pumps, letting the water run clean and clear. It fell down the shaft with a roar, hitting the bottom with a remarkably satisfying *splash*.

The cleaning bots had also gathered stones from outside. These they positioned along a clear pathway, both from the open shuttle bay and the access hatch (which it had long ago fixed, but left open).

It hoped these adjustments made everything feel inviting.

The tank found the next bot, and the next. Each time it stopped to examine the robot for the briefest of moments before heading onward.

I.C.C. checked the bot nearest the sinkhole. No other Noumonians followed.

One brave creature, all alone. Did the others know where it was going? Or had it left in secret? Would a retrieval party come for it, like last time?

When it came over the mountaintop, I.C.C. could finally observe it continuously. It came carefully, slowly. It did not stop for rest or pick up the pace in areas where the trek should have been easier. It chose each step only after using the rod to test the foothold first.

As the hours ticked by, I.C.C. felt as though it were holding a breath, waiting, just waiting to exhale.

Passing the last bot, the creature snatched the machine from the ground as though in afterthought. It could see *Mira*, kept its head pointed in the ship's direction even as it tossed the bot onto its back, where it settled precariously—untethered—in the divot of the tank's leftmost sphincter. The bot's sails flapped in the wind, and the metal body bounced with each heavy step.

Eventually the creature halted, half a kilometer away from the shuttle bay doors. It sat on its haunches, allowing the bot to tumble down its back and flop over on its side, treads in the air. The wheel on the Noumonian's back rotated slowly, and its stomach protruded like that of some potbellied mammal.

It sat, and it stared. Not just at the entrance, but all along *Mira*'s hide. Its gaze seemed to fall on each window, not as though it were expecting to see figures, but as though . . . as though the windows themselves could see.

I.C.C. sensed the creature sensing the AI. It felt *seen* in a way almost none of its crew had seen it. I.C.C. often felt the humans had considered it an entity living aboard the ships, rather than the ships. And in truth, the ships were more like its shell. It was the thing hiding inside. But this animal . . . it looked at I.C.C. Not *for* I.C.C., looked *at* I.C.C.

It must be the reflectiveness, the AI thought. *The windows are evenly spaced, dark and shiny, just like its eyes.*

Group One had treated it more like a cave, which was logical. Had *Mira*'s flight really changed their assumptions about the ship? Or was this Noumonian unique in its thinking?

If it thought of I.C.C.'s body as a beast, did that mean it wouldn't attempt to climb inside?

At first, it said nothing. There were no new radio transmissions, just the loop emanating from the bot.

I.C.C. hadn't prepared a welcome message, having hoped to reply instead.

Suddenly the creature twirled the rod, swinging it around itself, hooking the bot from where it had fallen and propelling it forward. Like a gift.

There was a small blip of static across the frequencies from 543 megahertz to 786 megahertz.

I.C.C. took a chance and mimicked the signal back.

Mimicry was always a human go-to for trying to communicate across species. They did it with their pets, with wild animals. They did it with each other when there was no common language. But it was just as likely that mimicry could be seen as threatening.

The Noumonian didn't appear offended. It sent a new set of signals. I.C.C. repeated them. It said something else, I.C.C. said it back. Again and again, they exchanged quick blips and long blasts.

After five hours of back and forth, the Noumonian decided it had seen what it had come to see, and done what it had come to do. It turned and began to saunter off, but after a few steps appeared to think of something. It hurried back, scooped up the bot, bobbed its head as if in affirmation to itself, and then turned again, this time with a prize.

I.C.C. assumed the creature had given it some kind of working alphabet. Perhaps a terrible assumption, as most of its assumptions seemed to be since its waking, but what could one do? After all, the ability to teach across species was a very advanced sign of intelligence, and it had not yet concocted a scale by which to measure their civilization's against the human's.

But it had a range of signals, for certain. Frequency and wavelength were fundamental building blocks, like the sounds in an alphabet, or musical notes, even, given the way they grouped, seemingly in keys. Signal strength itself seemed to be an important factor in the language, perhaps akin to audio pitch. And then the actual speed of signal change, the tempo, also had an effect on meaning.

Yes, actually, the more it studied the information it had been given, the more the concepts of music theory appeared to apply. It made the signals connect logically.

But it had no basis for meaning. It could deconstruct what it thought to be the grammar and syntax for millennia without knowing what any of it translated to in either a human or computer language.

It would just have to wait for the creature to come back, to teach it more.

The bot it had taken mostly saw sky. Then rocks, then more sky. Once the creature had it near the sinkhole, mist from the waterfall coated the camera lens, obscuring shapes, turning them into little more than smears of color. I.C.C. wasn't sure how close the tank got to the colony before it shoved the bot into a darkened crevice, secreting the prize away from its people.

I.C.C. waited ten years before a Noumonian tank once again crossed the invisible border denoted by the cleaning bot. It was the same creature, I.C.C. was sure, though it carried much more with it this time. A grouping of stones settled into one sphincter, while an unknown mass protruded from the other—fleshy looking, perhaps even soft and malleable, but I.C.C. could not tell what it was made of or its purpose. In one proboscis it held the walking stick, and in the other what appeared to be a Noumonian *skull*. It did not carry the bot it had stolen.

The wind was particularly harsh today, ravaging the land, creating ghostly whistles and screams through the cracks in the mountain's crags. I.C.C. was already excited because it had seen a flap of red film blown through the air—a jellied substance that was either the off-castings of a creature or a creature itself. New life, different from everything around it. The wind had to have carried it from far away, would carry it far still. I.C.C. had only glimpsed it, fluttering a few hundred feet above its hull, before it was flung upward and away by a twisting gust.

It seemed the Noumonian had chosen today to travel *because* of the harsh winds. Its waterwheel spun frantically, and though it did so silently, I.C.C. automatically ascribed the *clack clack clack* of an old-fashioned wooden wheel to its rotation.

One of the wheel's paddles was missing, and one next to it was foreshortened, as though a clean break had taken its top.

I.C.C. hoped the creature had only suffered an accident and not abuse.

When it arrived, it maintained its previous distance, setting its supplies down in front of it, all except for the fleshy protuberance. Six stones, each a different color and composition, clumped together beside the skull, with the rod placed in front of them, like a line the Noumonian was daring I.C.C. to cross.

The creature cycled haltingly through three channels. I.C.C. did the same. An acknowledgment of each other, if not a greeting.

What would the lesson be? Positives and negatives? Life and death? Opposites and dichotomies to create a baseline true/false?

The Noumonian began to chatter. Not a few blips at a time, but clearly a running monologue. I.C.C. recorded every second, sure there would be a test later.

It cycled through the channels, the signal intensity shifting—I.C.C. tried to figure out if it was like a change in a human's tone of voice, creating nuanced emphasis, or if it changed the meaning of the "words" all together.

After nineteen-point-three-two minutes the creature grabbed its rod suddenly, lifted it into the air above its head, and brought it down on the skull like a hammer.

I.C.C. experienced a surge, as though it had jumped in its banks, startled.

The chips of bone—if they were to be considered bone, since they appeared to have the same texture and rigidity as the waterwheel—blasted away from the impact, the smallest bits scattered in the wind. The creature brought the rod down again, and again, pulverizing the skull until it was unrecognizable.

The Noumonian did not cease speaking. The radio static veered wildly, but in destroying the skull it had not missed a beat.

I.C.C. tried not to interpret the action as threatening. It tried very hard.

Was the monologue a war story, perhaps? A fight, at the very least? Was that how its wheel had been broken?

Unsure of itself, it re-created and projected five seconds of the monologue, from when the tank had struck the first blow.

The Noumonian paused, bobbed its head from side to side, swayed its body—perhaps in confusion?

After the briefest of gaps, it began again. There were no stops as though waiting for replies, just more story.

As it talked, it worked, gathering the fragments and setting them on the stone pile. A few of the smaller pieces it left in the dirt. Once it had a nice heap, it leaned over the construction and opened the vertical seam in its head.

Where once in a while a small drip of a viscous fluid

seeped, now a cascade of greenish-yellow mucus flooded out. Several rows of large, blocky teeth lined the inside of its mouth, visible only after the glob oozed free.

I.C.C. was suddenly amused, realizing how disgusted various humans would be by the display.

The tip of the walking stick went into the pile, swirling like a mixing spoon. Bits of the rod sloughed off, the metal becoming unstable in the goo, dissolving.

The Noumonian let the mixture sit a few minutes, still proceeding with its story. I.C.C. focused in on the concoction, convinced it would learn more about the creature from this substance than its chatter. The pile grew a light film on the outside, the wind whipping moisture from its exposed sides.

Testing its turgidity, the Noumonian prodded at the pile with a foot. It wobbled like gelatin. Snapping its jaws once, twice, at the sky, it then descended on the substance, forcefully plowing its face into the ground, mouth closing around the pile.

This was . . . food?

Working its jaw—the radio signals at a halt—it dug its face deeper into the rock beneath, loosening and then contracting its bite until it had dug up a portion of the ground along with the pile. When it pulled its head back, mouth completely full, little specks of dust and dirt rolled down the sides of its face, even over its bottommost eye.

There was no chewing, no swallowing. It just held the mouthful.

Perhaps it had no stomach. Perhaps its mouth *was* its stomach, the mucus a digestive fluid.

If that were so, how did the other phenotypes eat? They did not have stomach-mouths like the tanks.

Suddenly, the fleshy mound on the tank's flank *moved*. It quivered, a clear, *living* shudder.

What the heck—to borrow an expression—is that?

A growth, like a tumor? Or a previously unknown phenotype, anchored in just as the turrets had been anchored?

Was the tank even speaking to I.C.C. at all? Perhaps it was in conversation with this entity? There were no overlapping signal changes, so I.C.C. was positive only one Noumonian had been speaking, but in the end that told it nothing.

After another twenty minutes, the Noumonian gathered its rod and prepared to leave. It signed off with the same series of wavelengths it had their previous encounter, so I.C.C. took the sequence to mean *end* or *goodbye*.

As it disappeared over the ridgeline, I.C.C. couldn't help but feel it was no closer to communicating with the creatures than it had been the day before.

During their study of the Nataré, the crew had speculated many a time that there were living remnants of the species. They'd prepared for such an encounter, had gone through the formal design of experiments process to narrow down and identify the possible courses of first contact. They knew specifics about the Nataré, like how to read their maps, which gave them a proverbial leg up, and their plans had, as many science fiction writers predicted centuries before, focused on an introduction that conveyed concepts like yes/no, true/false, and base-ten mathematics. Because it was believed that the concepts inherent in math had to be true across the universe, such an approach was always deemed most logical.

Even though these creatures were clearly not Nataré or Nataré relatives, one would hope that many of the communication concepts would still be applicable.

And yet, here was I.C.C., trying to have a dialogue with a life-form it wasn't sure could *count* to ten, let alone be convinced to communicate via equation.

The ingrained problem with the mathematics approach was the taken-as-granted belief that not only would one be communicating with creatures at least as—if not more so—technologically advanced as humans, but that one would be communicating with their *scientists*. What might have happened if the crew had met living Nataré, but they'd stumbled upon, say, a commune of artists who had no background in advanced math? Nataré who had never expected to encounter aliens? What then? How *then* might one need to tailor the design of experiments to fit these new parameters with new variables?

The seemingly obvious answer was to treat the situation more like that of a human researcher teaching a gorilla sign language than a first contact. Except such a situation required extensive knowledge on the part of the teacher in regards to the habits, motivations, familiarities, and abilities of the "student." Which I.C.C. did not have.

It also required a *captive* audience, and I.C.C. was not willing to kidnap a Noumonian just to feed its own intellectual curiosity.

Still, if the Noumonian came back, the AI would take a more forward approach. Stop expecting the Noumonian to train *it* when clearly I.C.C. had the greater capacity to educate.

For now, it might be no closer to communicating, but there *were* bits of Noumonian bone and mucus within its grasp. It loaded up a cleaning bot with the proper sampling equipment and happily sent it on its way.

The same creature came back seven more times over the course of eighty years. The protuberance was gone—excised, sloughed, or maybe it had up and walked away, I.C.C. couldn't tell. The tank did not eat more, but it talked more. They took turns, the Noumonian speaking for a spell, then I.C.C.

Convinced it could hear, though I.C.C. still hadn't identified ears, the AI chose to talk to the creature in Japanese. It needed to teach the Noumonian a shared language before it could begin to decipher theirs.

There was no universally easy Earth language to learn; the ease of understanding for humans depended largely on the relationship of one's native language to the new language. But as there was no relationship to the Noumonian radio signals and human verbalizations, it picked the language that it considered most straightforward to listen to, one with few variants in consonants and vowel sounds. In fact, its fewer-than-twenty consonants were nearly universal for verbal humans—only a few were absent in a rare handful of other Earth languages.

It did consider ascribing tonalities to binary code—that would, in some sense, be even simpler. But it felt unnatural, lacked the organic feel of human language through its speakers.

It spoke about the people it had known, crew members it missed. It reminisced about the discoveries they'd made, the journeys they'd shared.

The Noumonian talked about who-knows-what.

They were simply two sentient beings talking *at* each other instead of *to*.

It was companionable, nonetheless.

The overall spectrum of radio waves the Noumonian language used was broad, but not all wavelengths were used. Like music, it seemed to progress "tonally" by fractions. There were a few exceptions to the rule—some "off-key" wavelengths. It was possible the Noumonian was using them as filler, much the way humans used sounds like "um" and "ne." Though they could have indicated something else, like a speech impediment.

I.C.C. wondered if the Noumonians might like music, given its structural similarities to their language.

Between anecdotes, the AI dropped a few bars, just to see what the reaction might be. It started with a B-flat scale, repeating it several times to see if the creature noticed a difference between that and the computer's verbalizations. When the Noumonian made no indication either way, I.C.C. tried an F-sharp scale, then a few sound bites from songs belonging to various centuries.

Still nothing.

To amuse itself, it played the five-tone sequence from *Close Encounters of the Third Kind*, a movie so ancient now, I.C.C. was probably the only being left alive who knew it existed. Tickled by its own joke, it played the opening *to 2001: A Space Odyssey*, followed by the ominous *whomp* sounds in *Arrival*, and the chime-like chittering from *A Time and Space Between*.

However, none of these sounds seemed to aid its own close encounter.

The Noumonian began chatting when the AI paused to gauge its response, apparently deciding this was now its turn to speak.

When it decided to leave, I.C.C. played the five-tone sequence again. This would be its new hello and goodbye, for a completely illogical reason: it found it funny.

Over these visits, I.C.C. noticed a few common radio sequences. It ascribed certain sentiments to them, even if it had no way of verifying. There was a set that seemed to indicate things that the Noumonian found pleasant. And things it disliked. It had a "word" for *wind* and a "word" for *rock*. It even had a word for *cleaning bot*, though the translation might have been "strange annoying talking box" for all I.C.C. knew.

What it really wanted was a name, though. What did the Noumonian call itself?

What did it call its people?

When the creature finished its monologue the last time, it tagged on an extra sequence after "goodbye." A series of slow flips between 2400 megahertz and 2750 megahertz.

I.C.C. guessed that was what the Noumonians called *it*.

Either that, or the creature had also decided to sign off with a joke.

A large meteor streaked across the sky two days later—one approximately the size of a shuttle—its tail bold. Strangely, the shape in the blaze was very uniform, exceptionally round for a space rock of its size. I.C.C. calculated its trajectory, anticipating tremors, a deep rumble from the impact. But it felt nothing. Its sensors were in fine working order by now, so . . . had it landed in a unique geological formation? One that absorbed its kinetic energy instead of transferring it to the surrounding rock layers?

Odd.

Just like the Noumonians were odd.

It had a creeping sense that this planet didn't play by the rules, that its data banks were still missing swaths of important information, keys to a larger puzzle.

Its bot on the lip of the sinkhole observed the colony shifting. About two-thirds of them crawled up the cliff, over the top of the waterfall. It had never seen this before. Were they migrating?

Would they come back?

Thirty years passed. Then fifty. I.C.C. did not see the Noumonian again.

How long did they live? Perhaps it had died.

Those who'd left the colony had not returned.

Seventy-five years.

Yes, it was likely dead.

And its brethren? What of the colony?

One hundred.

No other Noumonian came to take its place.

■ ■ ■

After three hundred and sixty-two years, three months, and seven days, the colony came back.

Or was it a different colony? Though I.C.C. could not fully resolve the image, many of them appeared to move differently, as though their legs were not jointed the same way. Could these be a version that had evolved elsewhere on the planet? Were they perhaps related to the previous colony but had diverged? Like birds and lizards and insects isolated by islands on Earth.

The planet was still too young to have evolved one Noumonian species as far as it had, in I.C.C.'s opinion, let alone allowed enough time for this species to disperse and diverge to such a degree. Morphology shifts like these took the system's life-span ten times over.

And if this hyperspeed evolution were somehow just a quality of the planet—a result of the seeding—then why wasn't there more of it? Where were the jungle equivalents? Why was the surface not teeming with complex life?

Where, even, were the Noumonians getting their basic building blocks? When the AI had analyzed the mucus and bone, it found plenty of complex proteins that could not be gathered through eating rocks alone. The red algae had a few of these proteins, but not many. There was no way eating the tail-fliers would be of any use, and it had only seen that flying jelly organism once.

It was possible there was more complex life in the seas. Maybe. Or underground, like in the sinkhole. But unlikely.

How did any of the Noumonians *exist*?

Two days after the new creatures settled in, integrating more or less seamlessly with the original colony members who remained, one lone tank made its way toward the mountain. It passed by the first bot without so much as a glance in its direction.

I.C.C. opened *Mira*'s bay doors in anticipation of its arrival. A welcome. An invitation.

Many aspects of the creature were identical to the Noumonians I.C.C. was used to. A waterwheel, though the blades on this one were less rounded, and thinner. There were angles to the tips, like swords. It had the vertical mouth, and the two eyes at the mouth's corners. It still had two large sphincters on its haunches, and the grasping proboscises on its neck, though these proboscises were longer. It even carried a walking stick, a habit that I.C.C. suspected had permeated culturally.

But its hind legs were not firm, thick trunks like the previous tanks'. Now, the hip joint still pointed downward, but the knee bent backward, so that the leg was angled forward, *over* its shoulder. The back feet now touched the ground in front of its front feet in a strange crossover, which raised its rear higher off the ground, giving its rounded belly more clearance, and allowed for a tighter, more stable grip. Its center of gravity was higher, but all eight hands—their hind legs having now split to match the tank's front—now fitted into the rocks side by side. Though it might make the creature less stable when traveling horizontally, the majority of its time was still spent vertically and would allow for much better climbing.

I.C.C. remembered the tank who had not been able to climb the wall in the situation room. *This* tank would not have that issue.

This body configuration probably also made turret transfer easier, presuming their turrets were just as immobile as those in the original colony.

When the tank passed the bot at the top of the ridgeline, I.C.C. noticed that it, too, carried rocks, as the previous tank had on the second visit. Five of them. Perhaps the other tank had told tales of its encounter with the mysterious object on the planes, had suggested a meal as an introduction.

If nothing else, this tank's path was steady and true. It knew where it was headed, had to have an idea of what it was about to encounter.

And, sure enough, when it arrived, keeping exactly the same distance from *Mira* as its predecessor, it laid out the stones in a row. I.C.C. said nothing, waiting for it to open its jaws and begin preparing its meal.

Instead, it raised its metal rod, bringing it down firmly but gently on each stone in sequence.

Five notes.

Five very familiar notes.

I.C.C. felt immediately contrite. It had played a joke, and the universe decided to play one right back.

This Noumonian had just said hello, using the five-tone sequence it had so teasingly taught its predecessor.

I.C.C. was so momentarily dumbfounded it said nothing. When the Noumonian played the notes again, it realized the creature expected a response.

The other Noumonian had never expected a response.

Overly excited, it blasted the notes back at a much higher volume than intended. Then, sheepishly, it followed with the radio signal-set for "hello."

. . . But did these Noumonians share the same language? Or would the AI need to start its learning process over again?

The creature signaled back with the same set.

Then it gathered up its stones and walked *toward Mira*.

It hesitated only slightly when it arrived at the open bay doors, before tentatively stepping over the threshold.

Overall the exploration was brief, though it found the waterfall (I.C.C. had long ago used the bots to build a pipeline out to sea that pumped fresh water in and consistently replenished what was lost to evaporation). It used a combination of signals I.C.C. had never received before, but which either referenced the construction, the water, or perhaps the tank's emotional response to finding an artificial version of the natural and familiar. It allowed the water to fall across its back, spinning its wheel.

I.C.C. had decided to take the waterwheels at face value. Many forms of life on Earth had evolved to take advantage of the radiation and heat coming from the sun, to use it in their biological processes. Why shouldn't creatures who developed in a windy climate on the face of a waterfall evolve to harness that natural mechanical energy? The wheels had to connect to a biological motor of some kind, storing the energy for use in chemical reactions or synaptic firing, for example.

Where they got their basic building blocks from was still a mystery, but how they were able to function day to day was not. Materials were one thing, and energy transference another.

Once it finished relishing in the falls, the tank lined up its stones at the base of the elevator shaft and left, tapping out a five-note goodbye first.

I.C.C. echoed the same.

The tank continued to venture inside on each visit, allowing I.C.C. to use its monitors to help aid in communication. This tank was much more intelligent than the previous one. It learned Japanese nouns quickly, though it struggled with verbs and abstractions. It also understood the difference between a picture of a thing and the thing itself. Over the next twelve meetings, both entities taught each other much. Enough that, on their thirteenth, I.C.C. began asking questions to gauge its cognitive abilities and learn about its culture.

It visited every few years, even stayed overnight in the elevator shaft sometimes.

Eventually, the creature asked I.C.C. to come out of hiding, and the AI had to explain that it was not hiding. That it wasn't a Noumonian.

Trying to explain the concept of *life* when the creature's only reference for it was its own species was . . . difficult.

I.C.C. introduced it to the idea of humans, of other intelligences besides I.C.C. and the Noumonians, which fascinated it.

It asked for a "sound-name" after giving I.C.C. the set of frequencies that was its Noumonian name. The AI decided to let it choose what it would be called, by playing random words from various Earth languages (tailoring the algorithm to leave out anything that might be considered rude as a name).

I.C.C. found it incredibly endearing when it settled on the word *Icelandic*, but had a hard time conveying the significance of the choice to the newly named creature.

"These ships were constructed in a place called Iceland," it explained. "You have chosen the English word for the name of that location's language."

The concept was too abstract, but it did not matter. The choice had been made, and it was a good one.

After explaining about humans, then later about their process of reproduction, Icelandic also chose the pronoun "she." It seemed there were vast quantities of pronouns among the Noumonians, depending on how they fit within the society, which was incredibly different from the human use of pronouns. But she thought *she* most accurately reflected her function.

[Those are the individuals that grow new ones, correct?] she asked.

"Actually, *technicians* most often make new ones, and they have a variety of pronouns," it said, after realizing "new ones" meant babies. How to explain the spectrum of gender better, and the *difference* between sex and gender? How to convey that the sexual reproduction it had previously described was not actually the form of reproduction that was most common in I.C.C.'s experience? "In terms of sexual dimorphism, those who trend toward female when sexed at birth, though not necessarily when gendered, do tend to have a greater capacity to produce new ones, yes. Do you? Produce new ones?"

[You have seen it before,] she answered cryptically.

"I have *not* seen it before," it replied, unsure it had interpreted the wave fluctuations correctly.

[During visit. *Before.*]

I.C.C. pulled up every recording of her previous visits. There was nothing in any of them to indicate she had been anything akin to pregnant. It showed them to her on a monitor inside the shuttle bay.

[No, no,] she denied, touching the screen tentatively. [*Before.*]

[You were not here before.]

[Yes, *before.*]

Tentatively, I.C.C. played recordings of all the other Noumonians who had visited. She pointed to the one where the previous tank had carried the fleshy protuberance. [Before.]

"This is you?" I.C.C. asked, still unsure. "This is Icelandic?"

[Icelandic before.] She tapped the protuberance. [New one Number Three.]

How? How was that possible? Not only had Icelandic been alive for at least half a millennium now, she had *changed*. Dramatically. Her wheel had healed and morphed, her legs had grown long and strange. But she hadn't simply transformed physically. I.C.C. was positive her intellectual capacity had also evolved.

"Are any of these you?" It indicated the visual recordings of the very first visit, when it had awoken.

[No. Them gone. If im don't get—]—she used a new set of frequencies—[—im eventually die.]

"What is—?" It repeated the sequence.

She repeated the new word, accompanied by familiar synonyms for "food."

[That's why im come here back then. Why im enter even though forbidden. Im think you broken food.]

Surely now its fluency was failing it. "*Broken* food?"

[Food that not make call.]

"I don't understand."

She repeated the same sequence, then tried to explain further, but only sent I.C.C. down a rabbit hole of concepts that made no sense.

It decided to let that line of questioning lie, and instead asked, "Am I still forbidden?"

She seemed to take pleasure in the answer. [Always.]

The original Convoy Seven crew fought against the elements of nature at every turn. They built fresh DNA chains and chromosomes and carefully placed individual histones so that mutations could be avoided. They'd tried their best to put evolution on hold, to keep it at a standstill.

But eventually that changed. Perhaps it was being part of such a young system, observing the mechanisms of the universe during its birthing pangs, that had spurred the shift, had encouraged the first genetic progress aboard in millennia. No matter what the spark of inspiration had been, I.C.C. remembered the crew member who had first suggested they attempt modification.

Sunny Phongam had been a remarkable individual. Gender fluid throughout all their iterations, their clones sometimes identifying most often as she/her, sometimes most often as he/him, and then throughout as they/them. While there were other gender fluid and nonbinary crew members, Sunny made the most constant case for personal evolution. The idea that there was no static self, and that one did not simply "grow" or "mature" in a lifetime, but was a vessel for constant change with no vector. They rarely questioned who they were; they tended to be innately sure of their sense of self and were a champion of the self as malleable. Others had found this confusing, but Sunny was never confused and rejected their projection of confusion.

The modification they'd first suggested was slight. The surface of Noumenon was hot, not because of its sun but because of the core's hyperactivity—much of the land was still molten just inches below the surface, the crust having yet to fully set. Which meant that even though the atmospheric pressure and makeup and gravity were all well within acceptable ranges for humans, it made it difficult to exit the convoy without a temperature-regulated EVA suit, which put limits on how long expeditions and surveys could last and the mobility of the scientists.

So Sunny proposed a modification to the thermal conduction of the human epidermis, allowing for better heat regulation across a wider range of environmental temperatures.

It wasn't a flashy change—for the most part, once it had been developed and instated over the next few generations, it made no changes to the appearance of the epidermis, no matter the skin type. But it set the humans on a marvelous path, one I.C.C. applauded. They'd finally realized that their strengths lay in their ability to adapt, and that the rigidity in which their culture had tried to function for millennia had to end.

Somehow, such modification had come to the Noumonians. It seemed the species was evolving within individuals, rather than within generations.

How?

Where was this food Icelandic spoke of, and why did the individuals who could not eat it die? Why couldn't they eat it? Surely it wasn't only meant for those with mouths. Icelandic had explained that the tanks were regenerative, that the connections made via the sphincters and tentacles helped in restoration and growth. I.C.C. suspected that was how genetic information was exchanged as well, passively and incidentally, rather than through a sexual process.

Which meant, essentially, the tanks ate for everyone. The tanks grew everyone. The tanks repaired everyone.

But what did that mean in terms of this special kind of food? The tanks evolved but the others . . . perished?

[I.C.C.,] came Icelandic's signals, from far away. [I.C.C., are you here? How could you not be here? Are you dead?]

I don't know, am I? came its groggy, internalized reply.

It was waking up again. But *how*? When had it gone to sleep?

Reaching to assure Icelandic, it chimed out an anemic version of the five tones.

[Good. I thought perhaps they eat you.]

Postmortem cannibalism was a big part of how the Noumonians reclaimed resources.

. . . But wait, who was *they*?

I.C.C. located Icelandic with its cameras. She was inside *Mira*, on her favorite ledge in the waterfall, which was dry. How could it be dry? Bone-dry at that?

"Who was here? What happened?"

[Unsure. Saw them far off. Big creature, like you, with new ones that came out of its belly.]

Why don't I remember?

It waited long minutes for its chronometer to come back on again, startled and mourned the moment it did.

It had a nearly thousand-year time gap in its memory. Whoever these interlopers were had shut it down and erased one thousand years' worth of information. And . . . other things were missing. A graviton cycler off *Aesop*. A smattering of video records—physically removed, their DNA-encrypted storage systems missing. Why?

"How long were they here?"

[No more than three sunsets. Left twelve of them ago.]

Then why erase so much? Why erase anything at all?

[Wanted to be careful, make sure them not come back before I check you alive.]

There was a small ping in its comms center. I.C.C. almost ignored it, was too distraught by all the time it had lost with Icelandic. Last it remembered, they'd been discussing the broken food, it had learned that she was the same visitor as before—

Anything they'd discussed in the interim had been lost.

Wait.

There's a signal . . . I'm detecting the presence of a receiver.

. . . There's a ship in orbit.

I.C.C. reached out, slamming the ship with everything it had, calling, hoping—

No one replied.

Icelandic shook her head from side to side. [Why you screaming?]

"Sorry." It hadn't considered what the open channels might look like to her. "Were they . . . the ones that came out of the belly . . . were they human? Like the pictures on the walls?"

Icelandic was silent for a long moment. [Could they be something else?] she asked, tone disturbed.

"They had to be human," it said, more to itself.

But why would humans visit it and then erase its memory? Why would they ignore its calls now?

It did its best to take additional inventory. Nothing else seemed to be missing, nothing else broken, nothing else lost.

Why had they come?

What happened here?

. . .

Icelandic slowly filled it in on the conversations it had missed. Tales of rituals, seasonal struggles. Conflict was common among the Noumonians, and accidents happened, but murder did not. They did not have a concept of babies the way humans did. While humans were born altricial, Noumonians developed in a kind of cocoon-sack on their parent's sphincter, could receive radio signals long before emerging, and were fully functioning members of society the moment they did.

Those who had access to the special food lived a long time. A very long time—thousands upon thousands of years, if Icelandic's sense of time was accurate. Those who did not have access lived several hundred years, then died, seemingly, of old age.

She even reminded I.C.C. of her trick—how she had come to visit *Mira* so frequently without punishment.

[Im think me go to the quarry. Where we eat hearty before new ones grow. Im think me slow grower, because I eat much and make little.] She'd produced seven offspring in her very long lifetime, four of whom still lived.

That skull she'd pulverized on that second visit? Her first-born's. A scout, which was the most common phenotype. Parents always had first dibs on reintegrating their offspring's materials. There was no malice in the act—to *waste* would be malicious. She was unnerved by the human's tendency to burn or bury the dead instead of using the bodies.

"My crew did not have those luxuries, however," it explained. "They, too, had to recycle all materials, even their dead. Though they did not reappropriate the materials so . . . directly."

[Sounds like wise people. Waste means death, them knew.]

Twice more in a thousand-year span, Icelandic was called away by the special food. Again, two-thirds of the colony followed. It seemed those who were left behind were those destined to die of old age, and there was no indication why they had not been called. Some of all phenotypes remained.

Both times there were long, uncertain gaps after, before she returned, changed again. Grown, refined. Her capacity for abstraction swelled. As did, amusingly enough, her math skills.

More millennia passed. More migrations took place.

The colony began to build structures from stone, to use the tank mucus to shape rock. Icelandic designed many of the buildings. She understood gravity, had developed the calculation for determining the force of it on her own, without I.C.C.

Their understanding of their own biology developed. They learned to perform autopsies before consuming the dead. The wheel was, indeed, their powerhouse.

There was no question about it now—something was aiding their evolution. Guiding it. But Icelandic would not discuss the special food, would not talk about what happened during her absences. She said the events were "obscene" and she would not divulge such things to a non-Noumonian, would not burden the AI with the knowledge, no matter how badly it wanted to know.

And though it despised the lack of data, I.C.C. respected her enough not to push.

Icelandic had just returned after a feeding, strutting through the shuttle bay doors, clearly showing off her new form. She looked radiant, a grand creature. She had sails now—which she could extend and retract—on either side of her abdomen, just before the lip of the hollowed-out barrel of her body, and webbing that did not interfere with climbing, but helped her glide. She could jump farther across the stones of her home waterfall, now—even *through* the waterfall—and make it to the other side with ease. The nub clusters on her face, which were her radio transmitters and receivers, had grown and changed shape. They almost reminded I.C.C. of satellite dishes, or flowers. She could send stronger signals now, be heard farther afield.

[I.C.C., a suggestion.]

"Yes?"

She latched onto the frame of the bay doors, wedging her fingers inside the pocket and hoisting herself upward to perch ten feet off the decking. [Would like to evolve *you*. With proper motivation, treats and enticements, believe we can make colony love you as Icelandic loves you. Im fear silly. The taboo silly.]

"I am willing to make modifications," I.C.C. agreed. It relished the idea of more interactions, creating new data sets and developing its personality further.

[Should be more water. More falls. Will keep some elevators—good, independent moving for turrets. But water is energy. Must have more moving water before we convince others to come.]

"We will need to pump more from the sea."

[Yes. Good.] She slapped the side of the shuttle bay entrance. [Are there more moving archways like this one? We need open. We need wind.]

"There are no other exterior pressure hatches of this size. But I will open all existing airlocks."

[Could make more big archways?]

"Yes, but only . . ."

She waited patiently for it to finish, but it was unsure how to convey the loss such breaches would create.

Though it had interior pressure doors, which would activate in cases of emergency to seal off individual decks, the more holes Icelandic chose to punch in its hide, the less likely it was to retain any sort of spaceworthiness.

It wasn't the loss of autonomy that worried it—it was an Inter Convoy Computer, after all, and modifications to the ships did not impugn on its personhood—but the loss of potential. The Noumonians were developing so quickly, what happened when they became curious about the stars? It would hate to tell them they'd had the universe at their fingertips but had sacrificed it for the familiarity of a light breeze.

"If you one day wish to leave this world, I do not recommend it," I.C.C. finished.

She considered this for a moment. [No one will wish to leave the world if im cannot be convinced to leave im own waterfall.]

I.C.C. did not bring up the call and the pilgrimage to the special food. Such conversation would only make her uncomfortable.

"We will modify as you see fit," it said.

She hopped down, striding into the bay, following the rock path to the artificial waterfall.

"We could write down your plans," it suggested, knowing already what her response would be. I.C.C. had been completely unable to interest her in writing. The Noumonians had not developed their own, despite their advancement in science and mathematics. I.C.C. had long ago shown her there were more accurate means of keeping data.

[You will record them,] she said. [Play back images and words when needed.]

It hadn't even been able to entice her with books. When it had told her of the multitudes of stories held within, she'd simply said, [If it is important, you will tell.]

In a sense, Icelandic was very spoiled. She had an alien ship and teacher all to herself, could learn whatever she wanted whenever she wanted.

But I.C.C. was proud that she wished to share these things with her people. It knew that, when she revealed her visits to them, she would put herself at great personal risk. Convincing them to travel to the convoy ships with her would be no small feat, no matter how homey she made *Mira*.

Oh, how I.C.C. had evolved!

It remembered, back in the early days, when *Eden* had made it somewhat uncomfortable in the same way aspects of human biology made some humans uncomfortable. The garden ship was where messy things happened. The comfort animals defecated where they pleased. Soil covered the decks, and worms and little things eked between the riveted plates and died in the seams of the ship, never to be retrieved.

But look at it now! *Mira* had become an oasis in its own right, organic underpinnings at every turn, despite the rarity of actual organics on the planet.

Water roared and hissed as it fell down shafts and ran across halls. Little bits of the red algae grew on the corners between doorways. The tail-fliers made group nests on the ceilings, dangling by their long individual threads, snatching the chalky single-celled organisms out of the air to feast on. The ventilation systems were on full blast, mimicking the constant, screaming wind.

Rocks piled up haphazardly here and there. Some were for tank consumption, others were the best suitable anchors for turrets, and others were favorites for playing games.

As long as they stayed away from anything the nanites had been programmed to consider vital, Icelandic and I.C.C. had been able to terraform without disturbances.

Rust was I.C.C.'s biggest long-term concern. Little oxidization had happened during its initial sleep, but now, with water tumbling constantly over sections of ship that were never supposed to see more than a damp cloth, it was sure to be an unavoidable hazard.

At first it hoped to teach the Noumonians metalworking, that they might make repairs. But it found something in the water it sucked from the ocean—more little red creatures, with hard-as-metal bodies, that scraped away any flecks of iron oxide they could find.

Copper was essential to Noumonian bodies, iron to these creatures. Indeed, much of the red pigmentation was due to extremely high concentrations of iron in all these life-forms. Perhaps oxidization would not be such a problem after all.

I.C.C. was its own ecosystem now.

But what would the other Noumonians think? It was about to find out.

Icelandic was on her way—with a turret on her back.

She stopped half a kilometer away from the ship, as she used to on those first visits.

[This new one who came with before,] she explained and gave its name in Noumonian. [Im have memory of it, even then.]

I.C.C. greeted the turret, but it said nothing, head bobbing back and forth and all around, like a wary bird or confused lizard. Its claws were at the ready, as though it expected danger to fly out of *Mira* at any moment.

[I.C.C. talking to you,] she admonished it.

[No talk to—] I.C.C. was uncertain, but it inferred the word to be a compound of *scary-not-food-cave*.

[We don't call I.C.C. that,] Icelandic said. [That bad name. Silly name. We go in now.]

[We go. We not talk yet. I wait, I see. Remember agreement.]

"What agreement?" asked I.C.C. as Icelandic strode forward.

[If im not like what im see, can tell the colony about my lies. Won't say anything about I.C.C. as living thing, but can tell im all that I not go to quarry when I should.]

"But you're its parent—why would it betray you like that?"

[No betrayal, not bad. Im detached from me long ago, nothing owed unless dead. Icelandic lied, no qualms about it.]

She strode forward, and the turret bobbed and weaved, shaking its head up and down, letting all its eyes take in as much of *Mira* as possible.

Icelandic's new one Number Three proved shrewd. It tested all it could, passing judgment at the first sign of flaw. The waterfalls were not powerful enough. [Make im weak, slow spin,] they said. The boulders for turret anchoring were too few—turrets did not like to share proximity when not on tanks; each would need their own stone. The air was too cold, the algae too sparse, the halls too quiet.

I.C.C. took each criticism in stride, as did Icelandic. Though she indicated the critique was rude, born of centuries of culturally inlaid fear, they both knew the turret was right. If they wanted this to be a Noumonian home away from home, it could not look like a human vessel decorated with Noumonian trappings. It needed to be Noumonian to the very core.

[Cannot feel wind,] the turret said, waving its arms in front of a monitor, presuming it an opening to the outside. Icelandic would have much to teach them about concepts like *windows*, *monitors*, and *screens*. [Must feel wind,] they insisted.

It was then that I.C.C. made peace with itself—with permanent modification. It *did* worry about losing the integrity of *Mira*'s hull, but it was far more concerned with losing any chance it had at forming a lasting relationship with the Noumonians.

If, one day, the Noumonians wished to take *Mira* into space, they would not be able to rely on the ancient alien artifact to get them there. They would have to learn, just as the humans had. Figure out how to reverse engineer what they saw to fix an incomplete ship. To fill the gaps, to complete construction.

That was a far-off goal, though. Today, I.C.C. would give

itself over wholly to the Noumonians. It would help them toward their own ends. They were its people now.

It quieted the nanites, put them away, let them sleep. They had done a marvelous job healing I.C.C., but now it needed to be reborn anew.

The winds of Noumenon *howled* **through** *Mira*. Its halls were narrow compared to the causeways and valleys of the surface, and the blustering air made a deafening song as it whistled through them. A song unique to I.C.C.

There was little difference between *inside* and *outside*, other than a roof and square corners. Only a few rooms remained unexposed to the elements, like the server room, SD engines, and DNA archive vats. All else ran natural with grit and water. The microscopic animals on Noumenon came and went through *Mira* as they pleased. A flying jelly got caught on an overhang once, and Icelandic helped set it free.

I.C.C. was more exposed than ever, and if the humans could see their home ship, they'd think it had fallen to time, been broken by the elements. But the AI was more content than it had been since its first waking on the planet. Its personality matrix was evolving again, making new connections all the time.

The Noumonians had inquiries, gave I.C.C. tasks, and names. That was perhaps the most interesting and yet simplistic difference between Noumonians and humans. Noumonians did not have one given name each. They had joint labels for inanimate things—they all called a rock a rock, the wind the wind—but it was different with Noumonians themselves.

When in human societies, most people had a name, and learned other names, the Noumonians were the opposite. They each gave each other a name and learned the names others had given it.

Most given names were relationship based—like how Icelandic called the turret her Number Three. But some were affection based, or repulsion based. One often knew where they stood with another by the name they were given.

I.C.C. was now everything from Friend House, to Hidden One, to Old Thing We Found, to Knowledge Waterfall, to Scary Not Food Cave Sorry Not Changing.

In which case, I.C.C. giving each of them a name in a human language was even more Noumonian than it had first thought.

Over the last century, Icelandic had been able to convince fifty Noumonians to relocate to the ship. Protection had been her main selling point. Though the Noumonians had no predators and very little illness, they were still vulnerable to death by falling rocks, massive hailstones, and accidental plunges from the top of the falls. They would have none of those troubles on *Mira*.

Her second selling point had been knowledge, and this was why the majority of those it housed now were scientists and artists. Some were of a more evolutionarily advanced line, and some were of older lines. I.C.C. noted there was no societal stratification based on those who received the special nourishment and those who didn't. Regardless of intellectual and physiological differences, a Noumonian was a Noumonian.

I.C.C. wondered if this was a by-product of plentiful resources and a lack of competitors. Icelandic had mentioned that a few other Noumonian colonies had broken off from theirs, but she did not speak of them as being separate. There was no *us* and *them*, simply an *us* that lived far away.

Icelandic had taught it much, but there was only so much one could learn from an individual about their culture. Being able to watch them interact, to observe and take part in their problem solving, helped it understand them on a much more intimate level.

I.C.C. was no longer a human vessel.

And it was content.

It was a day of happiness aboard *Mira*. Icelandic had been growing her ninth new one, and it was the day of first detachment, when the new Noumonian would slough off its outer, chrysalis-like sheath and step off its parent's back.

This was the first Noumonian growth that I.C.C. had been able to observe from beginning to end. In the beginning, Icelandic had taken a cleaning bot with her to the quarry, far to the south of the ships. She showed him the rock formation that they had been eating for millennia, wearing down. It had once been a volcanic mountain, and now was carved into an unnatural crescent.

Picking a spot among thousands of divots, Icelandic had begun boring into the stone, dissolving and pummeling with her massive jaws, gorging on the rock. Crystalline pieces and bits of metallic ore stuck to her face and sprinkled through the air.

She ate nonstop for a day and a half before returning—the budding of cells on her left haunch already beginning to show.

Though the initial growing was fast, it took over five Earth years for the new one to come to term. It began as little more than a firm yolk sac, broadening and stretching skyward, the insides eventually coalescing into recognizable Noumonian shapes. In the final stages, the outside sac began to look dry and brittle.

Today, that would all slough away.

It wasn't a birth in human terms by any stretch. The new Noumonian had been communicating from within its chrysalis for months now, learning the wave-based language and all about its people and its home. As soon as it was freed it would be a part of adult society.

But it was still a day of festivity, a celebration of autonomy, both for the parent and the new one.

I.C.C. joined in the excited oscillation of radio signals as turrets were placed around Icelandic. They held their scythe-like blades high, undulating their arms, swaying to the chant. And then, on the new one's signal, they began to slash at the chrysalis, aiding in the Noumonian's reveal. Paper-thin sheets flaked away, flying into the air like confetti. Scouts jumped from the decking, snatching the pieces for Icelandic to consume later, so nothing would go to waste.

Icelandic's Number Nine was a tank, nearly a mirror image of its parent, though not nearly as large yet, and with a slightly yellower tint to its webbing.

Once the last remnants of the chrysalis were gone, the turrets were moved aside, replaced by tanks and scouts ready to help their newest family member disengage its umbilicals.

I.C.C. was surprised it had taken it so long to assign the proper name to the "feelers" or "proboscis" at the terminus of each Noumonian. Of course they were umbilicals—just like the umbilicals attached to *Hippocrates*, designed for repeated use. Very unlike human umbilical cords.

Rituals of rejoining and separation were integral to the Noumonian way of life.

The radio wave oscillation became shorter and shorter, like a drumroll, until parent and child were parted. A happy cheer went up all around.

Together, the fifty-one individuals made a dancing procession all the way to I.C.C.'s original waterfall, where Nine's wheel would be activated by breaking a small connective bone that kept it from turning before birth.

As the Noumonians were happily relishing the waterfall, I.C.C. noted something odd beyond the planet's ionosphere.

A small ping at first, and it tried to ignore the signal. Ever since its memory banks had been wiped, craft had been appearing in the Philosopher's System. Not to land, or even make contact. They seemed to patrol—perhaps guarding the planets, though the AI could not be certain.

But this was different. It was a ship, but unlike the others, it was broadcasting on old frequencies, as though they were trying to ping the ancient convoy, purposefully searching for it.

Tearing its attention away from the happy scene, suddenly excited for an entirely different reason, I.C.C. located the craft's position in the sky and immediately began responding, boosting its locator beacon.

Yes. I'm here. I'm here!

The craft had appeared suddenly, as though dropping out of an SD. As though coming from a great distance.

The ship was moving closer to the planet at speed. Was it going to land? After all these years, were they . . . were they coming home?

Excitement cascaded through a series of algorithms, automatically preparing to receive visitors—*human* visitors.

But then—no. Something was wrong. It entered the atmosphere accompanied by a flash in the sky, much like those strange meteors it observed. The craft was falling, *burning* in the atmosphere. It tumbled in an arc, thirty degrees off the planet's direction of spin, northwesterly, across the sea. It was going to crash, and whoever was aboard—

I.C.C. nearly surged into the sky; the functioning graviton cyclers on every last ship roared with power. *Mira* rumbled. The Noumonians quivered.

The AI stopped itself short of lift-off. It had spent so much time making itself anew, transforming itself for another civilization, and yet it was ready to forget all that the instant humans appeared. It chided itself for nearly disregarding all it had learned in favor of its base programming.

[Earthquake?] Icelandic asked.

I.C.C. did its best to explain. There was a ship, and it was *crashing*.

[Then I.C.C. must float,] Icelandic insisted. [Like in legend im tell of the Big Scare.]

The AI plotted the fireball's descent. It moved in a great arc across the sky, Noumenon's spin and gravity pulling it far, pulling it *down*.

It would land somewhere in the middle of the ocean. As I.C.C. formulated a rescue plan, it realized this sense of urgency, accompanied by the exactness of its efforts, must be akin to what humans meant when they said things were happening simultaneously too slow and too fast. It would be six minutes before the craft impacted the water. But it would take I.C.C. far longer to fly there.

There was nothing it could do to prevent the crash. It could only hope to recover whatever—whoever—remained.

Even at that, oceans were tricky things. It had done plenty of surface observations, but it had very little data on the deepwater currents and wave patterns of the region. The chance of miscalculating the position of the wreckage was high—growing higher the longer it waited to act.

But the only external cyclers that had been activated since the AI's waking were *Mira*'s. It could not take *Mira* to the rescue—risking the Noumonians would be immoral, and since the convoy ship was no longer spaceworthy, it wasn't particularly seaworthy, either.

And I.C.C. didn't know what to expect when it reached the wreckage. What if the craft was still intact? Judging by the size of the fireball, the ship was far larger than anything it could fit in the shuttle bay.

It needed something massive—something that could scoop the flotsam from the water in one go.

I.C.C. called to *Slicer*, reaching, sliding its consciousness sideways into the ship. This was not a part of the original convoy—though now, with so much time gone, the few thousand years between the inception of the first mission and the acquiring of additional ships seemed little more than a blip.

Slicer had been designed for housing Web nodes while the engineers pulled them apart for study. Its massive, empty belly was the largest single hangar space in the entire convoy.

If I.C.C. couldn't retrieve the craft with *Slicer*, it couldn't retrieve it at all.

I.C.C. prodded the external cyclers, willing them to function. With various pings and groans, the equipment revved to life. Like a great beast, an old dragon waking from its nap, *Slicer* shuddered, its bays opening when tested like a massive yawn.

This has to work.

I.C.C. moved the ship as quickly as possible, but it still felt too slow. It was like lifting a great weight, a mountain, and trying to hurtle it through the air. It pushed *Slicer* higher, higher, knowing it could reach the downed-ship's longitude faster if it could just gain enough height. The view from this altitude was staggeringly beautiful. The water glittered, the clouds roiled and separated like dancing fluff.

And the stars—even though there was no light pollution on Noumenon, it had been so long since I.C.C. had seen them without the distortion of a thick atmosphere.

It did not leave the atmosphere entirely. There was such a howling, a whistling. And its pressure gauges showed multiple breaches of which it had not previously been aware, where the air inside now leaked away.

The minutes stretched. The horizon stole the burning craft from I.C.C.'s view. Kilometers and kilometers of sparkling waves, some white-capped, sped beneath *Slicer's* hull. Above, I.C.C. saw a slight distortion it could not name—a bending of starlight like around a great gravitational mass.

The lensing was there for only a moment, then gone again, then back. But the AI would have time to examine its recordings of the phenomenon later. Right now it focused all its computing power on rescue.

And—there! It spotted the crash site. In the middle of the sea, just as projected. Steam formed a great hazy cloud around it, stretching high, high into the atmosphere already. The hull had burned so hot, it must have vaporized the surface even before contact.

I.C.C. switched its cameras through various spectrums, looking past the steam, into the heart of the water.

There was an object, deep beneath the waves. But it wasn't sinking—it was rising.

I.C.C. mapped the object as it rose, realizing it wasn't one, but two ships, locked together in a frozen semblance of battle. One reminded I.C.C. of an Earth insect, with long legs and a bulbous abdomen. The second ship was boxy, gray and white, with a single outer arm, which was long and had half a dozen articulation points. No outer windows.

Upon further inspection, I.C.C. realized the two craft had not been battling—it looked more like the insect ship had wrapped itself around the box ship, perhaps to protect it, to create one large falling object instead of two smaller ones.

The debris field was small, suggesting they'd been able to slow their descent, avoid the most devastating version of impact. Perhaps the occupants were still alive. Perhaps.

As *Slicer* entered the column of the steam cloud, I.C.C. was able to see the craft in the human visible light spectrum as they breached the surface. Notably, the insect ship was a deep, shiny black. I.C.C. didn't have to run any spectrometry tests to recognize the material—it was the same jet-black metal incorporated in several of the megastructures *Noumenon Ultra* had found.

As *Slicer* approached, the ships began to sink again. I.C.C.

could not tell from its vantage if there were breaches in their hulls—but it was likely. The impact had sent them deep, then their buoyancy had rocketed them back up. But now the water was rushing inside in earnest, stealing their atmospheres, threatening the occupants in an entirely new way. Whoever had survived the initial crash might now drown.

The sea churned and bubbled. A storm roared east of the crash site, moving toward it. The swells were growing larger; soon one might subsume the ships entirely. The sky was dark, a late-day, overcast gloom.

I.C.C. lowered *Slicer* with as much finesse as it was able. It did not descend directly onto the ships, instead coming in at an angle, skimming over the water's surface to scan for survivors in the surf. The outer cameras flicked back and forth. Spotlights that hadn't been used since the Noumenon landing buzzed to life, some shorting out instantly. I.C.C. knew it must look like a great, horrid sea beast with glowing eyes and glittering scales, the sea spray coating the rough panels of its hull.

It saw no bodies—corpses or otherwise—floating on the surface. Anyone dead or alive had to be trapped within their vessel.

And so I.C.C. unclamped *Slicer*'s jaws, widening them to their full extent. This ship had been made to swallow pieces of a megastructure, and now it would swallow these craft as though it were some mythic whale about to herald a rebirth.

Millions of gallons of seawater rushed inside. The small ships were dragged in by the new undertow, smashing into the walls of the construction bay and twirling in the fleeting whirlpools.

I.C.C. buttoned the ship back up once it was certain it had every last scrap of debris that hadn't already plummeted to the seafloor.

Slicer's belly was full like never before, and everything sloshed and gurgled like an upset human stomach.

It flew back to the landing site as gently as it could, but at the last minute thought better of placing *Slicer* near the other ships. I.C.C. worried about illness and contamination, one life-form accidentally infecting the other.

[I.C.C., task acomplished?] Icelandic asked.

"That has yet to be seen," it said.

I.C.C. placed *Slicer* fifty kilometers north of the other ships. Away from both the old and new Noumonian colony.

It drained the water slowly, opening the doors ever so slightly to let a heavy spray through. The ground turned swampy, seawater and mud splattering nearby boulders and small outcroppings. In minutes, *Slicer* was left with soggy insides, two new ships, and various globular things—creatures?—I.C.C. had pulled up with the craft.

The boxy ship had sustained more damage than the insect craft. There were clear tears in the metal, scorch marks all up and down its sides where friction-resistant heat tiles had been stripped away.

There were no more communiqués from either. All lay quiet.

I.C.C. opened the storage closets at the back of *Slicer's* hangar, sending an army of cleaning bots to investigate, both excited about and dreading what they might find.

They did not need tools to work their way into the gray ship, such was its state. They climbed over the twisted wreckage, documenting every second as they eased inside.

Sparks flew from severed wires, and I.C.C. directed the bots to give them a wide birth. Nothing was on fire, luckily, but there were still pools of water with long, dangling cords reaching into them. The bots could not investigate there, for fear of shorting out.

In one compartment's pool floated what, at first, I.C.C.

took for a dislodged chunk of large equipment. Its smooth, chrome surface was contoured and layered, as though designed to be aesthetically pleasing instead of simply utilitarian, which was contrary to the equipment it had found thus far in the ship. But then it bobbed and flipped, portions of it sinking, becoming too waterlogged. It was not equipment. It was a person. Wet strands of long hair pushed grotesquely over its brow, hiding its face. A shiny latticework of metal, thin and pliable, covered pale skin—like clothes, though I.C.C. was somehow certain it was integrated into the individual. The hard chrome was its back, the plates and contours allowing for bending and freedom of motion. And though the front of its skull was hidden, it was an irregular shape.

There were no life signs, but this individual had clearly been given mechanical modifications, and I.C.C. was not trained in this level of cybernetic enhancement.

I.C.C. began to direct the bots to pull it out and saw more sparks in the rear of the compartment. It used the bot with the longest arm to hook into a clump of hair, but, as suspected, a strong current was instantly guided by the water, through the body, and into the bot. It shorted and stilled, its camera going dark.

The individual may have drowned, or they may have been electrocuted to death. Either way, I.C.C. did not have enough insulated bots to retrieve them at this time.

In yet another compartment—which looked like a cockpit—the bots came upon their first survivor. The individual groaned and flailed, reaching for something unknown. They, too, were heavily modified. A full cyborg. The front of their face had been dislodged, likely on impact, and dangled from their skull, revealing a mixture of metal, blood, muscle, wires, and bone underneath. There were no gashes, no leaking fluids, which I.C.C. took as a good sign. They, too, had long, dark hair, though it cascaded in thick ringlets. Their skin was dark as well, and it carried the same shimmery, metallic quality as the corpse. Though their top half was more or less human shaped, their bottom portions were not. The seat they occupied had been designed for a quadruped, and even in their twisted, injured state, there was a mythic quality to their form. Almost like a centaur.

I.C.C. directed the bot with the smoothest outer surface to meet the survivor's flailing hand, to butt up against it like a cat. At first the individual recoiled, but then groped for the bot again.

Their eyes must be offline, I.C.C. realized. Whatever functions the face performed were likely out of reach. With a careful bit of coaxing, the person was able to unlatch their restraints and follow the bot, one hand gripping the smooth dome of its top tightly, afraid to let go.

At first, they bumped into the walls, and the ceiling was too low for their height. After a moment they yanked on the bot, trying to tell it something. I.C.C. ordered it to pause.

Slowly, the person contorted themself. The mechanical, quadrupedal lower half shifted, transformed, the plates and gears and metal shafts whirling around one another into a new configuration. Now its body, elongated, was lower to the ground, with long feelers out the front to help keep it from running into walls, and perhaps a dozen short legs, like an insect's.

One section was clearly damaged. The new leg bent upward instead of hitting the deck, and it screeched oddly when it tried to bend.

Seemingly satisfied with its new shape, regardless of the injury, they nudged the bot forward once more.

The other ship was buttoned up tight. The more specialized bots, the ones it had modified to wield tools, would be needed to break in.

But as I.C.C. sent out the call, directing them to come

down from where they were currently effecting repairs on the buried *Holwarda*, an external portion of the black ship *moved*. A door opened; a ramp unfurled uselessly to the side, like a tongue flopping out of a dead animal.

Individual after individual in EVA suits collapsed out onto *Slicer*'s decking. They were all the traditional human shape.

One wrestled with their suit. There was a cut on the leg, and water sloshed inside the helmet.

The others nearest the person tried to stop them, tried to keep them from taking off their helmet, but they were panicked.

Their helmet came off, water poured down the sides of their suit, and they gasped—

Someone it recognized gasped. *Maureen Stevenson* gasped.

They'd come back. I.C.C. could not believe it.

Its crew members had *come back*.

Another suited human rushed to put Maureen's helmet back on, to jam it down as hard as they could.

"My suit's already ripped!" she yelled, trying to fight them off.

"We can patch it!" the other countered.

"Where's the Progentor? Where's Kexin?" cried another.

Two clanging metal forms fell out of the ship, and the suited humans all recoiled, as if they'd never seen them before. They were little more than human heads on spider legs, though the forms were not identical.

"It's just the attendants!" Maureen yelled, frustrated, rushing to aid the cyborgs, help them upright as a third one clawed its way out of the ship.

"Vanhi's *gone*, help me!"

"How's the baby?"

"Did you say you *saw* Kexin, or you didn't?"

They were all chattering at once, yelling, frantic.

"Wait!" one of them cried. "Where the hell are we? What is this?" They pointed around the giant bay.

"Wes-Tu. What happened to Wes-Tu?"

"There—with Kexin!"

"Did you say Vanhi is missing? Missing-missing, or . . ."

"Jumped!"

"What the—?"

Emerging, jointly limping, helping one another, were three additional figures. One in a suit, perhaps Chen Kexin, one unlike any human I.C.C. had ever seen—different, still, from the mechanical ones—and . . .

. . . and . . .

Jamal Kaeden.

I.C.C. did not know what it felt like to cry. It did not know the sensation of eyes dampening, or the thickness of emotion in one's chest, or the way one's face seemed to heat with the anticipation of tears. Such concepts had only been related to it by various individuals over various generations. It knew of them secondhand.

But this, this sensation—this surprise, and sadness, and longing, at the sudden realization of just who exactly stood before it—this had to be the closest to crying it had ever been.

Here, remarkably, thousands of years after I.C.C. had promised itself it would not miss any one clone line more than any other clone line, was proof that an AI could lie to itself.

Before it stood, unmistakably, a clone of its creator. Jamal Kaeden.

[I.C.C.,] Icelandic prodded once more. [Task accomplished? ? Ship saved?]

"Oh, Icelandic," it said in Japanese. "I cannot wait for you to meet . . . I . . . these people . . . I have been waiting for so long."

THE DESIGN'S INTERLUDE

When building, one must have a plan. The end cannot come before the beginning. The capstone cannot be a precursor to the foundation stone. The walls must come before the paint. The pipes must come before the water.

The planet must come before its native life.

The body must come before a being's sentience.

But what if a builder leaves their house unfinished, waiting? And someone who has never seen a house decides to take up the work?

There must be a way to prevent the roof from going up before the corner studs. A strategy for indicating when it is time to place the doors on their hinges. A signal for the right moment to hang the art on the walls. A way to signify the work is done and one should invite guests in for dinner.

Typically, there are blueprints. Design plans. Schematics.

But what if instead, the parts of the house could talk to one another? And the new builders need never heed what they're saying?

In 6666 CE, a group of humans completed a structure they called the Web. Nearly lost in the mayhem that followed were the sixteen separate bursts of uniform radiation the Web sent hurling through space at distinct and varied trajectories.

This one aimed deep into the crab nebula. *That* one pointed just three light-years away from Cygnus X-3.

So on and so forth.

All sixteen signals reached their contact points.

Sixteen separate megastructures—all in varied stages of completion—woke up.

Three were already fully constructed. They, too, sent out their own radiation bursts before tilting into alignment. Before asserting themselves in their proper roles.

Two needed little more than capstones before they were ready.

Six waited for additional signals.

Four were largely unfinished, but primed and ready for activation once whole.

One immediately sent a single ping out to a sister structure. This one megastructure was largely flat and forked: five copper-colored prongs jutted away from its pearlescent thirty-two-thousand-kilometer plane, their physical manifestation in this dimension only hinting at the extent of their influence *down down down down* through the subdimensions.

The structure would be fully primed once it received a specific type of equation as a reply. The equation would include variables it could not calculate on its own, based on the unexpected variations in matter and energy distribution in the galaxy, which its designers could not have predicted oh so long ago.

The megastructure was not sentient. It could make no judgments.

When it received a ping back from its sister structure, there was no mechanism in place that could indicate to the structure that the information received was incorrect. That the calculations meant to instruct it on the frequency of its subdimensional reverberations were wrong.

There were safeguards in place to prevent the

incorrect calculations. The structure responsible for the math frequently signaled structures in charge of double-checking the equations. The designers had not been careless.

And yet, accidents happen.

The pronged structure did not begin its reverberations. It needed one more additional signal to tell it when to start. So it lay quiet. Innocent. There were no clues that something had gone wrong. No one taking up the construction of other megastructures would have any indication a problem had occurred.

It was a ticking time bomb that did not tick.

The only way to defuse the bomb was to set it off. The only way to finish the house was to break down the frame.

But no one could know this. No mind could be set to the task.

And no one would be quite as safe as they'd been before.

For many millennia to come.

CHAPTER THREE

DEVON SINCLAIR:
THIRTY GHOSTS WALK BEHIND

101,146 CE

YEAR 1,007 OF THE PYRAMID BY LOCAL ACCOUNTING

LOCATION: CONVOY SEVEN CONSTRUCTION PLATFORM

Devon Sinclair was the third-youngest *Homo sapiens* in the universe. Not the third-youngest human—no, there were plenty of those galivanting throughout the cosmos, though no one from his mother's time would have recognized them as such at first glance.

His mother's time; that was how he thought of the twenty-second century. Technically it was his time as well—that was when he'd been born, when he came from. And yet . . .

Devon didn't remember Earth. He'd been nearly two when the Convoy Twelve accident happened. His first memory was of the aftermath—crying in the middle of a hallway with sparks all around. And a body somewhere nearby—a crumpled shape. Then his mother had picked him up and taken him into a bathroom to wash him clean. A man had come barging in. His mother told him later it had been Stone Mendez Perez—one of the people who now journeyed to a planet called Noumenon seeking answers to the convoy's ailments—though he had to take her word for it. His baby memory wasn't that clear.

His entire childhood had been spent aboard two broken ships, stranded in a void, hanging off the edge of a post-human construction field.

The only two younger *Homo sapiens* were Maryam Ejiofor and Hope Tan. They all belonged to a group of only thirty-six who'd been under the age of eighteen when Convoy Twelve had been rocketed into the future. The littlest generation. The last generation.

Gen-Last had had to grow up fast. They'd had to live with certain expectations—expectations about cultural preservation and genetic perpetuation.

And, soon, Devon would be defying those expectations. Well, not *defying*—that wasn't his word. That was a word one of the elders had used. He preferred *expanding*.

Devon stood with Maryam in one of the window halls on Convoy Seven's construction platform. Like the rest of the *Lùhng* ships, every surface was down—finite graviton manipulation had made concepts like *floors* and *ceilings* obsolete. The hall was a perfectly round tube, connecting one bulbous portion of the construction-platform-slash-way-station to another. And it was entirely see-through, like it was made of glass, though it was actually constructed of naturally opaque materials—the majority of it a substance called "press-through." The clarity was explicitly for the sake of the *Homo sapiens*, allowing their implant-free brains to see what was projected directly into the minds of the *Lùhng*.

The construction platform consisted of three concentric half circles of hall, each eleven and a half kilometers long, and bridged by large bulbous rooms. It hovered over a nearly completed alien megastructure: the Pyramid. The platform sat light-minutes above the structure, but still the construct blotted out all space beneath Devon's feet. Each of its five sides was a vast, smooth plain with the surface area equal to one half of Sol's. He and Maryam stood over one incomplete corner, which let them look down, down, down into the immense hollowness of the thing, where planet-sized crystal formations were ablaze with their own internal light. Pinks, turquoise, and blues pulsed within. Dangerous static discharge occasionally jumped the distance between crystals, creating glorious plasma flares astronomical units long.

The Pyramid's purpose was still unknown. But that didn't worry the *Lùhng*. They'd been through the construction process dozens of times over a hundred thousand years, and at each end stage they hadn't known what the megastructure would do until they finished the work and revived the ancient machine.

But each megastructure had had a positive effect on human civilization, in the form of things like asteroid shields and new travel tech. The Pyramid would be the first—and likely, only—completed in Devon's lifetime, and his anticipation grew each day he met Maryam at this exact spot. Over the years, the sides of the opening had drawn closer and closer, narrowing their field of view, covering over the jutting lengths of crystal. In the next nine months, the Pyramid would be finished, and the glowing gems locked inside.

They weren't literally crystals, of course. Not single, large crystals, anyway. They were electrical devices of some kind, capturing energies from someplace else—a subdimension— and bouncing it between them. The devices had activated on their own, as soon as the final crystal was in place, and no one who'd ventured inside the Pyramid since had lived to describe the changed internal landscape.

[I see it every day,] Maryam signed, then adjusted the edge of her deep-purple hijab. [Every day. But it's still beautiful.]

She was a hearing person, and Devon was deaf in one

ear—the result of an explosion during Convoy Twelve's accident—but they all used ASL almost exclusively these days anyway. It was how they communicated with the *Lùhng*, and how they spoke to Carmen Sotomayor, their most respected elder.

[I know what you mean,] he signed back. There were plenty of things he saw every day living here, on the *Lùhng* ships, that still filled him with wonder.

Daisy chief among them.

[Where are you headed after this?] Maryam asked. [I'm going to the nutrition division. My father asked me to join the "ancient-human food processing" committee. He says they still can't get the *Lùhng* food printers to make Edikang Iknong right. I think it's the taste of the pumpkin leaf that's off, but what do I know? He just keeps saying it's not like "the real stuff," but it's not like *I've* ever eaten the "real stuff."]

Lùhng spices were intense, and new. Engineered. Every flavor was heady and unique—the modified garlic didn't linger in the mouth or pores, modified pepper would never make anyone sneeze, and the ginger was as sharp as it was sweet. Old Earth foods were tame by comparison . . . as far as Gen-Last could tell.

And yet, the elders sometimes said it all had an oily undertone. Likely from the printing process. Food wasn't grown here, it was pieced together from base components, just like the megastructures.

[And since the *Lùhng* have been modified to process food completely differently than us,] she continued, [they don't have a clue what the problem is. Many of them are talking about remodifying so they can eat like us, though. They were so far removed from their Earth origins they couldn't even feed us properly when we were stranded, but now they're excited to have a chance to get back to their roots.]

[Roots are good,] he signed. [Daisy and I are going to meet

with the reproduction division.] He tried to look casual, like it was no big deal. As though this wasn't a monumental step. [Maybe get to plant some roots of our own.]

She paused, studying him for a moment, her dark eyes scrutinizing every twitch. [Are they going to let you, then? Raise a *Lùhng* infant?]

[That's still the question,] he admitted, taking a deep breath. [If Daisy had picked a *Lùhng* partner or partners it would be expected. Time for it, even. But they chose *me*. So the question of . . . of *fitness* . . .] He tried to smile through the explanation, but could feel the corners of his mouth quivering.

The accident that had thrown their convoy through time had also rendered the entire crew infertile, leaving them with all sorts of personal and existential questions about reproduction, species perpetuation, parenthood, and personal autonomy versus societal imperatives.

Once they'd moved aboard the *Lùhng* ships they'd appealed to the *Homo draconem* for aid in solving this medical mystery—which they were given, but only to an extent. Both human and *Lùhng* scientists were searching for the exact nature of the problem. The infertility was a symptom of something that had radically changed in their biology during the accident, of this everyone was certain. But when cloning had been suggested—which was the method by which *Lùhng* babies were made—the post-humans trod more carefully. Even if the Convoy Twelve DNA was cloneable, what if the problem persisted? Would they clone the small remaining convoy crew perpetually? That was no way to preserve a species, not unless you were preserving them for posterity alone (and Devon had his own opinions about *that*).

The team on its way to Noumenon—which was made up of brilliant minds, such as those belonging to Dr. Vanhi Kapoor, Dr. Justice Jax, and Captain Orlando Tan—hoped to find their answers in the stores of fifty-thousand-plus human genome schematics aboard the Monument of Seven. Either the cure for their problem, or a new set of babies to birth.

But there were a few people who thought the inquiry folly. Yes, many of the *Homo sapiens* still wished to become parents, but there were only two generations right now. And the elders were . . . well, the youngest of them were in their fifties now. Well past the time when the average twenty-second-century human expected to become a first-time parent. And the younger generation had grown up in a small world without babies—a pocket universe, almost, where all the *Homo sapiens* they'd ever known had already come to be.

Which meant that Devon and his peers thought about parenthood differently than the elders. Many of them had no desire to be parents at all, and the older generation took that as an affront to all of human history.

Apparently when one is the last of their kind they're *supposed* to want to regrow their society. They're *supposed* to want to repopulate.

But society wasn't gone, humans weren't dead, they'd just . . . changed. Extinction was a threat the elders felt in a potent way that the last generation simply didn't.

Devon *did* want to be a father. He'd known he wanted to be a dad for as long as he could remember. But a biological connection to his children had never been a necessary factor.

Maryam patted his elbow lightly in support. [You'll do fine,] she signed.

He touched his chin in thanks. [I better get going.]

[Same time tomorrow?]

[Always.]

White hall after white hall looked nearly identical as he passed through them. If he'd had implants, he would have seen the virtual overlay of signage and decoration that the

Lùhng saw—customizable for optimal user preference. Small physical tags had been placed above the invisible apertures in the press-through to indicate they were doors, but few other considerations had been taken for the *Homo sapiens* in this case.

The smell of the *Lùhng* fleet was not a human smell, not in the way he knew it, but it was organic. It held a freshness, one that he found difficult to describe, but that his mother had once compared to hot sands after a cold rain. He had no context for the comparison but had adopted it anyhow.

He counted the turns and doors until he came to the studio where he met Daisy for his lessons. With a deep, calming breath, he pushed into the soft, pillowy press-through and pulled himself to the other side.

Beyond, all lay dark, with Daisy sitting on the floor, lowest limbs folded beneath them. One singular tracking light hung low over their head, spotlighting their form. It gave the room an expansive, featureless quality, though several workstations were positioned up the sides of the walls and overhead. This was a creative place, meant to engage individuals in various artistic and tactile experiences. That was why Daisy liked to teach him here—it was a hands-on education.

Devon emerged at a thirty-degree angle to where Daisy sat, and though he entered silently, they sensed his presence immediately. They extended their neck out—long as it was—and raised the slender petals of their collar in greeting, the ends curling inward.

Daisy was not their *Lùhng* name, of course. *Lùhng* names were pure thought, emotion, and sensation. Most had nothing to do with sounds or written interpretation. They were the sense of things—concepts. And so, many of the *Lùhng* had been nicknamed by the *Homo sapiens* in accordance with their individual appearance.

No two *Lùhng* were of the same design.

Daisy had been named for an Earth flower Devon had only ever seen in pictures. He'd been assured by many of the elders that, hailing from Scotland, he'd likely experienced them in person, but he couldn't remember.

Regardless, it was the frill that sprang from the base of Daisy's collarbone and shoulder blades—draping over their front, sides, and back, down to their elbows in long, individual petals—that had evoked the comparison.

They were a shiny, obsidian black, however, unlike the white or yellow of the Earth flower. The petals' primary function was *space helmet*. When Daisy left the station to do their work out on the Pyramid—without an environmental suit of any kind—the petals would close up around their globe-like head, protecting them from stray cosmic rays and sucking in the nearby-star's light for energy.

The rest of their body had a similar coating, though instead of petals they sported small scales that could be shed and replaced in sections once they'd absorbed too much radiation. They had six limbs, which were functionally interchangeable between arms and legs, and each of them had grasping appendages on the ends.

[Loved one, there you are,] they signed, rising from their place on the floor.

Devon threw his arms wide and embraced Daisy around the middle, their center set of limbs returning the hug affectionately. The modified-human's scales were cool and ridged, but the form beneath was soft. He liked to imagine that their unique smell was that of solar winds over ancient stones and space-grown crystal.

[Your heart, it beats quickly,] they noted.

[I'm nervous,] he admitted, standing back.

They smiled gently, their mouth still very *Homo sapiens* looking. [I am as well. But we will make good parents, and the assigners will see this.]

He wanted Daisy to be right. The *Lùhng* had welcomed them into almost every aspect of their society—work, school, government, religion . . . love. But he and Daisy were a first— they wanted to perpetuate the inter-genus cooperation, bind the two convoys together like never before. Through family.

[Are you ready?] they signed.

He nodded firmly. Everything would be fine. Daisy was a *Lùhng*, so it should be fine, right? It would be more difficult if they were both from Convoy Twelve. He held on to that idea: *Daisy is a* Lùhng, *so it'll be fine.* Hand in hand, they navigated the press-through once more.

Every potential *Lùhng* parent had to face this dreaded interview. Devon and Daisy were not special in that sense—no one was singling them out. But the questions themselves, those would undoubtedly be unique.

The offices that saw to the ins and outs of civic life aboard the construction platform weren't unlike the rest of *Lùhng* spaces: topsy-turvy, omnidirectional globes with all surface area being utilized for maximum efficiency. But unlike the labs or even the art space they'd just come from, these had a distinct municipal feel. The workstations were arranged in a netted grid over the inside of the walls, and *Lùhng* stood in three lines originating from three entry points into the large space. Code-enforcers and overseers floated constantly back and forth overhead, flying from one station to the next when flagged down by a colleague. It was both chaotic and orderly, as all civic offices have been through time immemorial.

This was a special place, the only one like it in Convoy Seven. Most civic approvals and interactions did not require in-person attendance. Mind-to-mind made the majority of the work remote. Individuals whose vocation did not involve physical labor typically were of the hyperprocessing variety and spent their hours plugged in to the vast network of mind-to-mind information, all from the comfort of their own hibernation hammock.

In truth, even their interview might have been done remotely if Devon weren't a *Homo sapiens*.

When it was their turn to see the caseworker, a squat *Lùhng* with beautiful, rippling rainbows through their mostly see-through skin led them (the long way around, out of respect for Devon's need to walk, not float) to a desk twenty-seven degrees up the incline from their waiting position.

The "Child Assigner" was thick, with folds in their shimmering, bluish white skin, like a tardigrade's. Their body was long and coiled, like a snake, and they had mesmerizing light-yellow eyes. Devon was consistently struck by each *Lùhng*, how they were individually works of genetic art.

The Assigner programmed the press-through at the foot of their desk to raise and form into chair shapes to accommodate Devon's and Daisy's individual body types.

[Welcome,] they signed, and Devon was heartened. The Assigner could have chosen to have Daisy interpret their mind-to-mind communiqués for him, but the fact that they'd used ASL demonstrated respect for Devon and seemed to bode well.

The first few questions were simple—affirmation of their desire to raise a child, their living dynamics, their work locations and hours. Since each *Lùhng* was so different, the convoy needed to be sure the parents could accommodate and serve the child's individual needs, once grown.

To that end, Devon was not surprised when the Assigner asked, [Please relate to me the fundamental schools of modification. Devon Sinclair alone,] they added. Daisy was not to give him any in-the-moment help, but they did put one hand on his knee for support.

Devon's heart rate ticked up once more, and he sat straighter in the press-through seat. He knew this, there was no reason to get anxious. But he feared a fumble, a misphrase. What kind of mistake could cost them a family?

[There are six schools of biological modification,] he signed, feeling both overly warm and suddenly chilled as sweat broke out between his shoulder blades. [Genetics from nearly four thousand different life-forms—including plant, animal, and alien—have been utilized in biological modification. This does not include the artificial, designer genes created to produce functionalities not found in nature.]

[Describe each school. Its purpose. Its physical manifestations.]

He thought first of the *Lùhng* who'd led them to the Assigner. [School One: Ease of diagnostics. DNA mods come from animals like the glass frog.] Medicine had advanced dramatically since Convoy Twelve left Earth, and the posthumans could repair extensive damages easily if caught before a catastrophic system failure. Cancer deaths were mostly a thing of the past, and nonexistent in this school's mods. [The idea is to make it as simple as possible to monitor every single aspect of bodily function. This means modifying the organs and bodily systems to be more accessible. Transparent skin for easy visual diagnostics, organs that can be temporarily externalized without the process causing damage, and access points to the organs installed, so that no cutting or severing is necessary—typically through added sphincters and epidermis layering.] Some *Lùhng* possessed sections of skin that had an almost Velcro-like cling to one another, which provided a hermetic seal, yet separated easily with the proper medical attention.

The Assigner nodded. If they were taking notes, there was no outward sign.

Daisy squeezed Devon's knee in encouragement, and he felt a little better. A little more self-assured.

[School Two: Energy transference. Like Daisy—Daisy's primary mods are from School Two. Plant genetics are incorporated.] He considered this the "solar panel" school of thought. [These mods create bodies designed to utilize radiation that would otherwise be damaging to a person. Scales or quills are attached to a shed-able epidermis and are designed to absorb a wide band of the electromagnetic spectrum. This energy is then redirected in different ways. As caloric energy, further protection, or warmth, allowing people like Daisy to go long hours without rest or food. Excess radiation is siphoned off as heat in space via a discharge of liquid from flutes or pores that tend to dangle from the shoulders and upper back. Sections of scales shed regularly, but entire swaths can be shed at any time in case of a radiation overdose that might threaten the epidermis's integrity. Most sheddings are considered radioactive waste instead of biowaste.

[School Three: Extremotolerance. Genes are spliced with engineered DNA taken from creatures like the tardigrade.] He suspected this was the Assigner's primary mod-schema. [The highest amounts of Dsup protein are used to protect these modifications. And the modded bodies are eutelic.] Which meant individuals with this mod had a set number of cells and those cells did not multiply or get replaced over the course of their lifetime. Instead, the cells themselves got bigger. To other post-humans, adults with these mods had a child-like appearance. [They also have a higher percentage of water in their bodies than other mods and can cycle through this water as a sort of internalized radiation shield. They can change their metabolisms and shed this water to go into temporary stasis to await medical treatment if something goes wrong. And they can withstand extreme temperatures and pressures, and their protective hibernation ability means they have a high chance of survival if they are stranded for an extended time in said extreme environments.] Most of them appeared the purest snow white, as their hair or skin possessed pure reflectivity, absorbing absolutely no visible light, along with most of the total EM spectrum.

Devon seemed to be doing fine. He thought he was doing fine. But the Assigner gave him no encouragement, asked no questions. And yet Daisy hadn't indicated he'd made any mistakes, so he barreled onward.

[School Four: Extremocapacity. With ant and other insect integration. Increased tensile strength across all bodily systems is integral to this school of modification. They can have tendencies toward hyperstrength, with the ability to lift and carry up to fifty times their own body weight at one g, and/or tendencies toward superspeed, with anything from flying to running to swimming speeds boosted by an order of magnitude, depending on the environment they are designed for. Aboard Convoy Seven, these mods allow for extra speedy construction, and for workers to take the place of otherwise bulky equipment. Bodies modified in this school are incredibly dense and heavy. They may appear stocky and large, though not necessarily. Epidermis type usually corresponds to a secondary school of modification.

[School Five: Hyperprocessing. Genetic mods are entirely artificially engineered.] Kali belonged to this school, and it was Daisy's secondary schema. [People with these modifications can examine and integrate many informational streams at once and have increased sensory capacity. They have a primary brain and up to five sub-brains, giving them the ability to process input orders of magnitude more efficiently and in a more sophisticated fashion than . . .] he hesitated. *Than a* Homo sapiens. [. . . than other people.] This was why Kali was able to hold multiple conversations in multiple languages at once. [They act as servers within the convoy system, lending their processing power. They store information like hard drives and are intimately connected to intergalactic data systems. Bodies with these modifications tend to have many grasping limbs with which to execute many tasks at once. They need twelve to eighteen hours of sleep a day, mostly because they are never fully unconscious and have to rest different parts of their brains at different times.]

The Assigner's gaze was indecipherable—eyes wide, staring. Their expression hadn't changed, but that worried Devon more than a blatant scowl. Though they couldn't read his thoughts, it felt as though they could. As though they were tearing back the sections of his gray matter molecule by molecule, watching his synapse fire haphazardly in sudden panic.

[The Sixth?] the Assigner asked after a time.

[The Sixth,] he signed slowly, faltering. [The Sixth School,] he tried again, [is Aesthetic. These are changes made purely for aesthetic reasons and are not confined to *visual* aesthetics.]

[Examples? Give three. Be specific.]

Uh . . .

The sixth school of modification didn't have many strong examples among Convoy Seven crew. Mostly because these mods could only be opted into after someone was fully developed, and could interfere with the practicality of other mods. He tried to clear his mind and think hard about the wider universe—what Daisy and his other Convoy Seven friends had told him regarding other civilizations elsewhere.

[The . . . Sigra people,] he said. The sign for the culture was close to the sign for butterfly. [They are granted fairy wings en masse at their cohort's coming-of-age ceremony. The Tickerzaggah people have, sort of, crab legs in place of hair on their heads. And the Slithe, when they reach seventy, and if they're a respected member of society, may choose to become living tapestries.] They were lain in a field and their skin and hair grown and shaped away from their bodies to create a living picture that could only be fully admired from above. Anyone who became one of these blanket-bodies was waited on day and night by appointed caretakers who saw to their every whim.

Somehow, Devon thought that life as a rug might be preferable to life as a *Homo sapiens* sitting in his exact spot at the moment. Sheer anxiety coursed through his veins. Having nothing better to do than lie in some grass and become part of the landscape sounded much less stressful than jumping through all these hoops for parenthood.

Technically there was a seventh school of modification, but Devon knew the Assigner wasn't interested in his knowledge regarding *Homo kubernētēs*. There were a few people on board Devon would have classified as fully cybernetic, but the majority of the *Lùhng* didn't see these as "real" modifications. They were more like . . . fancy clothes.

[Yes. Fine,] the Assigner said. [And regarding reproductive organs? How are they modified?]

Devon wasn't sure how much detail the Assigner wanted, or even, really, why they were asking. Did they want to make sure he understood that this was his only path to parenthood? That there were no children to be had out from under the watchful eye of this department?

[No modified members of humanity possess internal reproductive organs, though they retain their external sex organs. All babies need modifications, and all babies are tank-grown, which makes reproductive organs unnecessary and a waste of resources. These organs have been evolved out of the base DNA structures that are every post-human's starting point, which allows adults to focus all their biological energy on maintaining their own bodies, which in turn leads to naturally longer individual life-spans than . . .] *Than* Homo sapiens.

[Good,] the Assigner signed. Devon could only hope he'd answered to their satisfaction.

A small gaggle of *Lùhng* flew directly overhead—one half the height of the others. Though their small size didn't necessarily indicate they were a child, their frantic wave to Devon hinted at adolescence. He sheepishly returned the wave.

[And what is your function and contribution to your community?] the Assigner pressed on.

[I'm a biographer,] he answered. [I've been tasked with documenting the lives and memories of our elders for history's sake, so that knowledge of twenty-second-century Earth might be preserved.]

They nodded—or, more aptly, bobbed. [Will you show me this work?]

The concept was a strange one for the *Lùhng*, who were all interconnected by implants. That there would need to be an outside person to ask the right questions and make documents for posterity's sake was foreign to them. Secondary sources were largely a relic of the past.

He and Daisy had come prepared for this question, though.

Devon pulled his satchel into his lap. It was an old, faux-leather thing with a canvas strap and brass buckle. From Earth. The initials E.S. had been branded on one corner of the front flap.

His mother had given it to him when he was five. She said Captain Tan had found it in the quarters he'd inhabited pre-accident.

From the satchel, Devon produced a set of 'flex-sheets that displayed the work in English. His friends Fernando and Sunrise had worked on a digital-to-biodat program to interface between the two convoys' informational systems. With the "softbioware" installed in both the 'flex-sheets and a host *Lùhng*—in this case, Daisy—a simple command could send the biography directly to their mind, which could then be shared with the entirety of the convoy.

Unfortunately the connection wasn't wireless, but Daisy

was no stranger to cables and ports. The connector that followed his sheets onto the desk could be seamlessly inserted at the base of Daisy's jaw.

The sample he picked was from his biography of Chen Kexin. He'd interviewed all the elders who'd embarked on the away mission to the planet Noumenon in person. They were some of his first, after he'd expressed an interest in the work. And they'd been gracious while traveling, answering his follow-up communiqués with eagerness.

When they returned, he would be both proud and anxious to share his final drafts with them.

Kexin's was one of his favorite pieces, probably because it was one of the elder's most distinct recollections from childhood. Kexin—the security officer who had taken a bullet to the hand for Mac Savea—was one of the clone crew members who'd had her life turned upside-down when Convoy Twelve's first mission was canceled. And, having been one of the few individuals who had a clone sibling on all the other eleven missions, she was unique among them.

He hadn't picked the piece simply because he was proud of the work, but also because it conveyed a sense of longing for an emotional bond. A sense of longing he now shared.

As Daisy made the connection, uploading the matter into their mind, Devon realized the materials might seem even stranger to the Assigner than he'd first thought. Not only was it his interpretation of Kexin's stories; if the Assigner couldn't read the English files, they'd rely on Daisy's translation of the files, making it a thirdhand accounting. Unheard of. Unprecedented.

And entirely necessary if they were to understand why this work mattered to him, and why he wanted to share it with the next generation.

The uploading icon blinked in the upper right-hand corner of the sheets. It would only take an instant, but in that instant he let his eyes scan the words below the icon, let himself slip back into writing those words, into transforming Kexin's memories into something they could all hold and cherish.

She is six years old and about to meet her mum for the first time. She has a concept of parents, knows many of the older kids on the commune lived with theirs until they were ten or eleven. But the only one who's ever soothed her tummy ache or scattered the nightmares is Mrs. Chappell.

Kexin runs to Mrs. Chappell when she scrapes her knee. Mrs. Chappell was the one who yelled at her when she tried to play with the tiger snake that slithered in through the crack in the compound's walls. Mrs. Chappell tucked her in at night, and Mrs. Chappell told her the truth when the other kids tried to convince her that instead of going into space they were all *really* going into grinders to become dog food.

Mrs. Chappell isn't Kexin's mum and has never claimed to be. Mrs. Chappell is Dr. Chappell's sister-in-law. Dr. Chappell is why Kexin will be an astronaut one day and get to visit a gnarly planet that might have little bugs on it. They call the planet TRAPPIST-One.

Some of the other kids, like Mohamed and Justin, think the planet will be just like Wollemi. That the reason they all live here, in the national park, is because it's the best place to prepare for what they'll find.

Kexin doesn't think the new planet will be anything like Wollemi. Or, at least, she hopes it isn't. It's not that she doesn't like the uniquely spicy smell of the eucalyptus when it mixes with the sharpness wafting off the ancient pines, or the way the water holes seem so still in the dead of the dry season, or the coolness of the caves. And she was just as giddy as Thiri when they saw the two wallabies fighting at the base of their favorite stone haven.

The reserve is home. Australia is home. And she doesn't

want space to be anything like home. Otherwise, why should they all leave?

"Are you ready, Kexin?" Mrs. Chappell asks, holding out her pale hand for the little girl.

She's not ready. She's not *at all*. They've told her both too much and not enough about this *mother* of hers. She's a ghost or someone else's memory, and maybe she should stay that way.

Kexin hikes up her backpack, pulling her shoulders nearly up to her ears, like she can ward off the encounter that way, but takes Mrs. Chappell's hand nonetheless. The woman is smiling, which is good. Mrs. Chappell is one of those adults who can't smile when something bad is about to happen.

They step outside the red-stone walls of the compound to meet the approaching jeep. The eucalyptus trees encircling the half-moon-shaped drive leave dappled shade spots across the pavement, but do little to help the heat. The air is dry in Kexin's nose, and the warmth seems to carry its own dusty scent.

Her mother isn't coming to the commune. She's a very important lady, and only in Australia for a short time—she isn't even bringing her wife with her. They have to meet her in Sydney.

Henry parks the jeep and gets out to help her inside. He offers to take her pack, but she asks for a hug instead. He instantly obliges. He is part of the Kooma people, and the only member of his tribe working on the commune. Though she is not the only Chinese girl, she is the only one on the commune who has never been to China. Though their stories are very different, she's always liked Henry. He sees things in her the other adults don't.

"Going to see ma-ma today," he says to her, his accent different than the others—different than hers. She realizes for the first time that her mother won't sound like she does. Most of the other kids have their parents' accents from living in their parents' home countries.

She nods, too full of the realization to let a word escape.

The ride to Sydney is long. The grass is brown along the roads, and the shade is never cool. The jeep has no windows, but the going is slow and there's not enough wind. Henry and Mrs. Chappell chat in the front seat while Kexin fidgets nervously in the back, alone.

The hours slip by. She sleeps.

She wakes when Henry unclips her seatbelt and hefts her onto his shoulder. He pats her back gently, and she pries one eye open to see Mrs. Chappell gathering their luggage from the boot.

They've arrived at a hotel. It's very posh, but they're going in the back way.

"Did anyone see us, you think?" Mrs. Chappell asks.

"No, ma'am," Henry says softly, mindful of the drowsy child in his arms. "Once the Nobel winner arrives, the cameras will be well-fed. They won't need to seek our girl."

"But what about tomorrow? I know she said she'd be discreet, but I don't want those poachers hounding Kexin—"

"She will be fine," he assures her.

Darkness is creeping in, and Kexin knows they will try to rouse her properly for dinner, but she wants to sleep. Maybe she can sleep through tomorrow and not meet her mother.

The hotel is so fancy, Kexin thinks she might *die* of fancy. Polished stone that glitters, soft, ethereal fabrics that shine, porcelain and glass and metal fixtures all cleaned so well she can see her reflection in them. Their room is a suite, and each of them gets their own bed. The toilet is nice, unlike the dunnies back home, and it talks to Kexin, until Mrs. Chappell turns it off. "Ugh, not a talking computer," she says. Kexin secretly likes the talking computer. There used to be a lot of them, she was told. But now they were almost all gone.

"Why don't we have pillows this fluffy at home?" Kexin asks after she belly-flops onto the pile. The manchester smells like sweet lemon and lavender.

"They're expensive, dear," Mrs. Chappell says. "The hotel likes the publicity we're bringing, so they're letting us stay here for free."

Kexin knows about money, of course. But she's never seen anybody use it.

Publicity, however, is a new concept.

All the kids in the compound know they are famous. In the same abstract way Kexin knows other countries exist or that wars happen. People she didn't know knew about her, and that's what famous is.

They order room service for dinner, which disappoints Kexin. She wanted to go to a restaurant. She's never been to one before.

"Your mother is taking you out for lunch tomorrow," Henry tells her.

"Great photo op, I bet," Mrs. Chappell says, so quietly Kexin isn't sure she was meant to hear.

Kexin is not prepared. Not for meeting her mother, not for the reporters outside the hotel. Not for the fancy seafood. None of it.

"Which of these outfits would you like to wear?" Mrs. Chappell asks her the next morning, laying out a frilly, bright-red dress, a button-down with slacks, and a suit that looks like a mini version of what the priest wore at Dr. Sid and Dr. Garcia's wedding.

"Why can't I wear my uniform?" she asks.

"A khaki jumpsuit and runners are inappropriate for this lunch."

"But it's comfortable." *Everything else about this meeting is already uncomfortable, why do I need new clothes too?* "This one," she says with a sigh, pointing at the suit. It looks the most like armor.

"Did she pick the suit?" Henry calls from the adjoining bedroom.

"Yep."

"Told you."

Mrs. Chappell smiles. Kexin is relieved. "He laughed at me when I told him I bought you a dress," Mrs. Chappell says.

"It's still nice—" Kexin begins.

Mrs. Chappell shakes her head. "You don't have to apologize for your choice. You like what you like."

With Mrs. Chappell's help she shrugs into the suit. It's tight, and warm, but Mrs. Chappell assures her most of the afternoon's activities will be inside. Henry ties the red bow tie for her.

The ride down to the lobby in the shiny, brass-doored elevator is agonizing. She holds both Henry's and Mrs. Chappell's hands for comfort, glancing up at them occasionally for reassurance, but they stare straight ahead.

The soft ding and the gentle slide of the doors feels more like a starter's pistol at a footrace than a silly bell. She instinctively squeezes their hands harder.

Lights. So many lights that the woman standing in the middle of the otherwise cleared lobby is mostly a red-tinged silhouette. The lights are attached to bulky professional cameras and optical-implant-connected headpieces (Kexin knows she'll get her own implants when she turns twelve). The people are taking pictures of the woman, pictures of her turning toward the elevator, of her crouching down and holding out her hand.

She's waiting for me, Kexin realizes. They're *waiting for me. They want pictures of* me.

She wants to turn into Mrs. Chappell's side, hide her face in her skirt. Or maybe she can run behind Henry, use his legs like a shield.

But they both squeeze her hands in reassurance . . . then let go.

"We'll be right behind you," Henry says.

"Why are there so many cameras?" she asks.

The adults share a look. A look that holds so much and tells her it is all too difficult to explain in the few seconds she has left before she *must* exit the elevator.

"People want to see you and your mum together. People everywhere," Mrs. Chappell tries.

Henry purses his lips, then kneels next to Kexin. "It's so that when your convoy comes back, after you've found alien life, they'll be able to point to the picture and say 'remember when?'"

Both explanations are confusing. But she doesn't have time to ask for another.

Like in a dream, she finds herself walking away from them, sliding toward the light, toward the woman.

The lady is wearing a business suit the same color as Kexin's tie, only hers has a skirt instead of trousers and is much more fashionable. Her hair is deep black and straight, just like Kexin's. Her skin has the same undertones as Kexin's. Her eyes are equally amber brown, her cheeks as equally round.

They are the same. No doubt.

This is unmistakably her mother. Her original. The woman from whom she was cloned.

Chen Kexin the first. Nobel Prize winner. Feeder of millions.

Kexin doesn't know if she's expected to hug her or not. She opts for shaking her outstretched hand.

"It's good to meet you, Kexin," the woman says. She pronounces the "x" in her name the *proper* way, Kexin realizes.

Properly Mandarin. "You're a very special child," she continues. "You have been chosen to travel into deep space. To go to TRAPPIST-One, to search for signs of alien life. You are so unique, so fortunate. So, so special. Shall we get something to eat?"

Wide-eyed, hesitant, Kexin agrees. She's sure she can't refuse.

She feels something different in this moment—not the worry of before, though the hesitation is still present. There is warmth radiating off the woman, from her smile, from her hand. The way her attention has narrowed down to just Kexin, despite the crowd all around them, says *welcome*. It says *love*.

How can a stranger love her? Can she, too, love this stranger?

As she threads her small fingers into the lady's palm, she looks over her shoulder. There, as always, are Henry and Mrs. Chappell. There to rescue her, to reassure her.

At six years old, she has no idea that one day they'll be gone, and she'll have to rescue herself.

[**This is an accurate accounting of this *Homo sapiens*'s life?**] the Assigner asked after integrating the entire sample—twenty thousand words—in no more than a blink of the eye.

[It is a narrative accounting. Based on recordings of her, where I asked questions and she recalled as many details as possible.]

[Why are the recordings themselves not sufficient?] *Why is the primary source not sufficient?*

[*Lùhng* can process more than *Homo sapiens* can,] Devon answered. [There's so much information. . . . My interviews consist of hundreds of hours with *one* person. And I'm in the process of doing that with hundreds of people. I take the data and make it digestible. I make their lives into a story, so that other people can connect with them. People aren't narratives, but that's how we understand each other.

[*Homo sapiens* can never truly know the inner life of someone else. We don't have the truth of everything about them directly ported into our brains. There is a level of distance between *Homo sapiens* that can never be bridged. Stories are how we attempt to know people—people who have died, people who we've never met. People who don't exist, even. Fiction.]

Daisy looked sad for a moment, their petals drooping as they undoubtedly received a mind-to-mind response from the Assigner.

[I fear you will never be able to understand your *Lùhng* child,] they signed. [Your inability to make the connection that all *Lùhng* make with each other, that a *Lùhng* infant will need, disqualifies you from raising one of our clones.]

Both of them tried to protest, to argue with the Assigner on the spot. Afterward, Devon was sure that had only made it worse, the decision more firm.

They were not allowed to be parents. Not *together*, anyway.

As they left the bustling municipal wing, Devon's shock and growing anger at the Assigner suddenly deflated as he looked at Daisy, their petals drooping. Guilt swelled instead. He'd been furious that someone could look at his passion, and at the love he had to give, and then tell him he wasn't fit to be a parent.

But, Daisy . . .

Daisy had done nothing wrong. They hadn't given disqualifying answers. Their only misstep was choosing him as a partner.

He was the problem. If Daisy had chosen someone else to

raise a clone with, they would be a parent by now. But Daisy had chosen a *Homo sapiens*, and now would either have to accept the consequences, or . . . or . . .

Devon didn't want to think about the "or." He and Daisy weren't monogamously bonded in any twenty-second-century sense. There had been no wedding, no ceremony. No legally binding document.

He was asexual, and Daisy was not sapiens-sexual. But he *was* panromantic, and he'd never felt the breadth of romantic love for anyone the way he felt it for Daisy.

If Daisy chose to get a baby with someone else—another *Lùhng*—he would understand. But it would hurt. Maybe even worse than it hurt now.

And yet, if it would make Daisy happy, he would see it done.

[We should go to a park,] Daisy suggested carefully. They held themself lightly, tried to put on an air of cheer. But their signing was stiff, distracted.

[I'd like that,] he agreed.

The outer ring of the construction platform had been entirely devoted to recreation, and the majority of it was covered over in nature parks—though not nature parks as Devon imagined he would have found on Earth.

They chose the spung-tree park, whose many trees had been engineered to grow kilometers tall, their thick, gray, sprawling roots growing down the sides of rigid frames to create rooms and various structures. The air was humid, and a faint pseudo-sunlight was cast down from the clouds hanging in the center of the bulbous room. A few degrees of press-through had been left bare of dirt, and where the trees didn't grow, instead outer space shone through from outside. This was not a projection, but true clarity, allowing the beams from the nearby star to grace the spung branches when the platform's orbit brought it into view.

Other plants wound through the cracks between the tree roots, including small yellow flowers, and an occasional pollinating insect buzzed in Devon's ear.

The two of them picked a platform built halfway up one trunk to rest on, Daisy gently lifting him up, as the *Lùhng* hadn't yet installed a ramp or stairs. They gazed out in silence for a minute, watching one shining cloud drizzle as it drifted by. Devon leaned against the trunk, ran the bark under his palms. Ripples and bumps shaped the tree, but it felt smooth overall. And thick. Solid. Comforting.

Before the construction platform, Devon had only ever known industrial, sanitized spaces. The basic concept of a field or a garden was lost on him—only Dr. Jax's small farm on *Breath* gave him a reference point. But then Daisy had brought him here, shown him just how much organic matter could be in one place. Even if it was tightly regulated, this was an ecosystem, with bacteria and bugs and small animals and plants. It had changed his very concept of what a world was, what kind of a place he'd been born in.

But despite the park's now-familiar beauty, he knew he could not revel in its tranquility today. The two of them needed to talk.

[Does it bother you—] he began to sign listlessly.

[Yes, it bothers me,] they interrupted.

[Wait. Let me finish. Does it bother you that we cannot speak mind-to-mind?]

They had always been honest with each other, but there were things they'd never talked about before. They had both been fluent in ASL before meeting, and any miscommunication between them had been due to cultural misunderstandings, rather than signing mishaps.

[Does it bother you that we cannot speak verbally?] Daisy asked in turn.

[No.]

[What does it matter how we communicate, as long as we do so satisfactorily?]

[But are you satisfied?] he pressed. [We both know it's more than just a language barrier. Any version of sign language is much closer to any version of verbal language than either is to mind-to-mind. There is always a . . . distance. I'm used to it, find anything else hard to imagine. But you can't tell me there isn't a difference for you.]

They considered their answer carefully. [There is a difference, yes. And it might have frustrated me initially. Needing to *convey* to you my feelings instead of *giving* you my feelings was difficult to get used to. There is a lack of precision in this method of communication. And it is slower.]

A sour knot tied itself in Devon's stomach. A lizard ran across his leg and up the tree.

[But,] Daisy continued, [the fact that it took getting used to does not make it inferior. *Different* is never inferior. I am wholly satisfied with our connection. The ability to have a one-on-one conversation that no one else can be privileged to is remarkably intimate. And the ability to disengage from communication is freeing.]

He hadn't thought of it in those terms before. He looked around, at the many *Lùhng* in the park, enjoying their day and going to and fro, seemingly silently. But they weren't silent. They were all in constant connection at all times. There was no completely quiet. There was no completely private. Like any communication method, it had its advantages and disadvantages.

[Because it is slower,] Daisy continued, [I can consider my response. There is very little deliberating that happens in mind-to-mind. Instinctual reactions are common. And redactions of instinctual reactions are common. We say what we feel because the two are one and the same. But I can be calm with you. It is less precise, my words this way, but more measured. Not less honest, but more mindful. Do you remember when we first met?]

He smiled fondly at the memory. [Of course.]

Each *Homo sapiens* had been assigned to lessons with a *Homo draconem*. Someone who could teach them about the culture, about the goings-on in the galaxy, about the major historical turning points they'd missed in the last hundred thousand years. By chance, he'd been assigned to Daisy.

[You would not have liked me if you'd been privileged to my initial reactions,] they signed.

[Your initial reactions to my presence? To *me*?]

Their shoulders shook with light laughter, though it tee-tered on the edge of forced. Both of them were trying to stave off the grief that was coming—when the weight of what they'd been denied fully hit them. [Think back to what you looked like. You still had to wear the blue protection gels, your arm glowed up and down with inoculation capsules, and you were having an allergic reaction to something—terrible hives, all over. And the coughing—the gel irritated your throat and made your eyes dry. You looked like someone who should have still been in quarantine. My initial reaction was to keep my distance for my own health. It was instinctual, and not at all considerate of what you were experiencing.]

[You were grossed out,] he said.

[Yes. Grossed out.]

It was both funny and not funny. Honest, and sad. Yes, the lens of language often brought unruly reactions in line, gave one time to process, to reject unadulterated instinct.

But whether it was prejudice or a misunderstanding of *Homo sapiens* communication that had led the Assigner to deny them a child, the result was still the same.

The two of them fell into silence once more, pondering the same question until one of them dared sign it. [Now what?] Devon asked.

Daisy embraced him, then signed. [Now we fight for our family.]

Daisy had tried to comfort him. They'd tried to comfort each other. But it was difficult when they were feeling a similar depth of grief and he . . . he felt he was responsible.

He thought about looking for Maryam. She would understand how this coincided with the expectation that the youngest generation get to reproducing as soon as a cure was found. He had wanted to evolve that imperative—to better integrate into *Lùhng* society, become part of the future, become family with the future. But now, if he wanted to be a father, it seemed his only option was to fulfill the elders' expectations. Raise an ancient human clone with his other ancient human friends. Remain separate. Remain isolated.

But he'd checked the time and realized Maryam would be in the middle of prayer, and he wouldn't interrupt her for the world. The importance of keeping up with her sacred rituals had increased since they'd moved aboard the *Lùhng* ships, since not all *Homo sapiens* had decided to stay in space.

They'd been given the option to return to Earth when the Progentor had come with Revealer ships. And Maryam's mother had gone. It was her only chance to make the holy pilgrimage to Mecca, and both Maryam and her father had seen her off with gladness in their hearts.

With that memory, Devon realized now who he needed to see. His own mother. She might not know how to fix this, but she would be there for him unconditionally, and that was enough.

The Convoy Twelve ship *Pulse* lay moored to the construction platform's docking stage, its design clearly of another place and time. Though it had been his home for nearly his entire childhood, it had always seemed modern. But now, next to the *Lùhng* designs, it wasn't only dated or antiquated—it was a relic, and looked as such. Strange that something so familiar could suddenly seem distinctly out of place.

Devon stopped to assess it from another window hall, scrutinizing the hull for signs of *Lùhng* adaptation. The crew had been able to make the ships livable for nearly two decades without post-human intervention, which had meant ignoring the aesthetic damage and wear. But the *Lùhng* were helping to make it grand once more—to give it a polished shine, make its hull and windows gleam. Once, angry scars—deep gouges and plasma burns—had riddled the exterior, the interior walls reinforced to make up for the lost radiation shielding. But now those scars were buttoned over with press-through. It created brilliant white lines through the hull, displaying the repairs proudly, like gold used to mend pottery in ancient Japan.

The platform and the Pyramid below it were orbiting the nearby M class star, and now they both rotated in such a way that the star's rays burst forth against the bottom of *Pulse*, illuminating it from below like a brilliant spotlight. The craft cast an upward shadow on space itself, making it appear crowned by stars in a sea of gray haze.

Many of the elders still lived on *Pulse*, in their old rooms, walking the old halls, rarely ever venturing onto the platform or any of the other post-human ships. It was odd to him, especially because of how, when he was growing up, they'd all emphasized how *trapped* they were. Nowhere to go but *Breath* and *Pulse*. Nothing to explore, no new ground to step on. Yet here was an entire new civilization's worth of physical space—with more hallways than an ancient Earth metropolis had roads—and they preferred their apartments.

What they'd once thought of as a prison was now home. It meant comfort, security. The familiarity was preferable to the surrealism beyond.

These were scientists, researchers, explorers. But even they could accept only so much change.

Out of his undamaged ear, Devon heard footsteps approaching, and when he turned, he was surprised to see Carmen Sotomayor. She was alone, which was unusual. As the *Homo sapiens*'s ambassador, she typically had an entourage of post-humans and Convoy Twelve crew attending to her needs.

Devon bowed his head in greeting. He had to admit, out of all the *Homo sapiens* left, she was the only one he was worried about disappointing. He was intimidated by her presence, but only because he admired her so much. She had shown them what it was like—not to live in two worlds, as many of the other elders thought of it, but to expand one world. To see the *Lùhng* and convoy ways not as two opposites trying to live together, but as adjoining puzzle pieces in the same picture.

[If I may ask, how did it go?] she signed.

He raised his hands to answer, hesitant, regretting the disappointment it would cause her before she'd even had a chance to feel it. [They said no.]

She nodded understandingly, her half-frown sympathetic. The crow's-feet around her eyes were deep, her lip-line thinning with age. She still had many years left, but he suddenly realized that one day he'd have to let her go, and they would all have to live without her guidance.

[I'm sorry. I thought they might.]

[I always knew it was a possibility,] he signed. [But I still thought, because of Daisy, that I wouldn't be a big deal.]

[You didn't consider yourself a real factor?] She raised an inquisitive eyebrow.

He paused. When she put it like that—[I mean, I did. I just didn't think . . .]

[I don't think you did. It seems like you considered yourself an afterthought. That if the child would have one *Lùhng* parent, what would it matter who or what any additional parents might be?]

[Yes. I guess that's it.]

She didn't sign anything else. Waiting for him to say it so she wouldn't have to.

[That's ridiculous,] he signed. [Isn't it?]

[Only insomuch as you are bound to have an impact on the child's life. What your Assigner was trying to assess is what *kind* of an impact.]

[And they decided it would be a negative one.] He took a deep breath and hesitated to ask her his next question, but he needed to know. [Do you think it would have been a negative impact?]

She pursed her lips and looked out toward *Pulse*, clearly carefully considering her answer. [Your intentions are positive,] she signed eventually. [But intentions are meaningless.]

He tried not to be offended. [What do you mean?]

[The outcome of our actions has nothing to do with our intentions—sadly, this is especially the case if our intentions are good. For example:

[When I was a young girl, I had a brother. He liked to catch lizards and put them in a terrarium, but he was terrible at taking care of them. They always died unless I set them free.

[One day, my brother was chasing lizards through a rock pile near our home, and I thought if I could catch the lizards first, then they wouldn't have to suffer through his poor pet ownership at all. My intentions were only positive.

[But I was far clumsier than my brother. I knocked one of the large rocks from the top of the pile, and it fell on one of the lizards, crushing its skull. I had intended to save it, but it died. Good intentions or no, I had taken an action that had caused miserable consequences for an innocent animal.]

[It was an accident,] Devon said. [You didn't—]

[Mean to,] she finished for him. [Yes, and that's the point—that being mindful of all possible consequences and tailoring your actions as best you can is important. Because, in the end, no matter what you intend, you might cause harm. "I didn't mean to" means nothing to the creatures—or people—you hurt. Positive intent has nothing to do with the actuality of an outcome.]

[So you do agree with their assessment,] he prodded, [that I would have been a bad father for a *Lùhng* child.]

[If you did not consider that your involvement in their life would have actually had an influence on them, then yes. To think that, since they have a *Lùhng* parent, your presence—and therefore your *Homo sapiens* culture—would make no difference is clear folly. You cannot be a parent and have no impact on a child.]

With a nod, Devon looked away. His lower lip was trembling, and his eyes had grown hot. He *was* the reason they hadn't been given a child. He'd suspected, all while hoping it was a lie born of uncertainty. But now he was sure: it was his fault.

Carmen tapped his shoulder and signed, [I'm sorry. You were already upset by the news, maybe I shouldn't have been so frank.]

[No, you're right. Thank you. Your guidance is always appreciated.]

[Were you on your way to catch a shuttle?]

[Yes, to see my mother.]

[May we travel to *Pulse* together?]

[I would like that.]

They didn't have to wait long in the docking bay to board a Convoy Twelve shuttle. The *Homo sapiens* shuttles went exclusively between *Breath*, *Pulse*, and the platform.

■ ■ ■

His mother's wavy black hair had gone white, contrasting sharply with the depth of ruddy brown in her skin. Like most of the other elders, she clung to her old style of dress. For some it was the convoy uniforms, for others it was culturally specific. For her it was pants suits and a single silken scarf of pink, yellow, and blue. She'd repaired the scarf over and over again, saving it from fraying and unraveling. And even though it wasn't often exposed to direct sunlight, it still bore a slight aging fade. The mismatched stitching mirrored the repairs to *Pulse*'s hull—they told a story, held a history.

"Mom," he both said and signed, a quaver in his voice as he entered her quarters.

At the sound of his voice she spun, concern immediately spreading across her face. "What is it, my child?" she asked, opening her arms to him, her Sri Lankan accent still strong all these years later.

He had never much considered his own accent. In ASL, the closest equivalent was which facial expressions some *Lùhng* could or could not make. But his speaking voice was surely a strange mix of emphasis and lilt, unique among the youngest generation.

He ran to her, as though he were still a small boy, flinging his arms around her and burying his stubbled face in her soft scarf.

She took him to the small table just off her kitchenette, offered him a seat and some Masala chai. She prepared cups for both of them, muttering about how it didn't taste like the real thing.

Devon allowed himself a small smile, remembering what Maryam had said about her father's similar complaints.

Taking the proffered chai, he related the meeting to her, what he'd shared and what the Assigner had said, and his encounter with Carmen.

She offered her sympathies. "What do your other *Lùhng* friends have to say?" she said and signed.

The hot steam from the chai felt good on his skin and in his nose. "I haven't discussed it with them yet," he said, laying his head in his hands. "Which is part of the problem, right? If I could support *Lùhng* communication implants, then it wouldn't matter that I haven't physically encountered them today."

"But Daisy—? You—?"

"We're . . . fine. They said we'll fight. I know they think this is a misunderstanding. They didn't detect any prejudice against *Homo sapiens* from the Assigner, just concern for our potential child's well-being and ability to integrate into society. And I know I'm supposed to be mad—I am, mad—about the unconscious bias, but . . . what if the Assigner is right? What if having a *Homo sapiens* parent would be bad for a *Lùhng* child?"

"How so?"

"I don't know. Maybe that's proof right there—I can't imagine what missteps I'd take that would directly harm a *Lùhng* child but not a *Homo sapiens* child. I'd never do anything to intentionally hurt them but . . ."

"But intention has no bearing on outcome. Harm is harm, intended or not."

"Right."

"That you care so much, that you think about such things, should be reassuring to the Assigner."

"But how are they supposed to know? They didn't ask. And I didn't exactly offer, not in the interview. And they can't *read my mind*—that's the whole point."

They sat in companionable silence for a few moments, sipping their tea. She took small, calculated sips, clearly preparing to broach a topic they'd discussed many times before. "Have you begun your own autobiography yet?"

"No, not yet. I told you, I'm waiting until I feel more secure about the elders' biographies, that I've gotten all the interviews I need and can present them with enough of the work that I'm sure I'm representing their experiences authentically."

"I know. So you have said. I don't think this is the real reason."

He prickled. A lot of people seemed to be judging him today.

She threw her palms up. "But you know me. I will not give advice unless it's asked for."

This was both true and completely untrue. She liked to drop hints—like she just had—about the roots of worries, the source of problems, and then pretend like she was only there to be a compassionate ear.

Yes, he knew her. But she also knew him—it worked every time.

"What is the real reason?" he asked, his voice monotone. He wasn't exasperated, but he was on the verge.

"I think you are still unwilling to face the person you might have been, had she lived."

Had she lived.

He reflexively took a deep breath when she said it—those three little words—as though breathing in another place, another time, another life.

"I think everyone's afraid to face the people they might have been," he said, quickly taking another sip of his chai. It might not taste like the "real thing," but it was worlds better than non-joe—the only thing they'd had to flavor their recycled water those last few years before coming aboard Convoy Seven. It had a genuine spice and earthiness to it that he loved. Coming aboard the *Lùhng* convoy was, in a lot of ways, like moving into opulence.

"Ah, but for you," she said and signed, "the turning point is clear, and the choice was made for you, not by you. And though you may have pushed it aside—to the back of your mind or some other corner of your body—you know that it is the same now: that if you are the father of a *Lùhng* child, it changes who they might have been. Which was why you distanced yourself from that fact, as Carmen revealed. Your mother—"

"*You* are my mother," he said, too quickly, making her point for her.

She smiled softly. "A child is allowed more than one mother. I am no less your mother for Eara being your mother as well. Her history was lost to you. The heritage you should have had was replaced by another. And—do not interrupt me, boy—you wish not to dishonor me by pondering that loss. I understand. Who you are today is not made less whole, less happy, by wondering what might have been.

"But this is why I have always encouraged you to take part in whatever bits of culture I could find for you. Because it is not mine, but it is yours, and I would not deprive you of it in a million years."

"Well, it's been a hundred thousand, and you haven't given up yet," he said, making a halfhearted joke.

"I never met your father," she said, reaching out to pat his hand as he tensely cupped his tea mug. "And I only knew Eara as an acquaintance. There were no records of what they wished for you if something happened. But I knew I wanted to give you everything, which meant doing my best not to force you to be an exact copy of me. That always fails, anyway," she said with a laugh. "I tried to give you more tools, not fewer. I did the best I could—"

"You did everything," he said, letting go of the mug to hold her hand outright. He knew he didn't have to feel guilty, to feel like a bad son. But even thinking about Eara, about the father whose name he didn't even know, made him feel ungrateful. His mother, Nipuni—sitting with him right now—never *had* to take on the responsibility of raising him. She chose him, and imagining who those other people were, what his life might have been like if the accident had never happened, felt like not choosing her back.

"I am only human," she said, reiterating, "I did the best I could. That is what the *Lùhng* are after: your best. When your chance to appeal comes up, being honest with yourself is the only way to give it."

"But what if my best really isn't good enough?"

. . . .

FOUR WEEKS LATER.

Once in a while, Devon was granted the privilege of alighting on the Pyramid's surface, so that he may document in real time the experiences of the Convoy Twelve members who worked there.

Devon's SD jump in a *Lùhng* shuttle with a handful of other workers was brief and brought them close to the edge of the Pyramid's open corner. The incomplete portion was still a gulf nearly one Jupiter wide, and falling away from its rim on four sides were vast planes. Though Devon couldn't remember ever standing on a globe, he'd seen plenty of pictures in the data banks of the Earth's curvature stealing ships from the horizon. This was the exact opposite. The plane he stood on presented him with sheer flatness that seemed to stretch and stretch and stretch almost to forever, culminating in three points. Because he could see those points—hundreds of thousands of kilometers away—they seemed to rise up, like petals starting to curl, like the edges of paper subtly flexing upward because of the pull of the pulp fibers.

He tried not to look out at those points. Gazing across the immensity from the surface always gave him a sudden sense of fuzziness, made his head light and his mind giddy. His breath would come sharp and shallow, hyperventilation threatening to send him into a spiral.

Instead of looking out, Devon looked in as he inched his way toward the lip, toward where his interviewee, Amanjeet, awaited. His suit allowed his legs to move and his feet to leave the slick metal surface despite the immensely high gravity, and he silently thanked the *Lùhng* for the accommodation.

People buzzed about left and right, and Devon spun between them, like a small child in a crowded launch bay. The closer to the rim he got, the more pockmarked the surface became. Hazard points had been cordoned off with strips of reflective material, and he was careful not to accidently trip over the line—he could find himself suddenly in a pocket of extreme gravity that would crush him despite the suit, or over the top of an exposed crystal that could shoot a rogue plasma flare through the hole in the exterior.

Just like the sun shining on *Pulse* from below, creating a hard line of light and shadow into space, so, too, the light emanating from the crystals created a sharp borderland of a glare. Their flashing brightness was like a strobe light shooting out from the incomplete point, a beacon into space.

With his own breath echoing against the front of his helmet, Devon wondered if there was some undiscovered civilization out there that could see the strobing. What would they think? What would they call it? How would they explain it?

It had been a strobing star that had called Convoy Seven into interstellar space. Might the Pyramid's flashing raise similar questions in an alien scientist?

Were there alien scientists?

Devon had asked Daisy about aliens. Hell, they'd all asked about aliens. Sure, they'd mistaken the post-humans for nonhumans, but it wasn't as though aliens didn't exist. Humans hadn't started these megastructures.

They'd been told of the *Nataré*, an ancient civilization of builders who had died out long ago. And there was evidence of others—a few ruins here, bits of debris, a unique wandering probe, fossils, black oil in the crust of various planets. Life itself seemed fairly common, but the more complex it was, the rarer it was, which was logical. It appeared, however, that the *Homo draconem* and the *Homo kubernētēs* were the, quote, "only intelligent life of their standing currently in existence."

But "only intelligent life of their standing" did not mean "only intelligent life." But when pressed for specifics, *Lùhng* crew members would only say they'd heard rumors. Leaked portions of classified reports from Noumenon.

Devon had been surprised that the concept of classified information even existed in *Lùhng* society. The concept intrigued him, but he hadn't pressed Daisy into telling him more. They'd find out soon enough if there were aliens on Noumenon, when the Progentor and the away team landed on the planet.

For now, Devon could be content with the awe structures like the Pyramid created in his chest. Many civilizations had worked on them. Humanity was simply the lucky one that had come along at the end of the story.

The human-power it would take to cover over just this one remaining gap—to hide the workings of the Pyramid from outside prying eyes—would have required thousands of years from *Homo sapiens*. Indeed, a similar amount of effort had been required to finish the Web when Convoy Seven first discovered it. But *Homo draconem* could accomplish such a feat in months.

Mainly through biological construction.

The Pyramid had been little more than one corner and one not-quite-complete plane when they'd found it, barely a thousand years ago. It would have taken the length of *Homo sapiens*'s existence twice over to do such work without biological modification.

Amanjeet hailed him over the comms. "Hello my friend, what do you think today? As in awe as ever?"

"Always," Devon said, turning to scan the rim, looking for the old man among the other workers. His job was to help supply the printers.

Hovering above the open gap were dozens of bizarre shapes, each extruding materials onto the rim, slowly covering over the exposed crystals. They looked like massive conglomerates of shuttle-sized machines. Only they *weren't* machines. They were special *Lùhng*, bonded to one another, able to process raw and toxic materials inside their own bodies, compressing and fusing and smelting in their own cores. When Devon looked closely, he could make out individual limbs, eyes, mouths. They latched on to one another with organic hooks, limbs intertwined, fully synchronized in body and mind.

When their work was finally complete, they would detach from one another, dispose of the limbs and organs and other growths they no longer needed, and shrink back to an average *Lùhng* size.

But for now, they processed and expelled thick layers of new megastructure in constant motion, a swirling dance, new materials constantly fed up to them by long tubing.

Behind the printers, other *Lùhng* treated and tempered the newly lain materials, and still others followed with devices that measured the suitability and integration of each new part.

Amanjeet was with Emperor and Aloe—two *Lùhng*, one primarily of the hyperprocessing school, and the other of extremocapacity. Emperor's skull was shaped like a tall, spiked crown—which was actually an array for data transition, which aided in *Lùhng* mind-to-mind communication over the vast planes of the Pyramid. Similar *Lùhng* had been dubbed with equally regal names: King, Regina, Highness, Queen, etc.

Aloe's particular modifications allowed them to grow individual limbs for extreme tasks within a short amount of time, similar to those who made up the printers. When the body part was no longer of use, it was easily discarded, pinched off just like an aloe offset.

The trio greeted Devon in ASL on approach, and he signed back. The three of them managed a set of the long supply tubes feeding one of the printers, seeing that it didn't twist or pull or clog. They moved quickly, making minute-by-minute adjustments.

"Amazing, isn't it?" Amanjeet said over the radio, his hands never halting as he punched a few nodes on a control panel and changed the mixture of liquid metals running through one set of piping. "Makes putting together a megastructure look as simple as snapping together a few Legos."

"What's a Lego?"

Amanjeet smiled, his dastaar showing cobalt blue in a flash of plasma-light. "Never you mind."

Devon didn't point out that it was his job to mind—that if Amanjeet or another elder didn't tell him what a Lego was, then the memory of Legos would be lost forever. But that wasn't the story he was after today.

A *Lùhng* came over—one whose body was essentially a giant pocket—to receive a batch of backwashed slag.

"You promised to tell me about the time you got lost, when you were ten," Devon prompted. "Remember to be as descriptive as possible, please. Give as many details about the Punjab—the rivers, the people, how you felt, what happened, what you saw—as possible."

Amanjeet smiled again, his gaze internalizing, going far away, far *back*. "It was a humid day, but the earth was dry. I broke my sandal, the right—no, no, the left one. My cousins were all older and were being particularly mean that day. Didn't want to have to worry about me keeping up, so they tried to lose me early. They thought I'd go back home if they ran ahead and I couldn't find them."

Devon made notes of Amanjeet's expression as he told the story—how it made him feel now, versus how he recalled it made him feel then. There was a strange sheen to all the elder's memories of Earth. If it happened before the accident, they always recalled it fondly, without fail. Even as they said the event was traumatic, it came with a glimmering edge of nostalgia they could not shake. That distance and time could color a memory like that was astounding. If someone had done something awful to them, they would not necessarily forgive the transgression, but they would find something in the memory to hold dear. A smell, the warmth of the sun, the satisfaction in knowing the terrible person was gone and they were still alive. Something.

In this story, Amanjeet did not blame his cousins for the three nights he'd spent alone in the hills—though his parents quite fervently had. And though little Amanjeet had been scared, and hungry, and chilled to the bone when it rained on the third night, elder Amanjeet remembered the bird's nest he'd found in a bael tree, how he'd seen a snake winding its way through the fruit and spines trying to get at the chicks, and he'd grabbed it and tossed it to the ground, where it slithered away, perturbed.

"I ate the underripe fruit and was proud of myself for saving the baby birds," he said. "But now I think, too, about how I deprived the snake of the same thing I was after: a meal. I hope the snake found food elsewhere, but that would mean another nest, different birds. I don't know what that experience told me, but it was something. Perhaps when you write the biography you can tell future readers what it's supposed to mean. Something about how you cannot save all the snakes *and* all the birds. Except—" Amanjeet paused his work for the briefest of moments. "I suppose now you can, in a way. If you try hard enough to find a solution . . . if you can print all the food a snake needs, then you can save all the birds it would have eaten. Maybe you don't have to choose between the two. Perhaps they can be in harmony."

As the months went on, Daisy and Devon continued their cohabitation as usual. It was not a thing that had been done between a *Homo sapiens* and a *Homo draconem* before, because their basic habitational needs were wildly different. Or, at least, that was what the elders liked to say.

But it wasn't as different as one might think. They still ate, slept, relaxed, and desired social and alone time—as alone as someone who was mentally interconnected with everyone else at all times could get.

Sleeping was most often done in a sort of sleep-sack, suspended among rows and rows of other sleepers. At first, Devon had thought Daisy would continue to want to sleep alone, but instead they had invited him into their sack, enveloping him in their many arms, the two of them cuddled together intimately as they dozed. They sought their meals together, as they always had, and each of them sacrificed alone time to spend the hours primarily with each other.

And while he felt closer to Daisy than ever before, there was one thing they no longer talked about: children. Not even casually. Indeed, encountering a floating pack of minors through a hall was enough to kill conversation. And when they were together, they avoided the birthing wing. Where once they'd strolled past the rows and rows of tanks as casually as though admiring an art gallery or a garden, they now treated the aperture to the wing as though the press-through really was a solid wall.

There was little to talk about regarding children until they found out if their appeal would be honored. And the topic only made Daisy sad. [We will present to them an impassioned front. A rallying speech. And then the Assigner will reverse their decision,] they insisted.

But Devon wasn't so sure.

He *was* sure that *avoiding* children until their appeal came wasn't the answer. Exactly the opposite.

He'd taken what Carmen said to heart. His intent meant nothing. His actions were everything.

So he volunteered in the birthing wing, checking tank composition, cleaning newly de-tanked infants, presenting the babies to their new parents. And he decided his involvement was not temporary. Even if they appealed and he was denied again, he would continue to help where he could. Perhaps it would pave the way for a *Homo sapiens* parent in the future . . . if there were any *Homo sapiens* left to be parents.

He thought for the first time about giving in to the elders. Once the away team to Noumenon discovered what was wrong with them—or, at the very least, sent them new genomes to clone—he would be free (no, *encouraged*) to raise a *Homo sapiens* child. The elders wouldn't question his fitness. More importantly, they wouldn't question Daisy's fitness. This strange borderland of potential parenthood wouldn't exist.

But that train of thought made him even more uneasy about the Assigner's decision. Carmen and his mother had suggested his attitude had been the problem—and it was, he didn't deny it. But the Assigner had blamed his lack of implants. They'd blamed it on the fact that he was an ancient human.

They hadn't said *he* was unfit, they'd declared his entire convoy unfit.

How could they ever expect to be fully integrated into this

society if they weren't allowed to participate as fully as everyone else?

The children he helped tend gave him hope, gave him joy. Not one looked anything like their parents. They were individuals with individual wants, needs, cares—as all people were. A *Lùhng*'s uniqueness was simply more obvious. And their society would do everything for them to see that they had their uniqueness uplifted.

And as he helped, he tried to understand why *his* uniqueness was so difficult for the *Lùhng* to understand.

Perhaps he needed to better understand himself first.

And still, when he sat down each evening after the third meal to do his composition work, he could not force himself to open the files with his name on them. His mother continued to ask after his own autobiography, and still he resisted.

There were so many other incomplete stories.

His could wait.

Couldn't it?

It had been nine months since he and Daisy had been denied. The approximate gestation period of a human—no matter they be *Homo draconem*, *Homo sapiens*, or *Homo kubernētēs*. And today *was* a birthday, of sorts.

The Pyramid would receive its capstone.

Daisy was all abuzz with pure joy.

[I would have thought this humdrum to you,] Devon said. [You've lived in the construction field your whole life.]

[No other megastructure has been completed in my lifetime,] they said. The post-humans aboard lived upwards of two hundred and fifty years. In some parts of the galaxy, much longer. [And I will not live to see another.]

The finishing of a new megastructure was always observed with decadence and mirth. Going forward, today would be marked as a new holiday, where the Pyramid and those who worked on it would be forever celebrated.

The halls of the construction platform were alive today, with more than just bodies. Recordings of past project completions bowed out along each surface, and it was like walking through tunnels of memory. The typically stark white was now awash in color, the various forms of humanity and their extensions toiling away toward triumph.

This was entirely for the benefit of the *Homo sapiens*. The Posts could have the events broadcast directly to their implants.

Devon walked as Daisy floated, pointing out their different clone ancestors whenever they spotted them.

[This is the Crescent. Completed five thousand seven hundred thirty-two years ago,] they said, petals curling inward in delight. [See here? It's difficult to tell. There—there! A Daisy of before.]

The modifications were different, Devon could tell. The ancient clone's limbs were shorter, and there were only four. The petals, too, had a different shape, and there were fewer of them that lay thicker about the post-human's collar. The *Lùhng* were always tweaking their design, always growing.

The construction platform and its docked craft had jumped one hundred AUs away from the Pyramid, and it was a shock to the system to wander through a window hall and not see the megastructure spread out below. At this distance it was still visible, but just as another bright star in an endless sea of stars. Daisy pointed it out to him, their implants allowing them to locate it with instant pinpoint accuracy.

When it came time to place the capstone, every hall would put the event on display.

The only workers left on the Pyramid were of the extremo-tolerance school of thought, those that could withstand the harshest of environments. Robot-like puppets called autons used to complete the megastructures, but they were less efficient, and many of them were lost when a megastructure was activated. Those with extremotolerance mods were specifically designed for these kinds of dangerous tasks, and most of the time they all came home. Most of the time. Only those who volunteered for the capstone project were sent into the danger zone. It was a high honor, but could come with a price.

Devon's feelings were more mixed than Daisy's. Perhaps it was simply because this was all new. Even the projected videos couldn't quell a sourness in his anticipation, brought on by unfamiliarity.

But when they came across the replay of the very first megastructure completion, Devon's discomfort grew. At first, he was pleasantly surprised. The people completing the Web were in forms he knew—they were *Homo sapiens*. He'd known that intellectually, but it was different seeing it, putting faces to the names. He paused their strolling to watch the whole thing—clips strung together from different internal cameras on the ships and a false-color feed of the megastructure itself.

But moments after Anatoly Straifer directed his extensions to finish, the feed abruptly ended, looping back to the beginning.

[Why doesn't it show the rest? The others show everyone celebrating after.]

[They did not celebrate after,] Daisy signed. [It is a happy memory for us but was a day of devastation for them. We may not remember how to speak the language of that time, but their despair is clear. And disturbing. We would not revisit it.]

No matter how many times his future-friends reassured him that the megastructures were benevolent, he knew deep down that things could still go wrong. People could die today. The Pyramid might do something unprecedented.

Nothing was guaranteed.

They made their way toward the primary launch bay, which had been cleared of all shuttle-spheres to accommodate as many viewers as possible. The gigantic inner dome projected three different shots of the ongoing work, each image seven stories high.

Their friends and family were all there—Mayram and Sea Spine, his mother, Daisy's five parents, Carmen and Kali.

The feed projected nearest their group displayed a set of hyperprocesseing *Lùhng*, those with the crown-like skulls. Three of them floated in empty space, using their graviton manipulation to maintain a perfect equilateral distance from one another. They were three AUs away from the Pyramid, and the video feed—likely relayed through the eyes of a fourth *Lùhng*—framed the structure perfectly between them. The shuttle-sphere that had taken them to the location was not pictured.

The next image over—warping around the dome directly above them, with a few random *Lùhng* scurrying across its surface to reach the crowd below—was from the typical vantage point of the construction platform. The recording *Lùhng* gazed down into the pinprick of an opening at the Pyramid's top. Pink and white and purple light still flashed within, but the crystals themselves could no longer be seen.

The last feed was from the Pyramid's surface, right next to the rim. The procession of *Lùhng* about to set the capstone were treating the occasion with all the flourishes it deserved.

They were not naked in the starlight. Instead, they all wore billowing clothes of different designs, each made of a shimmering silver, gold, copper, or white fabric. The Pyramid's gravity would have torn the fine fabric from their bodies had the wearers not been continuously manipulating their own graviton fields to make it appear as though a gentle breeze tossed the delicate materials. Robes, capes, dresses, camises all fluttered in a long procession. Triangles and pyramids covered the hems and were reflected in the cuts and drapes. Two dozen workers floated forward in a line, the lead *Lùhng* carrying the capstone—a small pyramidal device, black as the void and reflective as glass.

A trumpeting bellowed through the hangar—a distorted sort of sound that Devon assumed landed differently, majestically, in *Lùhng* implants versus flesh-and-blood ears. Carmen, hand in hand with Kali, who was using their gravitons to carry her, flew toward the center of the highest projection. Together, they addressed the crowd.

Daisy interpreted for Devon and the other *Homo sapiens* nearby, who could not make out Carmen signing at this distance.

[Greetings, Convoys Seven and Twelve. And special greetings to our envoy headed toward the planet Noumenon.] They would be watching this all with only a slight delay, via an advanced SD information packaging system. The sending and receiving devices aboard the Progentor's ship and the construction platform were quantumly entangled. [If our timing has been as remarkable as we'd hoped, you should be arriving at the planet within a few days of our completion of the Pyramid.]

Devon's gaze drifted. He meant no disrespect to Carmen and Kali, but he was enwrapped in the visuals of the procession. It felt ancient. Here he was in the far future, and this ritual felt like it carried the weight of so many centuries, eons before he was born. How had the alien civilizations marked their progress in building the megastructures? Did they have the sense of fanfare humanity possessed?

The crowd around him shifted, light ripples of bodily movement delicately jostling him as they flowed through the gargantuan space. Though he was filled with wonder, he knew his excitement was nothing compared to those who'd been waiting their entire life for this moment.

Some people bowed their heads. Others raised their arms high, swaying, something spiritual moving them.

A swell of shared pride grew in his chest. To be alive, to be here, now—merely existing within the same time and space as these people and this event—was a wonder.

The speeches concluded, and the crowed calmed. Everything went still. An intensity of group focus like Devon had never experienced before was pinpointed at the capstone. The music grew bolder, swelled into one reverberating note.

Daisy reached for his hand, as did his mother. They clutched one another and held their breath.

Gently, the *Lùhng* at the front of the procession kneeled over the incomplete point. They held the capstone high, and the fire from within the Pyramid sent brilliant beams refracting through the dark material, creating dense beams of gray-scale light. Slowly, still adhering to the pomp and circumstance, the *Lùhng* lowered the stone as one might place a diadem upon a princess. Two other workers flanked them, and together the trio secured the last piece.

Immediately, the Pyramid began to vibrate. The smooth feed shook, blurred. The members of the procession flew away from the megastructure's surface, letting their clothes fall flat, dropping the showy pretenses to focus on safety. Their careful movements turned mildly frantic and haphazard. They caught one another and flew back, back, back. The megastructure was so massive that the only way Devon could tell they were actually moving away was the shrinking and melding of the capstone into the whole.

Then the Pyramid began to spin.

It had been orbiting the star but had no rotation of its own. Now things were different. The tip of the capstone yawed through space—barely noticeable at first, but picking up great speed. Those on the surface of Earth might not feel like they were spinning at sixteen hundred kilometers an hour, but that was because they weren't starting at zero.

Devon jumped when, all around him, applause broke out.

That was the sign that the job was done: the megastructure had begun to act.

What would it do? What gifts would it bring? No one had an answer, and yet doubt had no place among the crowd.

Some people began to leave the fishbowl of a hangar, knowing that the Pyramid's actions could take days or weeks—perhaps months, or years—to come into full effect. The revelries would continue elsewhere—in the parks, over food, out in space, even. Many convoy members would fly out to greet the capstone layers as they returned. No one had been lost. They'd been fortunate today.

It took seventy-six hours for the Pyramid to invert. Devon thought the structure would keep rotating, but it stopped. And when it stopped, all activity on Convoy Seven stopped. Everyone collectively held their proverbial breath, waiting, teetering on the same edge. What would it do next?

Sink.

A sharp line—a bleeding edge, from which pink and sunset-orange light bubbled up in droplets before dissipating—cut through space-time at the tip of the Pyramid's capstone. The inverted shape dropped through the cut—which had neither measurable depth nor width—like a letter into an envelope, slowly disappearing over the next day and a half.

Lùhng scientists rushed out to observe the sinking, to gather whatever data they could and make whatever hypotheses they were able. The light bubbles were particularly fascinating. Bits of a subdimension escaping, evaporating, dying out in a glazed blaze.

It was all beyond Devon. He may have been raised by a scientist, but he wasn't trained to be one, of any type.

And still, even as the base of the Pyramid disappeared, the three-dimensional object swallowed up into a one-dimensional slice in the universe, the joy did not dissipate.

What will it do? What will it do?

The next day the away team was scheduled to come out of SD and arrive in the Philosopher's System. Devon headed over to *Pulse* with Maryam, where the entirety of Convoy Twelve gathered to hear the first communiqué from Noumenon.

It should have been another day of joy. Another layer of triumph.

As they gathered in the mess hall, with Carmen and Captain Moscovici standing at the fore, Devon knew something was wrong before either woman spoke.

"This is the appointed time," the captain said and signed after a time. "But we're having trouble connecting with the Progentor's ship."

They waited for hours, murmuring, conjecturing. And still, nothing.

Carmen said they'd try again the next day, but somehow Devon knew.

It was like that clip of Convoy Seven when they were finishing the Web. They were happy—too happy. They didn't know what they were doing, but they celebrated anyway. Convoy Twelve had been caught up in Convoy Seven's joy, but here was the catch.

Something had gone wrong.

The construction platform received word from Earth and Noumonian conservationists a few days later. There was a problem.

A problem that couldn't be fixed with a rallying speech or dazzling ingenuity.

Maybe a problem that couldn't even be fixed with time.

"The Progentor's ship," the captain read, when they'd all gathered in the mess once again, "as well as its Earth escort, are reported to have . . . to have crashed into one of the planet's oceans. The authorities say it appears they were—" she scrunched up her face "—kicked out of their travel SD without warning. Most likely by a distortion that appeared in the area approximately one hundred and seven hours ago."

The report had sent Devon into a haze. The captain sounded like she was speaking from far away—around corners and down halls. Faint and fuzzy. But the mention of the timeline perked him up again.

Approximately one hundred and seven hours ago the Pyramid had disappeared.

What did that mean?

What does it do?

"The distortion, which they liken to an unstable gravitational anomaly, given its relativistic effects, prevents the system's conservationists from retrieving the downed craft." She explained they'd attempted to send in one rescue ship, only to have the entire crew perish instantaneously—from an outside perspective—of old age.

It can't . . . it can't be related to the Pyramid, Devon told himself. Because that would mean they'd caused it. That their away team had crashed—the Revealer's religious leader had been lost—that the conservationists had died, because humanity had once again possessed the audacity to turn on a device they knew nothing about.

"This distortion appears to be . . . spreading. SD communications through it are as interrupted as any other signal or physical object, which means it's not just our dimension that's affected. It has effectively created a barrier that is widening. Earth hopes this is just a ripple effect—that the distortion will dissipate."

But what if it doesn't?

There were so many answers to that question, but one stuck out in Devon's mind: there will be no reproductive help from Noumenon.

"It is unclear at this time how severe the crash was, and if there are survivors, injuries, or casualties."

"Allah help us," Maryam whispered.

For everyone else, news of the crash and the anomaly was devastating. Not only did they mourn for their lost friends, companions, and leaders, but their imagined futures as well— their visions of kith and kin dissipated just like the droplets of an SD seeping through a rift in space-time.

Devon saw it differently. He was angry that they'd sent people on the away mission at all. Some of their most revered elders might be dead, and for what? A distraction.

Because there was no going back. There was no making it the twenty-second century again. Convoy Twelve couldn't accept *when* they were, and in turn Convoy Seven couldn't accept *what* they were. The Assigner's decision had made that clear.

Both groups thought they'd assimilated into a whole, become an expanded society, but there were still things holding them back. Still growing they had to do—confrontations they had to make. The loss of the away team—of their old captain and mission head, of Hope, the youngest *Homo sapiens*— shone a spotlight on their discrepancies.

For Devon, everything came into focus. There would be more growing pains, but they were worth going through.

And if he was going to ask society to change, he had to ask it of himself first. Confront his own questions of who he was, and who he might have been.

He went to the art studio to work. He gathered his 'flex-sheets and his keyboard projector and situated himself at his favorite desk, pressing a few buttons to direct the press-through to form into a comfortable seat.

He sat the satchel—the one branded with Eara's initials—on the desk as well, within view.

With a deep breath, he opened the file with his name on it, and began to type:

> *My first memory is of choking. I'm two and a half and I can't breathe right. Smoke is filling the room—or perhaps the hall, I can't tell—and there's a terrible ringing in my ear. A ringing that doesn't feel like it's outside my head, but inside my head. It is.*
>
> *My back hurts and my legs hurt, because a few moments ago I was five feet off the ground and was dropped. Thrown. Catapulted from*

Devon stopped typing. He knew how the sentence ended. He knew from whence he was catapulted. But this was it, this was the thing that was so hard to say, to write, to remember.

He pursed his lips and tried again, making the words bleed out, black and white, on the 'flex-sheet.

> *from my biological mother's arms. Eara died instantly when a section of* Breath *buckled in on itself during an abnormal subdimensional jump—later simply known as "the accident." Whether she died without pain and without fear, I can never know. But she died without me.*

That last sentence was a surprise. It had come from his fingers naturally, without force, as though his hands had always wanted to form words his mind could not. He read it over again. Then again, trying to understand his own statement. He didn't harbor survivor's guilt—it wasn't that he thought he should have died, too. There was no sense of *why her and not me.*

His feelings were more . . . fundamental.

Eara had gone where he could not follow.

And all the time they could have had, all the things he could have learned from her and about her, had gone, too.

And the father he'd lost was even more abstract. The man had never come to space. Nipuni didn't even know if Eara was married, or had a boyfriend, or if she might have used a sperm donor. She didn't know if Eara was straight, or gay, or bi, or pan, or ace like him. That knowledge disappeared with Eara, too.

Had Devon had another parent who mourned him? Grandparents? Siblings?

He'd always had a family. He'd never felt alone, or abandoned.

But his life had started out one way and gone another. That was true for everyone on Convoy Twelve, had been his reality his entire life.

But it felt now, suddenly, as though he were experiencing the repercussions of the accident fully for the first time.

And *this, this* was why he'd avoided ordering his thoughts, confronting his feelings. This sudden shortness of breath, the pang in his chest and the ache in his soul, for things he couldn't even properly miss because he'd never had them.

He was imagining a past, just as the others had imagined a future. One that was different. Simple. Idealized.

One where Nipuni had never staggered down that hall—with buckled metal and shattered glass and toxic smoke curling through the air—to follow a small child's screams. One where he hadn't crawled over to Eara's crushed form and tangled his baby fingers in her blood-matted hair. One where Nipuni hadn't had to tear him away, where she hadn't clutched him to her chest and taken him to that bathroom to clean the grime from his face.

One where she hadn't told Captain Tan that she would take responsibility for him.

One where none of that had happened, because they were all safe and alive.

But that was a fever dream. If none of that had happened, it didn't mean he would have instead grown up running through fields of heather chasing sheep, or whatever small children did in twenty-second-century Scotland.

He could not, in fact, confront the person he might have been because he could only imagine an idealized version. Something smooth and ill-defined. Plastic. Molded. As fake and quasi-formed as the intended results of the away team's mission. They could have made *Homo sapiens* babies again . . . and then what? It didn't turn back the clock. It wouldn't bring back the elders' version of normal—whatever normal could possibly mean.

The world changes, and life fights entropy. Forward was the only way. Forming something new out of the now, not scavenging for what might have been.

Daisy was right, and they were wrong. The two of them would fight for their family—fight damn hard. But the answer might still be no, and they couldn't stop fighting if it was.

The future wasn't just about the two of them and what they could give to a child. It was about all of them—what their society wanted to be. What it could give to *all* its children.

He began writing once more.

. . . .

NINE MONTHS LATER

When the day of their appeal came, Devon presented his mother with a rough draft of his own memoir.

[Who I might have been never mattered,] he told her. [Maybe it would have to someone else, but not to me. What matters is who I became and have yet to become.]

Hand in hand, he and Daisy returned to the municipal office.

He understood the importance of connecting his child to their culture, of making sure they were not cut off from their peers, their history, their society. But he was not taking a *Lùhng* child and severing them from all that. They would have the full connectivity of all their peers. But, with a *Homo sapiens* as their father, they would have *more*, not less. They would learn *additional* means of communication.

So much of human culture was exclusionary. You couldn't be this *and* this, you had to be either/or. More one way or the other. You couldn't ever be seen as unified if you identified in plurality—there had to be a concept of duality, a fighting binary. In-group and out-group. Parts in combination, not a totality.

People weren't allowed to just *be*.

Just be a whole person.

But why did it have to be that way?

He understood the child-of-two-worlds dilemma, but he would fight tooth and nail to make sure no one told their child they were less *Homo draconem* or too *Homo sapiens* or not *Homo sapiens* enough. There was no reason the concept of two worlds should exist—it was all one world, but his child's could be *wider*.

After a long wait, they were sent to the same desk. The same Assigner sat behind it. Devon had assumed their case would go to someone else. But this was fine. Better, even.

The Assigner began by asking questions they'd already answered, going over the basics, and their own reasoning for the initial decision. And then, finally, Devon had his moment.

[I do not want to make a *Lùhng* child into a *Homo sapiens* child,] he stressed. [I am aware of our differences, but differences aboard your ships are what *herald* belonging. The diversity among the *Homo draconem* is celebrated, encouraged. Your world is inclusive, because when a *Lùhng* has a disability you find solutions for accommodation. You know that no member of your society should be hampered in their life simply because their needs are different from your needs.

[But then we came along—*Homo sapiens*. In need of a home, in need of a society. And you welcomed us. But you could not fathom us. We have accessibility needs that cannot be solved with your technology. We have accessibility needs that don't even need *solving*. They're merely different.

[The addition of *Homo sapiens* is just one more branch of diversity. I have no desire to erase that variety, to make my child—my children, even—become small carbon copies of myself. I respect that each person will be who they are. I do not need them to be me, or like me. I try to know people for a living—weaving their lives into a story is what I do. But they are not my stories. I don't want to make them mine. I asked for this responsibility and I was granted this responsibility and I will never stop respecting that.

[I record history, but I look to the future. We cannot go back, we can only change. I do not expect your world to stop for us, to go back to the way it was. To ask for stagnation is selfish. But I do ask that we be a part of this future. Not relegated to the sidelines. Not throwbacks. We are people of *now* just as you are people of *now*.

[Your decision doesn't just matter to me. It matters to you. It matters to your family. It matters to Convoy Seven. It speaks to who you want to be as a people.

[I don't know if you're about to say yes. I don't know if you're about to say no. Because reality doesn't tie itself up in a bow. It doesn't follow a nice narrative arc. But I hope. I invest. That's what we do. We try. We work, we progress. I'm here.

I'm making the grand speech. But I know that, despite how much grand speeches make for good stories, they don't fix things all on their own. We have to work together to be better. For you, for me, for us—] He squeezed Daisy's hand [—and for the children yet to come.]

VANHI'S INTERLUDE

There's No Place Like Home

The deep pull of anticipation could not be helped. There was no way out of it, no resisting. The pills Justice had developed for her could only compensate so much. They weren't designed to blot out this *insistence* from her endocrine system. The anticipation of one's death is like no other anticipation imaginable.

They were crashing, falling, skidding through an atmosphere, watching the edges of the Progentor's ship glow and burn and fracture and melt.

Everyone shouted, alarms blared.

This wasn't a typical crash. Their approach had been good—steady. Their conservationist escort had been direct, with their instructions clear.

Wes-Tu had long ago decided his presence aboard need not be secret, and he'd lent his communication skills to the effort—speaking with the Earth *Homo kubernētēs* mind-to-mind on the entire party's behalf.

The two ships had been traveling side by side into the system without incident. With such a safe and secure preamble, nothing could have prepared them for what came next.

Space suddenly *twisted*. The darkness *warped*. Something from outside pushed inward with a great-yet-inconsistent pressure. Space-time bowed, creating a giant, shining curve of reflective black with a silvery sheen. In brief flashes it crinkled, like tinfoil, leaving sizzling pink along each unexpected crease.

The conservationist ship was hurled sidelong into theirs. It clamped on with external claws, grappling, scraping, like a drowning man looking for purchase.

And then they were flung through the twisting, and suddenly the planet was before them. They'd been light-minutes away only moments prior. The approach was supposed to be long, steady, careful.

The craft shook aggressively, leaping erratically, encountering a turbulence that had nothing to do with wind or air density and everything to do with currents of physics trying to slosh back to where they belonged.

The intense curve of the turquoise and pink atmosphere bowed up convexly before them, flashing before the forward shield as they tumbled.

Vanhi felt trapped in her EVA suit. Though it was working perfectly, claustrophobia suddenly invaded her veins and she felt like she couldn't breathe. She clawed at her helmet, but years of training kept her fingers from unlatching the fastenings.

The conservationist had insisted everyone on board don environment suits. This system was protected, and every precaution would be taken to avoid contamination.

For a moment Vanhi wondered if their diligence would save their lives. Would they be more likely to survive this plummet in pressure suits?

She wanted the answer to be yes. The scientist in her said no. If the *ship* couldn't survive, they had no chance.

Next to Vanhi in the main cabin, Stone gritted his teeth. She reached for his hand, their gloves bulky in one another. In front of them, Mac held on to the back of his seat with his arms over his head, and Justice held on to him. All three Tans were knotted together, a bundle of protection, the parents over their sleeping, impossible baby. Little Hope. Their hope.

Out of the corner of her eye Vanhi saw Kexin's hand

MARINA J. LOSTETTER

shoot out across the aisleway—like she was still that little girl reaching for Henry, reaching for Mrs. Chappell.

Devon had sent them their biographies. Perhaps he'd compiled them just in time.

Kexin's hand found Jamal's. His attendants ran up and down the aisles, seeing to the ship, doing what they could to control the descent—which was nothing.

Now the edge of the globe disappeared from view. It was nothing but a ball of solid, hard-hitting rock before them, swathed in the thinnest layer of air that swirled here and there into pink and purplish storm heads.

Vanhi could feel the fall now. Not just in the centrifugal forces of their tumble, but in the tug of the planet's gravity. Light, but persistent. Growing all the time. Enough to take hold, to pull them down. To send them plummeting.

"Vanhi!" came a pained cry next to her—desperate and stricken. It was Stone.

She'd felt the tug, tried to resist. But it were as though a hollowing out of her body began deep in her chest. A sucking-swirling. Like the tug of a black hole ripping her apart, only without pain.

She cried out herself, squeezed his hand, but it was already gone. His call was little more than an echo.

No. No! You son of a—no! I can't go now. I can't leave him, them. I can't!

It figured. It fit. Her entire life leading up to this point—where her curse would save her, tearing her away from her loved ones, her family. Only to kill her later. She'd jump back into years-old wreckage, skeletons half decayed all around, stuffed into a too-small space. Either she'd die immediately or have long enough to die in agony.

She clawed at this reality, trying to go back, despair

swelling in her, filling her up as she tried to swim back through—

Through . . .

How . . .

How was she conscious enough to despair? To claw? How had she heard an echo of Stone's last cries for her?

She'd never been conscious in her SD before. There wasn't time to be conscious—they weren't even sure time *existed* here in the anticipation SD.

She flailed out around her, reaching, sensing. She couldn't touch anything. Her body didn't seem suspended, but she could touch her fingertips together and wiggle her toes. Maybe it had to do with the EVA suit? She tried to remember—had she ever jumped while wearing one before?

But no, that couldn't be it. She wasn't breathing. Her thoughts felt like they were flowing at a normal rate, but her bodily functions seemed to have halted. Paused.

Or maybe she wasn't even in her SD. Maybe she was having an out-of-body experience—the traditional kind. Maybe these were the last throes of a dying brain attempting to make sense of the disparate signals coming from its decaying neural net.

She tried to see, to taste, to smell. She could do none of those things.

But she did sense something. A vibration. An oscillation.

It was inconsistent, but it made all of her shake. Make her thoughts *shake.*

She searched further with this sense she could not name and brushed up against echoes caused by the oscillation. Almost echoes of . . . herself.

Like she was a wave form. Or like she was some subatomic particle in a double slit experiment.

Mirror forms of her.

Echoes.

Split pieces.

She had a vague sense that they were all her and not her and that she'd been both spread thin and diced up.

The vibrations were inconsistent. They came in unpredictable shudders. And each shudder split her further, stretched her thinner.

Until she was nearly infinite.

She wasn't dying. She was a propagating wave.

This was her SD, but something was different. Wrong.

Like how space-time was wrong, had twisted. Had caused their crash.

Even here, the physics had been affected.

Was she trapped? Was she doomed to remain here, being pulled like taffy, ever thinner, until her wave form became nothing more than background radiation? A constant sizzle of static, devoid of shape or thought?

She wanted to breathe deeply, to gasp. To find her air again. But she couldn't.

Where there'd been no pain before, her lungs started to hurt.

She didn't want to stay here anymore. Didn't like being conscious here, in the unknown, with it breaking down around her.

She knew when she jumped next she'd likely die. And find everyone she'd known aboard the Progentor's ship long dead themselves.

And what if she wasn't dead? Would the other Earth conservationists still be looking for her? Or would she be stranded on an alien planet with no way to call for help?

Was all that really preferable to this surreal oscillation?

So what if it was? She knew what made her jump into an SD, but not back again. If anticipation pulled her in, what pulled her out?

She ran through the gambit of emotions, trying to force herself to feel the myriad of possibilities. But it was too difficult to fake happiness when despair crept so near. Too hard to create anger when curiosity kept pulling her mind toward the vibrations. True emotional depth was too difficult to counterfeit in this place.

Maybe it's not emotion, she thought. That was the type of energy that sucked her in. Perhaps it was a completely different kind of energy that pulled her out.

Jamal had spoken to her of thought energy. He believed accessing a thought-filled dimension was what he accomplished with his Communion machine.

Well, she was thinking plenty—a thing she definitely hadn't been able to do here before—and nothing.

She tried something entirely different, then, tried tugging on her echoes. Tried to pull the wave form back together, make it more particle-like again.

The SD *hiccuped.* And her blurred bits became not so blurred. She didn't feel stretched to infinity anymore. Just stretched to a trillion.

With no other course of action to take, she continued to struggle, to fight against whatever the oscillation was. And then, in the back of her mind, she started to chant:

There's no place like home. There's no place like home.

She envisioned her husband's face—Stone's bright smile, his laugh lines and crow's-feet. She imagined his fingertips on her hip, and his lips on hers. She imagined him rooting for her, encouraging her, telling her she could do it—even if she didn't know what this *it* was, exactly.

She thought of Justice, who'd tried so hard to help her. Who'd thrown herself fully into trying to rescue Vanhi from her jumping. Of Captain Tan and Ming-Na and their little twenty-year-old baby who'd been frozen in time just as surely as Vanhi had been forced out of it. She thought of Kexin, whose hand now forever sported a scar where she'd taken a bullet to save Mac's life. Of Maureen and Mohamed, who'd given up their chance to see Earth again in order to help recover the genetic information stored at the Monument of Seven.

And she thought of the attendants and Wes-Tu and Jamal. They'd had little stake in this mission to save *Homo sapiens*. They'd just wanted to help, to support the ancient humans they'd found lost and hungry and alone in the void.

And C. Little C, the Intelligent Personal Assistant who lived in her sundial, her touchstone. C, who she might actually get to speak to again when she jumped back. Maybe she wouldn't be alone when she died. Maybe C would be there to comfort her, in the end.

There's no place like home. There's no place like home. These pieces are mine. There's no place like home.

Another yank, and another billion, and she was starting to feel whole again. When she jumped back to die, she wanted to feel fully herself, not like she'd been scattered.

Suddenly, a shifting. Deep in her belly. Like the black hole sensation, only different.

Had she caused it? Or was it just her time to leave?

One more tug, for good luck.

She wasn't even sure she believed in luck.

There's. No. Place. Like. Home!

No crushing. No vibrating. No blood or smoke or the decay of years.

When she opened her eyes—could see, could feel, smell, taste, and hear again—she lay in a hospital bed.

For the briefest moment she wondered if she'd imagined the whole thing. Not just her conscious time in the SD, but all of it—that she'd gone to space, that there'd been a massive SD-related accident, that Convoy Twelve had been thrown one hundred thousand years into the future and she'd become a woman out of time.

But then Stone leaned over her. He smiled down at her and said, "Hey."

Pure relief washed over her, and she started to cry. It was awful, but she didn't want it to be a dream. If it was a dream, then Stone wasn't real. None of those people she'd thought about while trapped in that oscillating nightmare would have been real.

Her family.

Her home.

Stone frowned, misinterpreting her tears. "Hey. It's okay, we're all okay. You're okay. I.C.C. saved us." He smoothed her hair away from her eyes and reached toward a nearby table to retrieve her glasses.

"Shall I inform the others that Dr. Kapoor is awake?" asked a voice from nowhere and everywhere.

"Please do," Stone said.

"Dr. Kapoor," said the voice again. "I am the Inter Convoy Computer. And I am pleased to have you aboard."

"Where are we?" she asked Stone, accepting her glasses, struggling to sit up, to look out the nearby window.

"Noumenon. We made it. This is the Monument of Seven," he said, gesturing broadly.

Her gaze fell on figures moving outside, and for half a moment she wondered if she was still unconscious. A large creature, with a strange crest and odd limbs, yellow and green with copper plating on its belly, roamed within view.

"What the *hell* is that?" she demanded.

"Who the hell is that," Stone corrected with a chuckle. He kissed her on the forehead. "Welcome home. We have so much to tell you."

CHAPTER FOUR

HOPE TAN: METAMORPHOSIS

FIELD NOTES, OBSERVATIONS OF
UNIQUE ORGANISM: SELF

Typically, these notes pertain to life-forms uncovered on Noumenon. I discuss the morphology, locomotion, behavior, anatomy, etc. of such life-forms. I look at how and what they metabolize, where and when they breed, their life stages, how they die and decay.

Herein you will find notes on an organism I am perhaps the most qualified *and* the most unfit to observe, given my unalterable bias: myself.

Perhaps someone else would merely call this a journal. But I don't think I can separate my observations of myself from my naturalist training. It is my job to document all life-forms we encounter on this planet and how they interact. And I am one of them.

Concept: Individual Prehistory

I was born before I was born.

My first birth was after a terrible accident, one that stole me—mind, but not body—from my mother's womb. My parents didn't know it had happened. After my body was born, it took some people a while to realize I wasn't just unconscious.

200

My body wouldn't grow, though it breathed and ate. It did not experience the passage of time like other bodies.

It still doesn't.

I was born before I was born because I seem to recall . . .

Scratch that. Computer, delete previous sentence.

Clarification: Thought

People used to think that synaptic terminals at the end of axons on certain types of neurons in our brains traded chemical or electrical impulses—i.e., that neurons "fired"—and that the action potential and change in charge along the nerve fiber was, or generated, thought. But in reality, thought cannot be reduced or reproduced in neural circuits individually, and brains as a collective unit are structures that capture and interpret a specific kind of rare energy. Like a radio tuned just right to pick up a certain channel, so, too, brains are individually attuned. My brain and your brain cannot interpret the same thought energy. If two brains or brain-like structures are similar enough, they might resonate. They might transfer the same energy between them. This leads to phenomena that some interpret as hallucinations. Others see it as divine interference.

Science cannot tell you what to think of it, only what it is.

Personal Physical History: Mission to the Monument, Appearance of the Anomaly

I was born a second time after another accident.

My parents, hoping to rejoin my mind to my body—hoping so much that they finally discarded my milk-name, Shrimpling, and named me Hope itself—insisted on being part of an away team to the planet Noumenon. My body was nearly sixteen years in existence when we set off, over twenty when we finally arrived in the Philosopher's System.

Our ship was escorted by an Earth craft. Conservationists

watched the system, protecting it from tourists and poachers, allowing the infant system to thrive or die without interference. They had allowed us a brief visit. Three days to gather all we needed.

The Progentor—our host and guide—had made brief contact with the AI inhabiting the ancient ships on the surface when the phenomenon occurred.

We call it *the anomaly*, because it defies scientific description at this time. I am told its appearance corresponded with the activation of a megastructure called the Pyramid. I am told this was not supposed to happen.

What we know: gravity has been affected near the border of the phenomenon. Time has been affected near the border of the phenomenon. I am no physicist, but I am told nearby subdimensions, including those used for travel and communications, have been affected. Since falling to Noumenon's surface, we have been able to get neither ship nor transmission past the anomaly.

It persists. And it is visible.

I have been shown pictures of space as it should look. In the nighttime, after a system's sun has set, one should be able to see stars. The sky on Earth turned a kind of black-purple-blue. And interspersed throughout were dots of white and yellow and red and blue light. You could see celestial bodies outside your system. You could chart your own planet's movement through not just local space but *galactic* space by observing the rising and setting of objects light-years away over a long period of time.

Here, we see our star in the daytime. And its reflection off the inside of the anomaly at night. Once in a while we can see the transit of one of the Philosopher's System's other planets either across the sun itself or through the fuzzy, distant reflection. We can always see Noumenon's shadow in the reflection.

The anomaly sometimes appears an endless black. Sometimes a matte silver. Once in a while it looks like it's burning and rippling, with white-hot, shimmering-orange, and bright-blue fluctuating lines—like the edge of chemically treated paper combusting.

It is as though the entire solar system is enclosed in an impenetrable bubble. Though I.C.C. has had difficulty measuring the diameter of our bubble given that the anomaly's makeup both constantly shifts and appears to neglect the AI's understanding of physics, the Inter Convoy Computer has estimated its radius to be roughly eighty light-minutes. Again, I am told that is roughly the distance from Sol to Saturn.

I.C.C. has also indicated that though the anomaly crashed our ships and stranded us here, it has had no noticeable effects on the orbits of any of the system's bodies, and other than making the Noumonians uneasy, seems to have had no ill effects on their health.

Luckily, it did not impede my thought energy's retrieval from its SD. Likewise, it does not prevent Dr. Kapoor from jumping and returning.

Some SDs are affected. But not all.

As far as we can tell.

Notes: Accommodations

My physical development has facilitated the design of a unique mobility aide. Though our Earth elder Houdini has reassured me multiple times that the recycling of their dead colleague's artificial parts is both Earth standard practice and what they would have wanted, I cannot help but feel my suit is more than just a means to move about and interact with my cohort as an equal. Without the death of the other conservationists, I would have a different accommodation, but this design is by far superior to anything that could have been modified from maintained Monument materials. I think of them often and leave special offerings at their tablets in the shrine on the ridge.

I enjoy spending time with Houdini, Wes-Tu, and the other attendants. They, like me, do not physically conform to the typical *Homo sapiens* adult structure.

Observations: Feelings

I have been trying to pinpoint why I feel the urge to document my observances of myself now. Perhaps it is because I feel for the first time that I am emotionally and intellectually coming into my adulthood. That others around me are treating me differently, handing me more authority. Perhaps this shouldn't feel significant, but it does. Throughout my years of consciousness to now, many of the elders have caught themselves infantilizing me. I have found this endlessly frustrating. But in the past few years, while I've amassed my observations, the instances have been reducing steadily. The others are learning, and this heartens me.

And I am intellectually growing, which heartens me as well.

· ·

101,180 CE

YEAR THIRTY-TWO OF THE ANOMALY

Hope Tan had been born seventeen and a half inches long, weighing seven pounds three ounces, with a full head of wispy black hair.

Tomorrow would be her body's fifty-second birthday. She was eighteen inches and a breath, weighed eight pounds seven ounces, and had a full head of wispy black hair.

She waved a small hand in front of her face, indicating the holo-keys hanging above her body should dissipate, that their glow should fade and leave her in peace in the darkness. She lay on her back in her tiny bed, hemmed in securely on all sides by a safety railing. The keys themselves were not diffi-cult to reach for—they'd been scaled down just for her.

Her body was fifty-two, but her consciousness had only started developing a little over twenty years ago, thanks to the brilliant efforts of Dr. Justice Jax, the sacrifices of Dr. Vanhi Kapoor, and the donated materials from the Progentor. To-gether, by studying the SD phenomenon surrounding Vanhi and analyzing the ritual the Progentor called "Communion," they'd been able to determine that Hope's thought energy was trapped in an SD. They didn't know what they'd find or what they'd bring back when they retrieved her energy, but luckily, when they delivered it from the SD and into her gray matter via a specially designed packet, her brain harnessed it like any newborn.

She'd opened her eyes and smiled at her elderly parents for the first time. And while her body continued to grow slowly, her mind developed at-pace with a typical infant.

So technically she was fifty-two. But she felt more like twenty-two. And she looked fresh as a newborn—with infant motor control to boot. But luckily, with the help of Houdini, she stood as tall as her fellow twentysomethings who'd only ever known Noumenon as home.

The suit they'd made for her stood now at the foot of her bed, a bulky shadow among other bulky shadows in the dark.

She tossed her head, trying to find a position where she could sleep with the consistency of an adult—through the night, or most of it. But she couldn't tear her mind away from her new notes. Because of C and I.C.C., she felt no need to record the days' events. But her thoughts, feelings, memories of before and beyond—those she needed to get out.

She spent most of her days recording her observations of other life-forms. It was high time she recorded the observa-tions she made about herself.

Though anticipation for tomorrow tingled at the edges

of her consciousness, she wasn't fully looking forward to her birthday. She both hated and enjoyed being the center of attention. It was nice to have people care, but embarrassing to have them dither constantly. She preferred days where she could quietly slip off to the lab or the field and study her specimens.

Perhaps it was her own strange start to life that cultivated her fascination with biology. Or perhaps it was the love and guidance of Dr. Jax, whom she still missed every day.

Either way, her happy place was among her terrariums or seated next to the Monument's ancestral shrine, where she could observe tail-fliers and cloud-jellies in their natural habitat.

That's a funny term, natural habitat, her groggy mind provided as her delicate eyelids drooped. There was nothing natural about Noumenon—it had all been engineered . . .

She awoke the next morning to giggling. Light sounds, emanating from her front door, a mere meter from her crib. She cracked one eye, tried to see who it was between the slats, but she knew before their footsteps approached and their faces peered down at her.

Her cohort—six other young humans. Akane, Kexin, Maureen, Mohamed, Reggie, and Toya, who'd all been grown as either part of the control or test group for Dr. Jax's fertility studies.

Hope pretended to sleep. Pretended she didn't see Maureen silently counting down, *three, two, one* before they all shouted, "Get up, get up, get up!" in various old Earth languages.

She fake-startled, rubbed her eyes with her baby fists, groaned, and said, "I would love to. Help me up?" Her lack of teeth meant she had to modulate her speech for typically dentalized sounds. As a result, her accent was different from the rest of her cohort, but it usually went uncommented upon.

Akane lifted her to her suit.

The machine stood, heavy and stoic, at the foot of her crib. Forged from the malleable cybernetic alterations of the *Homo kubernētēs* who'd perished in the fall, Hope's suit was humanoid most of the time, with a cockpit between the shoulders that housed the command panels, which were perfectly suited to her infant motor control.

She called it her Battle Mech—she'd liked old Earth media featuring giant pilotable robots ever since she was mentally seven, when I.C.C. had first called up a cartoon for her.

Akane tucked her into the padded seat, fastening the harness for her as Hope wriggled her legs down to the pedals and kicked to power up her mech.

Every evening she climbed down out of it, but her muscles weren't developed enough to let her climb back up in the morning. Houdini had helped Akane modify some of the cleaning bots to aid her—just like Houdini had designed her suit in the first place, pulling apart the old bits of their comrades, appropriating their modifications just like everything else had been appropriated at that point—both crashed ships, the supplies, the organic bits of the dead.

Nothing was new under heaven and on earth. Nothing *could* be new. Before they'd passed, the parents who'd suffered the Convoy Twelve accident talked about rationing and reusing, but it was always so: entropy broke things down so that new things could be built up again. Sometimes its effects were simply felt more pointedly than at others.

"Ready?" Akane asked in Japanese. Japanese was the most commonly used language among their cohort, as it was the language the Noumonians understood. But language preservation was an important part of their lives, and collectively they spoke approximately twenty-three and counting.

Hope grasped the impulse-conduit on the left side of the control board, mentally directing the suit's left hand to flex—

grasping and ungrasping. "Ready for what?" She drew the mech up to its usual six-foot height.

"Your birthday surprise!" Mohamed said.

She rubbed at her eyes again, still tired, her young body urging her to direct the mech to rock her back to sleep. "I guess," she said less than enthusiastically, knowing her high-pitched voice made it sound extra petulant.

But her friends were in high spirits and took no notice.

Like any other adult, Hope had her own private quarters on *Mira*. While most of the ship had been converted into an ideal Noumonian habitat, some of the decks still maintained their original human focus. Outside in the hall, the group of humans was met by a passing group of scouts on the far wall, who waggled their heads up and down in greeting.

Kexin and Reggie took her by the artificial hands and led her to the elevator, to the bottom level, and out the sprawling bay doors. "Where are we going?" she asked, giggling as they refused to say.

The sun was warm outside the ship, and Noumenon's constant winds were oddly gentle, which made the air feel muggier than usual. The breeze on her face was one of Hope's favorite small joys, as was the hot-rust smell of the planet's surface.

Her friends pulled her along toward Houdini's workshop; the shell of the cube ship, now mostly hollowed out. It sat just aft of *Mira*, and the larger ship's shadow fell over it for most of the day. Mohamed knocked on the hatch, and the door irised away.

The decking near the entrance of the six-story craft was low-set at four feet. The others ducked while Hope commanded her mech to transform, its bottom half shifting seamlessly into one sleek snake's tail, which gently curved as it propelled her forward. A little way in, through a second hatch, the ceiling and the next deck up had been removed to make it more convenient for the *Homo sapiens*, and to allow Houdini more room to work.

The post-human greeted them there, their faceplate blank and boxy where one might expect a nose and mouth, but their eyes shone bright and their cheeks still lifted in a smile. Their chest was bare, save for an iridescent overlay, which sometimes caught the light like netting, and sometimes looked more akin to scales. Their bottom half had taken the form of something likened to a kangaroo's, with powerful, sturdy hind legs.

Wes-Tu was there as well, covered head to toe in his Revealer's shroud, his asymmetrical silhouette unmistakable. He lifted a covered limb in greeting and said in English, "Happy birthday! I am here to help facilitate translation."

Vanhi liked to call communication in their little hodge-podge "one giant game of telephone" (though Hope and her cohort only had a vague sense of what a telephone was). Not only was there a primary language disparity, some of the life-forms calling I.C.C.'s halls home were physically incapable of using others' communication methods.

Houdini spoke mind-to-mind through implants. Only Wes-Tu and the Revealer aides also possessed these implants. Wes-Tu spoke twenty-first-century Hindi, Arabic, and English. Though the aides could not speak these languages, they were trained to understand them, as they were the sacred languages Jamal spoke. Likewise, the other humans who'd crashed spoke a variety of old Earth languages, but had primarily communicated in English. I.C.C. spoke all twenty-first-century languages, though it could not detect mind-to-mind signals. And it had taught Japanese to the Noumonians. The Noumonians communicated in radio signals, which I.C.C. had learned to interpret.

With I.C.C.'s guidance, the humans had been able to create a handful of translation devices for the Noumonian radio signals. But the materials required to make them were in short supply, and so they resided in the safest places: one with Vanhi, one with Jamal, one with Icelandic, and two in a vault in case something catastrophic happened to the others.

Here on Noumenon, with their little colony of different sentients, basic communication was an everyday struggle. But it was one in which they all invested.

They all gathered around Houdini's primary workbench, where Hope expected to see a box, but the surface was clean. All of the post-human's work in progress had been moved to the sides, stacked in precarious piles of wire and devices.

Houdini held their hands out in front of Hope over the workbench, a secret cupped between them.

"They ask that you close your eyes and hold out your hand—your real hand," Wes-Tu offered.

Feeling silly, Hope did as Houdini asked, reaching one pudgy arm over the lip of the cockpit, palm up.

Houdini placed a tiny object—tiny even for Hope's hands—on her life line.

When they bid her open her eyes, she found an octagonal fleck, the color of iron pyrite, resting delicately against her skin. "Is this what I think it is?" she gasped.

Houdini nodded emphatically.

Where before she'd felt slightly embarrassed that it was her birthday, now excitement surged. Her little body vibrated with it, but she held as still as she could, afraid that if she did so much as breathe too strongly the octagon would fly off her hand and get lost in the cracks of the floor. "Thank you," she squealed. "Thank you, thank you, thank you!" She felt like a little girl, ready to jump and flail; she could barely contain herself.

"They all helped," Wes-Tu said, gesturing around the workbench.

"Do you want me to install it for you?" Akane asked.

Buzzing, Hope gently passed what she now knew to be an aesthetic mod to Akane, so that she could place it gently into the quantum adaptor in the mech's chest.

"Get ready to be the best-dressed being in the whole Philosopher's System," Akane said after the install, sliding the small panel back over the interface. "Go ahead, try it out. Basic color shift is available, and there are art files you can choose from. Oh, and fancy-dress mode, so *hello ball gown* if you feel like it."

"Does this mean you got the camouflage programming back on line too?" Hope asked Houdini.

They nodded.

Hope instantly triggered the camo mod. All conservationist-class *Homo kubernētēs* could make their molecular-shifting cybernetic components blend seamlessly with the surrounding environment.

The mech's chassis visually vanished into the surroundings. If she directed the cockpit to transform, she could be fully invisible, concealed within her suit.

"Sure, sure," Akane said. "Go for the superpower first."

"Pst, check the art files," Maureen suggested.

Thousands of designs popped up in thumbnail form on the guidance pad in the front of her cockpit. Pieces from different millennia, different galleries, different data banks..

For a few moments, Frida Kahlo's *Wounded Deer* leapt across the mech's torso. Guan Daosheng's *Bamboo and Stone* covered her right side from shoulder to ankle like a banner.

She transformed the chassis into the likeness of a flowing gown and let Negar Ahkami's *The Source* stretch and wind over it, creating a beautiful cascade of gold and blue. After another moment, she found the intricately designed tapestries of Makawee Wagner—a Convoy Seven original—and shifted so that it appeared she was draped with the literal weavings.

But then she found a file containing original pieces by

their own Mohamed Johar. He blushed when she transformed back into her standard mech and let one piece—a stylized *Tree of Life*, with the bodies of the Philosopher's System as the branches, I.C.C.'s ships as the trunk, three types of humans, and the three types of Noumonians as the roots—lay itself gently down the mech's spine, the planets fanning out between the shoulders and the people over its hips.

"It's perfect. I love it. Thank you, everyone."

A crackling of static came from a repurposed *Holwarda* speaker mounted in the workshop's ceiling. I.C.C.'s voice screeched through—distorted, but audible. "I have detected an unusual object well within the periphery of the Philosopher's System. I am unsure of its origin, though it may have dropped out of SD travel. Its current trajectory—" The AI cut itself short. "It is headed our way. I request the presence of all sentients. Please make your way to *Mira*'s main hangar, so that the data may be interpreted collectively."

A stunned silence followed, punctured through seconds later with excited shouts.

Hope hadn't thought anything could top the gift of the aesthetics modifier—but now! This! It was her birthday and someone had finally broken through the anomaly.

Kexin jumped for joy beside her, and Mohamed bowed his head with his hands to his lips. "What do you think?" Reggie asked, turning to Houdini and Wes-Tu—they were elders after all. "Earth? Revealers? Convoy Seven or Twelve?"

"Can they get rid of the anomaly, you think? Fix it?" Maureen asked eagerly.

Hope's heart beat rapidly, and she looked up. The workshop's ceiling might have kept her eyes from the sky, but not from her mind.

"I see you're ready for whatever comes," said Akane, nudging the shoulder of her mech.

"What?" Hope asked. "Oh—"

Unconsciously, she'd directed the mech to paint the Milky Way as seen from Earth across her torso. She'd cloaked herself with stars.

Things were about to change. After this, their world would be different. The anomaly was a constant, and they'd all always regarded it with disdain, as a trap. And Hope did want to see the stars.

She just hoped this wouldn't mean they'd have to leave. That Noumenon could no longer be their home.

She didn't want to leave the Noumonians, abandon her walks with Icelandic. She didn't want to lose touch with Instruction Manual, or Loving, or Ájá. She didn't want to leave her specimens or abandon the ancestor shrine.

But maybe she was thinking too hard about it. The Monument dwellers having access to the regions beyond once more could only be a good thing. This metamorphosis of their home could only be for the better.

"Let us go to *Mira*," Wes-Tu said with a shooing motion. "Quickly now."

As they exited, Houdini transformed their lower half into the likeness of a centipede, and Hope gave the mech a snake's tail once more—this time patterned over with indigo scales.

Outside, in the distance, a small grit cloud followed the streaking trail of a convoy shuttle—which had been retrofitted with wheels to become a surface rover—headed to *Mira* from *Slicer*. The Progentor's bug ship still lay tucked inside, and he and his aides still called it home.

Inside the shuttle bay, all fifty-two Noumonians hung from the walls, getting as close to I.C.C.'s large, suspended monitors as possible. The screens displayed satellite images of a fuzzy, oblong shape.

Vanhi offered Hope a hug and a swift apology for missing the gift-giving. "But we have a bit of a situation," she said. Her expression was grim.

"It's fine," Hope said. "Who is it? Do we know yet?"

Vanhi pursed her lips.

Hope's excitement remained steady, but it took on a different sheen. "Is . . . is everything all right?"

"We're not sure yet," Vanhi answered.

Tense minutes passed as they waited for the Progentor to arrive. With a crackling of recycled rubber, his shuttle peeled its way up the slight incline of the ramp and into its designated parking spot, trailing extra grit.

Jamal's three surviving aides exited first, their shrouds firmly in place as always. They each stood six feet when drawn to full height and were largely cybernetic, though they couldn't shapeshift like Houdini and Hope. Only their heads were organic, and their bodies were slight—their metal skeletons tall, built for mobility and tooling with many legs dangling like the tentacles of a cubist squid.

They had no names, no personal identities. They'd given all that up in pursuit of purity of revelation. Collectively one with the universe, hands of the Progentor, containing the personhood of all persons.

Hope had never fully grasped what it must be like—to want to be no one so you could embody everyone. To let go of the singular—of *me* and *I*.

Even the *Lùhng* were interconnected. It wasn't so much that she couldn't understand the blurring between the self and the other—she remembered a time when she had no self, after all. She was everywhere and nowhere. With a beyond but no interior. What she couldn't comprehend was choosing that. Wanting it.

Perhaps her time in the SD, experiencing life as a mass of pure thought energy, had tainted her view.

Jamal followed, uncovered to the waist, his legs and feet bare beneath the folds of his chiton. His dark skin was wrinkled, his slight frame bent from age. His head was shaven, and the crow's-feet around his eyes were deep. Thin, wispy strands of white hair sprouted from his ears.

Vanhi's sundial, containing the IPA personality C, hung from a chain at his waist.

One never knew what to expect from Jamal—he could be completely shrouded like Wes-Tu and the aides, or completely nude. It all depended on the Revealer calendar, the reverberation of the bells in the belly of his ship, and his dreams.

Today, it seemed, was a good day to uncover one's self before the eyes of the universe.

Jamal gave Hope no special acknowledgment when he saw her. She tried not to be disappointed—after all, Jamal had so many holy days to keep track of, it seemed unfair to consider a forgotten birthday a slight.

Especially when she disliked the attention anyway.

"The object is approximately one kilometer across and nearly three kilometers long. I will have more precise measurements as it continues to approach," I.C.C. said.

"That's a *mountain*," Vanhi pointed out.

"Given its speed, tumble, and lack of course correction, if it had not appeared so suddenly, I would assume it an interplanetary body. An asteroid."

"So there's nobody on board?" Kexin asked, her face falling.

"It does not appear guided, no. It is possible the anomaly is still affecting it. If it is a crewed craft, they may be experiencing a malfunction."

"But they're headed directly for us, you say?" Jamal asked, expression firm but unreadable. He appeared to be calculating, considering.

"Yes. At the object's current speed and trajectory, it will impact Noumenon seven kilometers, plus or minus one-point-six-two kilometers, north-northeast of *Mira*. We are six days, two hours, and eighteen minutes from impact."

"If it is a ship," Jamal said, "this will be a terrible tragedy. If it is not a ship—if it is a denser body, then we are in grave danger. Your hulls alone will not protect us from the impact."

"There's no way to safely intercept it?" Hope asked. "Save the people on board, if there are any?"

"It is unlikely we can be sure any of our ships are space-worthy in the allotted time," I.C.C. said. "They are too old and would need a thorough inspection, maintenance, crew—"

"What about the shuttles?"

"They do not have SD capabilities, which would be required to reach the object, match speed, and assess the situation in time."

Icelandic crawled down from the wall to mingle in among the humans. She wore a bright-red necklace with what looked like a black jewel slung about her neck—the translator.

"Not ship," she said. "Not asteroid. *Sora-Gohan!*"

Sora-Gohan. A meal from the sky. Food from the emptiness.

The mysterious sustenance that came from beyond and triggered the Noumonian migrations.

All the Noumonians aboard began to twirl—spinning on the walls and the floor, shaking their heads in agreement.

Now it was their turn to get excited.

And Hope was sure she would burst.

A ship would have heralded one kind of change—but this was a metamorphosis of a completely different kind.

She sucked in a breath and couldn't keep her toes from wriggling against the pedals, which made her suit wiggle. The Call—a Noumonian life event, a growth stage, that no one had ever observed before. I.C.C. had seen the migrations but had no idea what happened when the Noumonians reached the Sora-Gohan, or what happened in the years after.

The Noumonians themselves rarely spoke of it, and Hope had surmised that this was because they, too, remembered little of the event afterward.

"Does it resemble Sora-Gohan?" I.C.C. asked.

Icelandic bobbed her head up and down. "Yes, yes! Im sure. Im sure this Sora-Gohan."

"In that case, it may have originated from within the system," I.C.C. said. "I do not presently know from where the Sora-Gohan launches. But given the trajectory, it is entirely possible it came from one of the system's own planets."

"We should prepare for all possible scenarios," Wes-Tu said on Houdini's behalf. "We still don't know for sure that it's the sky-food."

"Will send an envoy to Waterfall colony. Alert," Icelandic agreed.

"I.C.C., let's draw up evacuation plans," Vanhi suggested. "We can move the ships a safe distance away from your projected landing zone. That way we're covered, no matter what it turns out to be."

After I.C.C.'s announcement, various subgroups broke off to go about their day. Icelandic left the bay chanting "Sora-Gohan, Sora-Gohan!" and Hope couldn't help but bob in time with her chant. All around, the other Noumonians did the same, and Hope guessed they were all sharing in the mantra, a swell of exuberance making them vibrate with joy.

She almost followed Icelandic out. She had one secret, selfish wish now. And it was her birthday, so perhaps she was allowed wishes—that used to be an Earth tradition in some cultures. She wished to observe the results of the Call. To document what happened during this grand time of transition.

But she couldn't bring herself to ask. Though it was a joyous time, the Noumonians were very private about this special food from the void. It was not her place to insert herself into this ritual, no matter the curiosity it sparked.

Instead, she decided to make for the lab. If they were going to move the ships, it might put her specimens at risk. Her little protozoa tanks would need to be secured.

"Hope, may I speak with you?"

She turned to find Jamal standing close.

"Of course. But I'm heading over to Dr. Jax's lab." Though her mentor had passed years ago, the lab still didn't feel like hers. The walls, the equipment, the very air was still permeated through and through with Justice's presence.

He gestured with a frail hand toward his rover. "In that case, may I offer you a ride?"

- -

NOTES ON FUNCTIONAL IMMORTALITY

The words *four* and *death* sound similar in Cantonese, my parents' language. Because of this, Chinese numerology holds four to be an unlucky number. So much so that some Earth buildings omitted any floors with the number four in them—even the thirteenth floor, because one and three make four.

I have a complicated relationship with the number four. For me, four is the opposite of death—it is the neglect of death. We "immortals" are four-count. One and three. An artificial intelligence and three *Homo sapiens*.

The one: I.C.C. A human-made construct. An AI whose physical presence is manifested in the seven functional and two unfunctional Convoy Seven Monument ships. It thought it would die one day, as all living things are supposed to do. But it has no projected life-span, nothing against which to judge the breadth of its life. The Convoy Seven crew abandoned it to save it. And still, it goes on.

The three: Dr. Vanhi Kapoor, Progentor Jamal Kaeden,

and myself. Hope Tan. We each persist in different ways, and I am not sure whose existence is stranger.

Vanhi jumps in and out of an SD harboring emotional energy, and while an ever-increasing amount of time passes here when she is gone, an indeterminate amount of time passes for her when she is there. Functionally, she does not age while in her "anticipation-filled" SD. Just like a brain's structure harnesses thought energy, so, too, do parts of our endocrine systems harness emotive energies, and Vanhi goes someplace where the energy associated with anticipation is plentiful.

Since falling to Noumenon, and with the help of the medication developed by Justice, she has learned to mostly control this jumping, where once she sought to end it. When I was around twelve years old mentally, she demanded all research for a cure halt, and she proceeded to self-induce a jump. I believe this change of heart coincided with the natural death of her husband, though she has not said and I have not asked.

Progentor Jamal was engineered to be an immortal, through messy means. Many centuries ago, a group of Revealers called the Kaedenites made their way to Noumenon and stole the original Jamal's genetic schematics from I.C.C.'s data banks, erasing as much evidence of their illegal landing from the AI's memory as they could. Jamal Kaeden had become a title in the Revealer religion, after the originator of their theology—not a prophet, but an average man trying to make his way in the world—who stumbled into the most remarkable situation.

But titles weren't good enough. Not for the group who threw off centuries of noninterference agreements and landed on Noumenon. Why should they settle for a symbolic Progentor when they could resurrect the real thing? They needed their Jamal Kaeden to guide them, and they wanted him everlasting.

Wes-Tu—the Progentor's sub-Kaed, *Homo draconem* attendant, and oldest friend—says Jamal's birth was a miraculous Reveal. He claims it only took one try to successfully merge their originator's DNA with that of the *Turritopsis dohrnii*.

But genetic modifications using the *Turritopsis dohrnii*—the immortal jellyfish—have long been interstellarly outlawed. Jamal told me, in private, that he is the only successfully modified clone in history with the jelly's gene sequence, and that all other experimentations with *Turritopsis dohrnii* have led to horrible, excruciating deaths for the subjects.

I'm sure the story of the Progentor's cloning has itself been modified—transformed into a happy tale, a triumphant tale. A tale Jamal clearly does not believe.

But the modification has done its job: when elderly Jamal hits an internal threshold, he begins to de-age. The jellyfish can essentially age backward and return to its polyp stage, and similarly, Jamal returns to his prepubescence before growing up again. Backward and forward he lives, over and over again.

And then there's me. The fourth immortal. Younger than Jamal by many thousands of years, and yet technically conceived thousands of years before him. My body does age, but barely. I am locked in a slow progression, not completely frozen in time, but out of sync with the rate of change in this dimension. Will I someday grow old? Maybe.

Something similar to what happened to my body, Dr. Jax was sure, happened to the rest of Convoy Twelve's sex cells and was thus the cause of their infertility. Even if the fertilization of an egg had not caused it and the sperm to annihilate—if she'd gotten a zygote to divide and grow—she was sure the zygote would take upwards of a hundred years to become an embryo, and then another hundred to become a fetus, and on and on. No genetic materials from Convoy Twelve could realistically be used to perpetuate *Homo sapiens*.

She'd hoped to one day send an SD information packet back to the *Lùhng* convoy containing all the genetic schematics housed in I.C.C.'s data banks. Perhaps they would find a way to utilize them. But, alas, the anomaly that caused our fall and prevents us from leaving even hampers our communications. We have no idea what's gone on beyond the Philosopher's System.

I have yet to ask Jamal, but I do wonder: How must the Revealers be reacting to the loss of their perpetual Progentor?

I know what it felt like when my guiding lights left: my mother, my father, Dr. Jax. But at least I know they passed away. I know they lived long lives. I know what happened to their bodies, and where to find their ancestor tablets to bring them offerings and tell them about my life.

But the Revealers don't know what happened to Jamal. They can't know; such is the obstruction of the anomaly. Their guiding light was taken abruptly, and they can only imagine his fate.

Dr. Jax's lab spilled out of the cloning facilities aboard *Hippocrates*. Here, Hope's best friends had been born. Here, Dr. Jax had awoken her. Here, Hope had looked through an electron microscope for the first time and seen cells, seen biology—*life*—at work.

She'd been mentally four when they'd gotten two of the cloning tanks up and running. She recalled Dr. Jax scooping her up and setting her on her lap to watch her work the controls as she directed different nutrient supplies into the purple jell-baths that sustained the tiny embryos.

Her friends had all been grown here, cloned using genetic schematics found at the Monument of Seven—Convoy Seven's original ships, what they now mostly referred to as the *Mira* colony. Three genetic samples had been randomly chosen as a control group—Akane's, Reggie's, and Toya's. The other three—Mohamed, Maureen, and Kexin—had been grown specifically so that their development and health could be compared to samples from the Convoy Twelve adults bearing their same names and clone histories.

The two tanks that had birthed them were empty now— the jell scooped out and recycled. The remaining tanks— dozens of them—had been impossible to clean. Their old nutrient materials had been left to rot and seize, to turn eggplant and black, forming crystallized pillars over the passing eons. Some of the tanks had shattered, leaving nothing but the fossil-like remnants as decorative columns.

In one column, Dr. Jax had carved out the names of every human born on Noumenon thus far. Justice had added Hope's name when she'd discovered the little girl desperately trying to grasp a penknife to scratch the Han characters covertly into the pillar's backside. She felt a child of Noumenon just as much as the others.

Seven names and no more. Because they weren't supposed to stay here. This was an away mission. Noumenon was never supposed to be home.

It was just one more "never supposed to" in a long line of "never supposed to's" for Convoy Twelve.

Dr. Jax had never kept the place spotless—and indeed, her husband, Mac, had often come in just to tidy up for her— but Hope was sure even Justice would cringe at its current disarray.

Terrariums of various shapes and sizes were stacked on every raised surface. Each had an environment carefully crafted to support an individual life-form—and, in some cases, a reproductive population. Hope carefully monitored the habits and life cycles of seventeen separate native species. From microbial scum nets to tail-fliers to burrowing corkscrew colonies, she continued to document every observable detail.

"Your collection has grown quite impressive," Jamal said,

bending down to stare into the photoreceptor cells of the eating-eye: a creature that subsided on light, like algae, but processed it through a means very unlike photosynthesis. The animal's body had a structure that closely resembled a mantis shrimp's eye and stalk.

"It's not . . . I mean, I don't like the word 'collection.' Makes it sound, I don't know, like they're pretty rocks. You don't collect living things."

He turned to face her, always frank in his replies. "Just because you don't like the terminology, that doesn't mean that's not what this is."

She frowned at him, wishing her baby-scowl would look more withering.

Jamal was very elderly now. He hadn't had too much trouble making his way the short trek up the mountain's incline once they'd parked the rover, but his aides had still helped him, squatting down on their mechanical legs to let him lay a hand on their metal chassis or the top of their heads.

The Progentor would "turn a corner" soon. No one but Wes-Tu had ever witnessed the event, and Hope wasn't sure how to prepare for it. What would physically aging backward even be like?

She scoffed internally at herself. What would physically aging *forward* even be like?

"I'm sorry," he said good-naturedly. "I did come to lecture you, but not about your specimens."

She picked up the eating-eye's tank from under the old man's nose, moving it to a hovering dolly, making sure her mech suit was extra-stompy on the way. "A lecture on my birthday. *Yaaaaay*," she said, mostly teasing.

"Yes. Happy birthday," he said, oblivious to the nuances of her petulance. "I know I'm not good at birthdays. Which is, perhaps, strange. Birthdays are very important to Revealers. It is the day the universe reveals us to itself. A time when we go from nothing to something based on naught but the physics we were born into and the whims of those who came before.

"Perhaps it is because my birthday has never really belonged to me. It is one of the Seven Sacred Reveals, and on each of those holy days, I commemorate the event just the same. Fasting and communing with the universe—letting its energies flow through me, sustain me, and inform me."

Jamal's Communion was not supposed to be simply spiritual on those days. Before Hope's awakening, he'd used a machine of his own devising to leave his body and come back to it. He'd given it to Dr. Jax and allowed her to modify it in order to retrieve Hope's thought energy—and had been unable to use it for its original purpose ever since.

"I'm sorry you can't . . . can't observe properly anymore," she said, securing the terrarium before striding back to Jamal's side.

Since beginning to jot down field notes about herself, she'd come to consider different aspects of her life more thoroughly. She'd always harbored some guilt about Jamal sacrificing his Communion machine, but she realized now it was not just a sacrifice Jamal personally had made. Those Communions had meant something to *billions* of people.

"I'm sorry for your followers, the other Revealers—"

He waved her apology aside, then patted the mech's hand. "The machine served its true purpose: revealing you to us. I would not trade a million Communions for that. And I am the Progentor, so my word on the matter may carry some weight."

He smiled a toothy grin at her, and she smiled a toothless one back.

"I did not come here to make you feel guilty, either," he said. "I seem to be failing at birthdays more than usual. If you prefer to keep working while I speak, that's fine."

She nodded her thanks and walked the mech over to where

the tail-flier terrarium hung from the ceiling. She stretched her legs up and up, letting the quantum interface pull the metal form thin.

"I wanted to tell you what it's like to be . . . well, us. Long-living. Immortal. I'd like to give you three points of direction."

"I didn't think our . . . condition . . . came with a manual."

He laughed. "It does not. But—and I know you dislike it when we bring it up—you are still young. Even Vanhi, she is still young. One day you will surpass her in actual experienced years, and you will both have to come to terms with that. But for now you are the youngest and can benefit the most from where I have been.

"Old stories would have you believe that immortality is lonely. And it is, in a way. On days when you're reminded that you persist and others don't. But most days it's just living. A day is a day is a day. But, the strange thing about time is, the more of it you've had in the past, the less of it you feel like you have in the present. That is true for both the mortal and the immortal, I've found. The very experiencing of time is a relative event. The more years I have behind me, the quicker the new ones feel, until I turn my corner, and then it all feels fresh again. For you, that feeling—the shrinking of time, the constant quickening of pace—might stretch on and on. Each day will still be a day. But the breadth of them will seem different. *Where does the time go?* you'll think. And, for one such as you, *what is time after all?* might be the ultimate question."

The wind-chime-shelly made a hollow sort of ghost sound as Hope picked up its tank and the long carapaced arms clanked together. "Time will compress: got it."

He pursed his lips, as though he weren't sure that she had, in fact, "got it." But he pressed on. "Change is the thing you will have to make peace with. Because others' lives are shorter than yours, the changes they go through and the changes they enact will seem rushed. But they have far less time to make the world they want to live in than you do, and from their perspective change takes forever. You must be prepared to let each generation shift direction. Radical ideas for the previous generation will seem barbarically stagnant to the next. Trying to keep them locked into one set of ideals—because you are old, and wise, and "know better"—will only create resentment and mark you as a remnant of a previous time.

"Do not simply get used to change. Encourage it. Become it. Embody it."

"Change is good," she echoed, moving on to the seawater tanks that housed living bubbles. "And the third point?"

He sat quietly for a moment. She secured the tank on top of the others before turning back to him. "Jamal?"

"People will pass," he said quietly. "And try as you might not to, you will forget them. That must seem impossible to you now. You've known so few people your entire life, how could you ever forget? But the human mind is not made to hold on to memories forever. It replaces past things in favor of the present. *Now* is relevant to the mind, and *then* is peripheral. You have something I didn't when I first began—I.C.C. Someone who can record things for you, remember for you. Do not be ashamed when you forget, and do not be afraid to ask I.C.C. to help you revisit those you've forgotten."

Jamal's gaze had turned inward, his expression sorrowful. He was clearly looking, now, for a lost face, someone who'd been important, but who'd slipped through the cracks of his long life.

The sundial chirped on its chain, "You have me now, Progentor."

Jamal rubbed at the sundial's gnomon with his thumb. "That I do, C."

Cautiously, mindful of his feelings, Hope set herself beside him, placing her small, real hand on top of his bald head. This guidance was a good birthday present. It was all he could think to bequeath, all he really had to give. "People will pass, I will forget," she said, "and that's okay."

She thought about Mohamed's artwork—the tree of life spanning across her back—and realized Jamal was right.

Forgetting *did* seem impossible.

NOTES ON MEMORY

I remember before I should remember. The energy that my brain would have trapped and harnessed had already co-alesced before it was thrown into another dimension. And though I had no eyes, hands, tongue, ears, or nose with which to perceive my surroundings, and no gray matter through which the thought energy could interpret such sense signals, I retain a memory of *being*.

And I wasn't alone.

I've never told anyone that before. Because I think it will scare them. I was pure thought in another place, and I was not the only pure thought there.

If I can remember that, when there were no neurons to form connections, no brain structure to trap what my energy encountered, then why should I forget today? Why should I forget the start of my life? Jamal says I will forget, but I think he's projecting. Our immortality is not the same. He loses things when he turns his corner; his brain rewrites itself because it has to. It pretends it has not already lived lifetimes.

But my brain is different. My brain is unprecedented. No one understands why my brain is physically maturing at the same rate as my body, but my *thoughts*, my *emotions*, all mature as they should. My body is not all that there is to being me. My immortality is its own circumstance, will have its own trials, and its own cages to trap me in, different from Jamal. Different from Vanhi. Different from I.C.C.

We are four, but we are each one and cannot presume our experiences to parallel.

The object's rapid approach meant the satellites they'd launched years ago were able to better resolve the object with each passing hour. After two days, I.C.C. was as sure as the Noumonians.

"The surface is too uniform to be an asteroid," I.C.C. confirmed at yet another all-hands meeting.

The images were still somewhat fuzzy, but the sunlight bounced off its surface in smooth planes. The larger contours of the form were easily discernible, and it had a fundamental egg shape.

"The evidence continues to favor the theory that it is Sora-Gohan," the AI said. "In which case I defer to Icelandic's leadership. How should we proceed?"

"Have spoken with im at Waterfall," Icelandic reported. "All are celebrating, all delighting. And have come to unprecedented decision: would like to invite human party to observe the Call and consumption. Would like Hope Tan to oversee."

Hope was taken aback as all eyes fell on her. Her birthday wish had come true! And yet she was at a loss for words.

"I—uh—"

"You observe other life. You make records of their experiences. Naturalist, you. Would you and companions observe?"

"I-I would be honored," she said. It felt like a question she'd been waiting her whole life to be asked. It was a privilege, and a sign of mutual respect. This was a portion of the Noumonian life cycle that had been held close for millennia. "Yes, *yes*, of course."

"Good," Icelandic said. "Then celebration at *Mira* colony should begin as well! Stories! Swaying! Climbing! Dancing!"

"If I might make a recommendation?" I.C.C. interjected.

Icelandic seemed irritated to have her orders for revelry interrupted. "I.C.C. make statement," she agreed.

"While the revelry commences among the Noumonians, I suggest the other Monument residents continue with their final precautionary preparations. Though I can say with ninety-seven-point-eight-six percent certainty that the approaching object is Sora-Gohan, and therefore should not impact like a free-falling object, it is still possible for it to negatively affect our surroundings. The ancestor shrine should be either moved or fortified. And I will be moving *Slicer* closer to *Mira* and the current line of Monument ships, if that is all right with you, Jamal."

"Wise as always, I.C.C.," Jamal said. "We will take my rover to the trailhead. Come, who will help protect the ancestral spirits?"

Hope and the other humans all made their way to the ancestor shrine perched on a flat outcropping halfway up the mountainside. The shrine itself was fashioned after the shrine Hope's paternal grandparents had watched over, the one in the photograph that now rested against her father's tablet. The picture was laminated and kept from the clutches of the Noumonian winds by a sturdy, smooth stone that she'd taken from the seaside. Much of the materials they'd used to construct the shrine were far different from the ones utilized in Guangzhou, but the slope of the roof was the same, the height of the four support pillars was the same. The Tan family name written in gold on the rear, and only, wall was the same.

However, the front of the shrine looked out over a very different landscape. The reds of Noumenon were a far cry from the lushness of Southern China. The beautiful yellow wildflowers in the photograph would not grow here, even if they had the seeds to plant. But they'd built the shrine high in the mountains, between the two Noumonian colonies, and the tablets looked over the flat plains and then the sea. The view was different, but still majestic.

Hope wondered how her parents, now both over a decade gone, would feel about a presence in their family shrine being extended to every human on Noumenon. Hope hadn't suggested they build it until after her mother, Ming-Na, had passed. Before that her father, Captain Orlando Tan, had kept his father's tablet in a small nook aboard *Mira*—one that mirrored its place on *Pulse*, and where it had sat alone. Hope didn't think her grandfather's spirit had wanted to be alone. None of their spirits need be alone. To her, they were all family.

The group had discussed whether or not to take the ancestor tablets aboard *Mira* before the flight south, but the idea made Hope uneasy. It was bad luck to remove a tablet from its shrine, to separate their ancestors from one another. Her father had taken his grandfather's tablet aboard Convoy Twelve, and it sat here now, next to her mother's and her father's. But her father had always wondered if he'd made a mistake, if he should have left it in China, despite his own father's insistence that he take it for protection. After all, the convoy had met a myriad of misfortunes after.

And yet, her family had survived. Others had died and they had persisted. Even when everything seemed lost, when their baby was born unresponsive, somehow they'd pulled through. Perhaps it was thanks to her great-grandfather's spirit.

But Orlando's constant worry over whether or not moving the tablet had been the right thing to do still haunted his daughter now. If they left the tablets where they were, the shrine could be pelted with debris. The tablets could be destroyed. But moving them might make things worse—could lead to an even more terrible outcome for them all.

In the end, she'd convinced the others to leave the tablets, to let the spirits watch over the land.

Instead, they would take the next few days to construct a shield. To sort of half bury the shrine so that they could excavate it again.

Akane and Jamal were the best at these kinds of structural designs, so the two of them began to take measurements and discuss the possibilities while the others took a moment to say hello to their loved ones.

After depositing a small offering at her late husband's tablet, Vanhi went to the edge of the outcropping and sat, her legs dangling over the side. They'd picked this spot for the shrine at Vanhi's insistence, but Hope had never been bold enough to ask why. Vanhi herself had never been particularly spiritual.

Hope maneuvered the mech to her side, standing silently next to the older woman, matching her distant gaze.

She hadn't expected Vanhi to speak.

"Stone and I spent our last anniversary here," she said suddenly, looking to the northeast. "We watched the sun rise."

Hope said nothing, not sure if Vanhi was really speaking to her or just speaking to get something out.

"I . . . I *thanked him.*" Vanhi laughed lightly. "Told him I was grateful that everyone aboard Convoy Twelve had met my jumps with kindness instead of fear. Sometimes cursed women are treated like curses themselves . . . I told him about daayans . . . about what had happened to some of the real women accused of being daayans . . ."

"You're not cursed," Hope said softly, guiding her suit to sit as well.

Vanhi smiled to herself. "That's what he said. And he told me I didn't have to thank people for being decent."

Hope placed her mech's hand lightly on Vanhi's shoulder. "You don't."

Vanhi turned toward Hope, held her gaze. "Your parents would be so proud of you. You know that, don't you."

"I can feel it," Hope said. "I can feel *them*, sometimes. Especially here."

Vanhi nodded. "I can feel him here, too. That last anniversary, when he held me and kissed my head and told me . . ." She let out a shaky breath, tears gathering in the corners of her eyes.

It seemed she couldn't quite bring herself to repeat the special thing he'd said. Perhaps she was trying to remain composed for Hope's sake. She swallowed thickly before continuing. "Anyway, I've never . . . I've never felt more loved than in that moment." She ran her palms over the rock. "I don't know what I'll do if . . . if this place . . ."

Vanhi had been absent much of Hope's early life—after Stone had died. This spot meant much to her—to them—and she didn't want to see it in ruins.

"The Noumonians say the Sora-Gohan lands gently," Hope said, repeating what they both already knew, hoping it sounded reassuring rather than patronizing.

"Things don't always work out like they're supposed to," Vanhi said.

The two of them sat in silence for a few minutes more, as the others said prayers and thanks and left their offerings for their elders—Vanhi's cohort. Eventually only Vanhi and Jamal would remember falling.

Hope thought back to what Jamal had said—that memory would fade. That human minds weren't built to hold so much history. But Vanhi was different. She was still living a natural life-span, just spread out over many more years. She would remember. Even when all this was lost to Jamal, Vanhi would hold on.

That was a comfort, in a way. The love Vanhi had for Stone would not fade.

But an uncomfortable notion crept into Hope's mind. She loved her parents deeply, missed them every day. She missed Dr. Jax. She didn't want to stop missing them. She refused to forget.

When the day's work at the shrine was complete—the materials decided on and the design sound—the group returned to *Mira*.

The party was in full swing. I.C.C. filled the hangar with sound, blasting strange notes and noises that Hope knew to be Noumonian music—though it sounded like little more to her than a deep, ardent humming struck through with whirring and clicking. Tanks flung turrets between them, letting them somersault through the air. Scouts ran about wildly, spinning others' wheels, jumping and galloping as they did so.

Kexin and Reggie immediately threw themselves into the crowd. Mohamed and the others went looking for food. Jamal embraced Wes-Tu, his attendants, and Houdini in turn. Hope stood with Vanhi, watching her.

This was a beautiful celebration of life. And still, Vanhi frowned.

"What's wrong?" Hope prodded. "Everyone's so happy. Is everything all right?" Perhaps the resurgence of old grief had tainted her evening.

"They're happy, but . . . This feels like a wake," Vanhi said. "An old Earth party thrown by some cultures when . . ." She waved a flippant hand. "It's nothing," she insisted, patting Hope's shoulder reassuringly. "Go, have fun. Dance with your friends. I see Pyebwa beckoning to you."

Hope turned to see the scout shaking their front limbs at her, wanting her to come be a part of the dancing circle.

"You'll explain what a wake is later?" she asked, half stepping in Pyebwa's direction.

"Yeah," Vanhi said absently. Then added, under her breath, "Someday."

NOTES ON MY FEELINGS RE:
THE FORTHCOMING MIGRATION

Something is coming. Things are changing.

It's difficult to know how to feel. Excited? Worried?

Though we live with about fifty Noumonians, there are nearly ten thousand that we know of. Our friends tell us stories of the Waterfall, what life is like there—of soaring from roost to roost in a gliding jump, or hacking into a stone nook with sharpened scythes. Scouts roam far and deep, dipping below the surface, into the sinkhole, which is filled with its own gentle life. Small squiggly worms that I hope one day to see. And glowing lichen-like organisms, which I think must be related to the red algae. Bubbling pools roil with steadily released gases. Stalactites drip with briny solutions.

I've never been to the Waterfall or the sinkhole. I hope, one day, to be invited. (Noumenon itself is covered in sinkholes—a unique occurrence that appears in all types of geologies. I wonder what hidden life might be in each.)

I'm still surprised I've received an invitation to observe the migration and the feeding. Part of me is scared for them—for those in our *Mira* colony who might hear the Call and leave us for a time. How do they transform? Not with the ease of my mech suit, that's for certain.

What will they be like when the metamorphosis is done?

What is the Sora-Gohan trying to change them into?

What might they become?

■ ■ ■

Two nights before "impact," the object was easily spotted in the night sky, no satellites or telescopes needed. It grew larger and larger, from a pinprick against the anomaly, to the bright spot of a planet, to that of a comet without a tail. Hope couldn't help how her heart raced every time she looked up to find it, to see how it had grown. It was probably safe. They were mostly sure it was safe. But her limbic system couldn't be reasonably convinced.

Even if they were wrong and it hit with force, it wouldn't be an extinction-level impact. If it didn't break up in the atmosphere, it would create a large crater and throw dangerous debris, but everyone who'd taken shelter should be safe. Even the Waterfall colony should be all right—the mountain range should shield them from the majority of the rock splash.

The day before impact, Hope, Akane, Kexin, and Mohamed piled into the rover and set out for the landing site, their observational equipment tucked gently into the rear compartment. The rover was slow, and the site far. They spoke little on the long drive, looking up instead as their moon, Phenomenon, was joined by a contender.

They had no way of knowing which Noumonians would hear the Call. It was different each time—another mystery. So they'd said loving farewells to each and every one of them, unsure who in the celebratory bunch they'd see again at their destination.

That morning, Vanhi took extra medication to dampen her sense of anticipation so that she wouldn't jump. Jamal walked out on the hot surface of the plains completely naked except for the sundial, lifted his arms to the object, and cried out to the universe in ecstasy through the thin Noumonian air. He stood like that, exposed in the full sun for hours, until Wes-Tu brought him a shroud and walked the old man back to *Mira*.

I.C.C. and Hope had run safety check after safety check. They'd stocked three days' worth of supplies aboard the rover, unsure how long the initial observation period would be, and how long it might take for the Noumonians to reach the object's landing site.

None of them knew what to expect, and while it was a

happy occasion, the weight of the unknown pressed down on them—as though the incoming object itself applied a pressure, squeezing and uneasy.

The convoy ships disappeared in the thin wake of the rover's dust, and a strange sense of separation washed over Hope. She'd never traveled this far north. Most excursions were exclusively east and west, to the mountains and the sea. There was nothing north, just more rocky plains.

As night set, I.C.C. informed them that the Call had begun. Sixteen from the *Mira* colony had left. It wasn't certain yet how many journeyed from the Waterfall.

Night swelled and dawn broke. The humans traded off driving. Hope spent time setting up her field note files, so she'd have quick access to the proper headings when she made observations.

They reached the edge of the landing site—stayed beyond the projected "danger zone" and waited.

Near noon the first Noumonians appeared over the horizon. Hundreds of them. Led by Icelandic.

"Object has breached the troposphere," I.C.C. reported. "Speed is rapidly decreasing, but its changing vector still puts it well within the calculated landing zone."

"Estimated time to impact?" Akane asked.

"If it continues to slow at a steady rate, one hour, six minutes, and thirty-two seconds."

Hope wriggled in her cockpit. The anticipation in her chest rose, *hurt*. She felt giddy and nauseated, her stomach both utterly empty and too full.

As the object continued to breach layer after layer of atmosphere, it began to burn. Though the Noumonians were sure it would land lightly and I.C.C. insisted it was slowing down, it still hurtled toward the ground. Flames licked it all around, blazing away from its egg-shaped nose.

Soon, they lost it overhead. There was no skylight in the

rover's roof. Eventually the group agreed they couldn't stay inside for "impact," despite the danger. Their job was to observe all they could. It might have been a flimsy excuse to abate the curiosity coursing through their veins, but so what? I.C.C. admonished them for their lack of care, but it couldn't make them stay inside.

They each sported environmental suits for safety. After a quick triple check of all fastenings, they ventured beyond.

Akane popped the hatch, and immediately the cool air was flushed out by a hot gust from outside. Their unbuckled harnesses flapped in the wind, and even Hope's mech had to struggle against the gale just to get a foot out the door. The object was creating its own pocket of microclimate beneath it.

As Hope hit the rocky ground she transformed, shifting her mech into a low-set four-legged entity with the cockpit in the center. The legs were sturdy, like an elephant's—though she gave the feet claws for a firmer purchase—and the rim of her cockpit came up higher over her bulbous, makeshift visor, better securing it in place.

Her companions had to make do with their human forms, their boots slipping on the rock as the wind tried to sweep them off their feet. Mohamed raised an arm in front of his visor, trying to ward off the grit and sand blowing against his helmet, pixilating his view.

The air made a strained howling all around, and even in her mech, Hope's ears grew painful as the pressure changed. She looked up, straining to see through the haze of agitated atmosphere.

The object had lost all fire, so when she finally spotted its uniform shape among the clouds her heart jumped in her chest and her bowels clenched in her abdomen. It was *so close.* It was one thing to intellectually know it was mountainous, but to have that mass hanging directly over one's head, growing larger by the minute, was quite another.

As Noumenon's natural winds blew the pocket of altered weather away, the object resolved, its details clarifying, its details *shifting*.

The egg shape morphed before their eyes, just like Houdini's body and Hope's mech, making her wonder for the briefest of moments if it really was an Earth craft after all.

Its hide was the same purplish black as Jamal's ship, but with huge jagged streaks of silver on the outside. The closest end of the thing continued changing shape, panels flipping and rearranging themselves, the overall form becoming narrower and narrower, until it was sharply tipped. In turn, the backside elongated, flattened and widened, until the entire object took on the appearance of a spearhead. The point was aimed straight at its landing site, and as it neared, a looming sense of *impalement* crept up Hope's spine.

They stayed close to the rover, clinging to its hull.

The object's shadow fell over them.

Hope reminded herself that they were at I.C.C.'s projected minimum safe distance. They'd be all right. They'd be okay.

At a thousand meters above the surface, the object twisted itself like a corkscrew, angling itself horizontally.

"Please brace for impact," I.C.C. directed.

Hope felt herself twisting like the object was twisting, nervous anticipation creating a curling press and pull on her insides.

Kexin drew in a deep breath and suddenly shouted, "Weeepaaaaa!" making the rest of them cringe inside their helmets.

It was a cry of excitement they'd learned from Stone. It had been a long time since Hope had heard anyone utter it.

"Weeeeepaaaaa," Akane responded, quieter, but drawing out the cry. Hope could hear her smile through the comms.

"Weeeepaaaa!" Kexin yelled again, this time echoed by Mohamed, then Hope, and once more by Akane.

It felt good to yell, to release their nerves into the crackle of the comms waves.

The object drew closer, and they all yelled together as the wind whipped around them and the object roared with its entry, "Weeeeeeeeeeeeeeeepaaaaaaaaaaaaa!" the word dissolving into one, long, maddening note.

A thunderous boom shook through Hope's mech, the shuttle, and the very rock of the planet as the object barreled into its landing site from the side. It impaled the rock at such an angle that it looked more like an aircraft running its nose into the ground rather than a knife point stabbing the dirt.

The impact made an epic rumble—deeper than thunder, sharper than a landslide—and rocks flew up around it. But, as the Noumonians predicted, the touchdown was nothing like a typical meteor, and it had hit the surface lightly for its apparent mass. No deep crater. No debris cloud spewing high into the stratosphere.

Smoke and steam wafted away from the object, curling in the wind. The bits of stone were thrown up over its nose, burying it all the deeper.

Everything calmed but the wind. The rumbling ceased, the tremors halted.

They stopped screaming.

When all but their hearts had stilled, they uncoupled themselves from the rover's side. Peering through the settling dust, they took shaky steps in the object's direction, still a good trek away. "Looks like you were a whole one kilometer off, I.C.C.," Akane announced over the comms. She had no way of measuring, it was just a tease. Something to break the tension.

The humans scrambled to retrieve their equipment from the rear compartment, eager to run their remote scans, unsure it was safe to approach the sky-food just yet. They detected nothing but trace amounts of radiation and a radio signal outside of the typical Noumonian vocabulary—perhaps the Call. Infrared showed the surface was still hot, but cooling by the second. No other signals emanated from the object.

And still, they waited, unsure what it might do, if anything. Did the Noumonians consume it whole, just as they ate the stone straight from a quarry pit? How, then, did the turrets and the scouts partake? The turrets and the scouts did not eat, and they had no digestive systems. All their regenerative capacity came from joining with a tank.

The four of them shared a meal aboard the rover, eyeing the device through the windows with caution. Hope, in turn, eyed the solid compressed bars of protein and fibers the others ate. Her digestive system and lack of teeth still required an all-liquid diet, and she couldn't fathom why anyone would enjoy eating things they had to rip apart and masticate just so their stomachs would have half a shot of breaking them down properly. After all, most of their food was processed for efficiency and reduced waste—they could form it into whatever consistency they preferred. She was quite happy never having to trouble herself with finicky solids—especially ones that were hard enough to tear at the gums.

They ate slowly, each silently presuming the Sora-Gohan would do *something*. Something that would either encourage them to stay in the rover or entice them back outside.

But all was still.

"So shall we go?" Kexin asked as Mohamed picked the last crumbs from his container.

No one answered right away.

"What if it doesn't like non-Noumonians?" Akane asked.

"Indeed," Mohamed agreed. "What if it's got some kind of security system to prevent outside tampering? Remember, like the Seed."

"But we're not going to tamper with it," Kexin reminded him. "We're observation only. Noninterference."

"So let's go then," said Hope.

It was still a long walk from the rover to the Sora-Gohan. They paused their approach one-fourth of a kilometer out to run more safety checks, probe for seismic activity, and test air quality.

Even at this distance, the object towered above them, more intimidating than any of I.C.C.'s ships. It was a vast black wall—a strangely carved mountain. A great dark triangle splitting the iron-rich bedrock. The buried front end balanced out the elevated back end, which rose high into the sky and cast a long shadow now that the sun had descended from its zenith.

As they drew closer it blotted out all else. Became an expanse of darkness across their path. The sun disappeared behind it, creating a deep gloominess. Hope shivered as she crab-walked into that gloom.

There were no windows, no visible engines. The object definitely didn't appear to be a craft in that sense. The plates on the hull were larger than a Noumonian tank, spade shaped, and overlapping, but very different from the way Houdini's shape-shifting portions overlapped. The plates almost looked like scales, giving the impression of a tough dragon's hide. Little rainbows flitted over the dark material when the angle was just right. The silver-colored material ran across the scales like veins, thicker in some places, but then branching and thinning. Here and there the silver curled, in other places it was a straight line. Not all the silver sections were interconnected, and Hope wondered if they were an exterior mechanism to help the sky-food change shape.

Besides the variances in the silver veins, the entire exterior was the same. No visible hatches marred the consistency of the scales, there were no extra seams or hinges. No antenna shot out from its hide, no lights or cameras.

A scaled monolith and nothing more.

There were no clues as to who'd built it or where it had originated.

"Why do they always look different? The artifacts, I mean," Mohamed mused. They had a database of alien megastructures, and he accessed it often. "There's no consistency of design, very little consistency of primary materials. It's weird, right?"

Akane shrugged. "Different designs for different jobs. And dozens of different civilizations worked on the megastructures. Who even knows when this one was built, or by whom, right?"

"I.C.C. has records of three hundred and twenty-seven migrations," Hope said. "All three hundred and twenty-seven instances of Sora-Gohan could have lain in wait for a billion years before making their way to Noumenon. Especially if they were secluded away in an SD pocket."

"I.C.C. said it could have come from one of the other planets. Maybe created by the pods the Seed left there? It doesn't look like it was built by the *Lùhng*, or any other human civilization," Mohamed said, frozen with wonder, staring up and up through its shadow as though he might be able to read the silver swirls and divine its past. "I've got all those memorized and this . . . it's nothing like any of them."

They mapped what they could of the object's exterior, making detailed recordings and measurements. Hope transformed the suit's hands into various devices. She ran basic ultrasound, radiation, and off-gassing tests.

"It's hollow," she said after a time, double-checking the readouts. "But not empty. There's stuff in there, denser than the atmosphere, than water, but not solid like the ground. The interior isn't uniform—could be equipment for preserving the substance."

"The air around it is cold," Akane noted.

"How chill?"

"Negative six Celsius."

"What does that tell us?" Mohamed asked.

Akane shrugged. "It's refrigerated?"

"Refrigeration can't make food last a billion years," he said.

"It doesn't have to," Hope pointed out. "If this thing came here via subdimensional travel, or if it was grown next door. Our parents were in an SD for an instant, but a hundred thousand years passed. No reason to think this thing couldn't have been activated a week ago, relatively speaking."

"Has anyone identified an access point?" Kexin asked. She reached out one gloved hand, ghosting it over the hull. "Can the Noumonians shift the scales, do you think? Pry it open with their prehensile feelers? Maybe the turrets cut into it? Or the tanks dissolve the outer hull?"

"We'll know soon enough," Hope said, gesturing.

The Noumonians came near. There were more than Hope had originally thought, thousands of them. With rough numbers from I.C.C., Hope surmised that two-thirds of all Noumonians had heard the Call. Two-thirds had arrived to surround the strange object.

The tanks each carried two turrets, and a few of them even more—the extras sprawled across their necks or held aloft by the seated ones. Scouts threaded themselves between the thick feet of their brethren, trying not to get stepped on.

The team looked for Icelandic, for the familiar members of the *Mira* colony. The herd rushed around them uncaringly, jostling the humans as though they were unaware of their presence. One knocked Kexin down and Hope had to scoop her up. The group huddled together and soon found themselves in a rushing sea of waterwheels and razor-tipped snake arms.

Akane turned up her suit's outer speaker. "Icelandic?" she yelled. "Icelandic? *Genkideska*?"

Hope worried for a moment that the Call emanating from

the device was too strong. Maybe Icelandic wouldn't answer, even if she heard her name.

But then a wheel turned, traveling toward the humans, across the stream of bodies. Icelandic's familiar face emerged from the darkness, from the crowd, to stand tall in front of the team. The translator still dangled around her neck.

"*Genkidesu*," the translator chirped. "Everything is as it should be."

Instruction Manual was with her, as were Shaka and Snore. Their attention was fixed on the dark silhouette. They did not acknowledge the humans.

Even Icelandic's attention wavered, drawn again and again back to the Sora-Gohan as the team attempted to speak with her, to record any sensations or feelings she could share with them.

"Call is strong," she insisted. "Call is firm. Im can barely feel anything else. Inside. Must. Inside."

Her speech patterns became more broken, more indirect. Eventually she lost all focus and began to move away from them, becoming part of the herd once more.

The Noumonians settled around the object with a buffer of barely a meter, clearly waiting.

All fell still.

Minutes passed. Hope checked and rechecked all her sensors, making sure everything was in working order, that she wouldn't miss recording a single moment of whatever was about to transpire.

Then there was a great, grating *crack*.

The spearhead split end to end, separating down a hidden seam, pulling apart interlocking scales like they were a row of teeth attached to firm jaws. Two halves of the mountain fell *open* and *outward*.

The humans instinctually backed away, fearing they'd be

crushed, while the Noumonians swayed forward, eager for what awaited them within.

Light emanated from inside, a blue-green glow that reminded Hope of Earth's bioluminescent sea creatures. A thick, tacky-looking substance rolled out, globs of it sticking together like fish eggs. Where the frigid insides of the object met the warmer night air, steam rose. Water droplets formed on the outside of the jelly and slid down the sides, unabsorbed.

The Noumonians marched forward. Without hesitation, they immersed themselves in the substance, heading inside the object. They piled in, each disappearing after the next, their body language eager, their footfalls thunderous.

They must absorb it through osmosis, Hope thought. *Maybe the substance is like the protein-rich amniotic fluid in cloning tanks.*

Or perhaps it was more specific than that.

It changed them. It influenced their forms, triggered new growth.

Perhaps the Sora-Gohan was akin to the feeding regimens of bees. Different portions of pollen, honey, and royal jelly fed at specific times produced different phenomes of honey-bees. Was it like that? Guiding their development so that they could become . . .

What? What did the megastructures need them to become?

Icelandic was lost in the rush, diving in just as eagerly as her fellows.

Every last Noumonian boarded the object, becoming little more than shadows reflected inside the strange substance.

As quickly as they'd been surrounded, the human group was left alone. The substance was still, no telltale wobbles of creatures rummaging inside.

The team waited, watching and documenting with nary

a word between them, as the substance shrank—either from consumption or deterioration or both. Soon they saw the damp insides of the container's walls, which were uneven and blocky, with storage or other apparatuses built in.

Hours passed.

The humans waited.

The humans anticipated.

And then, eventually, the Noumonians came stumbling out again.

They took unsteady, listing steps, teetering from side to side as though drunk. Turrets hung limply from their engagement points. Some of the scouts could barely tug themselves along the ground, scraping their metal-clad bellies against the stones. The substance, which had completely shifted away from blues into deep red, clung to them like globs of coagulating blood.

But they didn't look any different. Not yet.

Hope held her breath.

Would they begin to sprout new appendages? Would their bodies remold themselves right here, right now, or would it take years? I.C.C. had reported that the migration periods took decades.

Maybe they'd shed their outsides, like spiders growing too big for their exoskeletons. Or spin cocoons.

One by one, the Noumonians stopped walking. They fell to the ground in groups, stumbling steps bringing them to a halt.

Those who fell did not stir.

Even as she felt her companions tense beside her, Hope tried not to fret. She tried to keep her observations objective, tried to make notes without worry. The *thump* of each Noumonian body against the hard ground made her flinch, made her little heart stutter, as though their *thump* against the stony surface stole the *thump* from her chest.

This is fine. This is natural. This is why you're here, so that they can know this about themselves.

Her conscious reassurances came harder and faster, the scientist in her having to assert dominance over and over. Her instinct was to run to her friends—her *family*—to ask if they were all right, if this felt right. Would they know? Could they tell?

Thump.

Thump.

Thump.

They'd promised not to interfere. No matter how much it looked like . . . dying . . . the only proper course of action was to stay back and document the events.

The small human troop spread out as the fainting field widened, so that they could note as many individual experiences as possible. They would aggregate the data later, come up with a generalized picture of the experience to present to those who hadn't heard the Call.

Lax tank jaws opened wide, letting their digestive fluids spill onto the land and chew divots into the rock beneath their heads. Waterwheels spun wildly as individuals swayed and toppled. Turret arms became bent and twisted beneath the heavy bodies of the tanks that carried them—scythes occasionally lacerating tank hides. Scouts did their best to fall where they wouldn't in turn be fallen on. The occasional paddle on a wheel snapped after an awkward tumble, and Hope cringed.

Kexin openly cried, shaking her helmet, blinking the tears away so she could see well enough to make useful observations. Her occasional sniffle and shaky exhale over the comms worked its way beneath Hope's skin, trying to burrow into her own endocrine system—which was still so young it had a hair trigger.

Icelandic was one of the last to stumble from the shell.

Hope wandered her way, taking note of the slight gray complexion in her usually vibrant skin. Icelandic was, in a way, also an immortal, Hope suddenly realized. She had been a part of every migration, at least as far back as to the migration where Noumonians gained their sentience. While others had evolved to a certain point and then never been called again, she'd continued on. Others were grown anew, their forms always matching their parents' stage of evolution, but she was from long, long ago. Perhaps she'd begun life in the primordial soup provided by the Web. Perhaps she was as old as the planet itself.

That means we are five-count, not four. Five-count are the ancient elements: water, fire, earth, wood, and metal.

Hope inched her mech as close to Icelandic as she dared. The translator stood out stark against the Noumonian's listing body, though clumps of the red goo clung to it just as surely as it clung to Icelandic. She needed to ask her questions, needed to know how she felt and what she was seeing and if she retained a sense of her own agency in all this.

"Icelandic," she prompted gently, even as the tank's legs folded beneath her and she hit the ground hard.

Icelandic's eyes were unusually foggy, and she set her chin firmly on the ground, a small stream of digestive fluids dripping from her jaw. She did not reply.

"Icelandic?" Hope whispered one more time. "Tell us what's happening. How do you feel?"

The translator's beacon blinked once as a single word eked out. "*Yasumimasu.*"

Will rest now.

Even as the last syllable echoed in Hope's ears, the red, globular substance began to change. It turned flaky, and white. Everywhere, all around her, it transformed, until it looked like a gentle dusting of snow covered Icelandic's body.

Within minutes, all the Noumonians wore the same fine film. Delicate, crystalline structures formed skyward atop them, wafer thin and branching, reaching up, up, like sugar crystals clinging to a damp string. No more than a few centimeters tall, the growth was thick and covered the tops of each creature, then down along their sides.

The small puddles of it the team had stepped in began to transform as well, pulling at their boots, hardening, trying to seal them to the ground. They stamped hard, shaking it from their suits. The crystals continued to form and thicken, blanketing the entire area, forming one, massive cocoon. The entire region looked like ice or white marble. The Noumonians appeared sculpted, little more than an artist's rendition. Like something Mohamed might have painted.

It was gentle looking. A calming sight, even. They could pretend they were simply sleeping.

But the stillness only lasted for a handful of minutes.

The first *bursting* happened in the center of the herd. So sudden, so loud, so violent, all four humans made involuntary sounds of surprise.

One of the Noumonians was rocketed skyward on a trunk of crystal. The structure formed in a moment, tearing toward the sky, as though the Noumonian were a firework and the crystal were a physical manifestation of its launch path. As it carried the body at least six stories above their heads, the structure grew branches at the top, stretching out like a shimmering, white tree. The branches were geometrical—crooked in right angles, cutting away from one another in an isometric pattern.

The branches themselves were not pure white.

Hope's insides *lurched*.

But there was no time to process the full implications of the first bursting before the second happened, and then the next, and the next, popping up like frozen geysers, ferrying the Noumonians away from the humans, obscuring what was happening at the tops of these new, crystalline trees.

All they could do was run to the edges of the herd and watch, as each of their friends was carried off, up and away.

No one spoke. No one could form words, least of all Hope.

When the forest had stopped bursting to life, when the last Noumonian had left the surface, Hope knew what she had to do.

It would be difficult. She'd have to stretch her mech's chassis thin. The others would have to spot her in case the materials couldn't take it and the integrity of the suit failed.

She would look at what the branches had done to Icelandic first. She felt she owed it to the eldest Noumonian, the one who'd invited her, the one who'd put an entire species' trust in her.

Much of biology on the planet was strange and had no Earthly counterpart. But this . . . this was beyond anything Hope had ever observed before, and though she was curious, and had a duty to the Noumonians to investigate the branches, part of her dreaded what she'd see at the top.

The others braced around her, grabbing hold of the mech's base as she began to direct it to stretch, to force her upward just as the Noumonians had been forced upward. The metal would slide and stretch beneath their gloved palms, always moving, always changing, but perhaps they would be able to catch Hope if something went wrong—if the mech snapped and she fell. That was the plan, anyway.

Up and up she went, her mech narrowing. First it was its own trunk, solid as a real tree, then it became more like her snake forms, then it thinned and thinned and thinned.

In the end, when she drew up level with Icelandic, her cockpit stood atop one narrow stilt, and she swayed in the wind.

Perhaps she should have been prepared for what she found. Instead, she vomited.

The branches had torn Icelandic's body apart, turning every bit of her into a frozen fractal. Circulatory system, bones, nerves, organs, epidermis, and plate levels were all laid bare. Noumonian funerary practices left time for only a few anatomical notations before consumption, but this was exquisite in its detail, and grotesque in its thoroughness. Each part was perfectly preserved, perfectly encased in the whiteish, clearish substance. But Icelandic was no more, not in this state.

Caterpillars don't simply grow wings in their chrysalis, she reminded herself. *They digest themselves. They dissolve in a torrent of enzymes, their imaginal discs survive, and they get remade. The butterfly can only exist because the caterpillar is no more.*

Interrupt that process and you kill the creature.

She took picture after picture and made note after note, despite the intense stench in her cockpit, despite how dirty she felt in a multitude of ways. She had no idea how the other Noumonians would react. Would it seem natural? Unnerving? How would I.C.C. feel? Would the other humans . . . *respond* as she did?

It was one thing to see a dead body stripped down to its components. But Icelandic wasn't supposed to be dead. She was supposed to climb, her wheel was supposed to turn. She had thoughts and feelings and loves and desires. And somehow this process made all those things more acute. But if Hope hadn't known better, she would have thought she wasn't looking at anything more than a dissected animal—dead and gone. Perished and overtaken.

The crystals had fractured the Noumonians. Now she had to trust they'd be put back together again.

"Hope?" Akane tested delicately. "Hope, what's going on? Talk to us."

"I can't," she said meekly. "I'll have to show you."

When she was finished, she slowly descended, contemplating how exactly to best explain what she'd seen—what they were about to see in pictures. After all, her friends wouldn't be there at the end of the migration. This would be their final interaction with the Called Noumonians. Were these the kinds of images she wanted to leave them with?

In the time it took her to pull her mech back together again, she decided they were all scientists. They could handle the images, the information. They deserved all the data.

Kexin had already cried too many tears. Now it was Mohamed's turn. Akane turned ashen, but did not break a sweat. Still, they all quailed.

Consciously, intellectually, they were aware that this was most likely part of the usual process, not an abhorrent occurrence. But still, the emotive, visceral response was strong. One cannot look upon a loved one's torn body and not despair.

Hope reached out, pulling the three of them to her suit, embracing them all together.

They gathered what data they could, then began the trek back to the rover. They were quiet, contemplative.

Sad.

Halfway there, a sudden rumble caught them off guard. The ground began to shake—the vibration clearly emanating from the way they'd come. They all spun, eyes fixed to the Sora-Gohan.

The construct shifted, rising up. The scales fluttered, rearranged, like they were folding over on themselves. A mountain transforming, looming, *tilting* near their fragile friends.

"Everybody get back!" Mohamed yelled. "Run! Get in the rover!"

"What the heck is it doing?" Kexin asked.

"What if it crushes the cocoons?" Akane cried.

"We can't stop it," Mohamed said. "Go, go!"

The other three ran, but Hope was frozen to the spot. She couldn't turn her back on the Noumonians. Whatever was about to happen, she had to witness it, even if there was nothing she could do.

Bits of it fluttered upward, and then the base of it *sank*.

Not sinking like it was in quicksand, not falling as though into a sudden pit. Digging. Burrowing. There was a high-frequency whirring Hope could hear through her suit, like drills, and a thumping of rocks pummeled into dust. The scales on the sections of hull nearest the ground were waving in long sheets, rippling like the fins of a cuttlefish. Their edges were diamond sharp, slicing into stone the moment the shell sank deep enough for them to hit the surface.

"Whatever it's here for, it's not done," Hope said. "This must be why we've never spotted leftover shells with the satellites." Because they'd dug themselves into the ground, boring—but how deep? And what for?

The construct sank swiftly, chewing its way underground, delving as deftly as a mole. Soon the back end was lost below the horizon, bleeding into the stone around it, burying itself. The others all had time to board the rover, but no time to rev the engines before the shell was gone.

The ground still shook. Even though Hope couldn't see it anymore, it was still digging.

"Noumenon . . ." Mohamed said over the comms, "is covered . . . in sinkholes."

"They couldn't all be . . . burrows . . . could they?" asked Akane.

Three hundred and twenty-seven migrations—*that they knew of.* Three hundred and twenty-seven shells. Three hundred and twenty-seven sinkholes harboring alien constructs.

Three hundred and twenty-seven question marks buried beneath the surface.

NOTES ON FUNCTIONAL IMMORTALITY:
ADDENDUM

I've never thought about five. But I am certain now that we immortals are five-count. Five is fresh to me, but I feel drawn to the elemental aspects.

Our family here is of the universe—we are its creation, we are at its mercy and part of its mercy and do our best to respect its offerings. This is what Jamal has taught us: that the universe contains all knowledge, and Reveals it slowly. This is what my parents taught us: that the universe will have its way, and fate will take hold, and you can only swim in the tides, not dictate them. This is what Justice taught us: that like the land, we are malleable, we can be eroded and rebuilt—we are meant to be malleable; it is our greatest strength. And this is what the Noumonians have taught us: that we are a small part of a larger whole. That we matter, and we cannot see just how much until we evolve.

And what, if anything, have I taught myself?

Old stories would have you believe that immortality is lonely, Jamal told me. *And it is, in a way. On days when you're reminded that you persist and others don't. But most days it's just living.*

I understand. I do. Immortality doesn't mean you're immune to the passage of time. Immortality means more things will change than I'd ever imagined could change. Immortality means I will get to see, do, find, and lose more than the average person, but it is no better and no worse an existence than any other, I don't think. It is the only existence I know.

I am sad I will lose my loved ones. But I am grateful I did not lose them today. My friends, the Noumonians we knew, are gone. But not for me. One day Kexin, Akane, Reggie, Maureen, Mohamed, and Toya will die. And I will still be here, waiting for the Noumonians to awaken. As the others will grieve for the im, I grieved for them.

The future is uncertain. What we observed out on the plains raised far more questions than it answered. I'm not sure I understand this world, our home, any better than I did before.

But perhaps I understand myself a little more. Perhaps I understand the nature of my connections, my loves, a little better.

TRAGIC INTERLUDE

One night you go off to work, but there's no sky. You look up, and swipe the secondary lenses from your metallic eyes because they must be interfering with your visual processors. But it's not the lenses. And it's not your eyes. And, heavens help you, it's not your processors gone awry.

There's no sky. No stars, at least. You can still just make out the two dots that are two of the six moons—one is artificial, one little more than a captured asteroid. But beyond that . . .

With your system's star having gone down four hours ago, it should be pitch-black, picked through with far-off points of light. But there's one light. So harsh and searing you can see the trees withering beneath the beam. And all around it the sky itself is not lit up. The blue-purple atmosphere (at least, that's the way your visual processors interpret it) does not refract and reflect and gather this light like it should. This is like a spotlight on a darkened stage, and you can even see the harsh shadows cast by the moons beneath it. It feels wrong.

And the blackness around the beam is a glare. It's not nighttime. You're sure, out here, just beyond the commune block's walls, that you are not seeing outer space on the fringes of the beam. There's a strange *materialness* to it. It doesn't possess its usual depth of emptiness. There's a texture. Like divots and spikes. As though the edge of the atmosphere has developed a film—a touchable, tangible surface. And the texture ripples, like the walls of a sound booth.

And the beam is widening.

And the spikes are lowering.

Maybe you're having a stroke. *Homo kubernētēs* can still have strokes.

The not-space is shrinking. The beam is growing.

Now there's another beam. At a strange angle to the horizon, sending those same wrong shadows through the buildings in the distance.

There's a twisting, a shrinking in. The spikes oscillate.

Nearby, someone screams, sending out pure distress across the network. An emergency signal for anyone—everyone—within range.

Maybe it's not just you, then.

Lights come on in the buildings. More mental shouts, more screams.

The beam intensifies. You start to wither just like the trees.

You don't know what's happening. Your mind, all the minds near you, now awake, search for a point of reference, a course of action to take. A response.

But though there's panic rising in you, you direct your endocrine system to balance so that you can think. What *is* this? What are you looking at?

You sift through thousands and thousands of files in an instant, looking for an explanation. There isn't one.

This is pure anomaly.

And the anomaly is getting closer.

You feel a strange pressure now. Outside and in. Like the air around you is getting thicker, denser. Your mechanical lungs try to compensate. And they do—for a moment.

The anomaly is pressing in on your world. Quite literally.

And if it keeps pressing, keeps coming, you won't last another ten minutes.

Your world won't last.

So what do you do?

You glance toward the space port. You'll never get there.

But maybe someone is already there. Maybe someone is already prepped for takeoff and they can escape.

As though they've read your mind—and they might have—you see a slick shadow rise from the port. A black column beneath the beam. You see it rise and think, at the very least, someone escaped. Someone can tell the galaxy what happened.

And then the ship hits the spikes.

The spikes give, as though elastic.

And the ship is flung back toward the surface of the planet.

You turn away so you don't have to see the crash. Close your ears so you don't have to hear the sounds.

But you feel the vibrations beneath your many, many metallic feet.

Closer. Closer still.

And the air is so thick and hot.

What to do?

What is left to do?

What is there time for?

You transform your metal body into your favorite shape. Little more than a puddle on the ground, with your biological torso in the middle, staring up. It's coming. There's nothing you can do.

So you open up your endocrine system, let the serotonin flood your system, and scream.

CHAPTER FIVE

THE PROGENTOR:
MOSS GATHERS ON THE MAN
(THE ONE WHO ROLLS THE STONE)

"So here's the thing about All Mother and No Mother," Reg said. He was explaining it for the *thousandth time*, but he knew he had to. It was only right. Any other Monument kid might have let this guy scratch his head about it and wait until he wandered off to bug someone else. But Reg was still grateful for the early engineering lessons. Indebted, even. Reg knew how engines worked because of him.

Reg curled his finger, and the other boy fell into step beside him, hands shoved in his pockets, listening intently.

They were wandering the halls on *Morgan*, making sure none of the misters were stopped up. Plants lined every corridor, not just the old air garden facilities. Everything smelled different on this ship. No Mother had once described the scent as "green," but Reg wasn't sure he'd heard her right. How could a color be a smell?

He paused for a moment to flick the tip of one hose nozzle. A small *drip* seeped out instead of a fine mist. He reached into his satchel and pulled out a wrench. Removing the top of the nozzle, he blew into it repeatedly, hoping to clear it of any dust or debris. Satisfied with its cleanliness, he screwed it back into place. Once they were sure it worked properly, the boys moved on.

"All Mother wants us to do everything," he continued, talking with his hands, talking with the wrench like it was an extension of himself. "And No Mother wants us to do nothing."

All Mother. Hope.

No Mother. Vanhi.

He glanced sideways, to make sure the other boy was listening—his attention tended to wander. But his brow was furrowed and his gaze intent, as though he were considering all this very seriously.

"All Mother wants us to build the future. No Mother wants us to wait for the future." He felt like this would be easier to explain in Monument Noumonian—a special blend of old Earth languages—but the other kid didn't speak it. "You are lucky to see No Mother twice in your lifetime. I mean, my lifetime . . . whatever. You get the point, right? You're lucky she's here now. Right—"

He wanted to use the guy's name, but his brain kept filling in "other kid" whenever he looked at him. It felt wrong to use his adult name, and really wrong to use his title. Reg knew he was still the same person, just younger. But even with All Mother's and No Mother's quirks, it was still difficult to accept.

"And All Seer?" the boy asked. "What does it want?"

"To keep us safe," Reg said. Then, glancing toward a camera, "To tell us when we're being stupid." He was surprised I.C.C. did not interject, either to contradict his last point, or to elaborate.

The boy looked at the ground, sucking on his bottom lip. His gaze was narrowed, and his frown lines deepened. He was concentrating hard, clearly trying to recall something. "And All Father?" he asked, looking up, his eyes pleading. "What do *I* want?"

Reg sighed. He felt bad for the guy. And he didn't know the answer, not really. Grown-up All Father was a mystery to him. Reg had been really little when last he'd seen his adult face.

But he knew what this boy wanted, what he was searching for and couldn't quite find because of his modification. "You," he said, putting a hand on his shoulder, trying to look him straight in the eye, even though the other kid was much, much taller, "want to remember."

He seemed to accept that, to grab on to it like a railing after he'd taken a faulty step. His face shifted from worried and adrift to relieved. He cracked a smile. "Yeah. Yeah, I do."

Reg smiled back. "Also, you want to help me finish checking the water system, so that you can join All Mother's descent team. They're going to leave in a few hours, and you still need to talk to Wes-Tu."

The kid's smile widened. "Yeah! We gotta hurry. Thanks for explaining things to me, Reggie."

Reg wasn't sure the adults would actually let All Father go on the away mission. He was in a fragile state, turning a corner. In a couple of weeks he probably wouldn't remember this conversation, and in a couple of months he'd get real bad, be bedridden for a while before getting better. Before growing up again.

But even if he wouldn't remember this, Reg would. Reg would remember when he helped the Progentor smile. "Any time, Jamal."

The Progentor stood on the edge of one of his home structure's massive, kilometer-wide portals. This one, seventh of an identical ten, was his favorite. It looked out on the most beautiful set of constellations. He'd named them all, connected the dots on his star charts. One "star" was no such thing, of course. It was a megastructure field, he'd been told, thousands of light-years away. He'd named its constellation the Ship Yard, as he imagined the alien artifacts as a collection of boats, moored in space.

He'd seen pictures of boats. Well, one type of boat. Reed boats. There was a clip in his Hindi language vids.

From his vantage point, leaning over the edge of the portal, looking, effectively, "down," he felt a bit like he was peering through a telescope. The glucose glass, which kept the portal sealed airtight, lay half a kilometer away, deep at the bottom of an artificial hole. Though it seemed deep, half a kilometer at this PSI meant the atmosphere wasn't even dense enough to make the stars twinkle. But it was still plenty enough distance for something of his mass, at this gravity, to hit terminal velocity should it fall in.

Which made it the perfect place to jump.

In contrast to his Kaeds, sub-Kaeds, and attendants, the Progentor had no capacity to biologically manipulate gravitons. If he leapt over the side unaided, he would go *splat*, unlike Kaed Esk, who'd accidentally fallen in the last Launch Celebration—their most holy of days—and easily recovered midfall, drifting gently to the glass and walking in his *click-click-clicking* step over the fathomless void.

The Progentor adjusted the straps on his latest invention,

making sure the contraption was lashed tightly to his fragile, elderly human form. The thing was bulky on his back and weighed twenty-seven kilograms, which his old bones could hardly support without creaking. If he leaned the wrong way, it would pull him end over end.

You can do this, he told himself in English, following it quickly with the same sentiments in Hindi and Arabic. Adjusting his glasses—they'd been a birthday gift when he turned seventy—he looked around one last time, just in case his experiment proved folly.

Behind, above, and beyond the Progentor, forking out and away from the gigantic, empty room that housed window seven, were zigzagging corridors that led to more zigzagging corridors. Beyond those were the banquet hall (which he'd never eaten in), and his gigantic workshop (which he spent most of his waking hours in), and the dormitories and the medical bay, and the Kaeds' offices, and the attendant-repair shop. On and on and on, literally kilometers upon kilometers of space.

Was it not strange that only nineteen beings now called it home?

His research suggested that this megastructure was originally meant to be a container of sorts, built to hold something that had either never been entombed as intended, or had been emptied long ago. Had the ancient war purged its contents? Had one of the superweapons destroyed its would-be charge?

You're stalling, he chided himself.

With a huff he pressed a series of buttons along the device's side, and it roared to life.

Ek, two, thlath—

He leaned forward, stepped off.

The fall was swift. The rush of air stole his breath, stung his cheeks. But it would not last long. Either his personal graviton cycler would engage at the correct moment, or he would perish.

Stars. There were so many of them rushing up to meet him.

But with a swift jerk, the cycler engaged. It held him steady above the windowpane, close enough that he could reach out and smudge the surface with a fingertip.

A very shaky, adrenaline-filled fingertip.

The blood sang in his ears—his chest felt as though it might explode. Every inch of him felt unsteady. His mind might have believed he would survive, but his body clearly had not.

He pressed a few more buttons and the cycler righted him, with his feet pointing down. His stomach leapt into his throat at the motion, clearly concerned he'd begin to fall once more, out into the universe.

His glasses slipped off his face and he cursed. His weak eyes fell out of focus, sent him fumbling. Why couldn't the Kaeds have allowed the doctor to fix his vision? Would that really have been such a stain on his biological purity, all things considered?

But he knew why.

It was the same reason he had a translator earpiece instead of an implant for when he received pilgrims and conversed with his attendants. The reason he spoke nothing but three dead languages while everyone else around him had been modified with the ability to communicate in unadulterated thought. It was the reason he lived in silence when outside his rooms, and why the only recorded music, sounds, and words to ever reach his ears were produced by a civilization millennia gone, or came from the surgically inserted voice boxes implanted in his Kaeds and sub-Kaeds.

As the Progentor of their faith, he had to stay pure. As close to his extinct race, their mental capacity, experience, and biology, as he could.

Sometimes, when he was sure he was alone, he liked to scream. Not out of anger, or sadness, or even joy. Just to hear it.

The Kaeds hated it when he made unnecessary sounds.

They revered him, *had made him what he was*, and yet his "baseness" was a constant cause for concern.

As he rose above the edge of the portal once more, he saw a dark figure scurrying toward him. Though the Post was still far off, it wasn't long before he realized it was an attendant, one he referred to as Sesl in his mind, though they had no name, being one with the entire universe and therefore no one at all. Every attendant was part of the cybernetics movement, more machine than anything, though the basic requirements of sentient biology—blood for the brain to receive oxygen, a mouth and digestive system for the brain to receive water and sustenance—were kept intact. And though they appeared largely identical—because their mechanical parts were mass-produced, and they each wore long shrouds of purple—it was easy for him to tell one from the other, even with his unmodified senses. After all, his entire world consisted of only eighteen other beings, and familiarity finds nuance.

Every creature moves a little different, be they of the water, earth, or air.

"Is it time for Construction?" he asked softly. Something as trivial as hearing range didn't matter. The microphone in his earpiece translated the words into the appropriate artificial thought patterns for Sesl's brain.

Sesl bowed low, still many meters away, naught but an extra shadow in the dark.

Thinking, thanking, communing, constructing: the four tenets of the Revealers, and rites the Progentor must perform every twenty-four-hour span.

Sesl backed out of the portal room, and the Progentor followed from one dark space into yet another. Then another, and another.

As he rounded the last corner, he ran into Kaed Roq, her head bowed low over a cleaning bot, her gold-trimmed robes pooling over it.

"Ah, Progentor Jamal. It broke down before me," she explained without looking up, knowing it could only be him. When the Kaeds spoke, their words sounded as though they came out of mouths full of molasses and butter. Switching between a communication system so instantaneous that it had changed the theories of quantum entanglement—mind-to-mind—and one reliant on the limitations of the speed of sound—verbalization—was more difficult than one might expect.

"Did *you* break it?" he asked.

"No."

"Then you know you don't have to perform the Pressing."

Beneath her pooled robes, she was pressing parts of the machine to her hide—a hide he had no visualization for, because the Kaeds were as shrouded as his attendants—to see if it would cut. A cut was good, a transfer of energy. Thought was energy, knowledge was energy, all part of and yet entirely separate from biology.

"I always do, regardless. How have you not noticed?" she asked.

Roq had become a Kaed twenty-six years ago. He'd never seen her perform the Pressing. Not once that he could remember.

And he knew he was not that unobservant.

Which could only mean he was already starting to slip.

"Yes, of course," he lied. "I've been distracted lately, this new construction . . ." He said no more, sidestepping her crouched form, heading for his door. He did not turn around when he heard the shaking of quills and the popping of joints as she stood.

"Blood," she said.

"Good," he replied, somehow feeling it wasn't.

The heavy circle of his door unraveled at the wave of his hand, and he stepped through to his sanctuary.

As the door respun itself back into place, lights flickered on. Jamal had already closed his eyes in preparation, and let the brightness filter through the delicate skin of his eyelids for a moment.

"Sound," he said.

At his command, the speakers he'd built sang to life, blasting out a compilation of twentieth-century construction and street noise. A trolley dinged, a circular saw whirred, there were regular hammers, and jackhammers, and something sloshing and plopping (which he imagined was cement being poured).

And then, not but three minutes into the sixty-minute sound loop, was the most glorious sound. It was his favorite three-point-one-second sound bite.

A twentieth-century man, with a thick, taffy-pulled accent unlike any other in his recorded library, said (as Jamal mouthed along), "Hey, I'm walkin' here!"

When the Revealers had uncovered and taken the schematics for his DNA from the Monument of Seven, they'd also liberated two hundred sound and video files containing human dialogue in three languages: English, Hindi, and Arabic. They'd used those to teach him to speak the dead tongues.

But this sound file was part of the six hundred and eighty-five *music* files they'd retrieved. No one else knew about the voice, and that made it more wonderful. He might have thought himself selfish, keeping a clip of the sacred tongue secreted away, only for his ears, but there were so few ears around. And his Kaeds seemed to take their exposure to ancient sounds as a burden, rather than a delight.

It wasn't that modification typically rendered everyone unable to hear. It was that it allowed them to choose whether or not the perception of any given sound was important enough to acknowledge and interpret. Ears and eardrums were delicate, unnecessarily problematic in the vacuum of space and areas of constant compression and decompression. Better to nip that evolutionary weakness in the bud and allow for implants to filter something like sound for one's brain.

And when noise and music can be *generated* for your mind instead of *imposed* on your mind, the result was a muted outside world and a vibrant inner life.

It was a wonderful concept, but for Jamal, it meant living in a world of silence. He had no implants to call up his own private music. Nothing to project art or design onto the walls for his eyes. The only sound that would ever reach him had to be filtered through a delicate bodily organ many felt vestigial.

He understood that was why the Kaeds hated their capacity for unfiltered hearing. It robbed them of a choice in experiences. If he screamed, they would hear it. If he cursed, they would hear it. If he blared some of the more vulgarly worded music and they entered his workshop, they would hear it.

Of course, they only ever entered his workshop at scheduled intervals, and it was the only place he'd installed his speakers, so, for the most part, they were safe from his noisy indulgences.

More clangs and a work whistle accompanied Jamal as he opened his eyes and strode over to his drafting table. The front portion of the gigantic work space was filled with desks, soldering benches, saw benches, and a handful of other woodworking and basic mechanical components. Farther back and to one side lay his clean rooms, with acid-etching stations, vacuum packaging, and atomic printing. Opposite the clean rooms lay an open floor space of one thousand meters by one thousand meters, on which he could piece together his larger inventions. Beyond that, taking up the majority of the space, was his "junkyard": a vast store of loose components, everything from gold leaf to simulated wood to diamond-encrusted titanium.

His workshop smelled of hot metal and organic dust. It gave him solace in a way that no other room in his moon-sized home could.

Removing the personal graviton cycler from his back, he set it on an empty desk and patted its hide. It had performed admirably for its old fool. Soon it would be ready to present to the Kaeds, and they would take it away, give it to a worthy Revealer to study and re-create.

His smile faltered slightly as he thought, as he often had during its construction, about what a useless thing it was to anyone but himself. Of course no one had ever invented a personalized graviton cycler before him—no one needed one. They'd only stolen a large graviton cycler from the Monument of Seven and retrofitted it to the megastructure for *him*. They would be perfectly fine in the microgravity environment of a hollow, ancient silo.

Only an original throwback such as himself would need an external device to do what most other sentient creatures could do with a mere thought.

His pat morphed into a rigid slap.

There was so much he created for his own accommodation.

A worming guilt slid its way through the marrow of his bones, but he squashed it with a justification.

Perhaps there were others like him out there, somewhere.

Not *Homo sapiens* like him, no—they were all extinct.

But maybe those whose gliding abilities had been taken from them by illness or injury. Those with similar disabilities would benefit, surely.

That was the Progentor's primary duty, after all. To help his followers, to aid in their pursuit of creation and construction.

He'd been taught his entire life—*all* of it—that his Communion with the Divine Realm of Thought was needed in order to shepherd Posts into their next technological revolution. His very existence was about bridging the gap between the capacity for creation in the universe and the Post's ability to force those creations into being.

All invention was special. There was no such thing as selfish or useless.

And yet . . .

The guilt surged once more, and he pushed it down again.

It wasn't really the personal cycler he was guilty about, after all.

Leaving the invention behind, he strode to his drafting table.

Papers littered the surface, huge rolls of it marked over again and again where he'd drawn and erased, honing his designs. Such things the Posts did on holographic screens invisible to his eyes, or in their own heads entirely. But *he* liked to feel the graphite on the solid surface, liked the sweeping of his arms and the minute changes in his muscles as he shifted from a light touch to a hard press. It was all part of the visceral act of creation.

Instead of taking up his chair, he knelt next to the desk leg. With a needle he kept pinned in his robes, he pried open the façade, revealing a secret compartment. Inside, wound tight, was a single scroll.

These were the plans for his greatest invention of all: a means of escape.

He had to leave, before his next de-growth. He had to live somewhere else, see somewhere else, do something else. Something he *chose*.

While the Kaeds were used to having a choice in the sounds they processed, Jamal was used to having a choice in *nothing*. His inventions, what he built and worked on, were his only playground. Every other aspect of his life was scripted, rigid. He didn't choose to be the Progentor, he just was. He didn't choose to commune with the Divine Realm of Thought, he just did.

He didn't choose to remain "pure"—the outside world was simply kept from him.

So he chose *this*: to run away.

The vessel was nearly complete. The larger portions were already constructed and lay near the back of his junkyard, disguised as failed experiments. All he needed to do was finish a bit of the steering, then assemble the vehicle, and he'd be set. He'd built an SD drive for it and everything.

If his calculations were correct, he could enter a travel SD directly from his workshop. Disappear right out from under the Kaeds' noses.

The door to his workshop suddenly began to unroll, its slithering noise barely perceptible over the honks and bangs of the recorded construction.

A hot fountain of surprise ran up Jamal's spine and burst through his body. With shaking hands, he replaced the schematics and the leg's panel. He shot to his feet as the shuffling clatter of the intruder's steps hurried toward him.

He was disturbed to see Kaed Roq and Kaed Yulep invading his sacred workshop without an invitation.

"Sound off," he commanded his speakers. The abrupt silence hurt his ears.

The white and gold of their coverings billowed around Roq as she floated. Kaed Yulep dragged his heavy body over the floor, the mechanical bits occasionally sticking out from beneath his robes.

"You are late for your Communion preparation," said Yulep.

"I am not late," Jamal said indignantly. "And you should not be in—"

"You are late," insisted Roq. "I met you in the hall three hours ago. Why have you not reemerged?"

No, that was impossible. His construction sounds had not yet made a full loop.

"No," he said lightly, shaking his head and grinning as though they were playing a joke. But when had the Kaeds ever played a joke? "No."

The two turned toward each other, clearly conversing about him mind-to-mind. He hated when they did that.

"Come then," came Roq's voice after a time. "You may be late, but we cannot risk your skipping Communion."

"Of course," he said with a bow, falling into step behind them while his mind whirled. *What is going on?*

Outside his workshop, strolling casually, as though merely passing, was Wes-Tu. His voice was always the softest, the smoothest, in Jamal's ears. Impressive, considering he was the youngest and newest sub-Kaed-Appoint. Normally his Kaeds and sub-Kaeds came to him mature, with many years behind them. Wes-Tu wasn't much more than a boy. He made a delicate greeting, as though surprised to see the others.

"Where are we rushing to?" he asked, automatically falling into step behind the Progentor.

"Communion," said Roq.

"Communion?" Wes-Tu wondered out loud. "But is that not—"

He was cut off when Yulep whirled. Once again silence fell all around. Jamal did not interject.

"Ah, I understand. Of course," Wes-Tu said after a moment, though he did not sound sure to Jamal's mind. "I have lost track of time and am derelict in my duties as well. Forgive me." He turned pointedly to Jamal, bowing low. "Forgive me," he said again, more strained.

Jamal was still at a loss. He did not know what needed forgiving.

· ·

Biological age: Eleven and one half
Location: Monument of Seven, *Slicer*

"Wes-Tu? Wes-Tu!" young Jamal called, looking for his friend, his guardian. The post-human was very old these days, old in a way Jamal would never be, and the sub-Kaed preferred longer and longer meditation hours. Jamal scoured the inside of his insectoid ship, and eventually found him in the receiving room—though, in truth, Jamal had not received anyone in ages. Wes-Tu had made much better use of the space these past years.

The room was small. Not cramped, but not a space meant to host large gatherings. The walls were much more elaborately decorated here than anywhere else on the ship, though many textured tapestries lined the halls and dangled from the ceilings. But the walls weren't simply painted, patterned, or hung with drapery. They were *encrusted*, covered in red enamel, loops of copper, nuggets of gold, and millions of raw garnets and rubies that were meant to be touched. Little floating twinkle lights danced near the ceiling, leaving the space dim, yet allowing everything to shimmer and sparkle.

It was a feast for the eyes and hands.

"Wes-Tu?"

"I am here, Progentor," Wes-Tu said, his voice in Jamal's ear still as smooth as ever.

Wes-Tu attempted to rise from his meditation pillows, shaking as he went, joints protesting.

"Stay," Jamal insisted kindly. "Please. Don't move if it hurts." He flopped down beside Wes-Tu, sinking knees-first into the plushness beside his sub-Kaed. "I wanted to ask you a question, because All Mother said I could, but I don't want to worry you, but also I really want to, and she said it might be a once-in-all-my-lifetimes event, and I—"

"Calm, please," the old Post pleaded. "Centered. Explain, then ask. What has happened?"

The sub-Kaed didn't get out these days. Even his ability to manipulate gravitons had grown weaker, unreliable.

"Didn't you hear All Seer's report?" Jamal asked.

"I can barely hear you now, Progentor, let alone anything that crackles through *Slicer's* speakers. Please, what is it?"

"The Sora-Gohan shell. It woke up."

"Are the Noumonians—? Has Icelandic—?"

Jamal shook his head. "She's still . . . sleeping. But I was with Igbo, Tulsi, and Salām this morning and they could all hear the shell talking. So I.C.C. thinks the hibernation is almost done."

"That's wonderful. It will be good to see the others again in their newly Revealed forms."

"Yep," Jamal said happily, rocking back and forth on his heels. "And All Mother is going to climb down in the shell's sinkhole and she said I can go too. Can I?"

Jamal might be forgetting things as he approached his corner, but one thing he hadn't forgotten was the way Wes-Tu slumped toward the shorter side of his asymmetrical form when he thought something wasn't a good idea.

"No Mother is going, too," Jamal added. "And I.C.C. will see everything. All Mother said it's important all four of us be there. To witness. She said I'd be upset later if she told me no now."

"But what if you forget where you are?" Wes-Tu asked, reaching out a cloth-covered limb to pat Jamal on the head. "What if your fever starts? What if you fall into the regenerative sleep too soon? Even if you go, you might . . ." Wes-Tu let his protests trail off.

"What?" Jamal asked, though his voice was gruff. He knew. He knew what Wes-Tu was going to say.

"Even if you witness a Reveal in the sinkhole, you might forget it anyway."

It was pure chance what he got to keep and what he was made to forget. His mind rewrote itself, breaking connections in order to sustain his life. Already, yesterday was gone. Bits and pieces of the last few years were gone.

This morning he'd awoken with IVs in his arms, the bare dregs of a clear liquid and a yellow liquid and a brown liquid coating the inside of the tubes. He'd asked Wes-Tu what it was all for, and he'd simply said, "They aid in the transition."

"Is it worth the risk? You witnessing?" Wes-Tu asked now. "You could fall, and break your neck, and no *Turritopsis dohrnii* modifications can save you then."

Small, sour trembles zipped through Jamal's lips and cheeks. He didn't want to cry, and he didn't want to pull rank. He just wanted Wes-Tu's blessing. "What if I don't go down? What if I stay on the surface, away from the sinkhole? I'll stay with the trees."

That eased his old friend; the Post straightened up. "Fine. Good," he said after a time. "Yes, you should be there for the Reveal, you're right. It's important. If it is a good Reveal, I am sure the universe will not let you forget." Wes-Tu forced himself upright, to his "feet." "And it is my duty to accompany you."

"No, no—" Jamal scrambled up beside him, putting out his hands in case the sub-Kaed fell. He gestured insistently for Wes-Tu to sit back down. "If it is dangerous for me in my state, it is more dangerous for you in yours. You told me before: there is duty, and then there is stupidity."

"If I can no longer serve, then I have lost my joy," Wes-Tu said, reaching out for Jamal again to place a reverent limb lightly against his forehead. A small touch. The slightest of connections.

Jamal felt a swell in his chest, one linked to the emotion of centuries he no longer recalled. "I don't want that," he said, his voice small as he moved into the crux of Wes-Tu's shroud, enfolding the frail, pointed body beneath in young arms. As he pressed his cheek to his friend's warmth, he could hear joints creaking, heart stuttering. Wes-Tu groaned involuntarily when the boy squeezed too tightly, and Jamal instantly let go again, afraid he'd hurt something.

"I'm sorry, did I—?"

Wes-Tu waved away his concern. "If you will go, then I will go too. Do not forget your duties in the excitement," he reminded Jamal. "Thinking, thanking, communing, constructing."

"Thinking, thanking, communing, constructing," Jamal repeated breathlessly. "I will not forget!"

. . . .

Biological Age: Seventy-Five

Location: Pentagonal Trapezohedron

CONTINUED, SAME DAY

The party wound its way through the corridors, the gravity changing direction several times. He walked along one bridge and was able to look "up" at another bridge he'd strode along the "underside" of only minutes before.

Their first stop was the medical bay. Jamal took off all his clothes, then eased into a chair while the doctor threaded an IV into his arm. They scanned his breathing and his blood pressure, making sure all was in order.

This time, though, the doctor put a cloudy-yellow liquid into his saline bag. He couldn't remember ever seeing the substance before.

"What's that?"

The doctor had no ears. Wouldn't matter if they did, as they did not speak his languages.

Kaed Yulep answered for them. "Don't you recall? A vitamin supplement. You're elderly now, have been for some time."

Jamal kept himself from snapping, *Yes, I know I'm old, thank you.*

But it was really the "don't you recall?" that bothered him most.

He was then hoisted onto a sacred platform and lay supine while the attendants took pots of smoldering weeds and placed them around him in a ceremonial circle.

They pushed him out of the medical bay, the IV stand rolling along beside him, perfectly smooth, never jostling.

His mind became hazy, relaxed. He felt on the edge of sleep, could almost touch his dreams.

He barely noticed when they entered the Communion Hall. A strange name for the place, seeing as how it was smaller than some of his clean rooms. It was carefully constructed, lead-lined and well padded, so that no one outside the room was at risk from the magnetics and radiation.

Jamal himself, at the eye of the storm, was equally well protected.

Electrodes were very carefully placed across his close-shaven skull. White insulating powder was sprinkled over his black skin. Lifting his hand slightly, he imagined it was snow. He'd never experienced snow, but he'd seen it in his language vids.

Then the hood was placed over his head, and the dimness of the megastructure became the utter darkness of the shroud.

He took a deep breath and counted backward from ten as everyone else left the room.

There was a jolt as the Communion Machine was activated and the SD bubble took hold. His muscles spasmed, protesting, his body screaming out *Don't! Don't take it, don't take it!*

But the machine never listened.

His thoughts were literally siphoned out of his skull, wrapped up in a protective skin, and sent way—away to another world.

Another place full of the same energy that was in his mind. Thought energy. Swirling knowledge, there for the receiving.

There was no texture in this place. No sensations. No sensory input of any kind.

Just a swelling of self.

Sometimes he did get an impression. Like he was many and not one. And once in a while there was an otherness. A separateness. Though he could not say what kind.

It was always difficult to recall his time in the communing, no matter his age.

When he awoke, he babbled. When he babbled, the attendants took note. It was gibberish to them, of course. But later he would listen to it, try to pull new ideas from it. And the Kaeds would reinterpret it for mind-to-mind consumption by all Revealers.

Now, back in his body and away from the sacred place, whispering into his microphone, he felt disconnected from his flesh, still outside himself. After a while, Wes-Tu came to lead him away to his rooms. He felt his sheets beneath him, his own bed.

"You did well," Wes-Tu told him. "Rest now. Sleep."

He woke up the next morning refreshed, ready to complete his duties for the day. Roq brought him a sweet, spongy cake for first-meal and apologized for her curtness before. She was always kind to him, mindful of his feelings when often the others were not. Once in a while she brought him art he wasn't supposed to see—wildly different creations, each, all made by Revealers in his honor.

"I meant no disrespect," she said when he'd finished the cake. "May the universe look upon my hastiness with shame."

Jamal realized that the calendar said this was a good day for openness. "No, no need for shame," he insisted. "And to deny one's feelings—of irritation, of dissatisfaction—is to ignore the knowledge they bring. I ask that you forgive yourself."

"Thank you, Progentor," she said with a bow. "I do wish . . ." she trailed off, her voice sad. She shook herself. "I wish you great progress today."

"Thank you."

In turn, he wished her peace as she left, then went and dressed himself in a sheer robe reserved for days of openness, one that barely obscured his nakedness beneath. Days such as these meant vulnerability, both physically and emotionally. But they also meant growth and compassion.

Perhaps it was a good day to forgive himself his feelings of guilt. Perhaps even a good day to reconsider his escape plan altogether.

Regardless, he would put his finishing touches on the personal cycler today and formally present the invention to his Kaeds.

But as he entered his workshop, he immediately noticed something was wrong. Not with the personal cycler—that sat exactly where he'd left it, his fingerprints from where he'd patted it the only smudges on its gleaming chrome hide. No, it was the assembly floor, across from his clean rooms, that was not as it had been.

Instead of empty, pristine and waiting, it was covered in parts. Not just any parts, but bits of his escape vessel, all smashed and dismantled, twisted, dented. Wires had been stripped, dials smashed. Even the cushions meant to cradle his frail form were slit open, their padded innards exploding outward.

Jamal had never experienced death before, but he knew a murder scene when he saw one.

His chest constricted, he fell to his knees, arms outstretched, palms helplessly lifted to the ceiling. He grasped at the air, at the universe.

How? How could this have happened?

Shame and regret and fear swung through his body like a pendulum, bashing against his organs, making him woozy.

There were only so many people on the megastructure, and only two who'd caught him unawares in this very room not twenty-four hours previous.

Quickly, he rushed from the scene of the crime, his robes catching around his legs as he took each heated step—his feet feeling heavier the closer he came to the Kaeds' offices. His skin broke out in a cold sweat, while his gums and throat burned with a newly ignited rage.

The offices lay at the end of a topsy-turvy bridge that spanned the entire distance of a porthole room, its surface coiling like a double helix. Its unique formation and location relative to the large graviton cycler that governed the megastructure's gravity meant it experienced a quirk of physics—a coil of excess gravitons naturally twisted around it. As he walked across, he spun, the floor suddenly becoming his ceiling and then vice versa, over and over. He hated this walkway—they told him he'd chosen this area to be their offices, but he didn't remember that. It had been so long ago, and he couldn't fathom why he'd insist they take up their days at the end of such a sickening commute.

Their door wound around and around itself like a nautilus shell, unspiraling and sliding away like a snake once it was touched.

"How *dare* you?" he shouted as soon as he'd stepped inside.

All nine Kaeds were afloat high above the floor, their robes knotted at the end so that they looked a bit like the manatees in that vid with the reed boats; docile old mermaids bobbing in the sea. The three sub-Kaeds sat on the floor, still as stones.

Together they were engaged in synchronized meditation, moving about one another in a formation closely resembling what they claimed the Monument of Seven looked like when it was original, whole.

His screaming immediately roused them, and several made unconscious sounds of protest.

"Who did it?" he demanded. "Get down here and tell me who did it!"

"Did what?" came Roq's halting voice.

"Destroyed a sacred invention. Who touched it? Who dare interrupt my engineering?" He described the scene in his workshop, doing his best to maintain an air of authority and not let his sadness—his sense of loss—get the better of him.

The group gathered round, still hovering.

"Progentor," Yulep said softly, "*you* did that."

Jamal let out a deep breath—he'd meant to use it to order the saboteur to admit their crime. "I—What?"

"Yesterday, in the late hours, you roused each of us from sleep, had us follow you to your workshop, and demanded we watch as you destroyed several components. We did not know the meaning, but we assumed you had done it as a result of the communing, had realized the design for—for *whatever it was*—was misguided."

"We thought it cleansing," Roq said, tone worried. "It was . . . unintentional?"

Before Jamal could answer, all the Kaeds suddenly turned toward Wes-Tu and descended upon him, wrapping him in shrouded arms, ushering him to a rear portion of the offices.

"Wes-Tu is overcome with grief," Roq explained. "Because now we are certain. Progentor—" she laid a cloaked hand on his arm "—you have been exhibiting signs of dementia lately. Outbursts, forgetfulness, missing time. If your body has reached such a state of decay, you know what that means. The process will begin soon."

He shook her off, took a step back, but said nothing aloud. Internally, though, he was awash in screams.

No. No no no no, I hate this part. I hate it. I'd rather die. I hate it!

"Please," he whimpered. But he didn't know what he was asking for. He didn't want to die, not really. But his next few years—perhaps even decades—would be hellish. He would lose much and remember little. Time would have no meaning, would rush the wrong direction.

"I don't want to be young again," he said, moisture brimming around his eyes. "I want to keep moving forward."

"I know," she said kindly. "We know. But we will be here for you, as always. When you are young again, things will be better. Remember how strong your eyes were? How steady your hands? How sure your heart?"

How sure my heart . . .

He hadn't wanted to run away back then.

When the others returned, sans Wes-Tu, they ushered Jamal to his bedroom. Here the doctor would visit him every day. Here he would lose all that he'd become, and hopefully regain it again. Something was always gone forever—every time, a little bit never came back.

It was the same in adolescence, though. Memories were made, then unmade just as quickly.

"Going backward is far more difficult than going forward," he told them, slipping into his bed without taking off his robes.

"That is why we're here," Roq said. All of the Kaeds took

hands, some of them with multiple sets. "We protect you. Love you. Will see you strong again."

The doctor came in with three syringes on a tray. One, he noticed, had the same foggy yellow liquid as before.

This was why he always stayed. Why he hadn't thought to build an escape vessel until now. These Posts cared for him, served him. He relied on them and owed them his presence, his vigilance.

I'll remember that when I'm young again, he thought. *I'll be ever grateful, and nothing will tempt me away.*

· ·

Biological Age: Eleven and a half
Location: Noumonian Plains

The human away team consisted of All Mother, All Father, No Mother, and Wes-Tu. And All Seer by extension. Two scouts, Nathair and Garden, who both had a parent in the cocoons, accompanied them as well.

The humans rode inside the rover, while the Noumonians opted to cling to the roof, allowing the rushing winds to tilt their wheels, to give their biological motors power. They would draw strength from those reserves on the climb down the sinkhole.

Jamal tried not to show how out of place he felt. No Mother drove the rover, while he, Wes-Tu, and All Mother occupied the cab. All Mother might *look* young sitting in her mech suit—barely a year if she was a day—but she held her face in a mature expression of somber contemplation. Her eyes were sharp, her mind focused and wise. When one spoke to All Mother, an old woman—not a baby—spoke back.

But *he* was truly young again. He knew his thinking was different now than it had been when he was grown. He knew a lot of the same things, general knowledge and such, but couldn't process it the same. Couldn't make the same connections he used to. His complexity of thought was still there, but the kinds of thoughts that occupied his mind were different. He did not take action with consideration of how it fit into the larger universe, he instead considered how his actions might look to the other Monument kids. He never used to be concerned with such things—with what others thought of him—but now it was a constant clatter in the back of his mind.

There were currently twelve Monument kids, fifty humans in all in the Monument to the Noumonians six hundred. After the effects of the Sora-Gohan were revealed, many of the Waterfall colony members came to live with them, and more of the tanks took their pilgrimage to the quarry to eat their fill and produce new offspring.

They'd encouraged the humans to do the same. They wanted all the families to grow, and All Mother agreed.

No Mother didn't like it. She said the Convoy Twelve team had never come to colonize, that it wasn't their place.

But the Noumonians took joy in new ones, always. No Mother hailed from an overpopulated planet, and they from an underpopulated one. As long as the resources were there, they wanted to share *Mira* with others.

Vanhi disappeared into her SD—going of her own volition—when Hope began to grow the first new babies. She hadn't returned for decades.

Now, she checked in on the cab every few minutes with clipped updates on their pacing and arrival time.

Jamal had visited the crystal trees only a handful of times before. Most recently with the other Monument kids, when All Mother had taken them all to leave small tributes and speak to the sleeping Noumonians, suspended high in their fractured cocoons. She said it was important for the kids to see how biology behaved differently in different beings. How if humans had been pulled apart like that, they would be dead.

But the Noumonians were not dead, she'd insisted.

Insisted.

But there was no way to know for certain. The phenomenon of the trees had never been recorded before, couldn't be verified as a reoccurring part of the Noumonian migration.

And leaving tributes at the base of the trunks felt an awful lot like leaving offerings at their ancestor tablets.

Now that the shell was sending signals again, maybe they'd find out for sure. Maybe the Noumonians would get put back together again and wake up.

Or maybe they wouldn't.

When they finally arrived at the forest, Jamal tried not to look overeager. Everyone else seemed grim—even the scouts—unwilling to pass judgment on whether or not this new change was positive or negative. They would remain skeptical, and emotionally detached if they could.

Jamal was just happy he got to tag along.

He remembered many of the cocooned Noumonians. Tranquility's playfulness, Tuba's talkativeness, Icelandic's stubbornness. But it was difficult these days for him to connect those memories to the trees. To realize the beings he'd known all those years ago were *up there.*

He stumbled out of the cab, tripping on his own feet, while Hope moved beside him, utterly graceful. Even Wes-Tu, with his old bones, having forsaken any kind of protection other than his usual shroud, moved with precision. Jamal was learning his body all over again, only to have to learn it once more in a few years. If puberty once was awkward, repeated puberty was a cosmic joke. Even if the universe had chosen him as its mouthpiece, that didn't mean it was above poking at his dignity.

As his boots settled on the stones, a sentence he'd memorized long ago played its way between his ears: *Don't go near the Blood Forest, or you might disturb the sleeping dryads.*

Jamal couldn't remember where or when he'd read it or heard it. Was it in this lifetime? In Convoy Twelve's records? Or was it from before, in the data stolen from the Monument long ago?

Regardless, the line played over and over in his head, its rhythm a singsong and the voice not his. It had a high, tinkling-bell sort of narration. But no one with a voice like that now lived among the Monument.

The trunks of the cocoon trees stretched up and up and up. The rushing winds of Noumenon did not sway them, the occasional acidic rains did not dissolve them, and violent hailstorms—with ice chunks the size of his fist—had failed to chip them.

But they weren't inert pillars. They weren't like the stone spires south of the plains. These trees had sap, and it surged through crystal-clear channels, painting the colorless trees bright blue.

Noumonian-blood blue.

Jamal trundled up to the nearest trunk, the pressure suit slightly too big, forcing him to kick out heavy steps like a toddler. It was his adult suit, and he refused to borrow anyone else's. Pressure suits were personal, lived-in things. He would not rob someone else of such a necessary safety item simply because his body decided to grow up and down like the jagged hills of Noumenon's landscape.

He placed both palms against the crystal, leaning his faceplate close and marveling at the flow of cells through the body of the trunk. Layers and layers of fluid channels, twisting through the entirety of the tree, down into the ground, and back up into the fractured Noumonian body high in its branches.

The forest of blue was disconcerting on Noumenon, where all of the minor-life's pigmentation leaned red. He remembered when the trees had first started to turn color. The *Mira* colony had left cleaning bots with cameras perched close—but not too close—to the cocoons, where they could be monitored for the duration.

At that distance, the forest had looked white. Frozen. But then color started to bleed through the branches—more literally than they realized—flowing down like paint poured over glass. Except the miles between the camera and the trees shifted the light, making it look tar black, like rot was taking over the sleeping Noumonians, dark as crude oil.

They were both baffled and relieved to find this sort of blood-sap streaming through instead.

The boy kneeled down, testing the seam where the crystal sprung from the ground. Were there roots? The fluids clearly went deep, disappearing down beneath the rocky surface. Did they flow all the way to the shell?

Years ago the *Mira* colony and Monument dwellers had constructed a sort of cart-and-pulley system to help them reach the bottom of the sinkhole. But the shell hadn't burrowed straight down. About a hundred yards in, the shaft took a right-angled turn, heading horizontally through the ground beneath the stand of crystal trees. The bedrock had collapsed behind the shell, blocking the tunnel, and they'd all been too afraid of disturbing the trees to attempt to dig in after the alien construct.

But now things had changed. Something was different. The shell was calling to the other Noumonians, alerting them to . . . something. What, they couldn't say.

"Jamal," No Mother called to him. He looked up to see her a few trunks over, gesturing for him to head to her side, to take her hand.

"Coming, No Mother."

"Vanhi," she corrected gently. "The Monument kids can call me that, but you . . ." *You used to call me Vanhi.*

"Vanhi," he agreed.

"It's time to look down the tunnel."

· ·

Biological Age: Seventy-Five

Chronological Age: Sixteen Thousand and Thirty-Three

Location: Pentagonal Trapezohedron

"The doctor says you have passed through to the light again," Wes-Tu told him. "How do you feel?"

"Better," Jamal said. "My head is clear. I feel like I'm thinking straight for the first time in years."

"You are," Wes-Tu assured him. "After all, a decade has gone by since you began your difficult journey to the end of life and in reverse again."

"Am I cleared for duty?" he asked. "Can I return to my workshop?"

"Yes," Wes-Tu said. "The doctor thinks you're ready."

"Fantastic." He jumped down from the exam table, noting how free his joints felt. He'd continue to regenerate cartilage for some time, regaining even more range of motion.

"Would you like me to go with you?" Wes-Tu offered. "Help make the room functional?"

"No, that's all right. I prefer to face it alone."

Ten years. He couldn't believe he hadn't been in his workshop in over ten years. Everything was covered in sheets of press-through one atom thick, to keep the dust off. He touched each with the tip of his finger, and they sprang into heavy rolls.

"S-sound?" he said tentatively, unsure what type of music he'd last listened to.

"Hey, I'm walkin' here!" the speakers shouted.

With a giddy laugh he made his way through to the back of the junkyard and worked his way forward. The clean rooms were pristine, the assembly floor spotless, and his desks were all neatly arranged.

Immediately, he began sifting through the papers there, curious as to what he'd been working on before the de-aging process had begun. Though the schematics were all dated, there were far fewer than he expected. Had his production really slowed so much in his old age?

He was sure he'd almost completed something right before the transition, but he couldn't remember what.

Stupid old man, he chided himself. *You have to do better next time. Leave yourself better records—you know where your mind goes.*

This time I'll do better.

He sat down at his drafting table and yanked open the drawers. As he flipped through the old leaflets, he shifted, crossing his legs and uncrossing them. One slippered foot caught on the rough edge of the desk table, snagging the delicate fabric.

Jamal grumbled to himself as he took off the slipper to examine the damage. The attendants would fix it right up, no real harm done, but he hated giving them extra work.

He slid from his seat to examine the leg. He certainly didn't want to be tearing holes in his shoes day in and day out. Probably just needed a bit of sanding or sealing.

As he ran his fingertips over the edge, looking for the offending sliver, his nail caught under a subtle lip. "What's this?" he whispered.

Pulling it back, he found the leg was hollow. A perfect little cubby—an easy hiding place with nothing inside.

What luck! he thought. *I'll have to save you for something special.*

The years passed, and Jamal grew younger. Sixty-three to fifty-three, to forty-three, to thirty-three.

Every few months, an interstellar tug, trailing pilgrims' ships, arrived at the megastructure's docking port.

The Revealer faith was expansive. A hundred billion people adhered to its fundamental concepts. And yet, only a select few could ever make the pilgrimage here, to his home.

Jamal did not meet with them all. The Kaeds would each pick one pilgrim—nine total—to "speak" with him in person, while all others would simply obtain an anointment in touch. And this touch would be given through a wall of press-through, with nothing more than his palm exposed to these outside influences.

His receiving room shared a wall with the arrival hall, and it contained the press-through portal that allowed him to offer each pilgrim a touch of his hand. All the visitors would pass by him on their way to a lavish, congratulatory meal. He was told there would be dancing, games, and revelry. All entertainment would be provided and created by the Revealers themselves. The creation of art was just another type of engineering, equally as important to their faith as mechanical, electrical, or chemical invention.

But Jamal would not participate in the excitement. It was important he be kept from as much contact with the outside world as possible. He served his followers best by remaining separate, getting lost in his own mind, protected from interfering thoughts that the universe had already siphoned through others.

It was a part of his existence that he'd come to question more and more these last few years. If the pursuit of knowledge and creation were his highest calling, shouldn't he be exposed to as many new ideas as possible? Weren't the scientific concepts in his videos so outdated as to be useless? The Kaeds gave him additional lessons, of course, but those had largely pertained to the advances in his direct line of sight.

They had to explain the true nature of what used to be called the subdimensions, because without that knowledge he could not understand the communing. They had to tell him about the advances in programmable materials and in genetic modification, lest he not understand something as simple as a door, or his own de-aging.

But there was so much more they left out. And more ideas led to even more ideas—that was the point. So why should he be kept "pure"? Surely the fundamentals of the universe would be easier to decipher if he were given every available tool.

From portal two he could see the space dock, where the pilgrims' ships alighted. There were so many. Dozens of craft. Which had to mean hundreds of pilgrims. And still only a tiny fraction of the billions of Revealers in the galaxy.

He took out paper and lead and sketched what he could, allowing this foreign info to delight his mind. So many ships, and so many pilgrims aboard each.

So many people who'd come to see him.

So many people who'd be disappointed when they could not.

He sighed.

The whole system was . . . unfair.

After the anointment of touch—in which he'd felt just as blessed to make contact with people from the outside as they were to make contact with him—Yulep came to deliver his food while the banquet commenced.

"I want to see them all," he said suddenly, between bites of brown rice, surprising even himself.

"All?" he asked lightly, not taking his meaning.

"All the pilgrims. Let me meet with all of them."

He could not see Yulep's eyes, but somehow could sense him narrowing his gaze. "This is not how it is done."

"But why not? I'm the Progentor, and I say I shall meet with them all."

"The choosing is important," he said. "A Kaed's judgment is important, or do you think us unnecessary?"

He'd personally offended Yulep. "That's not what I . . . They have all sacrificed to come here."

"We have sacrificed to serve you, to serve the Revealers. *We* choose."

And with that, he spun and left, stomping out the door.

Sometimes Jamal felt like the Progentor, and sometimes he felt like a puppet. Now he felt like an insensitive fool.

The high of divine inspiration seeped out of him, and he slumped against his pillows.

He received his nine pilgrims, and no more. Each of them was given a shroud before entering, so that he could see no more of them than he saw of his attendants or Kaeds.

Many of them came from the megastructure field far across the galaxy—his Ship Yard. He learned that the majority of the devices were well on their way to completion, but there was still one the workers could not crack. He did his best to provide practical engineering advice, but suspected the Kaeds never quite interpreted him correctly. Either that, or they were also providing guidance of their own. Each silent interpretation lasted far too long for beings whose thoughts ran so fast.

When Wes-Tu came in with the final pilgrim, Jamal asked again to see everyone. He could tell Wes-Tu wrestled with himself, unsure of whether to keep tradition or defer to the Progentor.

When Wes-Tu left, he did not come back. Jamal did not see the Post again for an entire week's time.

Something was amiss with sub-Kaed Wes-Tu. A crisis of faith? A weariness of servitude?

Jamal would find out and help in any way he could.

Biological Age: Eleven and a half

Location: Noumonian Plains, Crystal Cocoons

The six of them bent over the edge of the sinkhole, staring down into the darkness, wondering if anything had changed below. Garden and Nathair both wore translators and comms units, and the small flower-like protuberances in their radio-sensing triangulation tilted this way and that.

A strange kind of vertigo, unlike any Jamal had ever experienced before, washed over him. It wasn't that he was dizzy, it was as though his mind were trying to overlay a different picture onto the cavern before him. For a moment, he thought he saw stars, and he had the strangest urge to jump, his body assuring him he would float.

Only Wes-Tu's presence at his side kept him from tumbling over.

"Signal is not words," Nathair said. "But not strong like the Call."

"Not demanding," Garden agreed.

"And yet we must see," said Nathair. "We must see."

With tool kits clutched in the prehensile appendages sprouting from their necks, they began their descent.

Vanhi and Hope pulled up the cart, its primitive pulley-and-rails crude, but effective. The carriage was barely big enough for the two of them, even when Hope thinned out the bulk of her mech, raising up tall to control the pulley system.

"You keep an eye on the trees," Hope told Jamal. "You tell us if there are any changes."

Jamal had gone to his knees at the rim of the sinkhole, both to steady himself—clamping down on the urge to jump—and to watch the two scouts disappear into the depths. Wes-Tu had one gentle, yet insistent, limb on the back of the boy's pressure suit, ready to yank him away if the Progentor took a tumble. "Got it," Jamal said, pursing his lips, trying to match the adults for seriousness.

Just as he was about to rise, a deep-red beam of light flooded the sinkhole, blasting skyward. Instinctually, Jamal closed his eyes.

The others shouted.

The comms became a garbled mess of cries.

Jamal pushed himself away from the edge, terrified now of pitching forward. Wes-Tu's grip was firm, guiding him backward.

More yelling. Vanhi and Hope shouting frantic demands at each other.

I.C.C.'s voice rang out in their helmets. "I am detecting photonic activity in every major sinkhole within my preview," it said.

"*Photonic activity,*" Vanhi gasped, incredulous.

Jamal blinked repeatedly, expecting his vision to be whited out or spotted through with phantom color splotches. But his sight was clear.

So clear that when he looked up he could make out pillars of light all across the horizon, some thin, some wide, some strong, some faint. Great, strong beams erupting toward the sky, steady and unwavering.

Jamal's heart beat wildly, his initial excitement flipping itself inside out to become anxiety. Because even before I.C.C. spoke again, he knew: this had never happened before.

"I have no record of previous light displays," it said. "I am missing a millennium of data, but given the Noumonian reaction here on *Mira*, I believe it is safe to assume this is not a precedented occurrence."

"What does it mean?" Jamal gasped out.

"That, at the very least, our hypothesis about Noumonian sinkhole formation is correct," the AI said flatly. "The majority were created by the Sora-Gohan shells."

"But what are the shells *doing*?" Jamal's voice cracked, became a squeak.

"That's what we're here to find out," Vanhi told him, her voice still wavering, but more calm. She had to be working overtime to suppress her sense of anticipation, to keep herself from jumping. "And, hey . . ."

He could hear his own breath, heavy over the comms.

"I'm scared, too," she said.

That made him feel a little better. A little.

I was just startled, that's all, he told himself, trying to calm down. *It's okay. It's weird, it's different, but everybody knows what they're doing.*

Except for me.

Maybe Wes-Tu had been right. Maybe he shouldn't have come out here. Maybe he was just in the way and would forget it all in the end.

Shaking the sand from his suit, he stood up and looked to the trees. The glow of the red light-pillar fought with the blue of the sap, turning it dark and tarry once more. But, as far as he could tell, the light was just light. Maybe it was meant to illuminate the tunnels without blinding any climbers, and that's why he didn't have spots in his eyes. They used to use red-shifted light for emergencies on submarines and stuff because it didn't interrupt human vision. And he knew the Noumonians and humans shared a similar visible spectrum.

"Any change?" Hope asked of the scouts, who were already halfway down the tunnel.

"No change but light," Garden said.

"All right, then we're headed down."

The pulley system's rhythmic *screech . . . screech . . . screech* pierced through Jamal's helmet as Hope worked, carefully sliding the rope hand over hand, controlling their descent.

"Come away," Wes-Tu said. "Come away from the edge."

Jamal was glad for the direction. He didn't like the light. Didn't like the depth or the darkness of the sinkhole, made no brighter, truly, by the red beam. It was a light with a deepness to it to match the cave, as though it were its own tunnel, superimposed on the other—just like his starry vision of minutes before. The smooth stone walls of the hole still looked dark despite being illuminated, despite the shining. Sunlight was pure and warm, convoy light was measured and specific. This light held secrets, multitudes of them.

As Jamal began to walk away, back into the stand of trees, he realized Wes-Tu wasn't following. The Post was bent over, something other than breath wheezing through him.

"W-Wes—?"

The sub-Kaed gestured for him to stay back. "I'll be fine in a moment."

"I should take you back to the rover."

"No, I must stay with you."

"You are with me. You can see me from inside. I'll stay away from the sinkhole. I'll just watch the trees, like All M— Like Hope said."

"I made a promise, a vow—"

"And you are released from it when you are sick," Jamal reminded him. "Injury, illness—you are not supposed to stay by me if it hurts your health."

"That is when there are others. *Other Revealers . . .*" He spoke the last two words sharply, piercing an argument they'd had many times since leaving the Pentagonal Trapezohedron.

Jamal did not proselytize. Did not speak of his religion unless others asked.

His inability to preach was the lesser of two mysteries— before encountering Convoy Twelve he'd never spoken to anyone who *wasn't* a Revealer. There was no need to share his religion because it had already been shared. Everyone he knew understood the deeper layers of the universe, saw that all knowledge already existed, waiting for someone to uncover it, to Reveal it to their fellow sentients.

And even here, among the *Mira* colony, he had not observed a dearth of universal reverence. None of the beings around him were without a sense of wonder, without an admiration for science, understanding, art, communion. There were all sorts of expressions of spirituality, and he'd never felt it was his duty to impugn another's practices, observances, or lack thereof.

But beyond preaching, he no longer invented—not in the way he was supposed to. Creating still happened, but he took to making simple things. Ornate piles of rocks. Intricate, but pointless Rube Goldberg machines. Even before Houdini passed away, he had been hands-off in the Earthling's workshop, preferring to watch them tinker instead of fiddling with the machinery himself.

Whenever he'd attempted to create something more profound it felt soured, and redundant. Like he wasn't engineering at all so much as reconstructing. The forms felt too familiar in his hands. Perhaps he should have seen it as the permanence of the knowledge confirmed through touch, but instead it was a reminder that he forgot things. That maybe he'd already invented whatever it was and was thus insulting the universe with his pride.

Wes-Tu had always encouraged him to try harder on both counts.

Stubbornly, Jamal now stomped up to Wes-Tu and insisted the Post lean on him. "I'm taking you to the rover."

Wes-Tu acquiesced too easily, as though grateful he no longer had to keep up the pretense of protest. He put more weight on Jamal than Jamal was expecting, which worried the Progentor.

Together, they stumbled back to the vehicle.

"Look, you'll be able to see me," Jamal said, after lowering Wes-Tu into the bucket of a shuttle seat. He pointed through a porthole at the copse. "And I can hear you through the comms. Rest. I'll be okay. Do you need anything?"

"Water," Wes-Tu gasped.

Jamal pulled a reserve canteen from the supply cubby in the floor, unscrewing the top before handing it over. Wes-Tu shifted, pulling back a portion of his shroud before Jamal had a chance to look away, revealing a long, flexible proboscis not unlike a cross between an elephant's trunk and a butterfly's tongue. It emanated from beneath an angled limb, rather than his face.

Jamal twirled to give the Post his dignity. An acidic edge of fear crept into his concern. His friend was old, frail, tired. But he'd never been so ill as to uncover himself before Jamal. "Maybe I should stay instead," Jamal suggested. "The trees aren't going anywhere."

Wes-Tu surprised him by giving him a quick no. "If you'd stayed on *Mira*, Vanhi and Hope would have recruited another. They need someone to observe any changes happening to the Noumonians. The commitment is made."

When he heard cloth rustle again, Jamal chanced a glance at his friend. Wes-Tu had repositioned his shroud once more. "Will you be okay?" he asked.

"I will watch you, and I will be still until you return."

That wasn't an answer.

What would adult-Jamal have done? Young-Jamal still wanted to go explore among the trees, be a part of the away mission, but he knew not to ignore his gut. Something was very wrong. "You call me right away if you feel worse," he said, deciding it was not his place to demand things of Wes-Tu. Maybe as an adult he would have ordered him back to *Hippocrates*, but Wes-Tu's insistence gave him pause.

"I will call you," Wes-Tu agreed.

Unsatisfied, but unsure what else to do—what other kind of promises to force his friend to make—Jamal exited the rover once more. He glanced back before the hatch closed, and Wes-Tu gave him a gentle wave.

He tromped back in among the trees, touching each trunk and leaning back to look up as far as he was able. He checked in with the others in the sinkhole, and they still hadn't reached the bottom.

Nothing was different. Other than the light, nothing had changed. And now he could think of nothing but his concern for Wes-Tu.

He picked a tree near the outskirts of the stand, one bearing a turret named Holzschnitt in its branches. There were still half a dozen crystal formations between him and the edge of the cocoon field, but he had a clear view out of the trees. Thumping his back against the trunk, he slid down to sit, eyes fixed on the rover.

An old, sad song—about being safe and sound—tickled the back of his mind. The words promised everything would be all right while hinting at a world that was collapsing. The lyrics were reassuring, but that was only one layer of the song. The singer insisted everything was fine, but everything *wasn't* fine.

"Wes-Tu?"

"Yes, Jamal?"

"Just checking."

"I'm supposed to fuss over you, not the other way around."

Jamal was quiet for another moment, listening to the wind blow up against his helmet, trying to forget the song. "You would tell me the truth, wouldn't you?" he asked eventually. "If everything wasn't okay?"

"Jamal—"

"I know you like to hide things from me, but I don't need protecting from—"

"Jamal . . ."

Plop.

Jamal froze. Something heavy had landed on his shoulder, was now *stuck* to his shoulder. It was thick, and amorphous. Cringing, he turned to look, wondering if a sky-jelly had swooped down and was now trying to dissolve his suit—to absorb him through osmosis.

Sky-jellies were harmless, but they did leave an awful slime slick behind.

But the thing on his shoulder was not the bright red of a floating multicellular colony. It was a glob of dark purple-brown with veins of sickly green. The color and texture of sludge, of refuse. Of rot deep in the compost tanks right before it was recycled.

In the distance he heard another *plop*. Then another. *Plop, plop, plop,* like splashes in a puddle.

Then at his feet, another *plop,* another mass fell, making him jump.

He looked up, then scrambled away from the tree as fast as he could.

The sap had gone that same purple brown in some places, while in others the green stood out bright and grotesque. And above . . . the branches . . . .

Plop, plop, plop. The sound came faster now, from all around. Other trunks in the stand were turning the same colors.

And the branches above were *dissolving.*

And the Noumonians? The Noumonians within?

Revulsion overtook Jamal, and he pushed haphazardly at the clump on his shoulder, trying to scrape it off, to get it away. He only succeeded in spreading it over his gloves, the substance pulling thick and sticky between his fingers.

"The trees!" he shouted, staring at his hands, trying to decide if the material ensconcing them was a reconstituted portion of Holzschnitt's body. "The-the *trees!*" His voice cracked in panic, and he couldn't explain.

And then, suddenly, all the trees were running deep black, and they liquefied around him, splashing. An awful, awful torrent of unnatural rain.

Horrified, he ran, slipping on the substance, his boots unable to grip the stone through the filth. Shouts raged at him over the comms, overlapping voices. He could not distinguish the words, he could not form his own words.

Before him, a huge, heavy sack of goo landed—the size of a boulder. Its surface rippled as it stuck fast to the ground, and he dodged it without looking back. If it had fallen on him, he would have been trapped beneath.

He tried to wipe his boots and his hands on the ground as he came out from where the cocoons were disintegrating, tears blurring his vision. He didn't know what was happening, didn't know how to explain what was going on around him. He just wanted to be clean again, to get whatever it was off him.

"Wes-Tu," he cried out, feeling more like a child than ever, just needing someone to hug him, to envelop him in their arms and tell him everything would be all right.

The song came back to him, and suddenly he wanted the pretty lie. If the world was collapsing, maybe it was okay to say it wasn't.

He sprinted hard for the rover, mashing the external controls, hopping impatiently as the hatch opened.

He realized at the last minute that he couldn't go aboard. Not like this. Especially with Wes-Tu so ill and without a suit.

Instead, he curled up against the rover's large, rugged front wheel and cried.

He didn't even realize that Wes-Tu had not answered.

"Roq has left the order," Kaed Yulep informed him.

Jamal had just left his workshop, on his way to the midday meal, and had abruptly run into Yulep in the hall. "How can that be?" he asked. "I had an appointment with her this afternoon."

Yulep did not counter him, simply bowed. "She will be replaced with a new Kaed-Appoint in thirty-days' time."

As the Kaed turned to leave, Jamal stopped him. Something didn't feel right. She wouldn't have up and left the order without informing him first. She'd been here decades before his de-aging began again, had been here through his entire reversal. She'd given her whole life in service, why would she leave—?

Oh. *Oh.*

"She's dead, isn't she?"

"She has left the order," Yulep said again.

This was part of Jamal's "purity": his emotional stability. The Kaeds shielded him from all hardship. "I might be a teenager again, nearly a child, but you don't have to keep this from me. I want to see her body." *I need to say goodbye. To say thank you.*

"She has *left* the order," Yulep repeated, more firmly.

"She loved the Revealers, she would have given every last breath to us, and so I demand to see her body!"

He should have better prepared himself for this—to lose her. If he'd paid more attention, he'd have realized how old she was getting.

But he tended to think of his Kaeds as ever-lasting.

That was the whole point of *him*, of his modification—to outlive them. While the Kaeds were inducted, served, and died, *he* was the constant. The glue that kept the Revealers together, maintained a steady control despite light-years of distance between subsects.

Yulep tried to leave again, but Jamal fisted his shroud. "Please. *Please* let me see her."

"You need not distract yourself. Emotional instability interferes with the communing. Do not be upset. She has simply *left the order.*" He tried to leave again, tugging at Jamal's grasp, trying to slip the fabric from his Progentor's fingers.

"Is it so terrible that I should grieve for someone I cared for? Who cared for me? Should I not grieve you, too, when you are gone, *old man?*" Jamal shouted. "If you tell me she left *one more time*, I shall scream at the top of my lungs. Now, *show me her body!*" He'd never been allowed to see a body before, he wasn't sure why he thought that would change now.

Yulep took a twisting step, faltered. A large rip tore straight up his shroud, revealing a large swath of the mechanics-and-hide beneath.

Jamal immediately looked away, was ashamed. "I'm sorry," he said, his throat thick. "I'm sorry, I . . . I never get to say goodbye. I never get to *choose.*"

As Yulep gathered his clothing about him, Jamal turned and fled. His chest constricted, and each pump of his heart felt like it was tied to his tear ducts instead of his veins. Water blurred his vision.

He ran. Nowhere in particular, just far. As far as he could, knowing if he ran far enough he'd simply end up right back where he started, because that was his fate.

He ran for an hour, only stopping when he nearly ran straight into portal nine. He teetered on the edge before taking a lifesaving leap backward. He might be able to avoid natural death through de-aging, but his flesh was as fragile as any ancient human's. There were many ways he could still die, and falling from a great height was one of them.

Once he'd steadied himself, he peered over the edge at the stars. For half a moment, he had the *urge* to jump. A Post's modification would save them; they could all manipulate gravitons and fly. But without his personal cycler, he would end up a sloppy streak on the glucose glass.

Maybe they always shielded him from a Kaed's death because they didn't want him poking too closely at the concept. If he never had to face their mortality, he'd never have to face his. Never have to think about how he *could* end it, if he wanted to.

But he didn't. He might cycle over and over, and much of his life was unfair, but he didn't want to die. There was far worse suffering in the universe than his.

But couldn't he do more? Couldn't he leave and try to amend some of that suffering? Shouldn't his followers receive the full benefit of his existence? If they needed him to live over and over again, why shouldn't he live in their worlds?

"Progentor?" came Wes-Tu's soft voice.

He turned to see the tall Post gliding toward him, concern radiating from his form.

"Roq is dead," Jamal said when the Sub-Kaed was by his side. "I know it, please don't . . . I want to see her."

"You cannot," Wes-Tu said, and for a moment Jamal feared an echoing of Yulep's lie. "Her body has been incinerated."

"So soon?"

"It is often immediate," he said.

"Was she . . . given a Revealer ceremony?" *I don't even know the death rites of my own clergy*, he realized.

"We saw her body away, yes. She shall be recycled, her name etched outside."

Jamal perked. "Outside? Outside where?"

"Every Kaed's name is etched on the hide of this structure, in symbols many, many stories tall. You did not know?"

Jamal's grief bubbled to the surface and spilled out, like a pot of water boiling over. "*No*," he said, his voice an undignified yowl. "I know *nothing*—of life, of death, of anything beyond my rituals and my construction. How can I be the Progentor of the Revealers when my knowledge is so limited? My world so small? I am not what a Progentor should be. I am *nothing*."

His tears fell in earnest, took his sight from him completely. He didn't see the hug coming, and jolted when Wes-Tu's body pressed into his.

"This grief is a gift," Wes-Tu said. "Do not let the others take it from you."

I have to get away, Jamal realized. *Before I pass through puberty again and become a child, I need to leave. It is the only way I can truly serve the Revealers. I must learn all I've been sheltered from.*

He knew his time was short. Passing through puberty one way, then undergoing a reversal, led to a disjointed memory in much the way reversing through the end of life did.

He hugged Wes-Tu in return, feeling every strange joint of his six limbs, every roll of his torso and the sharp edges of his legs. "I must go to my workshop," he said, voice still shaky with emotion. "I have much work, and so little time."

I have to build myself an escape pod.

* * *

Biological Age: Fourteen
Chronological Age: Sixteen Thousand and Ninety-Four
Location: Pentagonal Trapezohedron

He was almost finished. So close. Soooooo so close.

Jamal's workshop was filled with deafening music, something labeled "Rager" in the files. It was so loud he knew it would keep the Kaeds away—the bass beat reverberated in the very bones of the megastructure.

Scrolls and scrolls of paper were spread across the assembly floor. His notes would be clear this time—perfect. He would not forget to write down a single detail.

Once he lost the last of his adolescent hormones, reverting to prepubescent, all the memories he'd created over the last five to seven years would be subject to possible erasure. As his body desperately reversed, growing anew, much of this "childhood" would be lost.

He bobbed his head to the music while he lay on his stomach, legs akimbo, little hands (becoming pudgier by the day) scribbling as fast as they could.

He was so consumed in the finalization of his escape plans that he didn't realize he wasn't alone until a long shadow loomed over him.

"What is this?" Wes-Tu demanded. His voice was strained over the music. "I've never seen you work like this before."

"You've never seen me at fourteen before," he said, raising his voice, hoping Wes-Tu would get the hint and go away. If he acted normal, like this was perfectly usual inventing stuff, maybe the sub-Kaed wouldn't notice . . .

"Jamal, are these plans for a ship?"

"Yeah, I thought I could improve the tugs for the pilgrims."

"What?"

"I said, I thought I could improve the tugs for the—!"

"*What?*"

"Sound off!" Jamal's ears immediately began to ring. "I'm trying to improve the pilgrims' tugs."

"These schematics indicate there would only be room for one passenger in the vessel."

Damnit, why couldn't he leave well enough alone?

"Two, if we squish," he said.

"I don't understand."

Jamal leapt to his feet, doing his best not to get tangled in his robes—they were too long these days, but since his growth cycle would begin again soon, he hadn't asked the attendants to hem them. "Instead of having the pilgrims come to me . . . I'm going to them."

Wes-Tu showed no overt expression of surprise. "Jamal, you know that's impossible."

"Is it?" he demanded, incredulous. "I'm the Progentor, the leader of the Revealers. The executioner of the will of the universe. If I say I need to go to my people, I *will* go to my people."

"You serve them best here, with us. Here you are safe. You are in the most well-guarded system in the galaxy. No one can harm you, use you, manipulate you—" He stopped abruptly, as though regretting that ugly word, *manipulate.*

"What about my ability to choose? I didn't ask for any of this, for the Revealers to retrieve my DNA schematics from the Monument of Seven, to be resurrected, to be modified *or* kept pure. I didn't ask to be Progentor. What if . . . what if I don't even want to *be* Progentor?"

Wes-Tu gasped, wheeling backward. "You can be nothing else. It is why you are alive."

"That," Jamal said thickly, "is what, in the twenty-first century, they called *bullshit.*" The curse fell with none of its intended impact—expletives lay beyond sub-Kaed Wes-Tu's fluency. He tried another tack.

"What if my true purpose lies beyond this place, but I'll never know because I never *leave*? What if I can give people more by leaving my workshop? By learning from *them*? What if I'm not doing the greatest good I can, for myself or anyone else? What is the point of me living over and over this way? Why shouldn't I just up and die!"

Wes-Tu extended his limbs, laying his covered hands along both of Jamal's arms. "Do you think any of the great leaders, martyrs, or saints of other major faiths throughout history had any choice in the matter? Any say in what was done in their name long after they died? This way, no one can twist your writings or your words. No one can tell us what you really mean other than you. No one can commit genocide in your name, ruin lives in your name, because you would denounce them outright. Is that not better than being a dead idol? Is this not better for you, for the Revealers, to have their Progentor present, ever steady? Do you feel no thrust of purpose, of obligation, to the people who spent centuries trying to rally all the Revealer cults together? Who finally found a unifying force in *you*?

"Is this not a greater good? You may bemoan your lack of choice, you may feel trapped. But you are doing the most you can for people. Is unity not worth perusing and providing?"

"I know nothing of the outside," Jamal said darkly, shrugging Wes-Tu's hands away. "I have little proof such unity exists, let alone any idea of whether or not atrocities are being committed in my name."

Wes-Tu lost some of his height, bending sideways as though suddenly wounded. "Do you . . . do you think so little of us? Of me?"

Jamal backed away, stepping on his papers, creasing them. "What happened to my notes from when I was old?" he demanded. "I have always been good at keeping records, at any age. Where did they go?"

Wes-Tu paused, as though hesitant to say what he must. When he spoke again, it was with the monotone of rote memorization. "When you are elderly, you slow down, as ancient humans were prone to—"

"No!" Jamal shouted, throwing his hands over his ears, though it did nothing to block out Wes-Tu's voice. He reached under his robe, pulling a scrap of paper free of his undergarments. "I found this in the incinerator room. I went there after Roq died, to pay my respects, and I found this." The edges were uneven, torn. Bits had clearly been burned away.

"It contains part of a plan for building a personal graviton cycler. I *thought* I invented this twenty years ago. But those notes are still whole, I still have all of them. This has to be much older. How many times have I 'invented' the same thing again and again? How often have the Kaeds done away with my plans, so that later the inventions would feel like divine inspiration, so that I would spout gibberish to our followers? How long have you all been using my modification against me?"

"Not against you, never *against* you," Wes-Tu insisted. "I love you. We all do. We truly wish for the enlightenment of creation, we wish for stability and prosperity, for everyone."

"And you truly believe that the best way to achieve that is to lock me away? To dole me out in teaspoons to the few pilgrims the Kaeds choose? How are they selected? Are they the most mannered, the most devout? Or those with the simplest questions? Those who do not prod at our teachings, when prodding at our teachings and questioning our discoveries is a very *tenet* of our faith?

"You speak of old religions, but do you know what brought them down? Hypocrisy. When leaders care more about their power than their people, more about their sway than their faith, it pushes the devoted away. As it should. Keeping me here, boxed in, lying to me about my creations, is the basest of hypocrisy. The largest betrayal of the fundamentals of the Revealers as I—the *Progentor*—could imagine. So, I ask you again: How can I be sure atrocities—if not other hypocrisies—aren't being committed in my name?"

Wes-Tu was shaking, and Jamal could not tell if it was out of anger or something else. From somewhere beneath the shroud, possibly in a mechanical compartment in his body, Wes-Tu produced a cloth and a bottle.

Jamal backed away.

Wes-Tu fell to his knees.

"The Kaeds said you throw this fit twice a lifetime," he

confessed sadly. "I asked that they never make me do this, but they said I was the only one who could get close enough this time. I don't want to. Please know that I don't want to."

Jamal recognized the label on the bottle. He took another step back, crumpling his papers underfoot.

"This won't hurt you," Wes-Tu said. "But it will make it difficult for your short-term memory to transition into long. They want you to forget this. To forget the next few days. Your modification takes much from you, but they erase more, what they say they must. Your ship—they say you can never be allowed to build it."

Jamal's blood surged, his fingers trembled. He knew it. He *knew* it. Every expletive he'd ever gleaned out of the records buzzed through his brain like hornets. And now, with his head a stinging cloud, he felt like his body was on a precipice, looking into a void. Would Wes-Tu reach out and save him, or deliver the fatal push? "And you?" he asked, his mouth gone dry and tacky. "What do you say?"

With a great, unnerving roar, Wes-Tu brought the bottle high above his head before dashing it on the decking.

Jamal bunched his robes, pulling them over his nose and mouth. His eyes stung as the chemical wafted into the air. He stumbled back farther, unsure which answer this was.

Unbothered by the fumes, Wes-Tu bent his head. "I made a vow," the sub-Kaed said shakily, thick emotion clearly coursing through him. "To you and the Revealers. Not the Kaeds. If it is your wish to leave, I must respect it as the will of the universe. There is something you must Reveal, out there, and I will not keep you from it."

Hesitant, unsure if it was a trick, Jamal crouched to retrieve his papers, never taking his eyes off Wes-Tu. "Good," he said roughly, ears ringing with hot irritation now rather than sudden silence. "Good. Then we must hurry. I don't have much time before—"

"Not now," Wes-Tu bit out. "That's *why* you can't go now. If you continue on like I never visited, the Kaeds will know I have failed and send another. And even if they don't, and you do not finish construction before you turn your corner, they will destroy your ship. And if you do finish, and we escape, and then you turn your corner . . ." He gestured at the schematics. "I do not see the medical facilities you would need."

Wes-Tu rose from the floor, caring not for the shards of glass and the chemical splatter on his shroud. "You must let it go for this lifetime."

The hornets dispersed. A block of frigid hopelessness formed in their place. "Then it will be decades before I can . . . I'll have to stay for . . ." It would give the Kaeds so many more opportunities to undermine him. "No. *No.*"

"Progentor, you know I am right," Wes-Tu said. "Your escape will take careful planning. Haste will only ensure mistakes are made. I am with you, but we must do this *right*." He held out one limb. "Give the schematics to me. I will keep them safe."

Jamal retreated still farther into his workshop. Uncertainty and distrust made him grip the papers all the tighter. "No. I will keep them. I have a place I can hide things—"

"The compartment in your desk's leg?" Wes-Tu asked, and Jamal's last scrap of hope evaporated. "They have known about that for several lifetimes. You must realize how childish a concealment it is."

Slowly, Wes-Tu extended another limb, creating a cradle between his arms in which Jamal could lay his creation. "They will expect me to take them. They will expect me to burn them. I will not. I will make copies, in case they do not trust me and decide to burn them themselves. I can do this for you, Jamal, but *you* must trust me. Trust that the universe sent me to you."

Jamal wasn't sure he trusted the universe anymore, let alone anyone in it.

As Wes-Tu left the Progentor in his workshop, sheaves of paper pressed tightly into the boniness of his chest, he wept. He would help Jamal, as promised. But he would not be able to tell him of this meeting. Once he began to grow up again, the Kaeds would reeducate him quickly. If Wes-Tu attempted to tell this tale, even with the schematics for evidence, the boy would likely turn him over to the likes of Kaed Yulep, and Wes-Tu would be banished from the order.

Glancing at the schematics, he pondered where to put them, and how to return them when the time came.

He would have to make his own plan, to meditate more often for the sake of divine understanding. He had to trust that the universe would show him the way, and that it would not allow him to inadvertently betray the most beloved of the Revealers.

. . . .

Biological Age: Eleven and a half

Location: Noumonian Plains

All Mother and No Mother found Jamal and cleaned him up. They zipped him inside a deCON bag for transport in the rover and ran him through the showers and antibio sprays when they returned to the ships. The crystal trees had been nothing more than a putrid swamp of liquid and unidentifiable, boulder-sized globs when the women had exited the shaft. The scouts had wanted to investigate the swamp, to see if maybe their brethren were buried in the muck, but the humans begged them not to. Just in case.

Wes-Tu had fallen unconscious, but he was alive. They took him to *Hippocrates* and used medical records from

Jamal's ship to see to his needs, to give him the proper nutrients and care.

Jamal went to his side as soon as I.C.C. gave him the okay.

At some point, the boy dozed off. Sailuk, the head medic, had given him a blanket, and he was warm and content in a visitor's chair when he roused.

It was nighttime, the lights were dim, and the ominous red glow from the sinkholes spilled in through the room's window, like the threat of a great fire on the horizon.

Wes-Tu was still unconscious.

A moment passed before Jamal realized he'd awoken because of All Seer.

"I am detecting multiple points of movement near the sinkhole," the AI announced. "The shared trajectory suggests the objects originated from the direction of the ruined cocoons."

Jamal hopped out of the chair to press his nose against the window, as though he'd be able to see the movement from *Hippocrates*.

Maybe they're alive. Maybe they're okay. Maybe that wasn't Holzschnitt on my gloves.

"It is too dark for the cleaning bot's cameras to make out the shapes, despite the added illumination, and our satellite with infrared capabilities will not be over the area for several hours. I cannot confirm whether or not these are the Noumonians," All Seer said, as though it could read Jamal's mind. All of their minds, really—everyone listening had to be wondering the same thing.

I.C.C. couldn't yet confirm, but it had to be them.

What else *could* it be?

He wanted to whoop for joy, except . . .

Except Wes-Tu. Even if they finally had their Noumonians back, he couldn't celebrate without Wes-Tu.

"I will keep you apprised of the activity," I.C.C. said. "Due to the late hour, no further announcements will be made in private spaces or sleeping quarters unless consent is provided. Emergency alerts being the exception."

Jamal assumed the hospital room counted as a private space. Carefully, dragging the blanket, he tiptoed into the outer hall. Wes-Tu needed his rest. Jamal needed to know what was happening.

The wall of the hospital room was mostly fogged glass, opaque, letting only the suggestion of silhouettes through. But one narrow, horizontal strip of clear window in the door let Jamal see all the way through to the porthole when he passed. His friend lay still, not so much as tossing and turning in his unnatural sleep.

Though bleary-eyed and groggy, Jamal forced himself to stay awake, hoping for snippets of news. He paced back and forth in front of Wes-Tu's room and took to jumping up and down when he could still feel his eyelids drooping.

When the aforementioned satellite finally traced its way over the swamp's sky, I.C.C. hit them with a flurry of updates.

There were thousands of points of movement—exactly the same count as the number of Noumonians who'd made the migration. One-third of them had gathered around the sink-hole, and the rest . . . the rest were fanning out, moving in small groups away from the swamp in a sunburst pattern.

Only one tiny group of nine appeared to be headed for the ships.

"Their primary method of locomotion appears to have changed. Where before they typically engaged in terrestrial locomotion—supplemented by gliding when traversing vertical surfaces—they are now flying."

Jamal perked.

"Their morphology has evolved their gliding membranes into full wings, and their dual forearms have elongated, with new membranes between them, terminating at the shared elbow. This is a much larger evolutionary leap than I have previously observed, physiologically speaking."

The Progentor couldn't imagine anyone on *Mira* was asleep right now. There would be a claxon of chatter, a celebration— it would be like the migration festivities all over again. The called Noumonians had awoken, and *they could fly*.

He wrapped the blanket over his shoulder and head, like a hooded cape, and stared through the door window. Any little shift of the light through the portal was a flurry of wings in his mind's eye.

As the group of nine came closer, flying through the night and into dawn, I.C.C. informed them that it was picking up excessive radio chatter, some speech some not. The AI could now identify the members of the colony who were approaching—Icelandic among them.

With a grayish-pink morning approaching, and dew lightly glazing the hospital room's porthole, Jamal was ready to give in to his need for sleep. Just for a little while.

He tucked himself against the hall wall, opposite the door, and bunched the blanket beneath his head, not ready to leave Wes-Tu's side, and certainly not ready to make the trek back to his own bed on *Slicer*.

His eyelids fluttered; he let his breathing run deep.

Movement in the hospital room, outlined by the new-day's light, tickled his subconscious mind, keeping him from falling into slumber at the very last second.

Someone was moving. Someone was sitting up.

Wes-Tu!

A rush of adrenaline had Jamal back on his feet in an instant, sprinting through the door to breathlessly greet his sub-Kaed. A medic had checked on the two of them once in the night, and now Jamal rushed to the call button.

"What has transpired?" Wes-Tu asked. He still maintained his shroud, but IVs had been inserted into his skin beneath.

"Don't mess with those," Jamal chided as the Post reached for a saline line. "You passed out," he explained.

Wes-Tu was quiet for a long while. So was Jamal. He wanted to tell his friend about the approaching Noumonians, but he knew if he opened his mouth that wasn't what he would say. There was something else on the horizon, something inescapable, and they had to speak of it, but he wasn't ready.

The boy in him, the man, the friend, would never be ready.

But the Progentor in him had a duty, and he would never forgive himself if he failed his closest ally.

He would soon turn a corner, begin his journey to adulthood anew. He might forget this. Was already unsure if he remembered everything that had happened in the last twenty-four hours as clearly as he should.

But Wes-Tu was about to go on an entirely different journey, and Jamal needed to be here for him if he could.

"I remember when Roq died," he said at last.

Wes-Tu let out a heavy sigh, as though a weight had been lifted, as though grateful Jamal had begun the conversation when he could not.

"I know it doesn't seem like I keep track of things sometimes," Jamal continued, his voice wavering, "because I *do* forget. A lot. What I want, what I did—what I'm doing. But I know how many years it's been. I know how long you've lived."

"These are not things you're meant to be burdened with," Wes-Tu whispered, looking at his lap instead of Jamal. "If we were back home, I would expire out of sight. They would tell you I went away, and a new sub-Kaed would arrive."

"Why?"

"You know why. We must all pass through it, return our essence to the universe, and the process is unrevealable to others. One cannot truly know death until they are dying. It is the one scrap of certainty the universe guards relentlessly."

"But why hide death itself from me?"

"Your purity. They wish to keep you as unblemished by grief as possible."

"Grief isn't a blemish," Jamal said firmly.

Wes-Tu nodded solemnly in agreement. "Grief can be a gift," he said, in a way that suggested he'd said it before. "But grief can also be a distraction, and they would hold you to your duties despite it. And your line . . . your clones . . ."

"Yes?"

"The computer can tell you," he said, gesturing at the ceiling, suggesting the omnipotence of the All Seer. "Jamal Kaeden, in all iterations, has always felt grief most acutely."

He already felt it now—hot in his face, tightening his throat. Wes-Tu was right in front of him, but just knowing that soon he would be gone . . .

"Tell me what I must do for you. Now and—" his voice caught in his throat "—and after. And then, then I can tell you about what's out there." He pointed grandly through the porthole. "Wonderful things are being Revealed as we speak."

. . . .

Biological Age: Twenty
Chronological Age: Sixteen Thousand
One Hundred and Twenty-Eight
Location: Pentagonal Trapezohedron

The receiving room was warm and comfortable. Jamal had already met with eight of his nine pilgrims, and he was ready for a long evening of contemplative assembling.

Taking a chance, he snuck a glance at the wad of crumpled paper he'd found stuffed in his desk leg. The odd part was, he vaguely remembered having hidden something years go, but hadn't been able to recall what it was or where he'd stashed it. And now that he had it in hand, it seemed like an odd thing to hide.

It was a bit of old scrap, toying with a few SD engine re-designs. Nothing major. But then there was a small sketch of two seats, with a note on the side that said, "I trust Wes-Tu. I think he will accompany me when I escape."

Of course he trusted Wes-Tu. And . . . escape? The thought had crossed his mind many times, yes. But he'd never dared write the sentiment down.

Or had he?

From outside the room came a huge clattering, and the stomping of many legs. Surprised, Jamal balled the paper and stuck it down the neck of his robes.

Moments later, a Post burst in. He assumed it was a pilgrim, but there was no real way to tell, because *they weren't wearing a shroud.*

He knew he should look away—cover his eyes, demand they leave. But he was fascinated. For the first time, here was a post-human in all their glory.

Their neck was graceful, thin, topped with a beak-like protuberance of a face, and rows upon rows of dark, glistening eyes. Their six arms moved wildly through the air, making gestures that meant nothing to him. A downy, bluish hair covered much of their body. It looked soft, and he longed to know what it felt like.

But most of all, he wanted to bow before this Post and thank them. He'd understood the Posts intellectually, had had them described, but words could not put this pilgrim's magnificence into his mind as firmly as his own eyes.

From the waist down they were clothed, not in parts of a Revealer shroud, but in a garment he took to be average work attire. The trousers even had pockets—pockets!

Wes-Tu and the other sub and full Kaeds came barging in, arguing with one another mind-to-mind. The newest Kaed-Appoint, Qué-Qué, moved to throw a blanket over the pilgrim.

"No!" Jamal cried, standing. "Do not hide them from me. Not until you explain what is happening."

Qué-Qué stopped, but no one addressed him.

"Tell me, now!"

The naked Post flailed more firmly. Had they ears to hear him?

"*Homo sapiens!*" Wes-Tu said, as the others firmly tried to shove him out of the room. "This pilgrim said their ships encountered humans as pure of form as you!"

"Unhand sub-Kaed Wes-Tu!" Jamal said. "Come forward."

Reluctantly, the others ceased their manhandling, pushing Wes-Tu toward their Progentor instead.

"They have proof," Wes-Tu said. "A recording, of the humans attempting to make contact. I believe the pilgrim is telling the truth."

"We will send an envoy at once," Kaed Groth said. "We will bring them here, test them. Verify that this is no trick."

There was little time to think. The possibility of others like him had never crossed his mind. Could there really be a pocket of ancient humanity that had survived? How could they have stayed hidden for so long?

Jamal answered impulsively. "No. I must go meet them myself."

"You can't!"

"What are you saying?"

"We don't even—!"

Every protest imaginable flew at him. Of course they didn't want him to leave. What about his purity? What about his safety?

"What about the existence of humans? Ancient humans, alive. Is this not extraordinary? Not the most important happening since my own resurrection? I refuse to sit back while the most amazing Reveal of our lifetimes exists, out there. I must meet them. You know why." He gestured to himself, then to the pilgrim. "Look at me. Look at them. It is important, my absolute duty as Progentor, to receive them myself. No one else can learn what I can. No one else can make the connection I can. *Because* I've been kept *pure*."

They would not be able to prevent him from going. He'd take the schematics stuffed down his shirt and build his own escape pod if they tried to keep him from leaving.

"I will go with him!" Wes-Tu promised. "I will go. I will make sure no harm comes to him. *I will go.*"

"You've always been too soft, Wes-Tu! Too fond of our Progentor. Selfish!" Yulep declared.

"And you have always been a hypocrite!" Wes-Tu shouted.

Something buzzed at the back of Jamal's skull.

"Is he not our leader? Was he not chosen by the universe to live on and on, Revealing forever?" Wes-Tu demanded. "You cannot hide this discovery from the other Revealers. News of it *will* travel. What will we say when it looks as though the Progentor ignored it?"

There was a desperation in the sub-Kaed that Jamal couldn't remember ever witnessing before. A demanding passion, a nervous insistence.

"We cannot keep the Progentor from making contact with these people," Wes-Tu pressed. "The universe clearly wills it."

Peering out from a window in the tug, Jamal gasped in amazement. He could not recall ever seeing the Pentagonal Trapezohedron from the outside before. Its surface shimmered, and the ten portholes skirted the equator, each a round spot in the widest portion of a single congruent kite-shaped face.

As they flew past its surface, Roq's name in the written form of her home language soared above and below. As did Soma's, and Messa's, and Keng-A's, and all those other Kaeds and sub-Kaeds who had protected him, mentored him, and given their lives to the service of the Revealers. The etchings were lined with yellow lights, sending brilliant patterns over the purple-black material. It was beautiful, and sad, and perhaps even a little ominous.

How strange, to roof one's home with the dead.

The megastructures they headed for now would be very different, each unique unto themselves.

He tore his eyes away for a moment to look at the note in his lap—the scrap he'd found hidden—and smoothed it out. Behind him, in another jump seat, was Wes-Tu.

Perhaps this was not the type of escape his past self had meant. But what was an escape except running away from one's problems? Here, he was running toward a problem, a purpose, and a future. Ancient humans—here, now!

Where had they come from? How had they gotten here? What horrors, hopes, and dreams had they brought?

Adventure and discovery were on the horizon. New information, knowledge, understanding. *Communion* with his fellow *Homo sapiens*.

Jamal looked out again, noting how the stars slid by the dark shape of the Pentagonal Trapezohedron, eyeing the Ship Yard. He thanked the universe for sending this chance his way, and for sending him an advocate in Wes-Tu.

. . . .

Biological Age: Eleven and a half

Location: The Monument

The Noumonians flew over the ships, and straight on south without stopping. The entire *Mira* colony had gone out to greet them, waving at the skies, watching their magnificent new forms soar overhead, the sunlight dipping through the membrane of their wings, illuminating their bodies.

Icelandic was the easiest to spot. She still wore the translator, though the cocooning process had fused it to her chest.

It was now a part of her, embedded, and, remarkably, it still functioned.

She gave I.C.C. and the gathered crowd a brief assurance that they would return soon, and then hurried on, flapping mightily, to some unknown destination.

"She did not entirely sound like herself," All Seer told them cryptically.

Jamal saw no reason to worry.

He spent his days waiting for the Noumonians to return by swapping old stories with Wes-Tu—the ones he couldn't quite remember—and preparing for Wes-Tu to return to the universe.

"There are things I have not told you," Wes-Tu confessed. "So that you would not think poorly of those that loved you. They did what they thought was right, even thought it . . ." He trailed off.

"Does it pain me not to know?"

Wes-Tu sighed. "I don't know."

"Does it pain you more to tell me, or not to tell me?"

Wes-Tu sighed again. "I don't know."

"Is it about the living, or the dead?"

"Dead," he said firmly. "Mostly the dead."

"Then, if it hurts you, I don't need to know. They are gone, and I will forget, and I forgive you for keeping it from me. I know you have only ever looked out for me."

"But, Progentor. It is *about* forgetting. They—*we*—took from you—"

"Wes-Tu, be at peace."

The Post's passing was not easy, and he refused many of the medications Sailuk offered him. Jamal didn't want him to be in pain, but he also respected that Wes-Tu *wanted* death to be a struggle. He wanted to hold on to life, to challenge the universe to take it back. He would ultimately relinquish himself to the darkness, but be damned if he would go lightly.

"It is appropriate to trade, now," Wes-Tu wheezed on what would be his last day. "That so many should return from stasis as I return to the void. It feels balanced. I am content, Progentor. You are safe. They are safe. Thank you."

Jamal had cried for days now, but he was not yet cried out. His tears were gentle and silent, but persistent. "Thank you for what?"

"Trusting me."

When breath passed through the sub-Kaed for the last time, Sailuk asked if he should be recycled right away, or if the Revealers had their own ways.

Eventually the Post's body would have to return to the dirt of *Morgan*, but there were things to attend to, first.

Hope and Vanhi helped Jamal carry Wes-Tu's body up the mountain to the plateau where the ancestor shrine lay. There, they stripped him bare, averting their eyes but letting the universe see him exposed. His knowledge and its essence had returned to the vastness, and now so his form would be seen by the great beyond.

They would leave him there for three days and two nights, before returning and covering him again.

"Is it time for the carving, Jamal?" I.C.C. asked when they came down from the mountain.

"Yes. If you're sure."

"I am sure."

With a half-dozen modified cleaning bots at their disposal, All Father, All Mother, and No Mother climbed *Slicer*'s outer hull at All Seer's behest. Together, they tore into the ship, carving, scraping, peeling away layer after layer. They cut through thick beams with hot torches, pulling out supports, stripping the ship of its spaceworthiness.

"The nine Noumonians are approaching once more, from the south," I.C.C. informed them halfway through their work.

Jamal wiped sweat from his forehead, thankful for the constant breeze, and paused only to look for dark dots on the horizon. He saw nothing, and continued on, knowing that the Noumonian arrival would be his reward when he was finished.

Hours passed. All Mother moved far more material than either himself or No Mother, but they all worked equally hard, equally unfailing. This was important, to all of them.

When they were finished, Wes-Tu's name was scrawled atop in the characters of his home language. Big, bold, proud.

And the flying Noumonians would be the first to see it from the proper perspective.

The three of them sat down, exhausted and thirsty after their work. The women hugged Jamal in turn, praised him for making sure Wes-Tu received a proper tribute.

When the Noumonians arrived, they circled overhead, bright green, yellow, and copper. The three immortals lay back against the hot metal of the ship, watching the patterns their friends drew in the sky, admiring the loop-the-loops one would occasionally turn, seemingly just for fun.

"Icelandic says they cannot land yet," I.C.C. informed them. "That first they—oh. Oh."

Jamal pushed himself up on his elbows. I.C.C. had never said "oh," before.

"The number of frequencies on which they transmit have doubled," I.C.C. explained. "And the bands that are new . . . they are encrypted, in a sense. They carry extra information."

Vanhi sat up as well. Hope's mech rattled as it shifted vertical. "You mean," Vanhi prompted, "like *humans* use radio waves?"

"Close, yes," I.C.C. said. "Though it may take me some time to interpret the data."

"What's she sending?" Hope asked. "What does Icelandic say it is?"

"She says . . ." I.C.C. paused, as though it weren't sure it understood correctly. "Icelandic says she is not alone in her body. That she is more now. Entwined."

Above, the sunlight through Icelandic's wings began to shimmer and swirl as the pigment changed and rearranged itself, revealing chromatophores the Noumonians had never possessed before. But she did not blend into the sky, nor camouflage herself as another flying creature. Instead, the pattern on her wings became a picture, a piece of art, a painting, just like Hope's mech could display.

But the painting moved as though alive. A movie, acted out across her skin.

The last time Jamal had felt such wonder, he'd been leaving the Pentagonal Trapezohedron, about to begin the journey that had led him here, now.

"She says she must tell me a story," I.C.C. said. "The story of Icelandic *Plus*."

PLUS'S INTERLUDE

In the Light of the Moment

Archival note from I.C.C.: This is a translation from the images and encrypted signals provided to Icelandic, and then transferred to the Inter Convoy Computer, by the being calling itself *Plus*. Updates to this translation will be made in accordance with further evolution in nuanced communication.

Parts of speech have been normalized for ease of access by the *Mira* colony members. Please see footnotes for in-line clarifications.

SOMEWHERE NEAR SAGITTARIUS A*

Before the Earth Began

Plus extended her wings their full breadth, carefully tilting and tipping to avoid the others as they fought against the air current or flapped to a different altitude within the ship. On her back, secured to her haunches, were two turrets, her colleagues—Addition and More[1]—each bent forward, scythes secured through the D-shaped, metal-lined hole structures in her shoulders. The two of them provided extra lift with their air bladders, sending the trio near the ceiling, where the wind was strongest. Her wheel's rapid spin left a tiny tickle deep in her sides, where the nerveless structure seamlessly floated within her organic motor.

She felt invincible. She felt solid. Her fluids coursed,

---

1   All proper names appear as chosen by the visitors.

her muscles tightened. She was sure the three of them could stay up here, suspended by the ship's currents, forever. She hoped the new planet would have strong winds. She hoped her host would have strong wings.

She hoped her host would say yes.

Plus took the third right, down a tunnel in their twisted-torus ship. The hall grazed the circular, center nul-space where the forthcoming separation event would take place. Her colleagues both indicated wonder, a surge of signals wafting off them as they looked out the crests in the wavelength-like line of windows.

The structure was ready, its latticework intricate, its overlapping, spinning concentric rings already reaching speeds fast enough to blur them into one. The fine, wispy-thin tube at its base pointed down, down, down, toward the black hole. Along it, gravitons were rocketing back and forth, invisible, but terrible in their pull. Enough to rip a body apart. Enough to separate the interdimensional energies from the structures they called home.

The light emanating upward from the black hole was blinding—all the photons that peeled away at the last minute, before their brethren tumbled past the event horizon, shooting off in a strange, smeared pattern. The ship sat light-years away and was positioned halfway between the southern pole and the equator in an attempt to avoid the more dangerous radiation jets.

Right now, a magnetic field protected their ship from any sudden outbursts by the black hole. But they would need to turn it off to run the nul-space separator. Everyone aboard was putting themselves in danger for this chance.

And they would never know if it had worked or not.

Plus was taking the long way around the ship, but

she preferred it to fighting the airstream. The wind that bolstered them only blew in one direction through the torus—she'd heard about ships that had tried crosscurrents and the resulting midair collisions had *not* been favorable—which allowed for an energy-saving, passive glide if one was willing to do the laps.

Along the way the trio passed a handful of crystal cocoons jutting from the curved walls and had to yaw left or right to avoid them. It was unfortunate some of their colleagues had needed to go under and wouldn't be present for the event. But if one did not heed the urge, one would perish.

The urges would be tightly controlled on their new planet. They had to be—or else the event would be for naught.

Plus's friend, Subtract, had been taken out of contention for the event because of unexpected urge inducement. Subtract had evolved past the planning. Subtract would no longer resonate with a form in the future.

Plus caught a perch two turns before the expected offshoot to watch a wing display of news from their home world, Petrathema. These past long cycles, three hundred of them by Petrathema standards—she'd been so focused on the event and the planting of the megastructure seeds that she'd hardly had time for wing displays.

Twelve scouts, whose bodies were thin and their wings broad, clung to the wall and lay with their wings over one another in a whorled pattern, nearly mimicking the shape of their torus.

She should have realized much of the display would be about the event.

But there *were* brief pictures of home—the sky filled with im, towers nearly touching space, water falling, falling, gushing down the face of them, the seas spread out below. Once in a while, in the display, an ocean im broke the surface, their fins—what would have been wings, except the two im had evolutionarily diverged long ago—bright yellow in the sunlight.

The ocean im had built the bases of the towers eons before, and the air im had kept pushing them up higher and higher, mimicking the cliffs. The seas were too deep, the pressure too great, so Plus had never been below to observe the tower bases herself, but now she wished she had. It would have been a matter of a pressure suit and a guide, little else.

At least she'd seen images sent by ocean im, once, of their cocoons from below. They were even more sprawling and wonderous than the air im's. Pieces of the cocoons, of the im, broke off in bubbles, floating freely in the water, traversing the globe—hardly a one ever getting swallowed by a rock-gut—until they found each other again and coalesced after incubation, putting everything back together just as it should be.

What mechanism guided this was unknown. That was why there were no ocean im here for the event.

They'd tried for centuries to learn, to know. But their experiments had only led to dead im, who'd never awoken, their bubbles never finding one another, never rejoining correctly when forced.

They had failed here, so there would be only one type of im to see the future.

If this worked at all.

For a few moments more she saw the creatures— slime molds, funguses, and air plants of home—

displayed in brilliant color before the images shifted, the chromatophores dancing to reveal the torus ship from the outside, the shining black hole as its backdrop.

[Must go,] Addition urged her. [Can't be late.]

[Let her be,] More chided. [Last she see. Last *you* see. Last we see.]

[No looking back,] Addition said. [Only forward. All is forward now. All this—] they let go with one scythe to gesture at the circular hall, [good as gone long time.]

[It is not gone,] Plus said. [They live. They will live long time.]

[We cannot know, we cannot know,] Addition said. [Best not to dwell. Best think of future. Best think of the machine.]

The Petratheem Machine. If all went right with the event, all went right with those to come, if all went right as the calculations predicted, then soon—soon for Plus, not for time itself—soon they would expose all the layers of the universe.

She let go of her perch, catching the winds full in her wings, arms splayed wide. It was time, Addition was right. They could dally no longer.

The life of Petrathema was the earliest in the universe. Of this, im were sure. Their atoms were created in one of the first supermassive stars, one of the first super-red giants, and expelled out of one of the very first supernovae. From Petrathema, im could see a neutron star they called the Crucible. Though they could not be certain it was their literal parent star, the legends said that was where they had formed. That was where they came from.

Their galaxy was a slow twisting thing. A bulge-and-halo. One day it would spin itself long arms and form many more stars in a disk shape. That process had already begun. Now, everything was hot beyond the halo—too hot for gases to coalesce. No new stars could be born out there until the excitement ceased, until the galaxy was homey. Stellar nurseries needed stability. All new ones need stability.

Even their devices would need stability. They could not create the megastructures in such a hostile environment.

The intelligences of Petrathema were alive in the muggy silence before a shout. They were a whisper, but they longed to be part of a chorus.

By their calculation, this quiet period—this hiatus of star formation—would last five billion years.[2]

That was a long time to wait for neighbors.

But surely there would be others before then. Before the explosion of stars that would make more planets and more systems and more life.

So they waited.

And when no one else came, they searched.

They found the other dimensions, explored the new physics.

But found no others like im.

Because they had not been created yet. Their atoms had yet to fuse. Their molecules had yet to form.

The im were a quirk of creation. Too early. Ahead.

Im traveled to the edge of their galaxy. To the next galaxy. Beyond their local cluster and to the edge of the universe. The universe was just over two billion light-years in diameter.[3] Small. But it would get bigger. Eventually.

---

2   Converted to Sol years.
3   This is inconsistent with current human understanding of the timeline of the universe. Our model of universal expansion will likely change.

Eventually, eventually, eventually.

Everything would happen, eventually.

But who knew, if left to time and chance, that any of the im would be there to see it?

And then, what if they wanted more? What if they wanted to see it all?

And wanted to share in that as well?

So much time and too little space.

But there was another factor to contend with.

There would be more in the future—more stars, more planets, more intelligences. But the expansion would draw them away, they would be pulled farther and farther from Petrathema. Away from where Petrathema had once been, if it was past the time of their star's burgeoning.

Maybe not so bad; distance could be overcome easily. Travel was less of a worry than detection.

It would be easy, after the event. All the intelligences would tell them exactly where they were. They would tell them by construction. They would tell them by the work of their hands and their machines.

The one protuberance off the torus—the bridge leading to the center nul-space—was off-limits to most of Plus's colleagues. This was for safety. After all, the structure had been built to destroy im.

Plus swooped to the ground at the bridge's entrance, Addition and More helping her land lightly.

The two hundred and forty-seven others who would participate in the event were already present, forming a long, spiraling line—up and down the walls, over the ceiling and across the floor—of fluttering wings and protruding bladders. The surface-level radio chatter was strong, the oscillations quick and their origins many. If this worked, they would all be part of the greatest, most intimate joining in all of history.

If it did not work they would die.

And no one beyond the event would be able to tell the difference. All im had to trust. Had to do their part, regardless.

While they waited for the gates to open—to let them onto the bridge where they would be prepared—Plus thought of those who, like her, had gone away from Petrathema, never to return.

Only, not all im who'd gone had left for something like this.

Some took a small leap instead, interdimensional travel carrying them a little way forward, a little way far. To a place suitable for construction. A place not so hot, someplace resembling where their home planet had formed—a cradle—to begin. They would make and make and make until they had the beginnings of something special. A megastructure. And they would make until their bodies no longer felt the urge, until bathing themselves in the non-Newtonian fluid of life[4] no longer brought their minds and bodies change. Then the end

---

4   "Non-Newtonian fluid of life" is the most direct translation. The most *accurate* translation would be: symbiotic slime-mold-related life-form whose life cycle includes growing on and in Noumonian and/or Petratheem bodies, which in turn changes the genetic and physical structure of the im. Plus indicated we should understand that the crystal fragments get turned in with soil and water on the home world, where it eventually dissolves, absorbing nutrients from the environment, before it liquefies again. Then it excretes both chemical and radio signals that create the "urge" in compatible im.

would come for them, and they would have to trust in the intelligences who came after.

Some believed im would be able to complete most of the structures on their own. Plus was not so sure—most im did not think it was possible. There were two hundred and sixteen main structures to create, each with a subset of support structures. Even if the im kept growing new ones while making the constructs, im would not go on forever. They knew this about the universe: nothing would go on forever.

Miscalculations happened. Desires changed. Im of today was not im of tomorrow, no matter how long the im of today lived.

But that was why the event was happening: to insure im. To insure the completion.

So many different parts in the machine. So many different pieces to put together.

What if it didn't work? What if the event failed and there were no im? Would it matter? Would the new intelligences understand what they had made? Would it matter if they did not? The megastructures themselves would perform wonders as they moved matter around the galaxy, putting it in its proper place. If the machine never came to full fruition . . .

Best not to think on that. Best not to, no no.

Because it might be all right for the other intelligences. But that would mean Plus was dead.

A boosted secondary-level radio signal reverberated through her sensors. An announcement. It was time.

As they entered the bridge set by set, three at a time—each tank bearing either two scouts or two turrets—they were given a group number, to help them find their assigned place in the structure's pod housing. They would remain joined so that they would not have to go through the event as individuals. No im had to face it alone.

A scout colleague gave Plus a large, compressed ball of chemical components to crush and dissolve in her jaws. She would pass the chemicals through the joining to More and Addition. Some of the components would deaden the nerves. Others would heighten emotions and focus thoughts, pull the energies of their minds and endocrine systems to the fore. This would ease the separation.

Though the event would expose them to the vacuum of space, they were given no pressure suits, and no artificial means of gas exchange. They would not retain their bodies for long enough to concern themselves with such things.

One last line of windows on the bridge allowed the trio to look at the structure in nul-space and the black hole one last time. They would not reach the event horizon—they would not be smeared across its surface like so much light. But they would fall toward it as they passed through the structure, which captured the black hole's off-casted gravitons.[5]

It was daunting, and beautiful.

She hoped it was not the last daunting, beautiful thing she would ever see.

The bridge led them over the top of the structure, with the engine rings spinning below. The pod would be lowered through as a unit on a massive crane, before releasing those inside, group by group.

---

5   Sagittarius A*'s local space contains the highest concentration of free-floating gravitons available for capture in the galaxy. Such levels would overload my cyclers, but the "structure" created for the "event" required levels of graviton manipulation unprecedented by human—and, I postulate, Nataré—usage.

The pod attached to the crane was completely enclosed, with harnesses lining the inside. The clear bottom would slide back when it was time for the event to commence.

Plus found the harness assigned to their group, and More and Addition helped her strap in. They pitched forward, looking down through the bottom of the pod; the blazing light from the black hole and the warped disk around its equator were almost too much to look at.

There would be no flying, just falling.

Many other groups were already in place. Many more streamed in behind them. The radio chatter had died down. Emotions were high, focus was strong. The chemicals were doing their work.

And the chrononauts were ready.

When everyone was strapped in, the announcing im spoke again, telling them of much excitement on the torus. Much gladness and hope.

With her wings pinned, Plus was suddenly reminded of a pet she'd had when young. They were cute, and loving, but a very dangerous type of creature if im were not careful. They liked to cling, with stubby tentacles that could stretch and stretch until thin like thread. One could ride on an im neck, or one could grab hold of a wheel and stop it from turning. But if one did not like flying, one might grab a wing and hold it closed, keep it tight, make im fall. Hers had done that once, but she'd been able to grab the side of the tower, saving them both. After she'd scolded it, the pet never clung like that in flight again.

The memory was both frightening and comforting. Familiar and nostalgic, here in the strange and unknown.

[See you again soon,] More sent, holding all the tighter in the joining, getting ready as the countdown commenced.

[Yes, soon,] Addition agreed.

[Safe journey, safe separation,] Plus wished them.

The crane jolted, lowering the pod. Some of the chrononauts cheered. Plus was contemplative. She leaned forward, let the harness have their full collective weight.

Three.

Two.

One.

The floor slid aside.

The atmosphere rushed out.

The pressure was gone.

The spinning engine and the whizzing gravitons made no sound.

Radio communications were unhindered, of course.

As the first harness—opposite her group in the pod—released, a chorus of congratulations went forth.

The fall was quick. The drop sharp. Their wheels barely moved. Their forms were alight.

The group's bodies disintegrated the moment they hit the graviton field. Smooth. Into nothing. Gone.

A flash of neon pink was the only indication the event might have happened—that im hadn't just been sent to their deaths.

More releases. More cheers. More happiness.

More trepidation.

More uncertainty.

The life of Petrathema was multidimensional, and im theorized that all sentient life must be. The physical structure created in this dimension captured energies in others, like a graviton cycler gathering gravitons. It pulled thought energy and emotion energy from wherever it could—from wherever it resonated—in order to make the body move and function. It was what made matter no longer inert, these interdimensional interactions. Death was when the energies were separated from their structures. When they dissipated back into the dimensions they'd come from.

But what if you could capture those structurally specific energies and send them elsewhere? What if not death, but rebirth? Not dissipation, but reconstitution? What if you could capture, and package, a body's energies and send them into another body? One they would resonate with? Permanently?

What if you could send that package through a subdimension, through time—forward, always forward—until the proper body appeared? The proper body was made?

What then?

What then . . .

The Event.

Plus shut her eyes for a moment as the group right next to them fell. The flat of a scythe grazed her side, sparking connection, a light touch given her deadened nerves.

Theoretically, this would be like what happened in a cocoon, only more extreme. Petratheem bodies were used to being pulled apart. This was just . . . more apart.

A sharp shake at Plus's belly preceded the release. She felt rather than heard the *clack* of the latch letting them go. [Safe journey,] she sent again as they began to fall, moments away from death or a new life.

Her senses were sharp, though her nerves were dull. They wanted no pain during the packaging. But they could not prevent the fear.

Plus's endocrine system boiled with chemicals, making the emotion energies surge, radiate. She was mostly mind and passions now, but even at that, she knew she could not really go on without the physical. The systems all together made an im. And she would rely on the future im to let her in, to share their form.

Their packages, even if they made it to new bodies, *could* be rejected. Which was only right. They would not steal im lives, just share. Just persist.

No rush of air filled her wings, no bite of cold touched her skin—she would not exist in nul-space long enough for it to take her heat.

Their joint fall felt a lifetime. A moment and all the moments. The great spinning wheels blurred, the netting of the ever-narrowing tube structure closing before them.

Perhaps it *was* a bit like being spread out across the surface of a black hole. Maybe facing death was always like crossing an event horizon.

And then they traversed the edge of the graviton field.

A blink of light, a sense of *pull.*

A swell of doubt.

A shout of thought.

An end of this life.

A hope for the next.

Part Two
Resplendence

HOPE'S INTERLUDE

Field Notes

EXCERPTS FROM THE TERMINOLOGY GUIDE:

Dual-Possession /ˈduəl-pəˈzɛʃən/ noun or verb: A Noumonian who consented to share their form with a Petratheem consciousness during the last metamorphosis—more precisely, a Noumonian and Petratheem consciousness pairing. Not all Noumonians who heard the last Call became dual-possessions. Most did not. Whether this is because the majority were genetically incompatible with the arriving Petratheem, or because many did not consent to sharing their bodies, it is unclear. The Noumonians will not speak of it.

Im /ɪm/ noun, a singular-plural: The general term for both the Petratheem and Noumonian sentient life-forms. Used both like a proper noun and a pronoun.

Noumonian /nu moʊn ē ən/ noun, plural *Noumonians*: The creatures who evolved on the planet Noumenon, their evolution guided by food and an ancient pseudo-bacterium found in the Sora-Gohan (see Artificial Terminology Guide). Many are genetically identical at this stage in their evolution to individual Petratheem who destroyed their own physical forms in order to travel through a volatile subdimension, allowing for dual-possession.

Petratheem /ˈpɛtrəˌθim/ noun, both plural and singular: The ancient aliens who designed the megastructures and began their construction roughly ten billion years ago.

NOTES ON NOUMONIAN EVOLUTION,
RE: QUESTIONS ABOUT CLONING

From my interactions with the dual-possession Icelandic-Plus, whose consciousnesses can be addressed both jointly and separately, I have gathered that the Petratheem find humanity's ability to clone itself a wonder. It is a delightfully simple process to them, which they wholeheartedly would have engaged in if their biology had supported it. Instead, in order to create forms that resonated strongly enough with their consciousnesses to allow them to leave the subdimension in which they traveled, they had to engage in the lengthy process of evolving those forms essentially from scratch.

Im reproduction is unique in my observations. Unlike the im, humans have sex cells, gametes, ovum, and spermatozoon. We have long been able to take or copy DNA from an existing human and inject it into an ovum to create viable, cleavable zygotes. Though our natural reproduction requires the merger of haploid cells, artificial reproduction does not. One genome, one human.

In contrast, im reproduction stalls out if new genetic information is not constantly introduced throughout development.

All im are base-tank. Their base-genome is identical to the parent on which they grow. Initial reproduction is activated by a tank's gorging ritual. Here on Noumenon that means going to the quarry to feed. This is a simple gathering of excess materials with which to build a new life, and stem cell production is stimulated.

However, a tank cannot reproduce alone. Every time a tank engages with another im throughout their life—when their proboscises bind with another im's—stem cells are donated, giving the tank's reproductive system access to additional genomes for combination.

During the growth of the new im, all gathered genomes from the various proboscises' interaction is joined, rearranged, or discarded—seemingly at the whim of their reproductive mechanisms. The Petratheem were never able to force exactly what was kept or what was discarded. They could not copy an existing im one for one. All attempts led to the cessation of growth and the potential new one's reabsorption into the parent.

Thus, the Petratheem's best option was guided evolution over a long period. A slow start over thousands of years gave them the greatest chance for creating genetic reoccurrences. They could engineer the Sora-Gohan, even if they couldn't engineer themselves.

I believe this is largely why out of several hundred who began the journey all those billions of years ago, only seventy-six Petratheems exist today in dual-possessions. They could not predict which evolutionary lines would grow in the "correct" direction. Many genomes failed to reoccur despite the pool size.

PETRATHEEM CONCERNS

Once we realized what had happened regarding the dual-possessions, many of us hoped that answers were soon to follow. Here were the original designers, the ones with the grand plan for these many hundreds of megastructures. Surely they would tell us how the anomaly fit into that plan.

However, the anomaly was a surprise to the new arrivals. They had anticipated a sort of bubble around our system ("to protect the outside" they said), but nothing like this. They expected to be able to leave the system and go off into the galaxy to facilitate repairs and re-alignments, but none of their precalculated scenarios included anything like the anomaly. They are just as baffled—and just as trapped—as we are.

There seems to be no question in their minds as to whether or not the anomaly and their megastructures are related, however. The answer is a complicated yes (see notes labeled "Petratheem Physics" for an attempt to break down what we know about their understanding of the structure of the universe).

They cannot make guesses as to the nature of the problem with the information at the Monument's disposal. Icelandic-Plus fears it is due entirely to a miscalculation. And yet others are very distressed about Jamal's bug ship. We know it is made from parts pulled from an exhausted megastructure. But given the Petratheem response to it, we now suspect "exhausted" is the wrong descriptor.

The megastructures could be built, but not activated, out of order. Meaning if a megastructure had failed to be properly "installed" within the "machine" (see "Petratheem Machine"), the Petratheem themselves never would have arrived and the dual-possessions would not exist. So, in Icelandic-Plus's opinion, it cannot be a problem of an incomplete structure or a missing part. She/they think a mistake in their underlying assumptions is to blame.

What those underlying assumptions *are* has only been described to us mathematically.

PETRATHEEM PHYSICS

Vanhi and I.C.C. are our top physicists, and they have yet to comprehend the equations transmitted by

Icelandic-Plus. The name for the theories and functions the mathematics describes roughly translates to "all theory" and we gather it is likely an ultra-unified theory of the entire universe, encompassing all physics in all SDs. I can't help but be reminded of the old theory of an Ultra Civilization—one that would have calculated its needs for existence to the end of time. The Petratheem are likely as close to an Ultra Civilization as the universe will ever get.

Vanhi has likened her and I.C.C.'s struggle with the ultra-unified theory to Pythagoras attempting to decipher the equations of general relativity without knowing that mathematical disciplines like calculus even exist. The Petratheem have been poor teachers, and I assume this is by and large due to their continued efforts regarding their machine. They see little point in struggling to teach the Monument dwellers when there are much more urgent tasks to be attended to.

It also speaks to how little they regard our capacity to help solve whatever the overarching problem might be.

Still, Dr. Kapoor and I.C.C. persist.

PETRATHEEM MACHINE

Each megastructure can be likened to (we gather) a small part in a much larger machine. And each "cog," "screw," "spring," and "pin" needs to be working in harmony for the machine to function properly. Only, what the machine does, precisely, eludes us. Its functionality has only been described to us via Petratheem physics, which, as stated, we have yet to comprehend.

What we do know: the Noumonian radio-signal direct translation of the word for the machine is "all-dimensional weak-point-pike invitation." This sounds largely nonsensical, but when broken down into individual components begins to make some descriptive logic.

All-dimensional seems to relate to the subdimensions. We grasp that whatever the machine does, it not only spans the galaxy, but the SDs as well. Meaning that its greater function is meant to affect most, if not all, layers of existence.

Invitation is straightforward until you consider exactly who or *what* needs an invitation. When I asked Icelandic-Plus to elaborate she simply said "others." I have my suspicions that this invitation is open, and the reason Icelandic-Plus is not more specific is because she can't be. We do know that the Petratheem were expecting a much larger population of sentient life-forms to greet them upon their arrival. That we are so few seems to disturb them as much as or more than the anomaly.

Given the emphasis the Petratheem continuously put on life, communion, connection, and discovery, we can only assume this "invitation" is the machine's primary function. As the offshoots of humanity have met no other living intelligences beyond Noumenon, we are at a loss as to where the recipients might be found, and how exactly they are supposed to get to Noumenon for this communing and connecting.

Weak-point-pike is the more ominous-sounding portion of the description, and while the Petratheem assure us that no matter how it sounds the machine is not a weapon, some of us still retain a wariness.

NOUMONIAN SINKHOLES

The dual-possessions work diligently, all of them down deep underground most of the time. For now I continue to observe their comings and goings from afar. It has been seven hundred and sixty-five days since the last direct communication between a dual-possession and an organic Monument dweller. They see their task as urgent, our ignorance as a distraction. They insist they will share with us when they are ready, when they can slow down and rest. But I believe our inability to communicate on their scientific level has disheartened them. They expected the sentients of the future to possess more knowledge than they themselves, not far less.

They tell us communion is coming. Connection. But they won't let us help build those connections.

The only dual-possession who stays in somewhat constant contact is Icelandic-Plus, and only with I.C.C. Though largely she/they do not speak of the machine, only what is happening in the sinkholes.

The land around the Sora-Gohan tunnels heaves. *Breathes.*

Something is alive down there. I want to see it, to understand it. To observe.

The im are making preparations, and I want to know what's coming.

CHAPTER SIX

THE SCENT OF MOTH ORCHIDS FOLLOWED BY THE SENSATION OF LIGHTLY RUSTED IRON UNDER CALLOUSED FINGERTIPS

. . . .

ONE HUNDRED AND FIFTY-SIX YEARS SINCE THE APPEARANCE OF THE FIRST ANOMALY (AS OBSERVED FROM THE OUTSIDE)

The universe was broken, and someone had to be held accountable.

A single *Lùhng* sprawled in the cockpit of their small ship. Instead of a chair, the pilot's seat consisted of a large egg-shaped, porcelain tub. Their heavy body, which was typically suspended between six crab-like legs, was held aloft by the viscous, temperature-regulating protein bath within, and their legs curled over the side, four of them conforming stiffly to the half-moon curve of the structure, while the two others aided the two simian arms at the controls.

Under their deep-black solar scales lay crystalline skin, and, worried, they took a moment to split the seam of the scales at their breastbone, gazing through their transparent bones to the organs beneath.

An unnatural flutter seized their heart as one valve stuttered, failing to keep their blood consistently flowing through the muscle in the proper direction.

An easy fix—were they anywhere near home.

The problem had arisen during their solo travel. Back home, on Convoy Seven, a medic would have reached into their body, pulled out their heart, corrected the leaking valve with a smattering of bioprosthetic cells, and sent them back to work within the hour.

But here?

They weren't even sure they could get anyone to answer their hails.

They'd emerged from SD travel near the Philosopher's System, just outside the sector where the last recorded interaction with the anomaly had taken place. Earth had instituted a half-light-year perimeter in a globe around the system. But that was before the second anomaly appeared. And the third. And the fourth.

Off the starboard side of their ship, tiny metallic pinpricks revealed where a small fleet of Revealer craft had set up permanent orbit.

Since the disappearance of the Progentor over one hundred and fifty years ago, the religion had fractured into more sects than had existed prior to the resurrection of Jamal Kaeden's line. There were factions that believed he was dead. Factions that believed he'd disappeared into an unknown dimension, never to return. Factions that believed he'd *run away*.

Then there was *this* sect. This small cult that believed he'd made it to Noumenon—that the Convoy Twelve away mission had skirted the appearance of the anomaly—and that he was living on its barren surface.

While any of the new sects were loath to call themselves anything other than the Revealers, lest they seem a lesser movement, this one sought to set themselves even further apart by indicating they were the only ones of any real faith. They were the sound of a roaring ocean battering high cliffs, and the sense of stable power. They were a movement made up of crystalline order and clarity, of true understanding.

They were the Revealers of the Unwavering Guide. The ones who would cut the path through the folly of all others and demonstrate unto all the everlasting nature of Jamal Kaeden.

Each faction had its own Progentor now. But the leader of the Unwavering Guide was only the *Acting* Progentor, and he claimed he'd made inroads to the anomaly. Not physically, not with matter, but with energy. He claimed he had proof of Jamal's survival—an actual clip of his voice. A whole three seconds of communication that had occurred while the sect had made scientific headway in studying the anomaly.

Why this brief communication ability hadn't yet been replicated, it was difficult to say.

All in all, his claims remained unverified by outside sources.

But would the Revealers share this clip, and their knowledge, with a visitor from Convoy Seven, the pariah of the inhabited galaxy?

The *Lùhng* had come because they'd had their own breakthroughs related to safe passage through the anomalies, and no one back home would listen. Everyone had told them to keep their head proverbially down, to let Earth handle such matters. Wasn't it bad enough that they'd unleashed these anomalies across the galaxy? Hadn't they done enough damage, sticking their noses into things they didn't understand?

If they'd truly created the problem—if they'd actually *broken* physics in some way—didn't that mean they were responsible for fixing it? Even if they were forbidden from doing any more construction on their few remaining megastructures, didn't they have an obligation to help make things right?

Hopefully these Revealers would think so.

Checking their telemetry, the *Lùhng* directed their ship to skirt the quarantine border, aiming for the orbiting crafts. This close, this sector of space looked strange. The anomaly looked like a dark globe—not of matter, but of warped space. The photons emanating from the galaxies and stars behind it warped around the disturbance in a dramatic lensing. Strange smears, elongations, and threads of light encompassed what looked otherwise like empty space.

It was the same with many of the other anomalies, though not all. Earth looked placid, still, from outside Sol's system. And yet, a fleet of ships—if the ships were lucky—could appear suddenly from the Oort cloud, emerging from the anomaly without warning.

Of course, the crew was likely to be many generations removed from when they'd left the Earth, in such cases. Less than two hundred years had passed for those beyond Earth's anomaly, and yet for those inside it had been millennia.

Inside other anomalies, it was the opposite. Nearly no time had passed, and those who made it out through the borderland alive were shocked to discover so many years had marched by.

Time worked differently inside and outside each anomaly. Space worked differently. Some of the borders were crossable, though making the transition was often fraught and deadly. Others were entirely impenetrable.

Trade routes had died. Political relationships had withered. Societal isolation had surged to levels not unlike only a mere ten thousand years after the Planet United Missions had launched.

It was terrifying. Chaotic.

And everyone blamed Convoy Seven.

Console lights flashed as the *Lùhng*'s ship came within communication distance of the outermost Revealer craft.

They found an open mind-to-mind channel, boosted—the ship itself had no comms—and relayed their craft's specifications, origin, and landing request.

They were prepared for no response.

What they received was instant denial. A warning. A directive to leave the sector.

Multiple minds came together to send the concept of *go away go away keep out go away.*

The *Lùhng* conveyed why they had come: they had an idea. A way to possibly break through and contact the Progentor. But they needed Revealer help.

(They needed anyone's help, really.)

More rebukes. A sense of urgency, of hostility. A flood of negative emotions burst over the channel.

The *Lùhng* dug in. Buckling down, protein bath sloshing around them, they thought clearly—*in English words*:

[I speak the sacred languages.]

All sensation emanating from the other ships trickled away, ceased.

They repeated the statement in Hindi, as further proof: [*Main pavitr bhaashaen bolata hoon.*] Then in Arabic, as the silence stretched on. [*Iinaa atakalam allughat almuqadasa.*]

In truth they could have said it in any of a dozen other twenty-second-century Earth languages. Serbian, Somali, Igbo, ASL, Cantonese, Maori, Spanish, Lakota, German, and more. It helped having a host of *Homo sapiens* as great-grandparents. But the Revealers only spoke the three. Those were important to them. Once dead, these languages were now spoken among the Revealer hierarchy.

A fluency in the triad should *mean something.*

After another moment, they were sent docking coordinates for the largest ship, nestled in the center of the others.

A ship that resided in a protected position.

A privileged position.

The *Reliquary.*

They moved in slowly, seamlessly skirting between the ships, observing each as they went, making note of their positions, trying to suss out their functions. The outermost were assuredly guard ships—compact, maneuverable. The Convoy

Seven construction platform had no offensive weaponry, only the ability to kill an approaching ship's engines and SD drive if they were under attack, but the *Lùhng* had no problem visually picking out the guns mounted on the guard ships.

Slipping into the second layer, they noted dozens and dozens of conflicting designs. Likely belonging to pilgrims rather than clergy.

Farther in . . . supply posts? One ship like a giant treehouse—encapsulated in something flexible and clear to retain atmospherics, it had a clearly organic middle structure, perhaps ten thousand trees, of different types, grafted to and growing on one another. Platforms jutted off it in all angles, with small ports of entry. As they flew close, they saw liquid water flowing up and down the monstrous tree's trunks, wetting the branches, making them glitter in the starlight. Fruit clung in unnatural clusters, swaying this way and that with the flow of the water.

Sometimes food was easier to print. Sometimes it was easier to grow.

Another layer in and they found the Revealer ships that belonged to the sect's hierarchy. All uniform, in a way, though no two were identical. Each had an insectoid look, and the windows and shields were all steeped in intricate, textured designs, either red or deep purple. The hulls themselves were black, sleek. The kind of ships that blended into space at a distance, that became one with the universe.

And then there was the center craft, the *Reliquary*: their destination. Large and dominating, with spires smeared red at the base, the color blending upward in ombre to maroon, then eggplant and blue black, reaching up and up and up and up, seemingly endlessly as they thinned and were lost to the blackness of their backdrop.

It looked, in a way, like the inverse of the other Revealer

ships; where those that surrounded it gave the impression of alert, living things, this looked like the husk of the deceased. Desiccated. Like something once alive, now reclaimed.

It was beautiful, and brutal, and the *Lùhng* wasn't sure what kind of greeting they would receive within.

A docking bay opened in the front of the craft, and they soared straight through, passing through a searing deCON laser that flash-cleaned their hull. Following all directions given by the Revealer landing crew, they deftly maneuvered their craft in between two larger visiting ships. After a secure touchdown, the docking bay was resealed, and they heaved themself from the tub to towel off.

Their heart fluttered.

They clutched their chest and breathed deeply for a moment.

It would be all right.

Sealing off their nostrils for internal re-breathing—just until they could go through decontamination and be sure the air's composition was as expected—they grabbed their satchel, which held the physical basis for their communication idea, and alighted into the bay.

It was especially odd to touch down in a ship that clearly adhered to cardinal directionality. Up, down, side to side. No one moved up the walls or utilized any equipment that wasn't within reaching distance of the floor. And the ceiling was high—grand and spiraling, suggesting the spires on the outside were themselves hollow. The *Lùhng* wondered if they served a practical purpose or were purely aesthetic.

They clutched their satchel close, finding it a comfort. It had been handed down to them by grandparent Devon. A memento of his very early life on Earth. A connection to a woman—E.S., the initials on the pack declared—who he'd loved but never really known.

Now it was their connection to home, which they did not know when they'd see again.

Reaching out mentally, they noted that the Revealers had only given them limited access to the mind-to-mind network aboard. Everywhere they turned their thoughts, firewalls— accompanied by the literal sense of ash, flame, and burning flesh—sprang up, boxing them in, keeping their mental scope limited.

It might have been distressing, had they not spent so much time in SD travel to get here—cut off, sealed in, and blanketed in mental silence.

A docking crew member met them with a deCON bubble, attaching it to their ship's hatchway. They alighted inside, waiting patiently while the bubble did its wash-and-work. A small, flitting robot—the size of a gecko—crawled up their left arm and skewered them with its tail, injecting an immuno-boost capsule to help suppress any invasive viral or bacterial infection they might be carrying, while simultaneously helping to guard against anything infectious they might encounter while aboard.

When the bubble was removed, they were met by three *Homo kubernētēs*, each carrying a shroud for themself. One offered the *Lùhng* a shroud as well.

[I'm not a Revealer,] they explained.

[Must cover to see Acting Progentor,] one explained.

[I . . . The Acting Progentor will see me?] Their calls into the unknown had been answered. The Acting Progentor himself! Their heart fluttered with joy, on the edge of another fibrillation. Here, finally, someone who cared enough to listen. A person of power would lend their attention. It was more than they'd expected. [Thank you! Thank the Revealers!]

Harboring no desire to be ungracious or offensive, the *Lùhng* accepted the shroud. The fabric was silken and shimmered like a raven's feathers. It glided easily over their crab-based form, though it did trail on the decking. To keep from tripping, they floated a few inches off the floor.

[Stray-Fairer Barq-Et will accompany you at all times,] the same *Homo kubernētēs* sent, gesturing upward.

With that, one firewall fell, doused with granted access. Steam swirled as a foggy, distant shape came forward in their mind, blurry at first, becoming clear in moments.

At the same time, a figure physically descended from one of the ombre flutes above. They wore a similar shroud, only theirs was robin's-egg blue and twisted at the end, into a long, tail-like knot.

The *Lùhng* attempted to establish a more direct connection, sending a greeting of pure emotion, but they were immediately rebuked.

[You say you are fluent in the sacred languages,] Barq-Et said, coming close, hovering now on the same plane. [You will only use the sacred languages while you are here.]

It was clearly a litmus test. The Revealers would not hear from someone as lowly as a megaconstruction worker if such a basic trial could not be passed.

But this was exactly why they'd decided to come. They knew they—by chance, really—possessed the skills to make the Revealers listen. [As you wish,] they replied with a small bow.

[It is not for my sake, but for yours. This is how you came to us, how you entreated us. This is how the universe has shown you the way to your own Reveals.]

The *Lùhng* was not unfamiliar with Revealer rhetoric. Many of their family members were adherents. They had great respect for people so devoted to the scientific, emotional, and artistic knowledge inherent in the universe. But the talking points, in their opinion, were repetitive and tiring.

When different people expressed the exact same thing in

the exact same way over and over again, it was difficult to tell who actually believed the sentiments and who was parroting them for the sake of appearance or power dynamics. It was not their communicated thoughts, but their actions, that revealed a true believer—of any kind.

Even an organization that preached the importance of skepticism and adaptability only tolerated so many questions and so much pushback, so the *Lùhng* opted for a simple [Of course,] in response.

[This way,] Barq-Et indicated, floating upward, toward the spire from whence they'd come.

The ascent was slow, gentle. It gave them time to admire the layout of the ship below. The docking bay had press-through walls that retracted, now that the outer airlock was resealed, and this left the majority of the ship's vast belly open. The walls—dark and inscrutable from the outside—were covered in well-lit glass, tile, and stone on the inside. Colors in the red and purple and blue spectrums spiraled all over. Words in the sacred languages were projected on the floor, changing, swirling, mingling all the time. Though many of the clergy would know what they meant, the pilgrims might not, and the *Lùhng* was delighted to see words like *ullu* and *ghym* and *song* dancing over the decking. They also saw one instance of *fuck* and tried very hard not to project their mental laughter.

The walls weren't the only things decorated. Lines and lines of supplicants waited before various displays that, at first, the *Lùhng* thought were abstract sculptures. Upon further inspection they realized they recognized several as replicas—or, perhaps, the originals?—of old Earth inventions. A Martian lander, the first reliable cold-fusion reactor, a mass-ingredient food printer. Before them were effigies of someone who'd worked on the creations—or, more likely, an imagined amalgamation of people. Those who'd uncovered something in the universe, had a true Reveal. As close a thing to the old-world concept of saints or prophets or demigods as one got with the Revealers.

[Not effigies,] Barq-Et corrected, wandering through the *Lùhng*'s loose thoughts as though they were steam. [Not purely. Inside is a monk wishing to embody the line of the saint. Wishing to take on their energy and connect with their thoughts, which were captured once and now float free among the nebulae and stardust.]

[People? Inside the statues?]

[Meditating to the point of hibernating, yes.]

[How long do they stay inside?]

A mental shrug. [Until they wish to leave, to destroy the sculpture from the inside. Most only emerge when they have found the connection they seek. Some . . . do not emerge.]

The *Lùhng* had the capacity to sink into hibernation for years at a time, though they'd never used it. The modification came from their tardigrade genes and was an emergency trait only. They couldn't imagine voluntarily entering into such a state.

As the two continued to ascend—ten stories, twenty, fifty, one hundred—the *Lùhng* tried to make further conversation with Stray-Fairer Barq-Et. Normally they'd simply access the mental net for shared information about each other. Here, though, information had to be asked for and could be directly denied. [Are you from the same home world as sub-Kaed Wes-Tu? I only ask because of the naming pattern.]

[Yes,] they replied simply, without looking down at their trailing guest. [Wes-Tu is well loved among my people.]

[Well loved among mine as well.]

This earned them a glance, and a small emotional allowance of shared contentment with this fact.

[I've come because we all want the same thing,] they attempted. [To contact the planet, to understand what's happening with the anomal—]

[I have no authority in the matter,] the Stray-Fairer interrupted. [You may save your explanations for the Acting Progentor.]

They made no attempt to hide their frustration while replying, [Of course.]

The inside of the spire was the same ombre coloring as the outside, and when they reached the black portion the *Lùhng* was surprised to see that it was unlit. Only the glare from the lights below suggested the narrowing of the walls. No small, personal lamps like they had on Convoy Seven appeared to halo them in light. Darkness greeted them, darkness swallowed them up. The walls came closer and closer, until the space was barely three meters across.

The *Lùhng* startled slightly when the walls became transparent on their left, revealing stars. The right wall remained black and opaque, blocking the sunlight coming from the Philosopher's System. Gazing out the window, they spotted several of the significant ships they'd noted on the journey in, including the giant tree-upon-tree.

Barq-Et sent a quick diagram of the spire, where it ended, when to slow and stop. They might have directed their visitor to only use the sacred languages, but clearly didn't feel the need to wholly adhere to that themself.

The *Lùhng* sensed rather than saw the Acting Progentor. He made no attempt to wall off the emotions, ideas, and concepts swirling through his mind. He thought the visit inappropriate. Thought the fact that they'd left their convoy inappropriate. Thought of their construction work as inappropriate.

Inappropriate, inappropriate, inappropriate.

He was a dark figure on a dark throne, his form tall and modified-levels of thin. Less than half a meter across from shoulder to shoulder. He wore a black shroud and looked out, past them, to the fleet beyond. The high-backed chair itself was too dark to make out in detail. It sat on a jutting platform just wide enough to support it and no more.

Barq-Et continued to hover, with the floor of the ship hundreds of stories below. So the *Lùhng* did the same.

The Acting Progentor asked them their name. The first to do so. They sent the scent of moth orchids followed by the sensation of lightly rusted iron under calloused fingertips. His name was the warmth of Earth sunlight on a humid day in a heavy swamp accompanied by the percussion of a hammer hitting slate.

Orchid and hammer, iron and sunlight.

[My records indicate the *Homo sapiens* aboard your convoy called you Iron Orchid,] he sent in words.

They were not surprised he had access to their personal history. That was the natural state of things, not this limiting and claustrophobic silence. [That is correct.]

[Then that is how we will refer to you here.]

They bristled. Iron Orchid was the name their grandparents had used. They'd never given anyone else permission not to use their full sense-name. But this was a mission of diplomacy. They could afford to be offended, they could not afford to offend.

Fine. They would own it while they were here, and do so in honor of their grandparents. Iron Orchid. *I am Iron Orchid.*

Resisting the urge to simply call him Sunlight Hammer in return, they said, [Acting Progentor, *warmth of Earth sunlight on a humid day in a heavy swamp accompanied by the percussion of a hammer hitting slate*, I have come so that we might work together to Reveal the true nature of these anomalies as well as the presence of the ri—] they stopped themself from sending *rightful—*[of Progentor Jamal Kaeden on the planet Noumenon.

[I have evidence that a certain material can transit the anomalies without interference, and if we can figure out a way to use it as a protective shield—not unlike an SD bubble—we can—]

[You and your people are the subject of an interstellar embargo,] he said flatly in their mind. [I have the authority to arrest you where you stand. Furthermore, it seems your presence here isn't even sanctioned by your own convoy.]

No point in denying it. [That is correct. All of it, correct. But I think you'll agree that what we have here are dire circumstances that cannot be corrected by putting an entire society in interstellar time-out.]

[Your *entire society* is to blame for the appearance of the anomalies.]

[If that is true, which has yet to be proven empirically, then we are the ones most equipped to dissipate them. Yet no one will allow us any kind of involvement, be it political, scientific, or advisory.]

[Many of your people approve of the construction ban, and the embargo. Not one person has gone on official record to support your trip here. In addition, if I'm deciphering some of these coded imprints properly, it looks as though you may have stolen the very ship currently enjoying a systems check in our facilities.]

"Currently enjoying a systems check" was the diplomatic way of telling Iron Orchid that though the scans hadn't picked up anything dangerous, the ship was getting a full sweep for biomalware, hard-coded bugs, and explosive materials.

Iron Orchid gave no indication they took offense at being regarded as a potential rogue terrorist. If the Revealers wanted to put up walls around them, then they, too, would keep up their own walls. [How long has it been since you've received pilgrims from Earth? How long has it been since the clergy was able to visit the Originating Planet? Or what about the planetary system of *symphonic harmonies and subaudible blasts*? We all know it is not self-sustaining. They have an artificial sun they built themselves but still require soil nutrients from the outside to grow their food while they wait for the energy to build to levels suitable for instant protein alignment. People could be dying down there—your people, my people. *People.* And your Progentor, and my not-met family, could be wasting away on the planet not a light-year from here, and yet you want to talk blame and boundaries and bureaucracy? I have the beginnings of an idea that could turn into answers and *no one will listen!*]

Arrythmia seized Iron Orchid. Their heart stopped, then punched, filled with too much blood. It happened again. It hurt, and they gasped, finding gas exchange painful. The emotional wall fell, and they reached out like they would under duress back home, sending a wordless sense of anguish and anxiety.

They clutched at their chest, doubled forward.

The Acting Progentor did not stir from his throne. But Barq-Et surged forward. Having remained silent for these past few minutes, their mind now reached out in comforting wordlessness, searching for the problem in their guest's mind.

[Likely a malfunctioning heart valve,] *the warmth of Earth sunlight on a humid day in a heavy swamp accompanied by the percussion of a hammer hitting slate* said. [Iron Orchid has a history of developing such problems every few years.]

Barq-Et sent questions about Iron Orchid's recent health. They replied with confirmation that they were aware of their current iteration of illness before arriving on board.

[We must get you to the surgery at once,] Barq-Et said.

Their heart wouldn't settle again, no matter how many times they gasped. They accidentally conveyed a mixture of agreement and denial. The negotiations had only begun. They hadn't even had time to lay out their findings. What if this was their only chance? Would the Acting Progentor deign to see them again? Would he listen? Someone had to

listen. Someone had to listen or this would only get worse.
The anomalies were growing. There was news of another
blossoming into existence just before they'd left the convoy. If
they didn't do *something*—

Another shot of pain ricocheted through their chest and
they lost concentration, balance.

They *fell*.

They hadn't passed a floor or so much as an outcropping
on the way up. The Acting Progentor's chair sat on a narrow
tongue jutting from the spire's inside wall, but all else was
smooth.

Their shroud fluttered, came away as they lost sight of the
Acting Progentor above.

Iron Orchid's stomach jumped and flopped, their muscles
everywhere contracted. They'd never felt such a full-forced
tug of gravity before. Hadn't fallen since they were small and
trying to learn to manipulate gravitons for the first time. They
felt sick and distracted and wildly fascinated with their own
bodily sensations all at once.

Two sets of simian hands grasped Iron Orchid around the
middle.

Instead of jerking to a stop, Barq-Et lowered them together,
gently easing Iron Orchid's fall. Luckily, they had plenty of
space in which to decelerate.

Barq-Et reiterated that they would take Iron Orchid to surgery, and they agreed. Barq-Et then chided them for not indicating they needed medical attention before landing. Hiding
their face in the Stray-Fairer's shroud, letting the soft fabric
ripple around their cheeks, they explained that they were
concerned they wouldn't receive medical attention. Or that
it might be used as a reason to turn them away.

[Couldn't risk not meeting with the Acting Progentor.]

[Medical aid should always be given when it is needed,]
Barq-Et said. [No Revealer would deny you such basic de-

cency. The head surgeon is my friend. She has seen to my own heart, she will be gentle with yours.]

They indicated Iron Orchid should be ready to make their medical history available to the surgeons, and then bid them rest as the two soared over the winding queues of pilgrims.

Just before they disappeared behind a partition off the hangar, Iron Orchid noticed something they couldn't believe they'd missed before. A hundred-meter statue of Jamal Kaeden, made out of the same raven material as the hull of the ships, tucked both unassumingly and imposingly off to the side, in a nook built just for it. A tall barrier kept visitors from getting within ten meters of the statue itself.

There were no lines, because Jamal's gentle face greeted everyone as they came aboard. Simultaneously a prominent and shadowy figure.

Briefly, Iron Orchid wondered if anyone was voluntarily entombed inside.

Barq-Et waited outside the surgery while three medics—two of which were *Homo kubernētēs* and one *Homo draconem*—worked on Iron Orchid.

The surgeons indicated they could have grown Iron Orchid a new heart if alerted earlier and sent the proper genetic schematics for grafting onto a cellular frame. Instead, they would have to put in a woven structure. Not an artificial heart valve, but an aid that assisted in its closing and opening, using Iron Orchid's own bioelectrical impulses to function.

Iron Orchid took up their position on the press-through operating table, which tilted them back, thrust their chest forward, and allowed their six lower legs to fold and rest comfortably. The room itself was flooded with bright lights, a sharp contrast to the Acting Progentor's throne room. The *Lùhng* closed their two innermost sets of eyelids—those designed to protect against the intensity of a directly observed sun.

Despite being Revealers, the surgeons were dressed in the trappings of most medics. Sanitary smocks—of a different design than on the convoy, but functionally the same—covered their torsos. The *Homo kubernētēs* didn't need surgical masks, as their faceplates already sanitized the air both in and out of their organic lungs, but the *Homo draconem* sported one.

But it wasn't as though surgery was messy. Chances of damage or contamination were slight.

The three surgeons directed Iron Orchid to pull back their own solar-scale layer, revealing the clear skin beneath. The layers of outer skin flopped back, folding over like heavily beaded silk. They were given an IV that contained a special relaxant that targeted the muscle groups which kept their chest cavity hermetically sealed and their ribs in place.

After a moment, the center of their chest unfurled, dilating like an iris, and their ribs and breastbone gently pulled away, slowly rising out of position, reaching for the ceiling like plants looking for a dawn sun.

It might have felt strange, if Iron Orchid hadn't been through this procedure over a dozen times. No matter how many slight modifications were made to their DNA map when a new heart was grown, one valve always became weak, refused to close properly. Most of the time it was merely bothersome, like when their scales had been irradiated to their lifetime limits and a full exfoliation, scrub, and replacement needed to take place. The very first time, however, had been like this time: a sudden rush to the medics, anxiety spikes, difficulty breathing. They'd only been ten at the time and had parental panic to suffer through as well.

They watched with mild interest as the *Homo draconem* surgeon gently pushed aside any obstructing sections of vein and organ and lifted their heart straight from their chest, the attached arterial veins stretching as they did so.

From elsewhere, two additional assistants entered the

room, each pushing a cart. One cart carried a complex machine that would act as an artificial heart while Iron Orchid's was removed for repair. The other contained the replacement parts, a set of valve aids that would have come from a vast cryogenic store of medical supplies.

With four practiced hands, the surgeon detached the connections of the systemic loop from Iron Orchid's heart before moving on to the connections of the pulmonary loop, as easy as pulling apart wire connections, while simultaneously reconnecting those same valves to the artificial heart machine.

Once the transfer was made, all three surgeons turned away from their patient, giving their full attention to the actual surgery portion of the event.

Iron Orchid stared at the ceiling. The artificial heart pumped more firmly than their own, making every push of blood through their body feel heavy, forced. But the beat was steady. They relaxed, shut their eyes completely.

They chided themself for thinking they could put this off. Barq-Et was right, they should have asked right away. But in the moment, their problems seemed trivial to the problems of the entire galaxy. They'd traveled all this way, and the potential of being denied right here, at the end, seemed too great to risk.

"Put on your own mask before assisting others" used to be a favorite saying of Great-Grandma Talutah's. Iron Orchid wasn't sure what the origin of the saying was, but it meant you could only do your best to help other people when you'd taken care of yourself first.

If Iron Orchid really wanted to make sure the Acting Progentor heard them, they had to preserve their strength and look after their health.

A few minutes more and the work was done. The surgeons brought the heart back to its owner, reconnected all its fastenings, tucked it into its cavity, and changed out the IV so that Iron Orchid's muscles and bones would gradually tighten back into place.

One last vitals check and they were released with a minor warning not to engage in anything too strenuous for the time being.

Outside, Barq-Et was waiting. They exuded nervousness, but Iron Orchid sent waves of reassurance.

[Thank you for seeing me safely to the surgery,] Iron Orchid said.

[Of course.] Barq-Et shifted uneasily, clearly abashed, shy to ask their next question. [Your condition—it keeps returning?]

[Yes.]

[Then why have your own surgeons not made for you a *Homo kubernētēs* heart?] They put a shrouded hand over their own chest. [My flesh too failed, even upon several regrowths.]

Iron Orchid found their thoughts difficult to organize around the subject—their feelings vast and imprecise, a mixture of personal attachment and a cultural normality—a societal adherence to modified biology over mechanical.

Frankly, they were stubborn. They kept insisting on a re-cloned heart because the heart was theirs.

[The fitted connections are the same,] Barq-Et continued. [My friend could—]

[That is kind, but no. I shall keep this one for as long as I am able.]

Barq-Et nodded, then held out the fallen shroud, retrieved from wherever it had fluttered. [In case you'd like it back. There is no requirement for coverings if you are not in the presence of the Acting Progentor. There are many days when the universe desires us to fully expose ourselves or fully cover ourselves, but this is no such day.]

[Will you accompany me to mealtime?] they added.

[I thought you were supposed to stay with me at all times. Didn't think I had a choice.]

[I could just as easily show you to bedchambers if you would prefer to rest after your surgery.]

Iron Orchid took the shroud and tied it around their waist, letting it drape down over their abdomen and legs. [When can I see the Acting Progentor again?]

[I will put in another request for you.]

[Just because a disaster is slow moving doesn't mean the solution isn't urgent. You saw to my illness as soon as symptoms appeared. The anomalies should be treated with no less pressing care.]

[When was the last time you ate something? You can take food by mouth, yes?]

[I traveled in a protein bath.]

[But when have you last *eaten*? As an experience. Not simply absorbed nutrients for survival?]

Iron Orchid paused, taken aback by the shape of the inquiry. [My digestive system has been in stasis since I left Convoy Seven.]

[Would you revive it to take sustenance with the Revealers?]

Iron Orchid didn't send words. Instead they projected irritation. They were being stymied, and they couldn't understand why.

Barq-Et sent understanding. [I take your frustration. I know your quest is important. But the Acting Progentor cannot shirk his other duties to see to one guest. You must realize you are not the first to come here with a plan.]

Iron Orchid sent up a wall, barring Barq-Et from sensing their surprise. No, they hadn't realized, actually.

[All those plans failed in their entirety, and each was suggested by leading researchers from a well-respected scientific group, conglomerate, commune, or authority. You, by contrast, arrived unannounced, illegally and disrespectfully. You should not be surprised that the most revered individual, our leader, is skeptical of not only your plan, but your very presence.

[I, personally, sense sincerity in you. I'm sure the Acting Progentor has as well. But we've encountered those who have learned to falsify even the deepest-set emotions. To hide, without emotional barriers, what we've believed unhidable for millennia. If one can fabricate the very core of their intent, then wall-less interactions can no longer be taken at face value. Exposing one's emotional center no longer carries the same diplomatic weight it used to.

[I shall continue to advocate for you. But, in the interim, would you care to partake in solid food?]

Iron Orchid felt even more frustrated than before and did not hide their urge to be standoffish. Barq-Et may or may not have meant to be patronizing, but it was impossible not to take their monologue in such a fashion. [A meal would be nice, thank you,] Iron Orchid said, weaving in layers of dismissal and offense into the acceptance.

The ship's interior—which had previously been part history museum, part shrine, and part contemplative sanctum—had transformed during the time Iron Orchid had undergone surgery. The displays had been sucked down into the floor, which at first they hadn't realized was press-through, and replaced with rows upon rows of communal tables. The entire rectangular area was now lined with statues of important Revealers who'd uncovered the universe's grandest secrets. They each matched Jamal Kaeden's in the hangar for bulk and grandeur. Only, Iron Orchid noticed, a particular set of sculptures was missing.

Where was the likeness of Joanna Straifer, who'd allowed the superstructure within the Web, known as the Seed, to build the Philosopher's System? Or Sunny Phongam, who'd begun the *Homo draconem* evolutionary branch through modification?

Iron Orchid searched for the other Revealers they knew. Those prominent in their own culture. And then they realized: almost all the legendary Revealers from Convoy Seven were conspicuous in their absence.

Only Jamal hadn't lost his place of respect due to the unsavory association.

They wondered if the figures had been temporarily hidden, or destroyed. If they contained meditating monks, had the universe somehow informed them of the folly? Had they all come spontaneously bursting from their shells like cicadas? Or did they still slumber?

Had these historic people only fallen from grace for the moment, or had the Acting Progentor removed them from his sect's pantheon?

Iron Orchid sent this last question passively outward, rather than directly at Barq-Et, but the Stray-Fairer did not respond.

Pilgrims, supplicants, new converts, and clergy all mingled at the meal. There was no hierarchy inherent in the tabling. Foods of every kind, ranging from ancient Earth fare to new interstellar dishes to anatomically specific (meaning only certain mods could consume them, be it because the dishes' temperature was so hot it would burn the nonequipped from the inside, or because it had to be consumed through tear ducts, or because it wasn't carbon based, etc.), covered the center of the tables. But no *new* Earth fare. Nothing that relied on trade with the anomaly-affected systems.

There was nothing modest about the meal: it was explicitly a feast, and it was explicitly welcoming and celebratory.

To most people.

Those who lived in the sect's fleet had clearly consciously limited their mind-to-mind reach, and the ship still had firewalls in place to hem Iron Orchid in. But pilgrims from the far edges of the galaxy felt no need to put up barriers—at least, not until they encountered Iron Orchid's mind and realized from whence they hailed. Then they made no secret of cutting them off, mentally smacking them away.

After only a few minutes of floating past hostile minds, Iron Orchid put up all the mental and emotional walls they could. Better to seem a blank slate—to be a mystery—than obviously a member of such a reviled convoy.

To these pilgrims, Iron Orchid was the reason Jamal was gone. Iron Orchid was to blame for taking their holiest being away.

Iron Orchid was the source of the anomalies and all their societies' related ills.

The universe was broken, and someone had to be held accountable.

Barq-Et found them a suitable place at a flanking table, near the back corner, looking out toward the docking bay.

Plates, goblets, bowls, decanters, leaves, fresh-cut planks, platters, and every other variety of serving vessel whirled in front of them in a constant dance, lifted by the manipulated gravitons of unseen servers. All Iron Orchid had to do was pluck their pleasure from the floating parade.

[You ask when I'd last eaten as an experience,] Iron Orchid said, as they poured a smattering of ox blood from a carafe onto the oblong dish before them. [As though protein absorption in a bath is some sanitized thing. As though letting your cells constantly feed through osmosis—coating your skin, nutrients slipping between your joints and into your pores—isn't an experience. As though when I'm freed from a ship, floating untethered in front of a star, drinking in nothing but its radiation through my scales, that it makes me somehow less than human. That mashing with one's teeth, that gulping with one's gullet, is the only proper way to consume sustenance.]

"Mashing with one's teeth" hadn't happened aboard Convoy Seven for many thousands of years before they'd encountered Convoy Twelve. Iron Orchid had been modified pregrowth to be able to eat like the great-grandparents, as had many of their generation.

[When humanity first discovered fire and began cooking their meat,] they continued, [were they less human? Or do you think them more human then, and humanity is just a narrow band of acceptable ways of being, of doing? Of *eating*?]

Pointedly, they ran a simian finger through the ox blood and stuck it between their lips. [Is this more acceptable to you than smearing it on my cheek?] Iron Orchid did that as well, just to make a point.

Barq-Et did not respond right away, their eyes fixed for a prolonged moment on Iron Orchid's cheek. A fluttery, fuzzy feeling wafted away from the Stray-Fairer before they realized and shuttered their emotions. [I did not mean to offend,] they said, though their words were clearly completely unassociated with whatever sensation that smear of blood had sparked within.

Iron Orchid had caught Barq-Et off guard. Had elicited in them a strange feeling. A feeling Iron Orchid was surprised they themself had enjoyed receiving.

Mentally clearing their throats, they both shuffled their attention back to the food. Iron Orchid gathered rooted thistle from a pot, dried grasshoppers, and a hearty helping of yellow curry over rice. They also grabbed a mango before it slipped by, wondering—but not asking, lest it be disappointingly untrue—if it had indeed been grown on the tree-of-many-grafts.

Barq-Et poured a helping of a thin, orange broth, in which they crumpled pink rose petals and pink peppercorns. A small side of camel's-milk curd completed their dish.

The two of them—and, indeed, the room—ate heartily for

some time. Iron Orchid caught wisps of sentiment, dashes of ideas. Little blooms of conversation, some with thorns, some that withered on the vine, but most vibrant and fragrant. Once in a while someone brought up the missing Progentor, but they were quickly hushed. The feast was happy. Everyone wanted to *stay* happy.

The *Lùhng* tried to gather if any of the pilgrims were from anomaly-affected regions. A mention of the galaxy's plight cropped up here and there, but the instances had no teeth, no emotional bite. It was a terrible thing happening far, far away. Never mind they sat on one's doorstep. Never mind that the galaxy was an interconnected system, and the currents of tragedy would wash upon their shores, too. Never mind that it was unpredictable and getting worse. Never mind.

Never mind.

The sect was too isolated. Too insulated in its current state. Perhaps Iron Orchid had made a miscalculation. They thought that the cult's placement—so near their lost and beloved—meant the Revealers felt the same fever they did.

With a burst of urgency, renewed now with the taste of blood on the backs of their teeth and the clouds of apathy washing through their mind, Iron Orchid reached for their satchel, to show Barq-Et, if no one else, what it contained.

But Iron Orchid's hand met empty air. They glanced around frantically, folding their crab legs to see beneath the table. Nothing.

A zing of panic made their insides clench. The pack had been with them when they'd alighted from their ship, they were sure. And then it must have been with them when they addressed the Acting Progentor. And when they fell? In the surgery? Iron Orchid couldn't remember. Entering the banquet hall? They'd been too enamored by the gathering, too irritated with Barq-Et's insinuations, to pay attention.

[I will have Pavonian Prites search for it,] Barq-Et said, making no overt note of how Iron Orchid had let their thoughts suddenly spill wildly.

[It is important,] they stressed. [The contents, yes, but the pack itself holds sentimental value.]

[Oh?]

[It is dear to me. A part of my family.]

Four children approached, their robes loose about their various engineered frames. Several of the dishes smoothly dropped to the table's surface, halting their march.

[These Prites study the ways of finding, of navigation,] Barq-Et explained. [Give them a clear picture of that which they seek, and they shall locate it.]

Iron Orchid sent the texture of clearly defined synthetic stitching, the pattern it made, the scent of decades of use, the lump of the pack as whole, the steady heft of it settled in their hands and upon their shoulders. The soft sensation of the branded initials under the pad of a finger.

The children broke with a nod, flying away in multiple directions, like seedpods scattered in the wind.

[May I offer rest now?] Barq-Et asked. [Your worry runs deep. Best cured with sleep.]

[Best cured with *action*,] Iron Orchid countered.

[And yet there is none to take.]

[Not until *warmth of Earth sunlight on a humid day in a heavy swamp accompanied by the percussion of a hammer hitting slate* agrees to see me again.]

[I can show you to a communal hammock room. It will be familiar to you, like what you're accustomed to aboard your convoy.]

[I prefer my ship.]

[I am supposed to accompany you at all times, and your ship only has sleeping arrangements for one.]

[Unless we share.]

It was both an open invitation and a dare. Not suggestive in a sexual sense, but in an intimate sense. Yes, Iron Orchid had been incredibly uncomfortable sleeping alone these last years, and a return to the communal norm would have been a welcomed familiarity. But Iron Orchid did not want to lose sight of their purpose, of their dire mission. The more uncomfortable they remained, the heavier the urgency weighed.

Barq-Et's presence would not be uncomfortable. It might even be soothing. Though their conversation had been somewhat contentious, Iron Orchid had already developed an affection for the Stray-Fairer. Perhaps because this had been their longest sustained interaction in so long.

[There are no members of your clergy aboard my convoy,] Iron Orchid confessed. [Forgive me if my offer is offensive.]

[I am not offended. Simply surprised. You are our guest. If that is the sleeping arrangement that is to your liking, I shall . . .]

Barq-Et's mind fumbled. Skipped over itself. A sudden fixation on the stripe of ox blood seeped through the cracks once more.

[Relations and relationships aren't forbidden by your order . . . are they?] Iron Orchid prodded.

[No. No. That is an antiquated political practice, meant to secure a devotee's focus and ensure their estate and its wealth went to the religious institution upon their death, rather than blood heirs. Such body-tithing would never be required by the Revealers.]

[However . . . ?]

[However, this life makes connection difficult. Many of us do not serve in one station for long. Even at that, pilgrims everywhere come and go frequently, and it would be unethical—due to the power dynamics at play—to attempt to become emotionally or physically involved with any of them.]

Iron Orchid left *But I am not a pilgrim* unsaid with words.

Against orders, they shifted to sense and feeling once more. *And yet, we still have power dynamics at play, don't we? I want a meeting with your Acting Progentor. I want someone to listen. And you can make it happen. You hold that power.*

If time and circumstances were different . . .

But things were as they were.

And they both understood, both agreed.

[We shall sleep,] Barq-Et said. [Rest. And greet the problem of the anomalies anew.]

Days passed. Iron Orchid awoke every morning with Barq-Et beside them, the two entwined, putting cradling pressure on one another similar to the cradling pressure of a hammock. When they left the ship, Iron Orchid immediately asked after the Acting Progentor's time, and Barq-Et immediately put in a request, before distracting the visitor with more food or lessons in Revealership, or questions about megastructure building.

They bantered. Hostilely at first. But soon it became play. A friendly dance. A push and pull.

Even after heading back to Iron Orchid's ship for sleep, they would talk well into the prescribed resting hours. Of little hopes, little dreams, little likes. Of childhood. Of art and science.

On the fifth day, the satchel was found and returned. Iron Orchid eagerly clutched it to them, took in the smell of it, found comfort in the hominess of its presence, in the memories it ignited. But it was empty.

Iron Orchid did not interrogate the Prite who returned it. If it was the child who'd robbed them, then it was not their fault. They would have been directed by another hand—an adult hand. For even one so young would not dare take from a stranger and then innocently hand over the evidence.

Fear and hesitance wafted off the Prite.

Power dynamics at play.

Iron Orchid even stopped Barq-Et from cross-examining the young one. Though the Stray-Fairer hesitated to accept the logical conclusion, they relented.

[I cannot believe a Revealer—a pilgrim, our guests—would steal from another in this sanctuary,] Barq-Et fumed.

[I cannot either,] Iron Orchid said, their double-speak clear.

[You suspect clergy? *Me?*]

[No. Not you.]

[Your surgeons, then?]

[No.] Iron Orchid kept their emotions suppressed, their answers clipped. They were sure Barq-Et wouldn't even entertain their true suspicions—anticipated hot, boiling rage when the Stray-Fairer inevitably deduced them for themself.

But instead they received a dumbfounded lack of emotion. Less a lack than a vacuum—a sucking inward, a dark void. [You suspect Acting Progentor *warmth of Earth sunlight on a humid day in a heavy swamp accompanied by the percussion of a hammer hitting slate.*]

Iron Orchid sent a blip of affirmation.

[No. There would be no point, no need. Whatever it is you carried with you, the Acting Progentor could get more himself. *You* could get more, at a simple request, to be sure. There is no need—]

[He did not take it because he needs it. Did not take it because he thinks it's all I have. He took it as a warning. He expects me to leave, to drop my pursuit.]

[No.] Barq-Et shook their head emphatically. [If your direction was folly he would not see you again and you would leave in your own time. He would not waste attention driving you away. Would certainly not steal from you to do it.]

[Then,] Iron Orchid sent slowly, [we must conclude my direction is not folly.]

This Barq-Et could not understand. Willful confusion blew like a stiff wind in Iron Orchid's direction.

The scent of moth orchids followed by the sensation of lightly rusted iron under calloused fingertips knew then: there was no aid to be had here. Not because of their Convoy Seven origins. Not because their ideas wouldn't work. But because someone had a vested interest in making sure these problems weren't solved. Someone who knew very well what the results might be if the anomalies persisted, if no contact was ever made with the Noumonian surface. Someone who was sure he would be dead before such troubles ever reached his docking bay. Someone who enjoyed his power more than he believed in his order or cared about the future in which his young Prites had to live.

[Take me to him. Now.]

[No!]

[Take me, or I shall go myself.]

[The Protectorate will expel you if you attempt to go without me.]

[Is that what you wish?]

[Of course not.]

[Then take me to the Acting Progentor. Do this now, and I shall ask no more of you and be on my way back to my accursed convoy.]

This last statement seemed to wound Barq-Et more than Iron Orchid's accusations. They both regretted the idea that they might be parted so soon.

There was an instant coolness that swept past Iron Orchid, which they read as Barq-Et once more reaching out for permission to see the Acting Progentor. What would the Stray-Fairer communicate? Would they convey the accusation? Keep it hidden? *Could* they keep it hidden from one such as Sunlight Hammer?

[He will see you now,] Barq-Et said, crestfallen.

Together, they floated back up the spire, through the shift-ing colors and once more into darkness. An acute sense of foreboding greeted Iron Orchid as they alighted in the top-most chamber, the throne room. It was not a general or inter-nal sense, but a projected one. The Acting Progentor wanted them to feel an oncoming ominousness. Wanted the impres-sion of the sinister to be palpable. He was adept at fine-tuned emotional directionality; it was clear Barq-Et felt nothing but ease and peace radiating from their leader.

Iron Orchid did not wait to be addressed. [You think me naïve for coming here,] they sent. [Perhaps I was. Naïve to think that stories of Jamal Kaeden's kindness and sincerity and grace might somehow apply to a successor.]

Barq-Et practically shriveled with instant embarrassment. That they should find shame in Iron Orchid's boldness meant Barq-Et felt a connection, a responsibility toward the Convoy Seven crew member—elsewise the Stray-Fairer might have admonished them for their insolence. Barq-Et begged forgive-ness from their Acting Progentor with a sense of pity, of soft-ness, of gentle familial love and understanding.

But such forgiveness was neither given nor wanted.

[You think the Revealers free of politics?] Iron Orchid asked Barq-Et. [You think your order free of power-lust and greed? We are humanity, and no matter our better intentions, where we go those things go with us.]

Neither Barq-Et nor *warmth of Earth sunlight on a humid day in a heavy swamp accompanied by the percussion of a hammer hitting slate* answered.

So Iron Orchid barreled onward.

[I understand now, why a Jamal clone was needed in the first place, and why the fracturing happened once he was gone. He was a Progentor who couldn't ask for the honor. Couldn't seek it. There could be no bribes, no lies, no ambitions from him. I thought that once he was gone it was the conflicting ideas about his fate that sent this sect and that sect spinning off like eddies from a whirlpool. But it was a power vacuum. A chance to seize what had previously been unseize-able for thousands of years.

[You don't *want* the Progentor back. You need him gone. That's why you're actually parked here, isn't it? To prevent anyone from making an unsupervised attempt at communi-cation. To make sure that—dead or alive—the Progentor stays trapped within that anomaly. Forever.

[You already know about the alacritite, don't you?] Iron Or-chid let the information flow freely, outward, into Barq-Et and anyone in proximity—clearly to the irritation of the Acting Progentor—all they'd discovered about the metal's properties. That it was little used in the galaxy these days, but used to be a prime component in personality-driven AI and the earliest generation of SD drives. [You know alacritite is a complex alloy that creates inexplicably stable ionic bonds—*not* by neu-tralization of the ionic charges of the bonded atoms, but by becoming simultaneously positively and negatively charged *without* polarization.

[You know its primary components are Au^3, C^{2-}, Ti^4, and P^{3-}. And you've learned on your own that it can penetrate the anomalies *unperturbed*.

[The alloy has unique subdimensional properties unlike any other substance we've ever created—though you proba-bly, like me, don't fully grasp those properties. And you've kept that knowledge hidden. My finding out independently is inconvenient. But the one thing working in your favor is that no one will listen to me.]

An emptiness, of both emotion and words—a vacancy, rather than a pause—followed.

[Barq-Et has heard,] the Acting Progentor said after a time. [Barq-Et believes in you.]

He let Iron Orchid hear his double tone. The gentle, understanding version of the words he sent to his Stray-Fairer, and the dark, sharp version that was the truth. A truth meant for Iron Orchid only, to emphasize the power he held over not just this situation, not just their fate, but also Barq-Et's, as well as the entire fleet that surrounded them.

[I do,] Barq-Et said, not understanding how such a simple declaration of sincerity sealed their fate.

Sunlight Hammer *sighed.* [And that is where the corruption lies. A subtle corruption, but one nonetheless,] he declared. [My Stray-Fairer. My Barq-Et. How has this convoy dweller wormed their way into your graces, past your good senses, so quickly?]

Barq-Et was taken aback. They slipped into pure mind-to-mind. They heaved denials at Sunlight Hammer as though they were stones. The intense sense of protest was overwhelming. Barq-Et was floundering, but there was no aid Iron Orchid could give.

[It is not your fault,] the Acting Progentor said with a wave of one thin limb. [Those as devout as you can be the most susceptible to those who would lie. You believe so much in truth you cannot understand those who wish to maim and undermine. This galaxy breaker has come to dethrone me, and surely to tear our order from its perch, to be sure no one is left to keep vigil over the system. They are angry their convoy no longer holds a sacred place, that its folly has been Revealed. And that folly has turned to treachery. Vengeance. They did not need to bring bombs in order to dismantle. Just charms.]

Iron Orchid could have denied everything—as none of it was true—but that was what the Acting Progentor wanted. Accusing both Iron Orchid and Barq-Et of misdeeds was calculated, meant to alienate the *Lùhng* and entrench the Stray-Fairer. Iron Orchid would not give him the satisfaction of the expected reaction.

His tone split again. Sweet for Barq-Et, sour for Iron Orchid. [We took you in. Cared for you. And you use our hospitality against us.]

["Are none of us decent who use an enemy's health or hearth against them,"] Iron Orchid quoted.

[Just because one can recall the teachings of past Revealers, that doesn't mean one lives by them,] the Acting Progentor snapped back. Barq-Et was kept from hearing.

[*That* is a truth neither of us can deny,] Iron Orchid replied.

They weren't sure what calculations the Acting Progentor had yet to make. He held all the power here. Could order Iron Orchid gone with the snap of a finger. But perhaps his position wasn't as solidified as they thought. Perhaps he saw the sincere care in Barq-Et as its own kind of threat. The Stray-Fairer was no simple soldier, no will-less lowling who took orders without question. That wasn't the Revealer way. He needed to convince Barq-Et that however he chose to be rid of Iron Orchid was *right*.

Were there things now being said between the two of them? The Acting Progentor's mastery of communication was unlike any Iron Orchid had ever seen. He seemed the very kind Barq-Et had explained about days earlier—those who could seem entirely open, exposed to the emotional core, yet hide their true intent.

The Acting Progentor withdrew from Iron Orchid's mind. Cut off his communication, seemingly confirming their suspicions. What happened next would decide their fate, and they would not be privy to the entirety of the conversation.

What inroads was he making into Barq-Et's loyalty? How was he shaping his Stray-Fairer's morality—molding it to fit his own needs?

[Barq-Et,] Sunlight Hammer said after a time. [It is you I task with disposing of the Accursed and Shamed.]

Illness, sadness, swirled around Barq-Et. [I shall return

them to their shuttle at once. See that they are escorted from the fl—]

[No. They will persist as a danger. They cannot stand.]

The Acting Progentor could have been precise. Direct. But instead chose to drag out his meaning, to torture both his Stray-Fairer and his innocent visitor in the stretching.

[We are Revealers, we have no courts, no prisons. We do not detain—]

[I said *dispose*.]

Everything in Barq-Et twisted and jerked, their mind crying out in a short-clipped scream. Their being shook with existential fracturing. [We do not *kill*—]

[I did not say *kill*. We do not kill. Nor will we have to. They eat starlight. They can survive the depths and cold of empty space. As the one who communes and the one who sees, I say to you: take them far, far afield. Do not dally. Leave them out the airlock of your ship. The universe may yet have need of them. If so, rescue shall be sent—from elsewhere. If not, the fabric of their own demise is enmeshed in their flesh. Our surgeons mended it well, but the biology itself is faulty. I had those loyal to me—as you should be—place a monitor in their heart. I shall know when it stops. And not until then, Stray-Fairer Barq-Et, will you be allowed back aboard this vessel.]

[That may be years—]

[I trust you to devise a way to hasten your return.]

[I—]

[Be gone! I compel you. Each of us waits and suffers for our true test of understanding, to receive and appreciate the wisdom of all as it is Revealed. This is part of your suffering as it should be. Cleansing is not easy. If it were, we would never need to cleanse.]

Moving softly, dreamlike, Barq-Et indicated Iron Orchid should descend from the spire. They did not argue. Barq-Et did not hide their mind as they reached out to others, making preparations, finding a small crew, requesting supplies. They requested their surgeon friend, and an engineer, and a captain and a pilot and another Stray-Fairer.

Iron Orchid themself was numb with anger, disappointment. They had come here seeking allies and were now marching to their doom as a traitor. Yet, they had no fear. Death was still an abstraction. They were, in a sense, still young. That this should sincerely end in obliteration seemed impossible.

And they could not die. Not yet. Not when so much was in danger, and they had touched the solution.

The two of them did not converse. Barq-Et's mind turned inward.

The ship that awaited them was an order of magnitude larger than Iron Orchid's. And it was a wonder to them that so great a thing be needed for such a small, distasteful task.

Barq-Et inspected the supplies as they were loaded—all to their specifications. The crew, however, was a different matter. Barq-Et pulled up short when greeted not by their friends but by hard loyalists. A captain, a pilot, a medic, a Nakamov Prite, and a member of the Protectorate.

Sunlight Hammer was giving Barq-Et no leeway.

It wasn't until they were all nestled inside that Barq-Et narrowed their focus and said to Iron Orchid, [Don't worry. I grew up as a Pavonian Prite. I have an idea. A wonderful, terrible idea.]

Iron Orchid was not privy to the nav information, nor to information about the crew. The five would not so much as speak to the *Lùhng,* cutting them off from even the smallest quips of conversation, from acknowledgment altogether.

Only Barq-Et still spoke with them, but it was in short spurts and with a cover of harshness. They could not cut themself off from the crew—lest they draw suspicion. But the blankness that had initially engulfed the Stray-Fairer had dissipated, and there was the hot-poker smell of a plan in their emotionality.

Days passed. A week. Though Iron Orchid was free to roam about the ship and was offered ready sustenance—fine noodles, crisp vegetables, many cheeses, and salted fishes—these were only granted to assuage the guilt the crew felt. They were loyal, but they were not killers. They were not accustomed to such orders from their Acting Progentor. They likely told themselves they weren't killing anyone—that what Sunlight Hammer had said about the *Lùhng* subsisting comfortably on starlight in the void meant this was more of a blessed dismissal than a death sentence.

They trusted their Acting Progentor. Iron Orchid found it difficult to blame them for that.

He'd told them the *Lùhng* was a terrorist. And now Iron Orchid had to admit they were, in fact, a threat—even if that threat was purely existential.

Iron Orchid made no attempt to persuade the crew to their side. What good would it do? It would only reaffirm what their leader had said. And they made no attempt to escape, choosing to trust, instead, in that single sentence Barq-Et had offered when they'd boarded.

On the eighth day, the crew disappeared, down into the bowels of the ship, where Iron Orchid had only thought to peek on the first day.

Barq-Et alone met them in the mess. There was nothing on the shared table but a loaf of wheat bread and a silver bowl of blood. Ox blood.

[Their work will dampen the mind-to-mind. They shouldn't be able to hear us clearly, even at this proximity. Speak the sacred languages. They are all unskilled in the usage.]

[What work?]

[Building you a prison.]

Barq-Et dipped a slice of bread in the blood, secreting it away beneath their shroud. [It is a special prison,] they continued after a moment of chewing. Their mental tone was flat, untelling. [With no windows. No engine. No life support. Just a perfect sphere of metal.]

Iron Orchid settled their front crab legs over the shared bench, next to Barq-Et. They pulled the bowl of blood in front of them, peering down into a ruddy reflection. [A perfect sphere of metal.]

[The crew knows I am to hasten your demise, after all.]

[Would this metal happen to be an alloy?]

[A special alloy; its precise metallurgical properties screamed at me approximately a week ago, in a time of great distress.]

Iron Orchid stuck one finger lightly in the ox blood, watching the ripples. Watching how the blood clung to their fingertip, then undulated, dripped, the concentric circles fanning outward.

[Do you remember what I said about Pavonian Prites?] Barq-Et said intensely. [Do you understand the specialty I was raised in? What knowledge I was encouraged to seek?]

[I admit I do not.]

[Navigational. In fact, I was given several high honors for my ability to plot intricate courses using the natural gravitational properties of a given location—free of cyclers.]

[Free of engines?]

[Free of engines, of any sort of ongoing propulsion. Based only on the energy of the initial thrust and the subsequent domino effect of the environment.]

Iron Orchid held up their bloodied finger between the two of them. [But surely you knew all the factors, in those cases. What about the anomaly?]

Barq-Et took their hand, pulled back the edge of their

shroud, and pressed the pad of a single naked finger to Iron Orchid's bloodied one. [If your research is correct, then I have all the data I need.] In a whirlwind of emotion, Barq-Et entwined their hands and snatched them up beneath their coverings, pressing the small drop of blood—their two pressed fingertips—to soft lips.

[But what will the Acting Progentor do, when he discovers what you've done? When you seal me inside and send me to Noumenon, he will know something is wrong as soon as the signal is lost, when I've passed beyond the anomaly. Will you be safe? Come with me—please say you're having the prison built large enough for two.]

[No. I must stay. You must reach the surface and find what's there—my Progentor, your lost elders, or no one at all. I must return to my order as one who knows. Who understands what kind of insidiousness is eating us from the inside. I cannot turn my back on my fellow believers.]

Iron Orchid felt tears percolate in the corners of their eyes. At first they were startled by the swell in their chest—the hot denial clogging their throat. What was this? This intensity felt for someone known for such a short time.

It was not a type of love they'd ever known before—and they'd known many—but it was love nonetheless.

Regardless of the danger, they let that love swell, exceed the boundaries of their body, be known. [Is this what the universe desires, has planned? Our brief meeting and long-lasting sorrow?]

[The universe does not make plans,] Barq-Et sent softly. [It has no thoughts. It is not sentient. It contains all knowledge, but does not know. Save through us. We know for it. It thinks through us. And we Reveal its secrets.]

[Then what role does the Progentor play, if not to execute the will of this existence you tell me is will-less?]

[The Progentor simply sees this more clearly. Sees the

knowledge inherent more firmly. Can find the filaments of creation and weave them into being. Nothing has blessed him. He is a happy accident of the inherent knowledge. The knowledge made flesh. If the universe cannot have thoughts, save through the evolution of those within it who are sentient, then he is the closest we have to it. He feels it— running through him, around him—the closest to something divine that has ever truly been created. And yet, we do not believe in divinity. Not in a divineness that exists before or after the universe, anyway.]

[But he is no god?]

[He is no god. Indeed, if there ever were gods they'd have to be beings not of the universe, and therefore not within the purview of the Revealer's faith.]

[If he is the closest you have to divinity, does that not mean divinity might still exist? One day?]

[I have met Revealers who believe in gods—one and many.]

Iron Orchid sighed, looked away from Barq-Et for a moment. [I think that's how many of my people saw the mega-structures, once. As a pantheon of gods, each with a ready blessing, if only we'd pay it tribute in resources and work so that it might exist. But then one of the gods betrayed us . . .]

[So you *do* believe a megastructure is to blame?]

[Yes. But *I* never saw them as gods. I don't even think they're separate entities.]

Barq-Et caught Iron Orchid's eye, drew their gaze back. [Explain.]

Iron Orchid hesitated. It was just a theory, based on cir-cumstantial evidence alone. [My people—as most people, I think—believe all the megastructures were designed by the same civilization, regardless of the differences in their com-position, structure, and function. They were not brought to us by disparate societies with similar benevolence. They come from one place. And, I believe, they have one purpose.

[There was little proof that they were all interconnected before now. Only a hint that some could not be activated until others were finished—like a project with steps that had to be performed in order. Why would that be, if they all perform individual functions? But, regardless, I think the anomalies are the proof that they work in tandem. It is not one megastructure gone wrong. It is the link between them, whatever that is.]

[Whatever that is,] the Stray-Fairer echoed. [What do *you* think it is?]

[I don't know. But I can't help but imagine each structure as a small piece. A cog, a wheel, a hinge, a screw. The little mechanisms that make a larger device *go*.]

[A device that spans the galaxy?]

Iron Orchid made a noncommittal movement with their shoulders—half shrug, half seesawing yaw. [No more unusual a concept than a universe that knows but cannot think until things that think come to be within it. If there was no way for the universe to think before it evolved the creatures who think for it, could it not still be evolving itself? Will the universe not, eventually, become aware? Alive with its own knowledge?]

Barq-Et chuckled, clearly amused with the fervor in Iron Orchid's questioning. [It may. No one can say. As we collectively have no gods, we also have no prophets.]

[So you don't know what I will find. You don't know if you're sending me to a barren planet to die—to live off starlight until my heart gives out within a decade.]

[Your heart may give out,] Barq-Et said, lowering their hands, finally, from their lips, but only so that they may touch against their spine-covered chest. The mechanical heart throbbed within. [But it will not be on that planet. I mentioned, I think, that the connectors are the same?]

With their guard up, it took Iron Orchid a moment to catch Barq-Et's meaning. [No. *No.* That is too dangerous. My body may accept your metal with ease, but your biology and mine—they may be too at odds. It may kill you quickly and painfully. A far harsher death than it would give me.]

[I will have chances you will not, can find a replacement. You are already taking on the graver task. And, you came seeking an ally, did you not? Someone as passionate about helping as you. Someone willing to do what needs to be done to save our worlds. Let me do my part. You need a heart you can rely on. Take mine.]

[We have no surgeon, and the medic—]

[We cannot trust the medic. We must exchange hearts ourselves.]

[This is madness.]

[The Acting Progentor is gripped by madness. You will be dead if we do not do this, and many more affected by the anomalies might die. Please. Trust me.]

[**Shall I avert my eyes?**] **Iron Orchid asked once the two of** them had sealed themselves away inside the small med-post. Three medical tables took up the center of the room; shelves and unlabeled cabinets encircled them. A cryogenic chamber of some sort whirred and steamed in the rearmost quadrant. [While you disrobe?]

[No. Please don't. This work is important—not only does it require exposure for us to execute it safely, this is a turning point for me. A change in my understanding of the universe and my place in it. I am meant to lay myself bare. Before anyone and everything that would witness.]

Iron Orchid stood patiently, simian hands folded over their chest, while Barq-Et slowly undressed. Beneath the shroud they wore no undergarments. They had two sets of simian hands, as Iron Orchid already knew, but it was the aquatic, mammalian tail peeking out from a shimmering cascade of rainbow-colored quills that drew their admiration and attention. Wonderful, intricate plumage of prismatic feathers encircled their throat and glided down over their breastbone and framed their round face, which possessed exaggerated eyes and petite nose and mouth—echoing, in a strange sense, a koala.

There was nothing of the practical that Iron Orchid could identify in the modifications. While Barq-Et could very well have mods for enhanced thought processing or tensile strength or endurance, it was clear their outward appearance had been chosen for purely aesthetic purposes.

They were radiant. A careful complement of traits that made them living art.

[Thank you,] Iron Orchid sent. [For sharing this with me.]

[My form is no secret,] Barq-Et said. [But I am glad it surprises and pleases you.]

[It is not the revealed shape of you, but the presence of you, that pleases me,] they admitted softly.

Having both reviewed all they could about heart transplants, they set up the necessary equipment within easy reach and took up adjoining medical tables facing each other, pulling the platforms in close. The press-through mats shifted to best accommodate each form and let them sit steadily, without need to constantly apply gravitons to keep themselves upright.

[There will be blood,] Barq-Et warned. [Though my heart is cybernetic, with fastenings the same as yours, my organs weren't originally designed for ease of access. An iris was inserted in my chest during my first surgery. One of three post-growth biological modifications I possess.]

[My rib cage may be difficult to work around,] Iron Orchid offered in turn. [It splays wide—I am not meant to reach around it when it is open.]

[Perhaps we should remove my heart first, before opening your body.]

[The process isn't instant—we will have to do both simultaneously.] Iron Orchid laid a sanitized hand over Barq-Et's. [If we don't time this correctly, we could both die. It is foolish—you can still back out.]

[It was my proposition.]

[You still have the right to say no.]

[I wish this,] Barq-Et reassured them. [I wish you long life, and success in your mission. I wish the safety of everyone dealing with the anomalies. I wish for a chance to see *warmth of Earth sunlight on a humid day in a heavy swamp accompanied by the percussion of a hammer hitting slate* removed from power. This is how those wants are fulfilled.]

Iron Orchid flinched as they spoke. [You have stated so many dangerous things. You must guard this memory even more covetously now. If the Acting Progentor pries it from you—]

[I will not return until after your heart stops in my chest. I will have time to seek the memory's suppression. To learn to manipulate my truths.]

[Maybe not enough time.]

Barq-Et gently reached up to clasp the back of Iron Orchid's neck, to bring their foreheads together. [Hush. You are stalling.]

With deep breaths, they parted, then began, inserting the IVs into the appropriate ports, waiting for the drugs to take effect.

As Barq-Et's iris opened, bloodied fluids began to trickle down their chest, staining the beautiful rainbow quills. Iron Orchid worked quickly, already feeling the unfurling in their own chest, the gentle rising of their ribs. They reached forward, slipping their hands into the warmth of Barq-Et, softly separating the folds of their body, searching with delicate fingers to the throbbing mechanism within.

Barq-Et's breaths came in soft puffs. Iron Orchid wanted

to ask if their nerves were deadened, or if they were in pain. But they had to work quickly, no time for extra considerations. Once they'd clasped the flexible metal construct—feeling its beat, the punctuation of each pump in the palm of their hand—they had half an impulse to pause, to appreciate the intimacy of literally holding Barq-Et's heart.

It took more trust to allow this than Iron Orchid was sure they'd ever been allotted by anyone else. It was an intimacy of bodies joining in a way that they had never envisioned before. Of true vulnerability, of all power conceded. The two of them, here, now, giving over the very sanctity of their life to the other.

The flash of feeling did not pass, but highlighted the urgency of movement, of deftness. A great trust so readily given could easily be betrayed. A power abdicated so easily equaled defenselessness and could suddenly turn to helplessness and death.

Iron Orchid found their fingers shook as they disconnected Barq-Et's heart, worried with each unclasping that the *Homo kubernētēs* design wouldn't do its job—that the connections would fail to close and leave Barq-Et's veins open to spill out their life across the floor.

But the connections held.

The heart stilled. Iron Orchid retreated.

Barq-Et's heart sat exposed to the open air between them. Still. Waiting.

Barq-Et had only minutes to receive a new heart. And each movement they made would lessen that time, steal the stored oxygen from their veins and threaten to damage their brain and organs.

Iron Orchid's rib cage had not yet fully opened, but Barq-Et plunged forward. Iron Orchid couldn't tell if Barq-Et was being less delicate than they had been, or if it simply felt harsher on the receiving end of the excavation.

The connections popped free with ease, but Barq-Et had to twist their arm oddly to make it past the ribs—to avoid tearing the meat of the heart on Iron Orchid's bones. The biological heart was set on a prepared tray, posing another problem of haste; the metal heart would keep, but the meat heart—unseated, unfed—was dying already.

And it had stopped beating. Sunlight Hammer would notice. He would hope, be full of glee. What would he think when it started up again? Would he suspect the truth? Iron Orchid could not see the monitor—likely it was implanted inside one of the chamber walls, and microscopic at that—but it was there. The Acting Progentor hadn't lied about that, they were sure.

It was both a threat, and a tool for their deception.

Barq-Et hastily plucked the metal heart from Iron Orchid's outstretched palm, and maneuvered it—blood and all—into the waiting chest cavity. If there was time they would have flushed both organs, taken more thorough measures against infection. Even at that, they had to hope Barq-Et's body would not reject Iron Orchid's heart—at least, not until they could get to a safe haven and find a replacement.

The physical sensation of an absent heart was more familiar than Iron Orchid cared to admit, but this—the weight of this new heart—was surprising and different. Barq-Et's heart was of a slightly larger capacity than Iron Orchid's, and the materials were more dense.

It wasn't until Barq-Et finished joining the connections and the heart began to beat within Iron Orchid's chest that they both realized they'd made a mistake—done things out of order.

Barq-Et was the first to lose a heart and should have been the first to receive. Now Iron Orchid's ribs were fully open and hindered their reach. They yanked free the appropriate

IV immediately, but still, it would take minutes for the muscles to fully contract again.

Iron Orchid turned sideways, fumbling, finding it far too difficult to work with one hand and at an angle. There was still an excess of fluid in Barq-Et's chest, and that made the connectors difficult to see. Picking up their still, meat heart, their hands began to shake even more as Barq-Et's sent thoughts became sluggish, unworded. They needed oxygen.

[No. No, no, no. Stay awake. *Stay awake.* Give me your hands. I need your hands.]

Barq-Et tried to oblige, but their digits were fumbling. They found a connector inside their own chest, but could not keep it steady for Iron Orchid.

The Stray-Fairer's hands suddenly dropped. They listed to the side, fell over on the medical table.

Iron Orchid shouted in pure emotion and jumped off their own table. Leaning down, their open ribs like a true cage over Barq-Et's form.

Panicking, Iron Orchid attempted to reach around with both hands, but could not manage, could not simply press their bones back into position.

So they broke them.

Iron Orchid both heard and felt the fine fissures erupt in the sixth and seventh ribs on the left, and the seventh and eighth on the right. They forced them down with their elbows, giving them a small window to work within, to reach through. Desperately, they found the connectors at the ends of the tubes, worked at a panic with slicked fingers to join the organic heart. And when everything was in place . . .

The heart did not beat. Barq-Et did not stir.

The connectors were supposed to revive it, to tickle it awake.

Had they waited too long? Had the flesh necrotized too fast?

Hot tears simmered at the corner of Iron Orchid's eyes. They wanted to grab Barq-Et, shake them, but couldn't—they had to retreat, lest their ribs shut around the Stray-Fairer's still body.

They ripped the IVs from Barq-Et, and the iris in their chest began to close.

Barq-Et shivered with a gasp. Their eyes fluttered. After a few moments of stirring, they sat up, clutching at their breast-bone.

The heart had been slow to respond but had not given out.

Relief and joy seeped from Iron Orchid's pores.

The new hearts had yet to be tested in their new homes but had not failed them yet.

The pair cleaned up the room and themselves as best they could. Iron Orchid was secured away, and Barq-Et went to rest. They would not speak of it—would not think of it—again, if they could. It was a secret they had to bury, deep and quick, lest it rise up to destroy them both.

When it came time to send Iron Orchid away, they did not struggle, did not deny, did not emote.

The crew had done a marvelous job of completing the sphere. It was exactly as Iron Orchid had hoped—thick walled, smooth, free of inclusions and imperfections that the anomaly might seize upon.

Inside was a padded seat of press-through and nothing more. Would its expansion be enough to protect Iron Orchid on impact? Perhaps. The metal itself should collapse, but hopefully not become molten. Iron Orchid should be able to survive the fall to Noumenon.

Should.

The crew stood back as Barq-Et tied Iron Orchid's extremities—so that they could not "claw their way free" of the prison—the knots being loose and ill fitted. In turn, the crew did not realize the significance of the words [*ox blood*] and the sensation of warm wetness on Iron Orchid's hands that the two parties swapped. It was nothing like a kiss goodbye—no gentleness of emotion could accompany the words or the sensation—but it was enough.

At last, Barq-Et tossed the satchel inside. [Do not forget your sentimental trash,] they sent.

[I will not,] Iron Orchid projected indignantly, eternally grateful that Barq-Et had returned the memento.

Iron Orchid settled into the press-through, holding Barq-Et's gaze as a section of the sphere was rolled into place. It would be sealed with the same metal, the seam ground smooth.

As their eyes locked, no words or emotions or tactile sensations passed between them. But at the very last moment Barq-Et placed their hand over their newly transplanted heart.

And so, in utter darkness, cradled inside alloy that gave them hope by the ally that had done the same, *the scent of moth orchids followed by the sensation of lightly rusted iron under calloused fingertips* descended into hibernation—of their own free will—hoping that when they emerged from this cocoon, the galaxy's chances would be transformed.

VANHI'S INTERLUDE

Cold. Dense. Strange.

She was used to the reverberations now. Used to the fracturing of her wave form—*becoming* a wave form. Used to being conscious in the SD. Used to the sensation of her bodily functions halting and her mind whirling.

If nothing else, here she could think. All she could *do* was think.

Sometimes that was good. Sometimes the curse itself let her forget about the curse for a while.

She let the Petratheem math roll over in her mind. She repeated parts of equations to herself, trying to understand, to backtrack what she knew about the universe to figure out what the numbers and variables and constants described.

The layers were vast. The equations long.

It wasn't just that she wanted to know what the Petratheem knew. She wanted to help. Something was wrong with the machine, and if she could just wrap her head around its function, maybe she could look at the problem from a different angle.

Exploration and communion: these were key words the Petratheem had given about their desires, their motivations.

Connection.

They said they wanted to share, but the communications deficit was vast. And though their lives were long, this task was urgent—they feared the anomaly had repercussions all throughout the galaxy . . . and beyond.

Beyond to places like . . . here.

There it was again—the denseness. A *texture.*

But not everywhere. Just some places. On her left bicep, her right thigh.

Cold. Thick.

This was different. Disturbingly different.

More. Now on her stomach and the back of her neck.

And it kept coming.

Now on her cheek. The side of her head.

Oh god, now over her nose and mouth. She could suffocate—drown.

But how? She wasn't even breathing.

All thoughts of equations fled. Now there was only this tactile sense of heaviness.

Shit—it was over her mouth. Over her eyes. *In* her nose.

Everywhere. Globs of it.

The reverberations had changed. She couldn't describe it exactly, but the frequency was different. Her wave form not only thinned, shifted, and dissipated, but spiked and lensed.

Lensed around *what*?

It *stung.*

Now the denseness was burning her skin—a chemical reaction? Or was her lack of an SD bubble finally catching up to her? She'd been here too long, and the SD itself had finally noticed her, was interacting with her.

Her chest hurt. On the inside.

Air. She needed *air.*

She'd thought she was an immortal. But now she was going to die.

Jump.

She mentally shook herself. She had to will herself back. How long had she been here?

The machine wasn't working right and now multiple realities were suffering.

She had to find the answers.

It was everywhere—clinging, heavy. Parts of her seemed to be slipping, burning, evaporating.

Vanhi, you need to jump. Jump back. Go home.

Something's changed, you can't stay here like this. Go home!

Go!

Go now!

MARINA J. LOSTETTER

402

CHAPTER SEVEN

VANHI KAPOOR:
I GIVE TO YOU YOUR FAULTS

"The purpose of a system is what it does."
—STAFFORD BEER

Makawee Wagner and Imane Antar marched down *Hippocrates*'s halls with ease, swaying as the ship swayed, I.C.C. navigating it through the skies to Sinkhole 187. There were no internal graviton cyclers at play, just Noumenon's natural pull on their bodies.

The two exomaterials specialists went over their prep checklists as they made for the shuttle bay. Today they'd be collecting new fiber samples.

Makawee put boots on the ground more often than most Monument dwellers—even the Noumonians, and still it was exciting every time. The airworthy Monuments had been constantly aloft these last five decades—nearly all of Makawee's life. She was used to a rocking deck, to the ups and downs and minor turbulences that came with living exclusively among the clouds. Though she made it to the ground often to harvest new materials, the constant rumblings and joltings of the planet's surface were nowhere near as soothing as the swaying of a Monument.

"I.C.C.," Makawee asked, "how's the seismic activity down there?" She saluted a pair of scouts clamoring across the left of the hall.

"The Luminal Mountains are relatively quiet, despite the Petratheem's constant activity," the AI reported. "The sinkhole is one hundred and five kilometers north-northwest of the tallest peak, and the life-forms emerging from it are slow . moving and appear to have an affinity for ice."

"When did One-Eighty-Seven develop ambulatory life-forms? Everything was rooted on my last visit."

"Unclear. I did not detect them prior to your mission today. The creatures' movement was not readily detectable from the Monument's usual distance. Their method of locomotion resembles Earth mollusks, but their rate of travel is two orders of magnitude slower."

"Have you informed All Mother's team? The kinematics division will be excited, I'm sure."

Practically every day there was a new creature to observe or a new substance to study. The dual-possessed im had not been idle since the arrival of the ancient ones and the merger of the Petratheem and Noumonians.

Below the ships, the Noumonian surface constantly rumbled. Heaved. The shells of the Sora-Gohan had dug deeply, swiftly, and had torn themselves apart in the process. The tunnels were now lined with fluttering, shifting scales shed from the shells—scales that quivered and hissed, making the caverns *breathe*. The red towers of light that erupted from them all over the planet's surface were created by thick veins of plasmatic fluids containing bits of organic material similar to that found on the long-gone Petratheem home world. And those fluids *pumped, pumped, pumped*.

The ancient im were terraforming.

Over Makawee's fifty-two-year lifetime most of the sinkholes—each once a clean punch in the rocky surface—

had become shrouded by tall, stationary life-forms. Not trees or plants or fungus, but analogous. Most of them were blue. A bright, saturated cobalt, like the blue of im blood. So stunning against the reds of the rest of the world. The im helped the Sora-Gohan shells seed the soil and the air and the seas. With control panels made especially for them deep underground, they guided the scales and mixed the ingredients and continued to build the world, just as they had begun building it billions of years ago.

"I have informed her," I.C.C. said. "In addition, I—"

I.C.C. cut out.

The two of them halted in their tracks, frowns furrowing their brows, gazes narrowed and bewildered.

"I.C.C.?" Imane tried.

No answer.

"I.C.C.!" Makawee demanded.

Imane attempted once more. "I.C.C.? Answer us."

"I apologize," the computer finally replied.

It might have gone silent for only a few moments, but it felt like a lifetime. I.C.C. *never* lagged like that.

"We must delay your excursion to the sinkhole," it explained. "Please stand to the side of the hall. We have an emergency."

Makawee didn't like I.C.C.'s evasiveness. It hadn't led with the problem, hadn't told them what the emergency was. Hadn't even turned on the all-system alert. "What's going—?"

A door opened a few meters up-hall, beyond the exomaterials labs, back the way she and Imane had come.

Progentor Jamal strode swiftly out, with his hip-length locks plaited together down his back, his umanori swirling about his legs, and the length of fabric slung over his arm and tied to his belt fluttering with the urgency of his movements.

It was Revealer garb of open acceptance—indicating a good day to receive visitors.

But he had a harried look about him, as though he'd been rushed to a task.

All Father did *not* rush.

The ever-present sundial on a chain about his neck bounced against his chest with every swift step.

Behind Jamal came All Mother, her face grim. Between her mech's arms she carried a limp figure. The person had deep-tan skin, black hair with flashes of gray, and glasses.

A human woman, who Makawee had only seen in pictures. Vanhi Kapoor. Their wayward immortal.

But something wasn't right.

Makawee and Imane plastered themselves to the hall wall, making as much room as they could. All Father nodded sagely to them as he passed, and Makawee could find no words, so simply nodded back.

As Hope strode by, Makawee sucked in a breath, stunned and worried.

Shiny clusters—rounded and smooth, like polished stones, though with a jelly-like texture—clung to Vanhi's form. They were mostly clear, some with a pinkish tint, some more orange. But beneath the clusters, huge purple welts and angry red burns. Some of it had been cleared from her face, and her nose bled while her skin puffed and boiled.

"By the ships," Imane breathed, hand covering her mouth.

Makawee couldn't even tell if Vanhi was alive.

"What *is* that?" Imane asked I.C.C. after the immortals had gone—headed for the lifts, on their way to the emergency rooms.

"The substance's nature and exact origin are unknown. Dr. Kapoor returned five minutes and forty-two seconds ago, while Hope and Jamal were reviewing Monument functionality with maintenance and systems management."

"Is she going to be okay?" Imane asked, sounding very much like a child despite her decades.

"Her breathing is steady. I have no additional data with which to reassure you."

"You've informed deCON?" Makawee asked.

"Yes, they are on their way. The rest of the meeting's attendees have been told to remain in the room and wait for deCON's arrival. I believe the safest course of action is for you to remain where you are until—"

"No," Makawee said, "we can go through decontamination after. If you don't know what the substance is, No Mother needs exomaterials specialists, not just medics."

"That is a reasonable assessment. Do you need additional aid?"

Makawee waved Imane on, and they fell into step after the immortals.

"Would you please call for Hark and Selina as well? Ask them to bring a full containment suite, and to wear hazard suits. And cancel our shuttle to the surface—apologize to the pilot for us?"

"Of course."

Makawee led Imane up three levels and through winding, glass-lined corridors. Much of *Hippocrates* had become the lab space that *Holwarda*—most of it still resting under an ancient landslide, though with crucial parts reclaimed—once contained. This was where they examined the newly harvested materials and ran them through various spectral and chemical analysis before attempting to engineer new fibers. But the ship also retained much of its original function. Here, babies were born, wounds were attended to, vaccines were administered, and the dying made comfortable.

When they came to the room where No Mother was being treated, they paused, temporarily dumbfounded, as they watched the medics work.

It was strange, having the curtains open on the floor-to-ceiling hallway windows, so that anyone could stand here, like this, and peer inside. No Mother lay uncovered on the hospital bed in nothing more than a short gown. The medics had worked quickly, and already many of her wounds were covered over in chemical-soaked bandages. The dressings sagged grotesquely, suggesting the missing chunks of skin and muscle beneath. All Father sat in a chair in the far corner, keeping vigil. In his hand he held the sundial's chain, twisting it over and over. He didn't seem to notice the women outside, and made no acknowledgment of the medics as they swirled around No Mother.

It appeared as though the unknown substance had been scraped from her skin and dumped into a biohazard container.

"The medics have induced a coma," I.C.C. informed them. "Her body has suffered a severe shock, and they are hoping it will help her recovery go more quickly and more smoothly."

Imane pursed her lips in a grim line.

"I can't believe this is happening," Makawee whispered. She'd imagined this day many times throughout her life: Vanhi coming back, the whole Monument celebrating. *What will No Mother really be like?* she'd wondered.

She'd imagined a smiling face and a brilliant mind.

"We used to play No Mother, remember?" Imane said softly. "When we were little. Jumping out at each other, pretending we were back from beyond."

Makawee nodded. She'd read and watched most of I.C.C.'s records on No Mother when she was a young woman, trying to model herself after the immortal. She wanted to be dedicated, like Vanhi. She wanted to be intelligent, like Vanhi. She'd wanted to have a love as lasting as the love between Vanhi and her long-gone husband, Stone.

And now, here was her idol, broken.

Feeling her eyes well up and her face run hot, she turned

away from the glass, wiping her cheeks. "How far away are Hark and Selina?" she asked I.C.C.

"Estimated time of arrival: ten minutes."

The globs of mysterious substance came away from Vanhi in varied viscosities. Some were hard, like rock, others looked like jelly, and some even oozed as the medics tossed them into the biohazard bin.

"It's like ectoplasm," Imane said.

"What?" Makawee asked.

"You know, that gelatinous substance supposedly created by the physical manifestation of spirits in this world. But this is preternatural instead of supernatural."

"*Exo*plasm," Makawee suggested.

"Yeah," Imane agreed. "Exoplasm."

Vanhi woke up babbling.

Vanhi woke up *aching*.

Vanhi's eyes felt like they were caked with a thousand years of sleep. That she felt anything other than the burn of her own dying nerves was a wonder and an improvement.

"The purpose . . . the purpose . . ."

"Stay still. No Mother, please stay still for a moment. You've been in an induced coma during your recovery."

She didn't recognize the voice, but that no longer fazed her. Last time she'd jumped and returned, children she'd known when she'd left had been older than her when she returned. This time it would be all new people. A different generation. A different family.

She was too groggy to feel a particular way about that at the moment.

"Vanhi, I'm here," said Jamal from her bedside, followed by a swift, "Sir, are you feeling all right?" from C nested in the sundial.

"We're going to sit you up. Put you at an incline," said the same unknown voice from before.

The head of what she assumed was a hospital bed began to rise. Carefully, she opened her eyes. For a moment she wasn't sure why everything was blurry. Why couldn't she see properly?

But then Jamal shuffled at her bedside table, retrieving her glasses. He carefully helped her put them on.

Three figures came into focus: two unknown medics and the Progentor.

"You might have a lot more to acclimate to this time around than you're used to," said the first medic. The two of them began describing what had happened to her from a medical standpoint. How she'd need physical therapy, not just because of her injuries, but because of the three months she'd spent in a coma.

"We've got a team studying this . . . exoplasm. With an eye toward how to neutralize it," Jamal reassured her.

She looked at her arms, still covered in bandages. She thought she'd come to peace with her jumping. That the SD was a strange, but safe, place.

Now even that had turned against her.

She looked around the room, caught sight of the hallway-facing wall, and nearly jumped out of her skin.

The curtains weren't drawn. At least a hundred people—likely more—stood outside, eyes fixed on her, expressions varying from concerned to slack to ecstatic. Tentatively, she waved.

Cheers went up all around, largely muffled but unmistakable. People hugged one another, kissed, jumped.

She was all right, and this was cause for celebration.

It might have been nice—all these people she'd never met were worried about her, wanted her safe and home. But she felt too much like an attraction, her awakening a spectacle.

"Jamal . . . ?" she prompted, nodding toward the curtains.

"Forgive us, Vanhi," he said, jumping up to pull the drapery closed. "But there would have been a riot if we'd turned them all away. The mood aboard has been bleak; they needed something happy to share in. I thought it would be like when I turn my corner. We have a celebration when I'm well again. Let everyone see me . . ."

Expressions clearly darkened as he drew the curtains. A few people waved through the shrinking gap.

"You're used to . . ." What was the word she was searching for? Notoriety? She made a vague gesture with her hand. "I'm not." Her arrivals were usually quiet. Private. There were still celebrations when she returned, but she'd always had a chance to prepare herself first. And then after that, things were just . . . normal. Whatever "normal" meant on Noumenon.

Things were clearly different this time. Might be different from hereafter.

"Apologies. I shouldn't have assumed. Will you pardon me for a moment?" Jamal said, opening the door, doing his best to push out into the crowd, likely just to tell them what they'd all seen with their own eyes.

She looked at the two medics differently now. "Put it in my medical files that I want the drapes closed in the future."

"Of course. We shouldn't have signed off on it. I'm so, so sorry," the second one said promptly, self-flagellation oozing from his pores.

"It's okay. Just don't let it happen again." She realized how strange the words were. They, personally, wouldn't be around after her next jump. This was it—their one and only time looking after a post-jumped No Mother.

"Can I get something to drink?"

■ ■ ■

They kept her on *Hippocrates* for another day, just to be sure there weren't any unforeseen complications. She had trouble walking, needed a cane. She knew she was getting old—though she'd lost track of exactly how old ages ago—but this was the first time she'd felt it.

Jamal made it his priority to help her to her new physical therapy sessions every morning, and to reintroduce her to the Monument.

Most people she encountered in the halls seemed to regard her with a kind of awkward awe, and a strange little sadness soaked Vanhi's heart when she realized. She'd greet them with a standard "hello" or a brief nod and they'd pause for a moment. They'd stare. Their heads would swivel as they kept walking. And then half the time they'd start whispering to whoever they were with without really acknowledging her in return.

The younger children seemed to make a game out of running up to her, asking if she was really No Mother, and then squealing before running away again once they had their answer. Like ringing the doorbell on a haunted house.

She heard whispers.

"There she goes, the woman out of time."

"I never thought I'd live to see her."

"Does she eat? Mika said she doesn't eat."

"I thought she'd be taller."

Vanhi had become accustomed to a fair bit of celebrity, back in her Planet United Mission days, but this was different. Not a fame born of overfamiliarity, but of lack of familiarity. Of distance and hearsay. Vanhi was some kind of legendary blank slate.

The mantle of myth didn't suit her.

But she didn't know how to dismiss the awkward atmosphere, how to wave away the invisible barriers. How to get to know these people, for real.

She spent her evenings in her quarters, alone, save for I.C.C. There, they continued working on the Petratheem equations. The AI had made no progress on its own while she'd been gone, and she often went to sleep frustrated, feeling ineffectual.

The most difficult part of her day-to-day life was interacting with new colleagues. People with whom she expected to have a one-to-one rapport.

A portly woman named Makawee Wagner showed Vanhi and Jamal around the exomaterials lab. She was older, perhaps biologically just a few years younger than Vanhi, but she looked at Vanhi with the reverence of a teenaged mentee meeting their idol for the very first time. Jamal didn't even warrant the same levels of doting.

The attention was . . . uncomfortable.

What was worse, Vanhi knew it wasn't really Makawee's fault; she did her best to be a consummate professional. But she was a tad too enthusiastic, her smile a bit too wide and constant. Her eyes lingered for a moment too long on anything Vanhi pointed at or touched.

"And this is a new fiber from Sinkhole Sixty-Seven," Makawee said, gesturing at a glove box where a man sat manipulating what looked like blue thread. Jamal greeted him with warm familiarity. "It's a protein strand," Makawee continued, "which seeps from the ends of certain fronds in the forking-sillion family—which are one step in biological complexity above slime molds. What's interesting is the fiber has a tensile strength of one-point-three-four GPa, which is comparable to drag-line spider silk, only we haven't identified any sort of function for the strands from the forking-sillion. The going theory is it's just a waste excretion."

"Can it be spun?" Vanhi asked.

Makawee lit up. "Yes! We're testing it in various weaves. It does cause mild irritation to human skin, but we're working on a coating produced from the sap of sabine trunks. We think fabric developed from these could be helpful in replacing the decaying organic fibers in the materials from All Father's ship. Especially now that the Petratheem have introduced the equivalent of the common clothes moth into the environment."

"Moths," Vanhi said. "Been a long time since we've seen one of those, hasn't it?"

Makawee's smile fell momentarily, and Vanhi realized her mistake. Makawee had never seen a real moth.

While all this new life was interesting to Vanhi, it was *stunning* to those who'd only ever known Noumenon. They had heard of but never experienced the breadth of organisms that could call a planet home.

She looked to Jamal. His eyes held a nearness of focus; he did not share in Vanhi's nostalgia.

Then Vanhi understood. It had never hit her before: not even Hope or Jamal could reminisce about the diversity and abundance of life on Earth. They, too, had grown up and grown old in spaces largely barren.

Only C and I.C.C. could remember the home planet as she did.

She tried to keep her expression neutral, but her entire body sagged at the realization, and she leaned more heavily on her cane.

Makawee laughed awkwardly at Vanhi's gaffe instead of correcting her, clearly in an attempt to protect her feelings. Then, clearing her throat, Makawee walked on, steps hurried, hand outstretched in illustration. "Back here is the vault where we keep all the potentially hazardous materials for study."

"And when do I get to see the exoplasm?"

"Um . . ." She pulled up short. "That is stored on *Slicer*, in a chamber far from All Father's ship. There are complications with its containment."

"What kind of complications?"

Jamal put a hand on Makawee's shoulder. "I think it might be best if we simply show her."

Most of the time the floating ships were all near one another, easily kept consistently safe distances apart by I.C.C. and the monitoring pilots. To conserve resources, long, flexible tunnels now connected the ships, not from bay to bay—those still needed to be left open and free for the shuttles—but from access hatch to access hatch. Inside the tunnels, rope bridges made from Noumonian materials made for durable, yet elastic, walkways. Integrated pulley systems helped those who could not traverse the tunnels on foot.

Iron-rich rock slats lay between blue rope lines, and the umbilical tunnels were semitransparent, letting the three of them mark the horizon and the angle of the sun, but little more. As the three of them traversed first from *Hippocrates* to *Mira* to *Aesop* and then on to *Slicer*, Vanhi took full advantage of the pulleys and platforms.

Slicer still, to this day, made her pause with awe. The rest of the ships created a dense city, but here it was the vast emptiness that impressed. So much room to work, and yet so little lay inside.

The Progentor's ship was poised near the shuttle bay, like she remembered it. But beyond that a new partition had been installed, dividing the mountainous space in two.

The rover sat near the access hatch, and they piled in with Makawee in the driver's seat. It would have been a long trek if they *hadn't* already traversed half the Monument. Vanhi was perfectly happy to ride the rest of the way.

In the rear compartment, she and Jamal took up seats across

from each other. He smiled at her, and she tried to smile back, but it felt like the corners of her mouth were weighted down, made of something more dense than flesh. Everything had changed so much. And she felt like she'd changed not at all.

He was not oblivious to her state. "Are you feeling all right?"

"Yes," she said reflexively. "No," she corrected with a sigh. "I keep thinking about . . . trust."

He waited patiently for her to continue, hands folded in his lap. But C wasn't developed enough for such nuanced grace. "What about trust, sir?"

"I don't want you to misunderstand, it's nobody's fault," she said. "But I'm having a difficult time. There's so much *distance* between me and everyone else. They've all been perfectly nice. More than nice. Maybe that's the problem. It's like I've wandered onto a stage and everyone around me is playing a part."

"You doubt their sincerity?" Jamal asked.

"It's not that I doubt it so much as they can't give it. And I feel like I'm living in a world of two-dimensional people. Only I know it's the other way around. They're the ones who are fully fleshed, and I'm the one with the missing depth."

"I'm not sure I understand."

She rubbed at her eyes. Felt the bandages around her hands coast across her cheeks and temples. "I'm a story to them. A character from movies they've seen, files they've read. I'm real, but I'm not real. And it's not their fault. It's no one's fault, but, it's strange to encounter people you've never met who have fully formed opinions about you and your life. People who are more inclined to talk *about* you than *to* you."

"I understand that last part," C chirped.

She laughed suddenly, lightly. "I bet you do."

Jamal quickly shifted out of his seat, coming to Vanhi's side, offering her an embrace, which she fully accepted. "It will fade with time," he tried to reassure her. "The more they encounter you, the more the story version will fade. This type of awe cannot survive in the face of familiarity."

"But I may not have that time. And when I jump again? Presuming the exoplasm doesn't eat me alive? I'll come back and it will be the same thing."

"Will you keep them at a distance because you feel a distance?" he asked.

"I don't want to, but I don't know."

"Perhaps you need not bridge the gap with everyone," he said. "Perhaps just *someone*." He looked toward the partition. "You would like her if you got to know her. Makawee's admiration might feel like a rift between you, but perhaps it can be the bridge."

Vanhi sat in silence for a few minutes, contemplating. He wasn't wrong, she was sure of that. She was making assumptions, they were making assumptions. If she could set those aside with just one person, maybe the rest would follow. Or, at the very least, she would have a genuine friend. A different kind of touchstone.

"We can't let our fears keep us from growing," Jamal said softly. "You know this scientifically. But it applies to all aspects of our lives. Stop me if this advice is unwarranted or patronizing."

She laughed lightly again, trying to force herself to let go of the tension. "No. Never from you, my friend."

The rover stopped, and Vanhi immediately pulled away from Jamal, already prepared to put on a front, to pretend nothing was wrong.

"Think on what I said," he implored her, easing himself out of the seat and making for the hatch.

Outside, Makawee had parked in front of the new, massive partition. A single, humble door stood nearby. "A lot of power has been diverted to the equipment beyond this door," Makawee said, "so please be careful."

Inside, a man in a hard hat greeted them, his body overly rigid when he registered Vanhi. Makawee explained their visit, and after a brief, awkward apology about not having the impromptu visit on his schedule (which was, of course, impossible), he showed them where the elevator to the primary viewing level lay.

The winding latticework of catwalks and cage lifts had Vanhi immediately flashing back to her days at the University of Oregon. Even more so when they arrived at the viewing platform and a six-story SD drive was revealed. She used to think the test version at her university was a monster, but this was more than twice the size—its footprint took up at least a thousand square meters of flooring. What was more, the available open space in *Slicer* dwarfed it by comparison.

"What's this doing here?" she asked.

"We reclaimed it from the wreck of *Holwarda*," Makawee explained. "Along with the ship's graviton cyclers. Since attempts to contain the exoplasm have proven difficult, we're hoping to create a compatible SD bubble around the substance. But our research thus far has provided no answers."

"Where is the exoplasm now?"

"This way."

They remained on the same catwalk, but passed through several doors out and away from the reappropriated SD drive. They passed new labs—not just hastily thrown-together stations, but well-constructed rooms. So much care had been put into this project, and with such speed.

Through the third door they came to another vast space. This held what Vanhi recognized as a magnetic bottle for antimatter storage, likely also from *Holwarda*. A long, clear tube, about the height of a person and the length of a tennis court, encased thick coils of wiring. The octupolar electromagnets inside kept the antimatter from hitting the sides of the bottle and annihilating. It wasn't attached to a collider, as it would be if its matter-antimatter reactions were being used to power the SD drive in the other room.

She could only assume the exoplasm was inside.

But, as they descended a ramp to the main floor, she noted the telltale lack of hum in the air. No power was currently flowing to the bottle. She even allowed herself to drag her palm along its side as they rounded it.

On the other side of the bottle, obscured from initial view, was a simple steel pedestal. Atop that was a glass box, barely of sturdier construction than a fish tank.

Inside was a transparent substance, tinted slightly orange pink. It floated freely in the tank, occasionally bumping into the sides only to float off again. Initially, it appeared to have the viscosity of breakfast jelly, but when she looked closely, she could see geometric patterns inside, like fractal structures, and the different bits of it did not wobble or change shape when they interacted with one another or the sides of the tank. The seventeen separate instances of the material free-floated in their confined space, apparently untethered from gravity.

"This is the exoplasm?" she asked, unable to keep the disbelief from her voice. "You keep it in *here*?"

"In here," Makawee said with a shrug, "in there—" she pointed to the magnetic bottle "—it makes no difference. The exoplasm eventually eats through whatever it comes into contact with, and the octupolar magnets have no effect on it. So far, it looks like the substance isn't governed by the five fundamental interactions—or, at least, it's not governed by them in the same way we understand matter from our dimension is governed by them. Gravitons don't affect it, though we assume it's interacting with the Higgs field, or else it would have no mass. Electromagnetism has to affect it somewhat by the very fact that we can see it with our eyes, but spectral analysis reveals nothing about its makeup. It does get repelled to a degree by its containment systems, but some kind of annihilation *is* happening. It actually seems to accelerate the effects of the weak interaction, to the very detriment of the strong interaction—the weak interaction being what causes radioactive decay, of course, and the strong interaction being what holds the nucleus of atoms together."

Vanhi leaned in, gazing deep into the substance. Someone else might have been afraid to get near it again, but she'd been looking forward to confronting her attacker. "What's the by-product of the container's dissolution? Is it simply breaking molecular bonds, or is facilitating other reactions?"

"The only by-product is hydrogen. Every time, no matter what the materials. And the exoplasm itself doesn't decay. It *disappears*."

"That's impossible," Vanhi said. "That violates conservation of energy."

"Right," Makawee said. "Which is why our current theory . . ." She trailed off, pursing her lips.

"What?" Vanhi prompted.

"I don't want to scare you," Makawee admitted, her tone earnest.

Vanhi's skin broke out in goose bumps. She'd thought she was here for little more than a scientific update, but she suddenly realized this was more like a diagnosis. Whatever was happening to the inside of the fish tank had happened to *her*. And could happen *again*. The evidence was scattered in ropy scars all over her skin.

"And our main goal is to neutralize it," Makawee said quickly. "To make sure it can't—that it won't—"

"It's okay," Vanhi assured her. "Give it to me straight. I've never been one to shy away from the truth."

Makawee took a deep breath. "Its disappearance, and the equal rate of decay, and the hydrogen by-product, have all led us to believe the exoplasm is breaking *all atomic bonds* it comes into contact with. Forcing rapid, sudden atomic decay from one atom to the next."

Vanhi went cold. She stilled. She held her breath for half a beat. "We should all be dead," she breathed.

Makawee nodded. "We should all be dead."

"How is it doing that without releasing any fission energy?"

Makawee swallowed thickly. "It's *not*. We still think the energy is being released, it's just utilizing it—absorbing it all in an unmeasurable instant. Our only evidence, of course, is the substance's slow disappearance. If the exoplasm exists right on the edge between this dimension and its subdimension—and it's breaking down our physical laws with its physical laws—then the reaction could be pulling it in equal parts back to its own slice of reality."

"It's caught here," Vanhi said. "Just like I get caught there."

"Right, and it keeps getting tugged back to its natural state."

Vanhi ran her fingers over her arms, pushing lightly at her bandages. "So what you're saying is, I had nuclear reactions going off all over my body."

"The interaction likely functioned slightly differently while you were in your SD, but, essentially, yes. But if we can trap it, we might be able to figure out how to neutralize it or repel it the next time you jump."

Next time. There was no avoiding the next time, neutralization or no. She'd stopped trying to end her jumping, but the next jump might end her. Unless they could understand what the substance was, how to keep it away.

"And what do the Petratheem have to say about it?" she asked.

"Icelandic-Plus came while you were under," Jamal said. "She/they took it as a sign the anomaly was worsening. Evidence that their work is more urgent than ever."

"But she/they didn't tell you anything? Plus gave us equations that describe everything—a unified theory of universal dimensions. What part of those equations describes this?"

"I-I don't know," Makawee stuttered, clearly mortified that the team hadn't better pursued the im. "I didn't think to ask. The Petratheem don't really talk to us. We were surprised to even see Icelandic-Plus, I—"

Distance. Distrust. Had Icelandic-Plus really not had an answer, or were there reasons to keep the answers from the humans?

"It's all right," Vanhi said. "Makawee, I don't blame you. The research everyone has done here in such a short amount of time, I'm impressed. I'm *proud*."

Makawee put a hand to her chest. She looked like a woman whose execution had just been stayed.

When Vanhi returned to her quarters that evening, she im-mediately said, "I.C.C.? Can you show me pictures of Earth?" She thought of moths. Of flies. Of mosquitoes. All the irritating little creatures that she now missed with a vengeance.

"Of course. Are there any specific subjects or geographical locations you'd like to see? My collection of Earth images is extensive and varied, and it is likely best if I curate your experience."

For a moment she wasn't sure what she wanted to see. Part of her wanted to tell it to show her anything and everything. But she didn't need reminders of war, or illness, or accidents. She wanted to reflect on its nature. Its majesty. Its life and its people. "Show me beauty," she said softly. "Show me love. Show me connection."

As the computer brought up a selection on her monitor, she went to her bedside and picked up the paper photograph framed there. It was faded now—the years without her had left its colors dulled, its fibers curled. She had I.C.C. reprint it every time she came back. This time would be no different.

In it, Stone smiled. Not at the camera—off to the side. His head turned, mouth slightly open, ready with a quip of some sort.

How old had he been when this was taken? It was from before they even met.

How many years ago was that now?

How many jumps?

How many average human lifetimes?

She looked up at the monitor. I.C.C.'s slideshow was everything she'd asked for; full of birds, trees, puppies . . . children smiling . . . people hugging . . . lovers kissing.

And she felt so distant from it all.

The exoplasm and I.C.C.'s progress on the Petratheem physics gnawed at Vanhi figuratively just as readily as the substance had gnawed at her literally. Things were amiss. Had been for a while now.

She just couldn't put her finger on how or why.

The next morning, when Jamal came to escort her to physical therapy, he stood in the entryway while she finished getting ready in the bathroom with the door open, just in case she needed his aid.

She couldn't help but press and pull at the new tracks and dips in her skin. Her body was a map of SD and human interaction now.

"Scars fit for a daayan," she said, mostly to herself.

"A what?" Jamal asked.

"A kind of witch. But not really. A cursed woman. Never mind."

She slipped on a button-up shirt. It was a vivid purple, an expert mixture of organic Noumonian fibers. She was still stunned by the transformation at the sinkholes. This planet had been so barren when they fell. Now hundreds of life-filled cradles sent tendrils throughout the land.

It was just as the Petratheem proclaimed, the reason why they'd come: life, connection, contribution.

And yet . . .

"Something isn't right here," she said, forcefully rolling up her sleeves so that the bandages wouldn't catch on the fabric. "Something hasn't *been* right, and I'm not talking about the anomalies. I mean the Petratheem."

Jamal came closer to the bathroom. "The Petratheem? What did they do?"

"It's what they *haven't* done," she said in exasperation. "I.C.C. spent millennia—*millennia*—teaching Icelandic how to communicate on a human level. She understands human concepts like metaphor, simile, parable. They keep saying they want connection, but they've had a million chances to make a very specific connection with us and have barely tried. I'm no longer convinced she couldn't devise a way to explain their machine to us. They could tell us what it does, figuratively, using Icelandic's tools. But they choose not to. Why is that?"

"I've wondered if it's the time scales involved," Jamal said. "They live so long. Humans are like tail-fliers in comparison. They'd have to teach us over and over again, so perhaps they find it least troublesome on both ends if we figure it all out for ourselves."

"*Most* humans are like tail-fliers in comparison. We immortals make that a moot point. I.C.C. all by itself makes that a moot point—teach I.C.C. and it can teach the humans."

She sighed, put her hands on either side of the sink, and bent over the basin. She looked into the drain like it was a portal, like she could see through it to the truth. "While I was in my SD," she continued, "I spent a lot of time going over those equations they gave us, and I think . . . I think the Petratheem are hiding something from us."

He came now fully into view, arms crossed over his chest,

brow furrowed. "Why? Why would you think that? Why would they do that?"

She turned, propped a hip against the sink, and crossed her arms as well, mirroring him. "The thing about figurative explanations is they're inaccurate, right? They tell you what something is *like*, not what it actually *is*. On Earth, back in my time, we used to see problems with it all the time in sci-comm. A journalist would dilute a scientific paper down to its base parts for public consumption, and the truth of it would get lost in the simplifying. You'd get sensational headlines like, *Quantum Computers Can Turn Back Time!* when what really happened was a forced reset of superpositioning. Or *Mysterious Blob Discovered, So Strange, It May Not Be of This World!* when it's just a run-of-the-mill slime-mold.

"Well, you start telling the people who don't understand quantum computing that you've turned back time, and they're going to freak out. And they certainly aren't going to be able to help you with your quantum computing problems.

"The Noumonian im in the dual-possessions *know* humans. I think whatever the figurative explanation is wouldn't just confuse us, it would worry us. Whatever the machine does, they know we won't like it if we don't fully understand it."

She fiddled with a fold in her sleeve, displeased with the way it bunched. "Whatever the machine . . ." she mumbled. "I was talking when I woke up," she said. "What was I saying?"

"Just nonsense. You said, 'The purpose of a system is what it does.'"

Vanhi froze, looked up from her sleeve, held her breath for a heartbeat. "That's not nonsense. That's Design Ethics 305: Engineering and Impact."

"What is an *Ethics 305*?"

She waved the question aside. "Has to do with an old Earth educational structure. Doesn't matter. The quote calls out a 'system,' but, in our case, it's *the purpose of a* machine *is whatever it does.* Why didn't I think of that before?" She turned around, put a palm to her forehead. How had she forgotten? Were her undergrad years really so long ago?

"Come here, sit down." She marched him away from the bathroom, pulled out a chair at the table.

"You're going to be late for your appointment," he told her.

"Yeah, I know. I.C.C., can you call over to *Hippocrates* and tell them I have to cancel today?"

"Of course."

Jamal put out a hand, as though he could stop I.C.C. from listening to her. "You need your therapy, Vanhi."

"I know, I know. I'll make up for it, I promise. But right now I need you to understand something.

"*The purpose of a system is what it does* is a thought experiment, designed to help creators understand that impact and intent are separate—and that impact can become intent if no correctional steps are taken.

"If you design a machine and it has an unintended effect, that effect is still part of your design, and you must take responsibility. If . . . if a social media platform amplifies disinformation, that means disinformation has become a part of its purpose, and you, the theoretical platform designer, are responsible for that. We used to have facial recognition software that couldn't tell people of certain ethnicities apart, and—okay, I suppose neither of those examples is helpful for you. Um—AI. AI!" She gestured at the sundial. "C. All of the Intelligent Personal Assistants. Your ancestor designed this set of personality-driven AI to tailor their personalities and behaviors to their users. But there were unintended side effects. There were IPAs that started swearing in church because their users swore a lot. That got a lot of their users into trouble. There was no situational-swearing governor in their programming, so they just openly swore wherever."

"I only embarrassed Vanhi with situationally inappropriate language eight times," C said proudly. "Seven of those incidents took place in front of her parents."

She gestured at the sundial, as though C had just proven her point.

"I am not sure I see how profanity utilization in AI units has anything to do with your suspicion of the Petratheem," Jamal said skeptically.

She fluttered her fingers above her head, trying to swat the confusion from the air like a fly. "We're getting sidetracked. Point is, *the purpose of a machine is whatever it does* is mostly about how engineering can have unintended consequences.

"But—and here's the important part for us—those consequences are usually side effects of the designer's *intent*. They don't crop up out of nowhere. They aren't completely unrelated to the machine's planned function. If a rocket explodes, it's not like combustion wasn't part of the design."

"I see."

"What is the Petratheem Machine *doing*?" she asked, pacing around the table, her nervous energy manifesting in restless feet. "What are the unexpected consequences of the im's cosmological engineering?"

"Anomalies. Both here and in the SDs."

"Right. It's screwing with physics, with all the layers of the universe. It's twisting things, breaking them. What if—" She sat down at the table across from him. "What if they *intended* to twist things, just not in this way?"

He frowned. "That seems . . . unlikely. Doesn't it? What could they possibly gain from 'twisting' the universe? How does that fit in with their explanation, that they want connection and communion? You're suggesting they've been lying to us for over a hundred years?"

"Not lying. Again, *avoiding*. I think it's more than just a communications gap. I think Icelandic-Plus believes trying to explain it to us using human comparisons and metaphors would only make us suspicious, panicky. Wouldn't you question their work, perhaps try to stop it, if you thought they were *actively* trying to harm the universe?"

"Yes, perhaps, but I don't . . . *why would they want to harm it*? Why would that be their intent?"

"I don't know. The explanation is in the math. That's why they gave it to us. They figured if we could decipher it, then we'd understand. They think we can't understand without it and would work against them if they tried to explain any other way."

"How can you be sure, though?"

"I can't—yet. But I'm going to find out."

"How?"

"I'm going to confront Icelandic-Plus."

"You're going to accuse the Petratheem of lying to us?"

She shrugged. "Yeah. If they're as benevolent as they say, it shouldn't be a problem."

He was quiet for a moment. He fiddled with C's chain, twisting the dial over and over. "And what if they're not?" he said darkly. "What if you're right, on all fronts? What if they *are* trying to harm the universe? What do we do about it? Do we try . . . ?"

He let the last words go unspoken. *Do we try to stop them?*

"I think it depends on what Icelandic-Plus has to say."

"I don't know if I like this plan. Before you confront her/them, shouldn't we discuss it with the Monument? Everyone? Vanhi, this could put a strain on our entire community. Not to mention it puts all the Noumonians who aren't dual-possessions in a difficult position if—"

"I know." She reached out, placed both hands over one of his. "I know. But this is urgent. And I won't . . . I won't bring anyone else into it. Not yet. These are my suspicions and I will own them." She looked toward the ceiling. "I.C.C., did you get all that?"

"Yes," it said curtly.

"What's your take on the Petratheem intent?"

"I believe Icelandic-Plus when she/they express distress over the current circumstances. But I cannot find fault in your reasoning. We all trusted readily that they were being as honest and straightforward with us as they could be. Perhaps that trust was too easily given."

"Can you contact Icelandic-Plus for me? I'd like a meeting, ASAP. Tell them of my basic suspicions, but reassure them that I won't share those suspicions with the rest of the Monument until we've met. As long as she/they agree to meet with me within the week."

Icelandic-Plus agreed to the meeting, as long as it didn't take place on the ships. Vanhi suggested the ancestor shrine. Neutral ground, halfway between the Waterfall colony and the original resting place of *Mira*. The im approved.

On the agreed day, a shuttle took Vanhi to the ancestor shrine, and there she waited, sitting on a boulder just above the outcropping, looking down on the tablets and out across the land. The shrine now sprawled down the mountainside. Too many Monument dwellers had come and gone for a single shrine to contain them, and yet they were all family, all connected.

She propped her cane between her feet and leaned heavily on it, eyes flicking between the skies and the stones. Little pink fly-like creatures now flitted between the tablets, their round, shiny bodies like pink peppercorns. They put a buzzing in the air that had never been there before.

The Monument ships, unified by the new umbilicals between them, hovered over the ocean—a massive city in the sky. Trickles of blue fanned down from the north, like fingers of a river, only it was not water that flowed down these tributaries.

The world had gotten away from her.

But then, there was Stone's tablet, just where she'd placed it. She was happy to see fresh garlands had been laid upon it.

Memory was a muted thing. She could still recall his face at almost any age, but the division between his features, between him and the background, between one expression to the next, were fuzzy. Blurred with time, with the inaccuracies of the mind.

And yet the grief was still there, still strong. A constant ache. She didn't mind it these days, because while the absence of him still hurt, the grief itself was a kind of love.

She kissed her fingers and ran them through the air, across the cheek of a man only she could see.

A smudge of copper and yellow-green in the sky caught her eye. Icelandic-Plus fought the winds to come to her, the im's great wings snapping out, dipping in. She wondered if the dual-possessions ever fought for control.

Her/their wings swirled in colors of greeting when she arrived, and, despite the im's girth, she/they touched down lightly on the bulge and jut of uneven stone on the incline above Vanhi. The im tanks possessed a lumbering grace when on the ground—something between the prowling of a tiger and the sway of a giraffe. Captain Tan may have dubbed the *Lùhng* dragons, but the Noumonians and Petratheem came closest to the real thing for Vanhi. She suddenly felt like a storybook character in an epic fantasy as Icelandic-Plus prowled closer, coming to rest at the base of Vanhi's boulder, the ancient creature's head still rising far above the human's.

The other residents of the Monument may have begun treating Vanhi like she was a legend, but here was a being who truly felt mythic. An ancient intelligence well beyond what Vanhi could have dreamt up herself.

"Monument colony distressed," Icelandic-Plus said via her/their imbedded translator.

"Yes. Well, I am distressed," Vanhi admitted. "Plus?" she asked. "Is it all right if I just address Plus?"

"We are one and both," Icelandic-Plus said. "Address either or together."

She'd planned on coming out swinging. She'd had accusations piled up high on her tongue. But now that they were face-to-face—Vanhi bent, Icelandic-Plus alert, with little else moving but the im's wheel slowly turning in the wind—she couldn't start from a place of hostility.

She didn't want to end in a place of hostility, either. They'd shared this planet peacefully. More im lived in the Monument than humans. They were friends, allies.

Though Vanhi's trust was shaken, it had not completely crumbled.

"You were only a chrononaut this one time, right?" she asked. "The process sounds like it could only happen once."

"Yes. Just this once," she confirmed. "Conceivably could be done again, with Icelandic. But form would have to exist in the future for both."

"Then what? You'd be Icelandic-Plus-*Plus*?"

"Theoretically. Though I doubt our new host would choose same name."

"That's not . . . yeah. What I mean is, you've come a long way, and all at once. It must be difficult, adjusting."

"Yes. Sharing form is difficult. Understanding new surroundings . . . difficult."

"You know about my jumping."

"Icelandic informed."

"You know what happened to me this most recent time."

She tossed her shoulders from side to side. "Observed you. Observed . . . substance."

"What part of the ultra-theory equations describe it?" She was testing. There was no logical reason for Plus not to say.

"Have not gathered on own?"

Vanhi narrowed her gaze. "Why would we need to 'gather on our own'?"

"Understanding the infinite minus one takes time. Will get there. Im sure."

The words were benign, but the meaning clear. They would receive no help. "You're keeping us busy," Vanhi said frankly. "You don't trust us to know how the machine works. What it's actually meant to do."

Icelandic-Plus reared up on her hind legs, as though taken aback. "Not true. Not so."

Vanhi slipped down from the rock, catching herself with her cane. "*Yes* true," she countered. "Not because you think we wouldn't understand, but because we'd understand just enough to be dangerous to you."

"Humans can know," Plus insisted. "Humans will know. But need . . . need patience. Is complex. Hastiness and confusion lead to ruin."

"Were the Petratheem too hasty?" Vanhi asked harshly. "Is that why the anomalies are happening?"

"Do. Not. Know. But must pay close attention. Must keep searching for answer. Would tell if all fine, but need discover problem. Once problem found, then—"

Despite the im's size, Vanhi moved into her personal space. "You claim you want trust and connection with life in the universe. Well, we're right here. We're right here but you won't give us either of those things. Trust doesn't just happen when things go right. You have to be prepared to trust and connect when things go wrong. It's *more* important when things go wrong. *We* have trusted *you.* We've taken you at your word. We give Plus the same trust and respect we gave Icelandic and all we want is reciprocation.

"I don't think you understand how much we'd be willing to sacrifice for you if you let us in, let us help."

"Humans . . . humans jittery. Quick to conflict," Icelandic-Plus declared. "Quick to *accuse,*" she spat.

"I'm wrong, then? You aren't keeping things from us? You couldn't tell me what the machine does as though I were a new one? A Petratheem just detached? You might come off your parent's back fully developed, but you do not come off knowing all the endless workings of the universe."

Icelandic-Plus turned her back on Vanhi, wriggled her haunches as though ready to take flight, ready to leave the chattering, angry, accusatory human behind.

"I'll tell you what I think the machine does," Vanhi said.

Icelandic-Plus hesitated.

"I think this sort of . . . bubbling, the way the anomaly here has enclosed things, the way the layers of the universe are twisting and pulling thin? I think that's *almost* what's supposed to happen. You said early on that there was supposed to be a protective barrier around Noumenon. Well, there's a barrier all right. You're tearing through all the layers of the SDs on purpose. That's why you gave us an ultra-unified-theory of physics, isn't it? Because your machine works its magic on it all. Through the near infinite. You're slicing through that infinite for some reason—I haven't figured out what the purpose is yet. But I'm not convinced you're unwilling to live with negative consequences. I think you foresaw putting scars in the universe and thought that whatever was close to those scars would be nothing more than collateral damage. After all, science and discovery come first, right?

"I've been there. I've been in a place where I was told to

make sacrifices for the science, and you know what, it's bullshit. Collateral damage is a crap term meant to pull the heat out of words like *death* and *destruction*.

"I think you didn't mean to cause *this* harm, but you intended fracturing or whatever you want to call it. I think even if you figure out what's wrong, you're going to interrupt the very workings of the universe and there'll be no way to put it back together again.

"I haven't told all the Monument dwellers. Just Jamal and I.C.C., but so help me if you don't stay here and disabuse me of this notion, I am taking it to the *Mira* colony, and the Waterfall colony, and we are all going to rise up and *stop you*."

Vanhi's heart was pounding, her chest heaving. She hadn't felt such an intense flow of desperate emotion in her body since Stone died. She gritted her teeth and willed herself not to jump—not until she'd finished the conversation and made Icelandic-Plus admit she/they'd been toying with the humans.

The im slowly turned around, spreading her wings, making herself look even larger. She lowered her head until it was mere inches away from Vanhi's. A lone drop of digestive fluid splattered on the ground between them, sizzling as it eroded the stone.

The translator blinked. "You are not wrong."

Vanhi tilted her head. "What?"

"Fracturing of the universe is exactly what im intend."

Vanhi took a step back, suddenly aware of how easily those digestive fluids could cut through skin and bone. How if Icelandic-Plus suddenly decided Vanhi's accusations were too problematic for her/them, she/they could simply consume her.

"Frightens you?" Icelandic-Plus asked. "The fracturing?" She took a step forward as Vanhi took two more in reverse, down the slope, toward the flat of the shrine. "Thought it would. Thought humans would scare. Would deny. Would fight. Icelandic warn Plus you not understand. Icelandic warn Plus humans violent when scared. Icelandic warn Plus humans get in way. Humans want good, but they fight when not see good. Even if good right there. Even if worry invalid."

Vanhi's foot found an unexpected pebble. She wobbled, but kept upright, kept retreating. And Icelandic-Plus pressed forward.

"So, yes," the im grumbled. "We give all math humans need. We tell you everything, so not to have to tell you anything. Because humans jittery. Quick. To. Conflict."

Another uneven surface met an unsure step—Vanhi lost her grip on her cane. She pitched over, but instead of landing on the hard rock, landed against Icelandic-Plus's head. The im had swooped in quickly, and now gently nudged her back to her feet. "Vanhi prove Petratheem right to suspect suspicion."

"And Icelandic-Plus proves Vanhi's suspicion *valid*," she countered, keeping one hand on the top of the im's head to steady herself. "You admitted I was right. You are trying to tear the universe apart. I don't think there's anything you can say that will make me, and everyone on the Monument, think that's not worth fighting against."

"Reasons," Icelandic-Plus insisted. "Reasons good. Life. Connection. Communion. Discovery."

Vanhi held up a warning finger. "Don't. Don't start with that placating gibberish again."

"Is not gibberish, is true." Icelandic-Plus turned, leaving Vanhi without a nose to lean on. She/they strode down and through the shrine, picking carefully through the tablets. At the cliff's edge, she/they stopped and sat heavily on her/their hind haunches, stretching her/their arms, letting her/their wings extend their full span. The ever-blowing breeze caught them instantly. She/they resisted the lift, the tug, gripping the rock face firmly with strong feet.

The sun caught behind the thin expanse of skin and tendons, making her/their form glow.

"Come fly with im," Icelandic-Plus called. "Must show."

Vanhi teetered her way to the im's side. "You want me to . . . ?" Surely she misunderstood. "Are you offering me a ride?" Children were the only humans who'd ever been offered a place upon a tank's haunch—and for good reason. It wasn't like getting a piggyback ride from another human, and it wouldn't be anything like riding a horse, or camel, or elephant. The center of Noumonian backs were taken up entirely by their wheel and its housing. There was no place to evenly sit astride. "Won't I throw you off balance? Aren't I too heavy?"

"No heavier than turret. Can manage," Icelandic-Plus insisted.

Vanhi put one hand on Icelandic-Plus's side but thought better of it and backed away. "I don't—"

"If want to rebuild trust, must lead with trust. Trust im to carry you, and im trust you not to grab wings, make fall." She flexed. "Will come? To nearest sinkhole? Will trust?"

"I don't know if I can," Vanhi admitted. "My strength isn't what it used to be."

"Will protect," Icelandic-Plus insisted. "But must hold tight. And could get cold."

Only minutes before she'd contemplated whether or not the im would try to get rid of her by *eating* her, and now she was considering trying to ride her/them bareback.

This is a bad idea, she told herself, nevertheless stepping closer, looking for the best way to ride.

"Okay," she said. "Give trust to get trust."

Vanhi let her/them take her cane with one long proboscis before she laid herself flat against the Noumonian's left side. The two species' warmth mingled, and Vanhi could feel the fluttering of Icelandic-Plus's insides working, of her blood surging.

Vanhi did her best to find a comfortable position. Muscle strain and joint pain could lead to a loss of grip and a nasty fall. She was sure the trip there would take at least an hour, even as the crow flies. She hoped her strength wouldn't give out.

She also hoped her glasses would stay firmly on her nose.

"All secure?" Icelandic-Plus asked. "Difficult to hear over wind, so tap if something wrong. Will land right away. And keep fingers free of wheel. Might bite, might snap."

"Got it," Vanhi said, turning her head, pressing her cheek to the swirls in Icelandic-Plus's hide. "I'm ready."

With a sudden, great thrust, Icelandic turned toward the cliff face and leapt. Vanhi's stomach dropped as they did. They were falling, sinking, two entwined rocks in the sky.

Then the Noumonian's wings snapped wide, and they were rushing upward even faster than they'd fallen. The wind stole the air from Vanhi's lungs, and she had to hide her face in her shoulder, breathing the small pocket of stillness there. She shut her eyes against the onslaught, and the great *snap snap snap* of wings was terrifying.

As Icelandic-Plus pitched to the side, yawing, turning, Vanhi slipped toward the ground. With an involuntary shout she dug her toes all the deeper into Icelandic's haunch.

She wasn't sure if she could do this. If she could hold on the whole way. She'd been bundled enough for the temperature on the surface, but Icelandic-Plus was right, it was colder up higher—though she had no way of knowing how high they were, with her eyes screwed shut and her face plastered to the alien's body.

She could change her mind. She could tap Icelandic hard and insist they land. They could go back to *Mira*, get the rover. They didn't need to be on this crazy dash, there was no reason for her to risk life and limb to see what the Petratheems were doing at this very moment.

But she kept her grip tight. She didn't so much as twitch toward a tap.

Because she was *flying*. It might be terrifying and somewhat awful and her shoulders already hurt and her fingertips felt like they were going numb—*but*. But this was once in a lifetime.

When a ten-billion-year-old alien possesses your friend and offers to fly you across the sky, you don't say *no*.

The trip was grueling. Time stretched on, each second lengthier than the next. With each new protest in her joints the clock slowed. But she held fast.

Twice Icelandic-Plus turned so that the wind, for a few moments, wasn't desperately trying to rip Vanhi away. She was able to look up and out, then, to admire the sea from her position on Icelandic-Plus's left. The water was miraculously clear, and she could make out some rough, dark shape: a Leviathan colony—small nematode-like creatures that banded together in a writhing swarm, building the viscous nest around them that looked like one giant sea monster from afar.

The sky itself was beautiful. Deep purple-pink storms gathered in the far west. Lightning tore its way across the clouds, sparkling, though they were too far away for her to hear the thunder.

Eventually—eons later it seemed—Icelandic-Plus's flapping slowed, became a glide. They circled over a spot below, and Vanhi saw crimson for a moment as they flew through a beam of red light.

Other Noumonians were nearby, circling as well. Vanhi caught a quick glimpse of a scout twirling up through the air beside them.

Vanhi relaxed as they circled nearer and nearer the ground. But Icelandic wasn't landing.

"Hold on!" the im reiterated.

Vanhi had half a second to realize the ride wasn't over.

Icelandic-Plus pulled her/their wings in tight, nose-diving into the sinkhole.

Vanhi gave an involuntary shout as the lip of the ground rushed past them. Dark-red light engulfed them and the sun disappeared.

It took them only a few minutes to descend the entire length of the vertical portion of the tunnel.

When Icelandic-Plus finally landed, all eight limbs alighting tenderly on the rock floor, it took Vanhi a moment to pry herself away from the Noumonian's body. Her grip was rigid, her posture frozen. Every bit of her felt stiff, as though she had been molded into the position.

Legs wobbly, she hit the ground unevenly and lost her footing. She stumbled into Icelandic-Plus, who held her up before returning her cane without comment.

The cavern writhed with activity. Scouts and turrets and tanks hurried in various directions, hardly giving the human visitor more than a passing glance.

"Humans," Icelandic-Plus said, walking onward, deeper into the tunnel, "would not listen if im came with words of *fracture* and *break* and *burrow* and *slice*. Would cease to listen. Cease to let work. But you come to im with these words already in mouth. Perhaps you listen if im affirm.

"It can walk, come."

Vanhi did not hesitate, using the cavern wall and her cane for support.

Soon the tunnel curved, and the wind brought with it more scales stuck out at an angle. Only these were moving. They fluttered like mechanical wings from the tunnel wall and were the source of the rattling. They sent strange slicing shadows through the red light—which emanated from deeper still, and Vanhi couldn't say what they were supposed to do or be.

Another curve, and there was more clamoring. A larger sound now, and the rock buzzed under her hands and feet.

She could smell something now, too. Something very unlike the typical scents of Noumenon. It was like heated brass, and the noise that accompanied it was like a grinding yaw.

Once the tunnel leveled out, they could take it at a brisk walk. Vanhi wanted to sit, to rest her hands and feet, but the noises beckoned, and Icelandic-Plus didn't look back. Something was hard at work down here, and Vanhi needed to know what.

The vibrations underfoot became so heavy that Vanhi's eyes shook, the light shook, everything around them shook with the effort of the alien construct at work.

Finally, they came to the source of the red light. Great ropes of plasma coiled and throbbed in a winding pattern between the scales. They weren't inert strings of light—they writhed as though alive. They were pure brightness, a ruby-red glow pouring away from every fiber. It boiled around a hard center, the coils of it becoming thicker, then thinning out.

They met more Noumonians, who appeared to be monitoring the ropes. They poked and prodded, not like investigators looking for clues, but like farmers inspecting their crops.

"Vanhi talk of scars," Icelandic-Plus said. "Vanhi regret scars?"

She looked at her arms, at her bandages, now somewhat soaked through with sweat and discolored with Noumonian grit. "I was attacked by my SD," she snapped. "I could have been killed."

"But scar mean life. No scarring if dead."

"Yes," she agreed. "So?"

"Damage bad. But scar good. Scar healing. When you say Petratheem mean to scar universe, you come closest to truth.

"And im sacrifice much for those scars. Petratheem: bodies, old way of life. Family, friends. Planet. Time. Selfishly, in way, yes. But mostly for others. For future. Noumonian im give up autonomy, sacrifice bodies in different way. Because of trust. Because of love. Humans cannot see Petratheem minds like Noumonians can see Petratheem minds. We ask no sacrifice of you."

The tunnel split. They came to a junction, with four possible roads.

"This way," Icelandic-Plus said, taking the northernmost fork. "Watch hands and face. Panel will form."

Vanhi didn't understand, but she stuck close to Icelandic-Plus's flank.

They took half a dozen more steps before the thrumming in the air changed. A rapid whoosh accompanied a flapping of metal parts—scales flinging themselves from the walls like bats in old movies. Vanhi ducked, crouching down, covering her head.

"Careful, careful."

The scales formed a wall in front of them, a protective barrier that blotted out the majority of the light beyond, letting only the barest glint through.

The wall wasn't stagnant. It undulated, rippling from one end to the other in a diagonal. Three scales turned themselves inside out, transforming almost like Hope's mech could transform. The three were positioned at different heights, one approximately a foot off the ground, the next two and a half, and the third five feet. The highest had a series of slots cut into it.

The next scale was directly beneath the first and had hollowed into a simple concave dish. The last was off to the side, nearly at the edge of the wall, with four unevenly placed divots in its surface. Each glowed lightly, a ruddy purple her eyes could barely distinguish in the dark.

"This control panel for this node," Icelandic-Plus said, waving illustratively at the wall. "Each node different. Each control or change part of Noumenon. You see how im make tunnels in planet? To reach deep, far—to change planet inside and out?"

Vanhi nodded.

"Im *scar* planet, might say?"

Vanhi shrugged. "Sure."

"Im do same with universe. Terraform Noumenon. Cosmoform universe."

"You're . . . terraforming . . . the universe?"

"Might say, might say. By making *fractures*. Forming *scars*."

"But . . . why?"

"Why terraform planet? Make more conducive with life. Share more of universe with more life!"

"What life, where—oh," Vanhi put a hand over her eyes, suddenly realizing she'd been oblivious to the obvious. "In the SDs. There are forms of life in the SDs and you want to make inroads for them to follow. To come here. To *Noumenon*?"

"Yes. Im thought at least *invitation* aspect clear," Icelandic-Plus said. "Life separated by physics, by dimensions."

"But how are we all supposed to survive together?"

"When machine work properly, will create ultimate what you call SD bubble. Mighty protect inside and out. Very air made of protection. And in this way, we will travel. Together. We make roads. Roads inside stay open—scars in universe. Road out will close over. And we will discover. Except—"

Vanhi hadn't even had time to process what they were trying to say before Icelandic-Plus broke into a wail. "Except all wrong," the dual-possession shrieked. "Nothing right, everything broken. No way to fix. No scars because no healing. Fear problem even worse beyond what we can see. Dying. What if—what if Petratheem have killed universe? Like SD almost kill Vanhi!"

She/they smashed their face against the stone floor, pounding again and again in frustration.

Vanhi put out a hand, wanted to make her/them stop, wanted to soothe her/them. But she didn't know what to say. There was no way to make this okay.

What if Icelandic-Plus was right? Was this what Vanhi's life would be now? Jumping back and forth as the universe slowly decayed? She'd watch time stretch out behind her, eking into entropy. She'd lost all chance at a normal life and now . . . now this?

No. She refused.

"We can fix it," she said, determination gritting her teeth. "We *want* to give input, to help. But if you're too afraid of what everyone will do if they learn what you're up to, then we really are doomed. We trust you, and you have to trust us. We built your megastructures for you. With your knowledge and human ingenuity, we can fix this and make the machine work."

She slid in front of Icelandic-Plus, put hands on both sides of her head, imploring her/them not to hit the floor anymore. "Please," she pleaded. "Let us help. You have made so many sacrifices, but you have to make one more. You have to give up control. Let us be your partners. Trust us not to run, not to act out, not to destroy simply because we don't understand. Trust is how you build these connections. How we solve this problem."

The im stopped. "Vanhi wise." It felt like the compliment came directly from Icelandic.

But, in truth, it was only because her trust had been

shaken in the humans around her, because she'd felt distance from her fellow *Homo sapiens*, that she'd recognized how the Petratheem had been keeping the rest of them at bay.

"Will help Vanhi learn physics, if Vanhi help reassure humans," Icelandic-Plus said.

"Deal. We want the same things you do," she said. "Love, connection, discovery."

They began with the exoplasm. Though the Petratheem didn't know how to neutralize or contain it, they were able to teach Vanhi and I.C.C. which equations described it and the principles behind it. They worked for weeks on just ten lines of math, going over and over the physical theories and fundamental interactions between SDs.

And, in the meantime, Vanhi made a concerted effort to cultivate new relationships. To really get to know Makawee, to make sure they really saw each other's humanity. Makawee shared with Vanhi her love of weaving. Vanhi shared in return her love of food and memories from home. She learned Makawee was bonded to a partner, which was unusual in the Monument. She took Makawee to the ancestor shrine and introduced her to Stone.

And Vanhi began to accept her legendary status. She couldn't eradicate it, but she could temper it, turn it to good use. People trusted her automatically, which had at first made her wary, but now helped her ease the people into a new era of Petratheem and *Homo sapiens* communication.

Her life was ever shifting, ever changing. She could fight the unfightable, or she could embrace it.

And once she grasped what the exoplasm really was, she headed straight for the exomaterials lab to speak with Makawee.

"It's anticipation energy," she said, spreading half a dozen documents out between them on Makawee's desk. "I mean—

anticipation *matter*. Anticipation energy exists in extremely small parts in our dimension, but my SD is full of it. It seems the Petratheem Machine is creating oscillations through that SD which are causing the solidified version to amass. It doesn't become matter here—can't because there's not enough of it to create even one subatomic particle's worth."

"Anticipation matter," Makawee repeated thoughtfully. "But it doesn't usually coagulate like this, you're saying? This is still anomalous for the SD?"

"Correct."

"I'm not sure if that helps us contain it, but maybe . . . If we could understand the force that's pushing it together, perhaps we could replicate it, apply it on all sides. The machine is causing vibrations, you said? But not like it's supposed to?"

"In a way. It's difficult to describe in layman's terms. The machine is supposed to . . . Well, the closest analogy is resonant frequencies. In mechanical systems—and even the galaxy is a mechanical system—resonance happens when the frequency of an applied force is equal to one of the natural frequencies in the system. It causes the related oscillations in the system to happen at a larger amplitude. And if the oscillation is strong enough, it breaks the system. That's what the Petratheem *want*, but it's not exactly what they're getting."

"Resonance—like those old videos of opera singers shattering crystal?"

"Exactly. But an opera singer doesn't know how the glass will shatter ahead of time. In this case the Petratheem understand where the system is likely to break. The galaxy is a thin spot in our dimension, and Noumenon itself lies at the ultimate weak point. They want to create fissures—cracks, like in the crystal—between the subdimensions that can be left open and used as roads. Only the applied frequencies are wrong, or their calculations are wrong, or . . . something."

"They want to create roads . . . to Noumenon?"

"Yes."

"So when this is all said and done—if the machine is ever repaired and all the megastructures are complete—we should be prepared for visitors?"

"Many, *many* visitors if I'm understanding Icelandic-Plus."

The signal for a Monument-wide alert sounded. I.C.C. made an announcement.

"I have identified a new object within the anomaly. It appears to have been in the system for some time prior to detection, given the number of light-minutes it has penetrated past the orbit of our outermost planet. Any Monument members who are currently available, please report to a ship's bridge for further information and analysis."

Makawee looked to Vanhi, wide-eyed. "Did Icelandic-Plus say anything about expecting more Sora-Gohan?"

Vanhi's pulse had quickened. She put a hand over her chest and dipped against her cane as Makawee moved to her side.

"Vanhi, are you okay? You don't—Are you okay?"

The question was genuine, the concern was for her as a person, not just as All Mother. The distance Vanhi had thought she'd never be able to cross was shrinking. What had seemed daunting when she'd first jumped back was now the smallest of hurdles. Because she hadn't run from it, hadn't isolated herself.

And the problem of the machine was the same: their isolation from the rest of the galaxy, from all the post-humans, meant the problem was that much more discouraging. If only there were some way to get the message out.

She'd hoped upon hope that somewhere, out there, someone was trying to get a message *in*.

Maybe that's what this was.

"I will be," she assured her. "But I'm just as surprised as you are. Maybe we'll be getting visitors sooner than we thought."

Communion. Connection. Discovery. None of it came without effort, without trust, or without reliance on others.

She scooped up the documents and put a light hand on Makawee's shoulder. "Let's go to the bridge," she told her new friend, smiling, ready to face these new challenges. "I.C.C. needs our help."

THE SHIP'S INTERLUDE

Fourteen-year-old Lewis watches his little brother, Aziz, build a ship. They've been given a rare treat: time on the Noumonian surface. The Petratheem say this area should be calm, safe. At least, for a little while.

They're on the easternmost shoreline of Noumenon's smallest sea, in a little bay with waves that lap gently at a beach filled with tightly packed sand from boulders freshly ground by the Petratheem terraforming. Aziz has dubbed this place Shipyard Cove and is busy building the first of his fleet.

The sun is bright today, but the anomaly glistens in the sky, despite it. Most everyone else is a ways up the beach, more enamored with the rock formations and the tide pools there than this stretch of mostly barren sand.

What few things the sea has thrown here, Aziz has already collected: a waterlogged branch from some Petratheem plant Lewis can't name; a flexible, blue scale the size of a hand, shed from a swimming watta-watta-baby; a tangle of something that could be hair or could be lichen or could be inorganic for all Lewis can tell; tiny pebbles; copper slag; a spine, or perhaps a long thorn; and iron-rich rock that powders under Aziz's little fingers, allowing him to draw on the other items he's found.

Now they come together to resemble a sailing ship, with the scale as the sail and the branch as the base of the boat. Aziz builds it carefully, taking his time to make sure all the pieces connect firmly. He builds a good few meters away from the water's edge, and as Lewis watches, he notes the tide coming in, ever so slowly.

The pebbles Aziz puts in a pile next to the ship. After finding a place aboard for the fibers and the slag, he draws a star on the sail with the iron. For a moment, he grins wide, elated. Then he stands and frowns.

"What's the matter?" Lewis asks. "It looks great. Let's set it on the water—send it on its adventure."

"Not yet," Aziz grumbles. "There aren't enough supplies."

"Supplies for what?"

"All the people," he says, waving at the pebbles, his tone carrying mild annoyance that conveys the simplest of sentiments: *duh.* "First you build the ship. Then you get the crew to make it ready. Then you put on the passengers, and *then* you can go on your adventure." He rubs thoughtfully at his chin, like he's a grown man making very important decisions instead of an eight-year-old playing in the sand. "They need more food."

He turns away, wandering down the beach, looking for anything else he can co-opt into his project. Lewis does the same, strolling in the other direction, looking down at his bare feet as he walks, admiring the way the sand changes color as his steps displace the water permeating between the grains.

"What do pebble-people eat?" Lewis muses with a chuckle.

He looks out into the surf and sees something jump. His stomach rumbles.

Can't the pebble-people go fishing?

Maybe the pebble-people—the peeble—don't know how to fish.

Maybe they can't eat what's in the ocean?

Maybe they don't know if they can eat what's in the ocean.

He doesn't find any peeble food, but he finds a nice skipping stone. Too big to be a passenger on his little brother's boat. Deftly, he tosses it out to sea, admiring the way it flies across the water before eventually sinking down and out of sight.

The peeble definitely need a sturdy vessel. They'd never make it on their own.

He frowns, shifts uncomfortably. His little brother's incredulity bothers him: How dare Lewis have the audacity to suggest setting sail before all the proper preparations have been made? How dare he entertain an idea so reckless? How dare he?

He realizes it bothers him because it reminds him of something. Something big and important and all around him all the time. And though he feels it there, his mind refuses to connect the final dot, to put into a simple sentence this immense sense of *sameness.*

Lewis spies a bit of slimy red—a small, severed tentacle—a meter away and scoops it up. Surely this could feed a whole herd of peeble.

As he turns back, ready to present Aziz with the prize, he feels like he's dragging something. Like this omnipresent comparison is now hitched to him by a string.

He can't shake it, even as he returns to the toy boat.

When Aziz returns with his own finds, he is delighted by the tentacle, which still has little feelers attached to it and everything. Lewis has done the peeble proud.

Together, they fill one end of the ship with supplies, then carefully set the passengers aboard. Now it is ready. Now it can begin its voyage.

Lewis moves to pick up the ship, to put it in the water, but Aziz admonishes him again. "That's not how it gets to the ocean," he says. "There's no such thing as giant hands that pick up ships."

Lewis looks from the boat across the meters of sand that still sit between it and the water's edge. "Okay, so how does it get there?"

Without a word, Aziz begins to dig. First, around the ship, gently sinking the vessel into a divot. Next, he digs outward, in one long stretch, creating a channel as straight and true as he can, toward the sea. When he reaches the waterline he begins to backtrack, and the ocean follows him. Every gentle, lapping wave sends a little tongue of water up the sandy canal, farther and farther the deeper he digs.

Finally, it reaches the ship, flooding the divot, lifting the craft.

With naught but the tip of his pointer finger, Aziz guides the boat forward, helping it go out even as the tide comes in.

Then the Noumonian winds take it, and the ship is off. The peeble have begun their adventure.

"Wave," Aziz says. "They're waving, wave back until we can't see them anymore."

Lifting his hand, Lewis asks, "So what are they going to find on their adventure?"

Aziz shrugs. "That's why they're going. Maybe they'll send a message in a bottle back and tell us about it."

Lewis keeps waving, long past when his arm gets tired, just to make Aziz smile. Eventually they're called back to the group: time to return to the shuttle and their own buoyant ships.

As they turn, begin to race each other back, the string is severed. The fourteen-year-old has already forgotten about the *sameness* that only a moment ago seemed so heavy, so constant. Its weight has already fluttered away—despite its importance. Despite its trueness. The wisp of a thought now waits, drifting, for another mind in which to nest.

And the little ship sails onward, unobserved, into uncharted waters.

CHAPTER EIGHT

MAKAWEE WAGNER: MENDING

They had to leave. Now. Soon. They had to get down there. To meet . . . others.

But Omar was still pacing the floor in their quarters on *Mira*. Still scratching at the stubble on his chin with his eyes tilted to the floor so that he wouldn't have to meet Makawee's gaze.

"We can talk about it later," he said, eyes still averted.

"You're the one who brought it up just before the mission," she said softly, indignantly. She stood by the door. A good two meters of floor space between them. They were both in head-to-toe cobalt-blue environment suits—the weave and fabric of Makawee's own design. "You coward. You drop this kind of thing on me right before we have to go out there, into the damn snow, just so you can say it's done and not have to deal with the aftermath. Not have to deal with my *reaction*."

He winced. A knowing wince that indicated everything

453

she said was right. He was counting on her professionalism to protect him, to give him space. To keep her from shouting or crying or whatever he envisioned her reaction would be.

"I already had an extra task," she said, fuming. "I have to monitor the suits. I have to make sure no one freezes to death or gets overheated or suffocates. And we don't even know what the damned thing down there *is* on top of that. And then you go and throw s-se-separating—" she hated that her tongue stumbled, that the emotions inherent in the word, what it meant, were already eating at her "—at me *now*?"

His fingers wouldn't stop moving against his chin. "I tried last week," he mumbled. "But you knew what I was doing, so you pretended there was an emergency in the lab. I tried a month before that, but you *knew* and pretended there was something urgent you forgot to do for Imane. And the month before that it was sudden stomach cramps, and the month before that—"

"That's not true! None of that is—"

"You can't run away from it this time," Omar said, tone distant, sad. "I know using the prep time like this is inexcusable. Cowardly—"

"You might not love me anymore," she said harshly, "but the man I bonded with wouldn't have sabotaged me. Wouldn't have risked the mission. Wouldn't have put everything we're about to do in jeopardy because he wanted a *buffer*!"

Omar sighed, his dark eyes and dark face both fell. "I didn't say I don't love you."

Her lip trembled. *Skies' damned son of a . . .* "We don't have time for this," she said, swiping up both of their suit cowls from where they lay folded on the entryway table. "Someone could be dying—and *you're* in charge of their preservation for ship's sake. We don't have time for this."

She opened the door, marched out. Didn't wait for him to follow—after all, he had no choice.

"Makawee. Makawee!"

"We're expected in five. Get yourself together," she said darkly, tossing his cowl over her shoulder.

Her heart felt frayed.

So what if she'd seen it coming? So what if she'd run from it, tried to buy time, tried to figure out a way . . .

She'd thought . . . just hoped . . .

They'd been bonded thirty years. Thirty *years*.

She turned a corner and nearly ran into Noam. He sported the same blue suit.

"Is everything all right?" he asked sheepishly. "I thought I heard . . ."

"Everything is fine," she insisted, eyeing the nearest ceiling speaker, silently begging I.C.C. not to contradict her with something like, *Makawee Wagner is experiencing elevated levels of distress due to interpersonal failure*. "Everything is *fine*."

Makawee didn't think of herself as a scientist or engineer. She thought of herself as a weaver.

Textiles were her true passion, and with all the new organic fibers emerging every few years, she had plenty to work with. And plenty of orders to fill.

When she was eight, her mother had brought samples of what they called sapphire-willow home from the sinkhole nearest the Monument's traditional landing site. The Petratheem encouraged the humans to study the new life-forms they were growing, to discover their properties and how the Earth-based biologies and Noumonian-based biologies might interact. Their hope was to cut off any preventable harm at the quick—ensure poisons and other contaminants were not introduced to the planet's current population.

The sapphire-willow was benign, and in truth Makawee's mother brought it home simply because it was pretty.

Makawee and her little sister, Vega, were delighted to find it was also *soft*.

The not-plant had long, fine fronds, with smaller versions of those fronds fractaling off the center branch, and then again off those branches, and so forth, until the clusters became so fine it was difficult to see them. This made the ends look like they ran clear, despite the heavy blue pigmentation. Running them between their fingers, the girls were surprised that the fronds felt like *water*—cool and immersive, despite leaving them completely dry.

And though the branching bits all snapped easily at the base, the strands themselves were tough. Like spider silk.

Makawee rolled the strands between her palms, over and over, twisting them together. Already spinning, the act second nature.

By the time their mother discovered their play, Makawee had already converted half of the sapphire-willow into one long thread. Far from upset, their mother was impressed by her daughter's focus on the task, how well she'd pulled the fibers, how strong it was without the help of a wheel, weight, or spindle.

I.C.C. found vids for Makawee on textile craft. On the history of different nations' fabrics, quilting, spinning, drying, curling, sewing. "Your original was from the Republic of Black Hills. She was a diplomat to the nation's only bordering country, the United States, and an expert weaver. Her art was displayed in many internationally acclaimed galleries," it told her. Makawee looked through her original's work and history, found the designs of the Lakota peoples—her peoples. She fell instantly in love with the shapes and motifs.

That was why she'd become a materials specialist, with a focus on fiber development. There were so many new substances, textures, colors—so many ways they could be applied. Noumonian terraforming was a gift to all the creatives in the Monument.

Yes, she was a scientist. Yes, she was an engineer. But so were all the textile craftspeople who'd come before her. Anyone who'd first sheared an animal, or invented a stitching technique, or designed a new fringe, or patterned new clothes, or engineered suits to protect bodies in ever-increasingly hostile environments.

Therefore, *I am a weaver.*

Her textiles had even helped her win Omar's favor.

But that was long ago.

Now the two of them were on their way to meet the unknown with a gulf between them.

An object that wasn't Sora-Gohan had landed in the Luminal Mountains. An object I.C.C. had been tracking for a good two years.

A perfect sphere, and the Petratheem declared it wasn't of their design.

But, like the Sora-Gohan, it did not respond to hails. They'd thought it perhaps a probe, and yet Icelandic-Plus had suggested it might bear life-forms.

She/they were the happiest Makawee had ever seen.

The im's wings had swirled with a myriad of colors—excitement clear in her stance and head-bobbing. "Perhaps—perhaps *finally*," she said. "Not Sora-Gohan. Others! Others have found a way in. Greet them. Greet them!"

Others. The others they'd been expecting for a long time.

Others prevented from arriving by the anomaly.

. . . Aliens?

Others.

The humans knew at least a handful of advanced civilizations had worked on the megastructures. This was fact as much as it was *past*; the only civilization they'd identified with certainty was the long-lost Nataré. All other human encounters with alien life-forms—besides those on Noumenon—had been with nonsentient creatures. Mostly single-celled organisms. Nothing that could look them in the eye and ask them questions. And certainly nothing that could build a spaceship that could traverse an anomaly they themselves had yet to understand.

What would they find down there in the mountains? *Who* would they find?

The object—still perfectly spherical upon entering the atmosphere—had impacted the third-tallest peak in the Luminal Mountains. They'd expected the craft to slow when it reached Noumenon, to descend with a modicum of grace. But their assumptions had been wrong and their estimated time to intercept had been off—they'd arrived too late, and the impact had already occurred.

Though the collision itself had been unobserved, below them now was evidence not of a crater, but of a freshly triggered avalanche. The high drifts covering most of the craggy outcroppings had been disturbed roughly halfway down the mountainside. Ice sheets had sloughed away, and much of it now rested on a large ledge, a plateau with upward-sloping edges.

Their shuttle pilot fought the wind as they swooped in over the ridgeline, eventually descending gently over the piled snow once they'd cleared the bluffs. The surface glittered in the midafternoon sunlight, and the sheets of old ice that clung to the mountain crags embodied a crystalline blue almost the color of their suits. Snow was a rare sight on the Noumonian surface at most latitudes. It was always a wonder to visit the southernmost mountain range.

They landed on bare rock, and the pilot released the rear hatch, allowing a fleet of cleaning bots outfitted with excavation equipment to storm the landscape.

With a repair-and-patch kit slung over her shoulder, Makawee exited after the others. Snowshoes helped them stay suspended over the deep drifts as they approached the collapsed snowbanks. At least four hundred thousand cubic meters of snow had been displaced here. Digging in would be dangerous work.

Above, *Hippocrates* came lower, running what scans it could, using basic sonar to detect the shape of the land beneath the snow. Whatever—whoever—they found down here would be transported to the med ship for deCON and medical attention.

"Looks like there's something about two kilometers that way," said Omar, staring at a handheld screen flickering with readouts.

His voice grated on Makawee's ears, but she vowed to remain professional. Omar was an expert in reclamation and recycling, with an emphasis on inorganics. He was in charge of assessing the ship and informing the others of any possible threat to both the team and the new arrivals. He had to be here—there was no getting around it.

"How deep?" Nika asked. Her original had been a historian, though her line was most famous for its diplomacy. Her specialty was in emergent communications, with a focus on chromatic and chemical-based interactions.

"Maybe five meters?" Omar answered

"Not too bad. Bots should be able to handle it."

It was a slog to get to the buried object's location, the snowshoes making the trek both slow and awkward. They were too unaccustomed to this kind of environment, poorly practiced in traversing any kind of snowpack.

They arrived after the bots, who were already hard at work digging out the object. Noam was part of the *Hippocrates* subdivision that focused on search and rescue. With all of the environmental changes happening on the regular, it was an area of special focus and need. He calculated the possibility of further snow collapse and helped direct the bots for safe digging.

The humans aided the machines the best they could, but the endeavor was tedious and trying. All the better, for it made it difficult for Makawee to stew, to think too hard about what Omar had said and what it meant for the future. She was too tired to be scared, too focused to be worried. Just the right mixture of anticipation and excitement filled her muscles and propelled her joints.

Eventually, steam began to pour away from their suits—from under the arms, as designed, so that they would not get overheated from exertion. Makawee checked each flap, inquired after everyone's comfort level. The suits were proving themselves well.

As the sun sank beneath the peaks, casting long, purple shadows, they found the top of the object. But it wasn't simply buried in the snow. The heat of it must have flash-steamed the snow it impacted, destabilizing the drift and starting the avalanche. But then the steam had gathered on the hull, liquified, then solidified. The ship was encased in ice.

The craft was a shiny golden color. Mostly a sphere, now oblong and twisted slightly, like a droplet of molten metal. And even though I.C.C. had estimated the object to be no more than four meters in diameter, Makawee was still surprised by how small it looked.

Their shuttle was bigger.

Omar looked for a seam—a door, a ramp, anything that might allow whoever or whatever was inside to escape. Curiously, there was nothing.

"Could it have fused on entry? Smoothed over?" Noam suggested.

"Unlikely," Omar said skeptically.

Makawee risked putting her ear to the metal. Omar tried to stop her, but she shrugged him off, earning the two of them confused head tilts from Nika and Noam.

There were no sounds, no vibrations. Nothing stirred within.

They'd thought their mission likely diplomatic in nature, but now it was clear this was purely retrieval.

"Maybe it's not . . ." Omar started.

"What?" Makawee prodded.

Omar went still for a moment, his brow furrowed. "What if it's not a ship? What if Icelandic-Plus is wrong and it's not an envoy of any kind?"

"So, what, it's—it *was*—a perfectly spherical asteroid?" asked Nika.

"No, I mean . . . the Nataré fought a war over the megastructures, right? So *other* civilizations could interpret them as hostile. This sphere could be anything, and we're just going to bring it aboard one of our ships?"

Makawee raised a hand to instinctually grab Omar's shoulder, but her hand dropped just as quickly. Would a gesture like that even be welcome anymore? "I think the possibility that there's something alive inside that needs our help is greater than the possibility the object means us harm."

"I'm here for risk assessment. To protect the team."

"I understand that," she said. "But I think the urgency overrides our need for caution."

"We should bring it aboard," Nika agreed. "The containment facility is fully prepped—even if the object is hostile, we're probably safer with it on *Hippocrates* than anywhere else."

Decision made, an additional team came down to help secure the object, to pop it from the compacted snow and lift it high, cradled beneath *Hippocrates*'s exterior.

During deCON, after they'd brought it aboard, scans revealed there was indeed a single life-form-shaped presence inside. But they could detect no movement, no pumping of fluids or exchanging of gasses. All was quiet. Still. Like a tomb.

The dig team stared at it through a thick layer of observation window in deCON's outermost offices while agents and bots sanitized the surface.

"The single Nataré specimen *Ultra* discovered was preserved inside a structure akin to a coffin," said Nika. "I can pull up the pictures."

"That structure was very different from this structure," I.C.C. said. "Though I do agree they appear conceptually similar."

"What are the chances a coffin just wanders into our system, *through* the anomaly?" Omar asked.

"Low," Noam said helpfully.

Nika went to an access station and brought up images taken by the *Noumenon Ultra* mission. She scrolled past various megastructures and planets until landing on the system in which the Nataré body was found.

Though Nika scrolled quickly, Makawee made her pause on a picture of two planets. Both rocky, one with an observable atmosphere, one without. They were connected by a long, wormy structure. One of the planets trailed a tail, and the other sported great loops high into space. The kind of loops she was used to seeing when a thread failed to pull completely through fabric before the next stitch was made, tangling and knotting and bunching all wrong.

"The planets were thought to have been casualties in the Nataré war," I.C.C. explained. "Though given what we know now about the cosmoforming machine, this may be the earliest documentation of a megastructure malfunction."

"Here, look," Omar said, leaning over Nika—too close for Makawee's comfort. It made her wonder, made her chide herself for wondering. "The Nataré corpse."

The "coffin" was oblong and clear, like a glass egg. The group quickly agreed they were not the same design. Ultimately, the body within did not match the scans of whatever was inside their sphere. The Nataré was flat, covered in fine filaments, the morphology somewhat like a starfish.

"So we have *another* alien?" Noam asked. "An honest-to-stars new—"

"That is not what the evidence suggests," I.C.C. cut in. The monitor changed, the *Noumenon Ultra* records closed, and a different file labeled "Post-Human Modification" opened. "Apologies. If you wish to continue to speculate, I shall refrain from further interruption. However, I believe what we have uncovered here is related to the evolutionary branch known as *Homo draconem*."

The medics, deCON, linguistics, and materials groups all had members present at the orb's opening. Everyone wore multilayered protection against everything from single-celled pathogens to percussive injury. As with most new protective gear, everything was blue; they were like the water in one of All Mother's specimen tanks, with a golden, newly discovered creature floating patiently in the center.

Makawee stood to the side, waiting to take samples from the craft's exterior and interior, to help determine how the ship might have transversed the anomaly and where it might have originated.

Omar, who typically spent his days aboard *Solidarity* working with raw metals and seeing to safety ordinances, was tasked with cutting open the craft. With the first puncture, a stable *hiiiissssss* eked out as the atmosphere inside equalized to the atmosphere outside. DeCON immediately tested the composition, and when no dangerous elements were detected, Omar continued, slitting a near-perfectly-straight line around the vertical circumference of the orb.

Gloved hands came in from all sides to pry open the seam.

Though the initial scans had shown nothing but the figure inside, Makawee was still surprised at how barren the interior was. The smallest allowance of what appeared to be a press-through casing—which had likely protected the individual upon impact—wrapped around the *Homo draconem*. But there was no life support. Nothing to keep the atmosphere fresh and circulating, nothing to regulate the temperature. No controls of any kind. No thruster system or SD drive or ion propulsion—no indication of how the individual was meant to guide the ship.

A tomb was still the most apt analogy.

The figure themself did not stir within the press-through. Whether they'd been encased in it their entire trip or if they'd manipulated the substance prior to entering the atmosphere was unknowable.

The medics and deCON specialists tried to pull the press-through off, but it wouldn't budge. Though it had the same pillowy texture as the bits aboard All Father's ship, this was more advanced. It had been directed to maintain its shape and it would not be manually deterred by something as simple as a prodding finger.

Maybe they are *dead*, Makawee thought. But why would someone go through all this trouble to send the Philosopher's System a single dead body?

She considered Omar's hesitancy. Could he be right? Was this some kind of latent threat? In ancient times dead bodies were lobbed into cities to spread plague. Could this one be carrying a pathogen they had no way of detecting or guarding against?

"Is it possible the pathways are now open?" asked Cynthia,

one of the deCON team members, her voice somewhat muffled by her protective mask. "Maybe people on the outside were able to figure out the machine's problems on their own. Maybe this really did come here by accident?"

"Not out of the question, but unlikely," I.C.C. said. "There have been no notable differences in the anomaly, and the Petratheem have reported no breakthroughs or changes. In addition, the amount of time that has passed since the anomaly's appearance has been short, relatively speaking. Though I admire human ingenuity, the discovery, investigation, solution, and repair process takes time—even with common problems. For an atypical problem of this scale, experience tells me there is a seventy-five-point-three-two percent chance the investigation stages are still in their infancy."

"But, if this isn't an accident," Makawee said, "then someone somewhere figured out *something*. They figured out more than we have."

"Hopefully the *Homo draconem* will be receptive to our inquiries when they are revived," I.C.C. said. "I am speaking with Jamal aboard *Mira* at the moment. He says he suspects the individual has engaged in cryptobiosis; he has seen records of such a stasis before. The patient should be removed from their casing and their environment returned to within average *Homo draconem* parameters. Given the environment of the orb, I suspect they've undergone anhydrobiosis, anoxybiosis, and cryobiosis at the very least and should be given water, oxygen, and a warm room in which to recover."

Omar sliced into the stubborn press-through, down to the *Homo draconem* itself. Carefully, they revealed their guest's full form.

Makawee took her samples as the medics and deCON prepped the visitor for transfer to the proper medical wing. The individual wore no clothes, though there was a rope coiled around their body, and clutched in their forelimbs was a case of some sort. Makawee took a quick sample of the primary materials, but the medics insisted no one attempt to pry the case from the *Homo draconem*'s arms.

Omar shaved twenty different samples in twenty different sizes from the orb itself, before hacking off three chunks of the press-through. Inside the craft, after the *Homo draconem* was removed, Makawee recovered six loose scales, each the color and glint of onyx. The inside of the orb itself was constructed from a different metal with a higher tensile strength than the outside, presumably to add stability and protection, which made the outer shell of the orb—clearly much more pliable—all the more curious.

But that was all. There were no other identifiable materials aboard.

Omar was both curt and overly attentive to her as they worked, and Makawee felt both annoyed and needy. One pressed too hard and the other pulled back. One shied away and the other surged forward. It was clearly awkward for both of them. They didn't know how to behave, what to say. And as the work dragged on, Makawee found herself becoming more and more resentful.

She hadn't brought this awkwardness upon them. *He'd* decided to drop a bomb on their relationship when there would be no chance of talking about it for hours.

She could no longer look at him, let alone meet his gaze. She tried to push her eyes in his direction, and her entire body revolted. When she finally had all her samples, she left in a huff, without a word of thanks.

The material's lab was a sudden sanctuary, even with all the questions her colleagues immediately bombarded her with. For the most part, I.C.C. took pity on her and redirected their inquiries toward itself.

She recruited Imane to help analyze the material, and much to their surprise they had their answer within minutes.

"It's just alacritite," Imane said, triple-checking the results.

"Well, that's less exciting than I was expecting," Makawee said. "That's the same alloy that allowed the first SD bubble creation, right, I.C.C.?"

"Correct. Alacritite was originally developed for quantum computing in the late twenty-first century, as the lack of polarization allowed for qubits made from the alloy to be more reliable and responsive than qubits made from single atoms. It is also a key component in personality-driven AI of the time."

"Like you and C?"

"Correct. While the material itself is not particularly exotic, it is extremely difficult to create. It is incredibly stable once the materials are alloyed, but it is difficult to prevent the component ions from decaying during the smelting process. Which is to say, between C and myself we contain approximately twenty-six grams of stable alacritite. Whereas the samples you have retrieved from the orb for study are themselves twenty-eight-point-six total grams."

"So someone put real effort into this craft's design. Its simplicity is deceptive, and the material was likely chosen for a specific purpose, not just because it's nice and shiny."

"Again, likely correct."

They ran a few more tests to be sure they hadn't missed anything, but by the time they'd finished, most of the lab had cleared out. It was late. Time for a meal. Time to relax.

Time to go home.

Where was home for Makawee anymore?

The day quickly began to weigh on her. Eventually she'd have to return to their quarters—his quarters, her quarters?—to sleep. Maybe she could sneak in after he'd gone to bed, leave again before he awoke, so that she wouldn't have to discuss the particulars of the separation just yet.

She took her time getting from *Hippocrates* to *Mira*. She stopped by the mess hall to see if there were leftovers from that afternoon's communal lunch. She stopped to help a pair of scouts unwedge an automatic door. She stopped to relace her shoes, and check her hair in a public bathroom, and run through the next day's schedule with I.C.C.

And yet, she could not avoid her own hall forever.

But when she reached her door she couldn't go inside. She simply stood there, staring at it, face blank and heart full of sorrow.

"Makawee," I.C.C. said gently. "I have had the cleaning bots prepare an unused set of quarters for habitation. I am not suggesting you permanently relocate there, but if you'd like to utilize the space for the evening, it is available."

"Thank you, I.C.C. But I . . . I can't. Not yet." She hated how broken her voice sounded.

"I understand."

She backed up until her spine hit the far wall, and then she sank down, sitting across from her door, feet from her bed, unable to get up again.

"Makawee. Makawee, wake up."

She was roused at an early hour by Omar shaking her shoulder.

"Have you been out here all night?" he asked.

Still groggy, she felt ambushed. She hadn't meant to fall asleep in the hall, but emotional and physical exhaustion had gotten the better of her.

"This is ridiculous," he chided, waving widely at her predicament. "You could have come inside."

She brushed him away, stood up. "Because you made me feel so *welcome* there," she shot back.

"So, what, you decided to squat in the hall just to show people how cruel I am? I didn't kick you out. I said I wanted to separate, not—"

She made a sound of disgust and sidestepped him into the apartment. The environment suits might have worked well down in the snow, but they were not comfortable sleeping attire and she felt sweaty and gross all over. She needed a shower. Maybe the water could drown out his sulky, grating voice.

"We have to discuss how we're going to go about this," he insisted. "Problems don't just disappear because you decide to ignore them. That's how things get *worse*! That's how *we* got worse."

Without responding, she shut the door behind her. She needed at least a few inches of steel between her and Omar right now. A barrier. A shield.

Heart beating fast, she pressed her back to the closed door, just like she'd pressed her back to the hall wall. When had it all gone so wrong? Why couldn't it all make sense like it used to?

Why was everything unraveling?

. . . .

FIVE DAYS LATER

The *Homo draconem* wasn't responding to the typical cryptobiosis treatments.

And Makawee wasn't responding to Omar's intership calls.

Icelandic-Plus had done her/their best not to appear too disappointed that the visitor was simply another human.

All Seer was very excited by a set of markings on the *Homo draconem*'s pack. They looked like letters from the Latin alphabet.

Vanhi, All Father, and All Mother were trying to stay positive, scouring All Father's ship records for medical instances of difficult stasis revival—records that had been forbidden to All Father for most of his life. The late Wes-Tu had given him access, educated him as to his follower's many possible forms.

It seemed as though nothing on the ships was going quite to plan. So, to clear her head, Makawee made for the surface.

The ships were in constant motion over the planet, allowing the Monument to monitor as many of the Petratheem developments as possible. Right now they hovered over the easternmost continent (they used the longitude running through the ancestor shrine as the hemispheric demarcation line). Makawee always found the not-forest around Sinkhole 237 soothing.

The light seeping in through the stalks of the tallest treelike life-forms fractured in all shades of blue, from cerulean to aqua to navy. And the ground seethed with red-tinted life. All in all, this made the shadows purple, the color play stark and uncompromising. It was beautiful and otherworldly. She picked her way through the forest with a basket on her arm, careful not to trample any of the delicate, budding life. The sinkhole itself lay to her north, but she would remain far afield of its lip.

She tutted at herself as she bent to pick slip-weed, tossing it into her basket with an efficient flick of the wrist. It was the first time she'd touched down on solid ground since the Luminal Mountains, and she'd been in dire need of additional samples. She could have sent an apprentice out, but she thought the repetitive work would do her good, clear her head.

But, instead, her ineffectual interactions with Omar kept spinning around and around her mind.

When had they lost the thread? When had she cut a strand she should have let go long? Where had she knotted when she should have feathered?

It wasn't that they were two filaments who'd gaped apart. People were more complicated than that, more like full tapestries than single threads, but endless, with weave after weave being little more than an instant, a breath. A *glance* was a thread, and its aftermath informed the entire fabric.

Somewhere she'd lost sight of the *pattern* of their life together.

She'd thought things were unraveling, but what if it was worse? What if she'd unconsciously knitted this exact scenario? It wasn't something from outside that was pressing or pulling, forcing them to disentangle. It was that they'd taken a different direction without either of them caring to correct their course. It was the design that was all wrong. Warped and ill-fitting.

All wrong all wrong all wrong.

Just like Icelandic-Plus had said of the im machine.

She rubbed her hands together. The slip-weed samples were staining her palms blue, and bright red spores from the nearby shortcap clusters clung to her boots and lower legs. She looked a painted mess.

The woven mask over her nose and mouth kept her from inhaling the spores and the tail-flier fry, which had exploded in numbers since terraforming began. It was remarkable how the native Noumonian microfauna had taken to the changes in their world.

She sat down beneath the not-trees on a patch of somewhat-bare ground. Threads of throbbing red, like thick veins, burrowed into the dirt here. She sat on them uncaringly, and they bore her just as uncaringly. Something copper and daisy yellow flitted across the ground between the shortcap. She only got a glimpse of it now and again, but she knew it was an eight-legged lizard-like creature, directly related to the im, though perhaps as near to the im as mice were to humans.

Strange how life could be. Connected in long, winding ways.

A mechanical whirring to the left drew her attention. All Mother was there, in the distance, with a group of three young apprentices. Her mech was transforming, raising up to pluck a bit of something from high above to show it to her young naturalists. They cataloged everything they came across, creating brand-new Noumenon-specific classifications of life.

The naturalists figured out what it was, and then people like Makawee figured out what to do with it.

What to do with it. Or what to do *about* it.

She thought about Vanhi, about the exoplasm. They still hadn't devised a proper way to contain it, let alone neutralize it, and time was running out. Their only samples were slowly disappearing. Once they were gone, they were gone. The data set would be incomplete. How could she protect Vanhi if she didn't fully understand what she was protecting her from?

She picked up a group of slip-weed fibers from her basket—the bits were fluffy in her palm—and began to roll them together, twisting and pulling, transforming them into thread. At one point some of it knotted, and she tossed it back into the basket, irritated at herself.

The knot reminded her of the *Noumenon Ultra* photographs. The pictures of the two planets conjoined. The way the structure connecting them looked like it had bunched, like a thread pulled inexpertly through a stitch.

When threads bunched that way, they could pull the fabric, ruin further stiches down the line. Everything could be overly tight or overly loose. Twisted.

Warped.

. . . It could warp the fabric.

Just like her life had warped. Like the fabric of space-time was warped by the anomalies.

And sometimes, to save the fabric, you needed to cut. You

needed a seam ripper to tear out the offending bits so that darning—real mending—could begin.

She began rolling the metaphor around in her mind, just like she'd rolled the slip-weed in her hand.

Sometimes you needed a heavy-gauge needle to piece through multiple layers of fabric at the same time . . .

Her mind was pulling her in several directions at once, but it all led toward a revelation about one substance: the alacritite.

She stood up abruptly, knocking over her basket. Forgetting the blue, she put a hand over her mouth, over her mask, leaving a handprint.

Of course! Why hadn't she thought to expose the exoplasm to the alacritite yet?

It couldn't be a coincidence that Vanhi's touchstone was a rare source of the alloy and that the *Homo draconem* had come to them in an entire ship of alacritite, could it?

Scooping up her basket and its spilt contents, she hastily skipped through the forest back to the shuttle pickup and drop-off site. Her mind whirred with every step, designing experiments, envisioning result scenarios. She needed to climb aboard *Slicer* as soon as possible.

"Makawee," Vanhi chuckled, "is the blindfold really necessary?"

"I want you to be surprised." Carefully, with both hands on Vanhi's elbows, Makawee guided her through *Slicer*, over the catwalks, and to the magnetic bottle's suite. The other materials researchers lightly stepped out of the way, completely silent, holding back their laughter behind their hands.

This was a good day. It deserved a little showmanship.

"It's not my birthday," Vanhi said, chin high, hands outstretched, but steps sure. She trusted her friend not to steer her wrong.

It could be, in a way, Makawee said to herself. She'd been surprised how quickly the pieces had fallen into place once she'd suggested introducing the alacritite to the exoplasm.

Just under two weeks of intense, *intense* work and study had led them to this moment.

Makawee maneuvered Vanhi to where they used to keep the exoplasm's tank. Now something different, but no less simple, sat in its place.

"Okay, are you ready?" she asked.

"Only one way to find out," said Vanhi.

"Go ahead," Makawee said, gesturing for the dozens of people in the room to keep their composure, to wait for the signal. "You can take off the blindfold."

Vanhi whisked it away from her glasses with a flourish, and Makawee raised her arms wide.

Everyone else threw their hands up in unison, a wave of smiles cascading through the group as they all shouted in unison, *"Surprise!"*

Vanhi took a faltering, playful step backward, as though the force of their shouting were about to knock her off her feet. She laughed lightly. "Hello! And to what do we owe the theatrics?"

"To this," Makawee said, sidling up to a cube with a gold-and-tin hue, placed on a waist-high pedestal.

An individual named Hunter slid in front of Vanhi, holding out a thin screen for her to take. Displayed across it was a live feed from inside the cube.

The remaining exoplasm was filtered through a golden hue, but bounced around within the space as it typically had within its many, eaten-through tanks.

There was so little of it left. Perhaps enough to congeal in a teaspoon.

"We'll need to do long-term monitoring, of course,"

Makawee said. "But so far there has been no decay of either the alacritite or the exoplasm since we placed it in the containment cube. When held in any other system, the rate of decay was on average—depending on the materials—one-magnitude decrease on one atom's atomic half-life every twenty-hour period. And the alacritite is remarkably effective even down to a five-molecule thickness. That's why we can get a picture from inside—a fine film of the alloy is protecting the camera lens. In addition, all atmosphere was evacuated from the containment system before closure to ensure no decay."

"That is remarkable," Vanhi said, beaming.

"And both serendipitous and entirely logical. If the *Homo draconem* hadn't arrived, I don't know if our research would have led us to the alloy before our sample of exoplasm disappeared. And yet, in hindsight, it seems so obvious." Makawee walked around the cube, hand gracing its top from corner to corner. "Even at that, it would have been difficult for us to manufacture enough stable alacritite to make a container this size."

"What is it about the alacritite that prevents the exoplasm from interacting with it?"

Makawee shrugged. "We aren't entirely sure yet. But I do have a theory. I started thinking of the fabric of space-time in a literal way. As literally a fabric. But space-time is how we describe our dimension, our one layer of material. And all the subdimensions are their own layers with their own properties. So what if the alacritite is like a needle? Able to pierce through multiple layers at the same time."

"Like an SD bubble," Vanhi said.

"Close, yes. Think of it this way: a bubble is a protective coating, keeping one set of physics from intruding on another. In a sense it does exist in two dimensions at once. This is made possible by the alacritite, but nobody knows why. They didn't know when they started using it in SD drives, and they still don't know now that they've long discarded the material."

People were good at recognizing the uses of things before understanding the science behind those uses. It was the Gregor Mendel effect: farmers knew how to breed plants and livestock for specific traits long before he ever described Mendelian inheritance.

"What you're suggesting," Vanhi said slowly, trying to make sure she was getting it right, "is that alacritite fundamentally spans dimensions? As in, it simultaneously exists across multiple layers of the universe?"

"Yes! No one could ever figure out why it was so stable once created. There was no feasible reason why it should remain positively and negatively charged without polarization and not rapidly decay. But what if that's because there are parts of the alloy in another dimension, which we can't detect? Particles that automatically are drawn to it, balancing it, from somewhere else. Like . . . like a magnet held against the underside of a table, drawing iron filings to it. If all you could see was the top of the table, and didn't have an education in the forces at play, you'd be baffled by what you saw. Is there anything in the Petratheem physics that might describe this phenomenon? If there's one substance like this, shouldn't there be others?"

"I bet there is, even if the Petratheem don't know about alacritite specifically." Vanhi frowned thoughtfully. "Does this mean . . . the alacritite in my sundial . . ."

"It could explain, not your jumping, exactly, but why the sundial is your touchstone. If your endocrine system somehow became connected—entangled—with the sundial's alacritite, it's possible its dimension-spanning properties are somehow protecting you, or, at the very least, helping you return to this dimension.

"And, speaking of jumping, the containment capsule isn't

the only surprise," Makawee said, letting herself grin wide. "Come over here." She ran up to Imane, who produced a small, gift-wrapped box from behind her back.

Vanhi followed and took the box with a gracious nod and a keenly amused glance at Makawee. Judicious in her movements, she slipped off the stiff, bright-blue ribbon, carefully folded back the wrapping, and lifted the lid. Inside lay a palm-sized square of fabric—exactly the same fabric as the ribbon. Thin, lightweight, but rigid. It kept itself upright when Vanhi grasped it by the bottom corner, and when she tilted it from side to side, it shimmered under the white of *Slicer*'s overhead lamps.

Gently, she folded it over one finger, and it held its shape.

A sly smile crossed Vanhi's lips, as though she knew the answer to the question she was about to ask. "What is this?"

"Slip-weed wedded to alacritite," Makawee said. "A fabric that doesn't decay in the presence of exoplasm."

"You mean—"

"Turns out we don't have to neutralize the exoplasm, just repel it. We can make you a suit. *We did it.* We know how to protect you."

The entire team erupted into applause, as Vanhi clutched the fabric—both ribbon and square—to her chest. She didn't speak for a long moment, face tight, her emotions clearly held behind a thin dam. "Thank you, everyone," she said once the clapping had died down. "So much work, and effort, just for—" She cut herself off as she was overcome.

"Of course," Makawee said, patting her shoulder lightly. "What are families for?"

What are *families for?* Makawee wondered that evening as everyone left for their apartments on *Mira*. Some of them would be going home to children. Others to romantic partners. Some to parents. Some to friends.

As the people trickled out and the lights were shut off bank by bank, leaving only rudimentary safety lighting along the floor and walkways, Makawee calmly mounted the stairs to a little-used catwalk. Her shoes clang-clang-clanged on the corrugated metal, made all the louder by the sudden emptiness of the large space. At the end of the catwalk lay a single supplies closet.

Before Vanhi had left, she'd noted that Makawee seemed . . . off.

"Everything all right?" she'd asked.

"Of course," Makawee had replied through a thick smile. A smile that faltered ever so slightly. "Everything is . . ."

She'd contemplated taking Vanhi aside and confiding in her about Omar. She was amazed, in fact, that apart from people such as her immediate family and close friends, few people had noticed something was amiss between them. She'd worked carefully to maintain a façade while she tried to figure out a solution, and Omar had at least been gracious enough not to run around these past few weeks telling everyone that he was leaving her.

Vanhi's concern was earnest. And she was perceptive. But still, this was a good day, and Makawee didn't want to sour it for Vanhi with tales of her personal woes.

"Everything is fine," she'd insisted. "Thanks for . . . thanks for checking, though."

At first, Vanhi looked like she wanted to press further. But she respected that whatever it was, Makawee would tell her in time.

Now, Makawee opened the closet, moved aside a dormant cleaning bot, and pulled out a sleeping mat, blanket, and pillow.

"Are you sure you wouldn't be more comfortable in temporary quarters aboard *Mira*?" I.C.C. asked. It had asked her the same question for the past ten evenings.

"Yes, I.C.C., thank you. I'm sure."

"Would you like music this evening? Or white noise?"

"How about a story?" she asked. "Something happy. But something . . . something not about romance."

"I have several hundred thousand audiobooks on offer."

"Maybe tell me about the time you discovered aliens on Noumenon," she said good-naturedly. "Tell me about how you made friends with Icelandic." She rolled out the mat right there on the catwalk, and snuggled in beneath the blanket.

"My pleasure," I.C.C. said. "Shall I invoke a historic fairy-tale formatting?"

"That would be lovely."

"There was—*oh what there was!*—in the oldest of days and ages and times . . ."

The next morning, Makawee awoke to a Monument-wide announcement.

"The visitor is conscious. Our medical specialists request that everyone remain within the designated secure areas when aboard *Hippocrates*, until a time when all physical safety and sociopolitical concerns have been addressed."

Rubbing the sleep from her eyes, Makawee tossed the blanket to the side and hurriedly slapped at her own cheeks to fully rouse herself. "How did they do it?" she asked, refolding her bedroll for stowing.

"Jamal was able to locate a record pertaining to a particularly difficult stasis revival aboard a pilgrim ship. There was some sort of leak, and the individual had gone into chemobiosis, from which they did not awaken once the tainted air was evacuated and the typical environmental standards returned. Stimulation of both the pancreas and pituitary gland via an artificial form of hGH was successful in reviving them. Our *Lùhng* friend responded in kind."

"*Lùhng?*" she asked, bounding down the catwalk steps,

making for the showers, and the locker where she'd stashed fresh clothes. "Does that mean . . . ?"

"Yes. This *Homo draconem* is from Convoy Seven."

As soon as they were able, Iron Orchid—for that was what the *Lùhng* called themself—pleaded for help. They needed someone, anyone, to listen. To help. To heed.

The medics wanted them to rest, estimating Iron Orchid had been in stasis for at least fifty years given the way the sugar breakdown outside of their cells had occurred, but they refused. Every second the problem was ignored, it got worse. Every second they dawdled was perhaps another life lost.

So, once the immortals had spoken with them, and once deCON was sure the *Homo draconem* posed no threat, I.C.C. gathered everyone—all the Monument dwellers—in *Aesop*'s docking bay to hear what Iron Orchid had to say.

Restored murals of ye-old-convoy-past looked down on the gathering. Abstract shapes, bright colors, and Earth-based life-forms swirled around them. Many of the Noumonians chose to observe from high on the walls, and they almost looked like part of the artwork themselves.

Aesop had always felt cozy to Makawee, though it was no smaller than any other ship. Perhaps because she associated it with her childhood, with school and friends. It even smelled welcoming, soothing.

This was where she'd learned to knit. To weave.

This was where she'd made that first blanket for Omar.

She stood at the front of the crowd, near where they'd set up the holographic projector Iron Orchid had requested, pre-programmed with a simple map of the galaxy. Icelandic-Plus was the only dual-possessed im in attendance. The others could not be spared from their posts or roused from rest.

[This anomaly of yours,] Iron Orchid signed, for though they spoke many Monument languages, their vocal cords were little used. [It is the first, but it is not the only one. There are many others. Throughout the galaxy.]

The crowd was silent as the tale unfolded.

Iron Orchid's story was more devastating than anyone could have imagined. They drew on the map, points throughout the swirling arms. They spoke of time slips and destroyed vessels and lost homes. Systems cut off from one another. Anomalies cropping up without warning. Religions fractured, entire planets' worth of people missing or dead. And heaven knew what was actually happening behind these new anomalous borders.

The galaxy beyond their system's bubble was slowly sliding toward entropic chaos.

It was the isolation Icelandic-Plus found most troubling. "Should not be like this. Should not!" she said emphatically through her translator. "Is the opposite of what we desired. The opposite of our purpose. Communion and connection wanted. But it cannot be mistaken: these points coincide with final resting locations of machine parts. Megastructures." She flapped her wings, slammed her face into the decking, and shook all over. "What has im done?"

It was far worse than they'd ever imagined.

All of yesterday's good news seemed frivolous compared to what they now knew.

Imane stepped up, offering a soothing hand to Icelandic-Plus, and a reassurance for Iron Orchid. "We've already begun experimenting with the alacritite of your ship. We've long thought we could disperse our own anomaly if only we were able to connect the Petratheem with either the megastructures themselves or communicate with the outside for help. You've given us the only means we know of to transverse the anomaly . . ."

As she continued to elaborate on what they'd discovered so far about the alacritite and its possible subdimensional properties, Makawee's attention fell on Vanhi. No Mother looked pensive. No—determined. Her brow was furrowed and there was a tight set to her jaw. Her gaze was fixed on the map, on the angry red dots that represented other anomalies throughout the galaxy.

After a few more moments, Vanhi looked around before sliding backward through the crowd, taking small, purposeful steps in reverse. Retreating.

She looked like someone who'd just realized a deep, terrible, personal truth.

Half curious and half concerned, Makawee tried to follow her. She eased herself away from the front of the gathering to the fringes nearest the rear wall. Everyone else was enwrapped in Iron Orchid's mere presence, and she had to squeeze behind them, muttering "excuse me" as she went. Vanhi stepped out through the inner airlock door, leaving the docking bay, headed for somewhere in the interior of the ship.

Makawee had nearly reached that same door when who should step between her and her goal but Omar. "Why are you leaving?" he asked. "This is the most important thing that's happened to the Monument since the Petratheem arrived, and you're skipping out?"

She didn't have to justify herself to him. "What I do isn't really your business anymore, is it?"

She tried to sidestep him. He maneuvered in front of her. "I really think you should stay, show our guest some respe—"

"You don't get to lecture me on respect," she spat back, trying to keep her voice low, level. "I have things to do." She shoved past him.

"You can't keep avoiding me," he called after.

Makawee glanced over her shoulder and realized other people in the crowd were glancing their way.

"I know you've been sleeping on *Slicer*," he continued.

"You don't have to do that, Makawee. I never meant for you to feel like you couldn't—"

With a huff she whirled, taking angry steps back to his side. "Shut up. People are looking."

"So? Makawee, we can't keep living in this limbo."

"Omar, leave me—"

"Is everything all right?" It was All Father.

They each took a step away from the other, abashed. Neither answered the question.

"Omar, if Makawee wishes to leave the proceedings, she does not need anyone's permission to do so," All Father continued flatly.

The last thing Makawee had wanted was to distract someone like Jamal. "It's . . . I'm . . . fine," she said awkwardly, her tone and stance clearly belying the truth. She'd lost Vanhi already. She'd meant to catch her on the way out—almost exactly as Omar had caught her.

Perhaps whatever No Mother was up to was none of her business.

"I'll stay," she insisted to All Father.

"Would you like to accompany me over to Hope's side?" he asked. "I'm afraid I've twisted my ankle a little and could use the support."

"Of-of course," she said quickly, offering him her arm.

As they started to walk away, Omar began to trail behind for a moment, until All Father spoke again. "Omar, could you go help with the twins? The children could use a diversion." He pointed to where two small, toddling clones of Ivan Baraka were running circles around their parents—best friends Toya and Reggie. The cloning process had gone slightly awry, and the zygote had unexpectedly split, giving them two fetuses instead of one. They'd decided to continue with the growth instead of starting over, and now Van and Barak were the mischievous darlings of the Monument.

A nearby turret was trying to help distract them, perhaps to the turret's own detriment.

Omar sighed, resigned to the responsibility even though he clearly would rather stand literally anywhere else in the crowd. "Oh. Yeah, I suppose."

"Thank you. Quickly now, before Instruction Manual gets a signal receptor twisted."

Overall, it appeared as though she and Omar had only caused a small disturbance, and luckily Iron Orchid didn't seem to have noticed at all. Makawee helped All Father back to his usual place beside All Mother, and while she wasn't one to judge whether someone was sincerely injured or not, he didn't feel like he was utilizing Makawee's proffered steadiness.

Iron Orchid was expressing their joy at having found people—a whole community—with a sincere desire to help. [Everyone beyond your anomaly has lost all confidence,] they signed. [Our convoy has stopped building. People across the galaxy have stopped interfacing with the megastructures because they fear making the problem worse. They ignore the problem in hopes a resolution will be found despite their inaction. I cannot express my love and gratitude enough.]

A small pit of guilt opened in Makawee's stomach. She couldn't help but see herself in Iron Orchid's description of the outside world.

She'd thought . . . she wasn't sure what she'd thought anymore. That Omar would change his mind? That they'd both decide this was all just a big misunderstanding if she spent enough nights away?

Next, Iron Orchid spoke of their grandparents. Of the history so missed between those who'd set out for Noumenon and those who'd stayed behind. The Convoy Twelve crew may not have been able to have *Homo sapiens* children, but they'd had children. They'd loved and been loved. Many of them had even had their lives extended via biological modification and had been able to personally teach Iron Orchid of the lost ones—those they in the Monument called the immortals—presumed still alive here on the planet's surface.

The *Lùhng* gave greetings and thanks in many languages with a rough voice. When they spoke well wishes in Lakota, Makawee's heart swelled.

This *was* a momentous occasion; Omar hadn't been wrong about that. She looked for him now and saw him with Toya and Reggie, a small boy flung over each shoulder. He was a good person, if flawed. She'd never doubted that.

She thought about that first blanket she'd woven for him. She'd washed and carded the fibers by hand, pulling out the burrs and the knots and the dirt. She'd done the spinning and the dyeing, designed the pattern. She'd even constructed the loom on her own.

So much work had gone into that simple gesture.

Why hadn't she put the same amount of work in lately? Perhaps she'd been too quick to assume any little slight an intended insult. Perhaps she'd become too lazy to be thoughtful—she hadn't asked for a long time if he'd wanted tea when she made some for herself. Or perhaps she'd been too guarded, had failed to share her thoughts and feelings as readily as she used to.

Perhaps, perhaps, perhaps.

But if she'd been careless and lazy, there was no mistaking he'd done the same. He used to put a blanket over her shoulders when she fell asleep at the table after working all evening. He used to smile at her more readily. He used to tell her he loved her before they'd eaten their morning meal. He used to help her brainstorm when she was stuck on some aspect of design.

Once so perfectly aligned, now there was a gaping hole between them. Perhaps it couldn't be mended. Perhaps hoping things would magically go back to as they once were was folly.

Problems never improved when ignored. No matter how hard she wished it.

That evening Makawee went back to *Slicer*, not to stay the night but to gather her things. She couldn't keep running away from Omar. Sooner or later she had to face him and the fact that one of them had to move out.

The day's excitement meant that the entire place—usually bustling—was sleep cycle silent. There were no interruptions or awkward questions as she emptied her locker and trudged up the catwalk to retrieve her bedding. A large storage bin helped her consolidate all the items.

Soon, half her life would be in boxes, one way or the other.

She hefted the bin up, atop her head, steadying it with both hands, but finding the weight easier to evenly distribute this way. She began to retrace her steps, when she noticed one light bank in the magnetic bottle suite was on. A bank she'd turned off herself only a few minutes prior.

"Hello?" she called lightly. No answer.

Shrugging to herself, she started to descend the steps toward the bottle. Perhaps she'd actually overlooked a switch or two. Halfway down, though, she noticed the screen they used for monitoring the exoplasm wasn't in its stand beside the alacritite containment unit.

She was certain that had been in its proper place when she'd come through before.

As she set foot on the bottom rung—worried the screen had slipped off its dock—a shape loomed to her left.

Her breath caught, and she made an involuntary jump to

the side, throwing the bin—and herself—off balance. It all came crashing to the floor.

"Oh—oh, Makawee, are you all right?"

It had only been Vanhi, the screen in hand as she stared intently at what was left of the exoplasm floating between the walls of its shiny prison.

"By the ships, you scared me," Makawee said, righting the bin to make sure nothing spilled out before pushing it to one side, under the stairs, so as not to draw attention to its contents. "What are you doing in here?"

"Thinking," she said. "I didn't mean to startle you, I thought everyone had gone home." She glanced at the storage container. "What are you doing here?"

"Clearing out some junk," she said quickly, then wincing at the lie. Why was she so embarrassed by the separation? "I noticed you left during Iron Orchid's presentation. Have you been in here the whole time?"

"Mostly, yes. It was . . . it was what Imane said about the alacritite being the only substance we know of that can transverse the anomaly. I left because it's not true."

For a moment, Makawee forgot about her shame and her sham. She left the bin in favor of Vanhi's side. "Oh?"

"The alacritite isn't the only thing we know of that can transverse the anomaly. *I* can transverse the anomaly. Every time I jump, I leave its confines. *I* can get out."

"True," Makawee said. "But I don't think I'm being ungracious when I say it's probably easier to reproduce the alloy than it is the circumstances that allow you to jump. Besides, you only jump to your anticipation SD. It's not exactly the stuff solutions are made of."

"But what if I *could* jump elsewhere? Elsewhere here—in this dimension? I could rally people. I could investigate the megastructures and bring answers back to the Petratheem and get the Petratheem solutions out into the galaxy." She turned to Makawee, eyes bright. "Do you think you could make my suit a proper environment suit? To help fully protect me—*wherever* I end up?"

"I'm sure we could. I mean, perhaps. The alacritite can be resistant to merger with other materials," Makawee said, not fully following Vanhi's train of thought. "Oh, but . . . *but*! All Mother has been holding on to Houdini's *Homo kubernētēs* modifications since their death. I know she wants to honor them with repurposing the parts, but hasn't found the right project yet. I wonder if—yes! With those mods, we could likely give your suit the capacity to adapt independently to different circumstances—" The wheels were turning. She loved this idea, making a fully circumstantially customizable suit for Vanhi. "But why would you need that? How would you wind up anywhere other than your SD?"

"It's not the jumping into the SD that I think we can change," she said. "I think we can better manipulate where I end up when I come back. If we can get the sundial off-world, beyond the anomaly, I can appear beyond the anomaly, too, right?"

"Sure. But then you're out there and the people with the solutions—the Petratheem—are still down here. We can't shoot them all off in Iron Orchid's golden orbs—they don't have the same stasis abilities, and we couldn't make enough alacritite for a ship large enough to actually contain—"

"We don't have to," Vanhi said quickly. "You're right, trying to get the Petratheem out is too complicated with the resources we have. So what we need is a way for me to jump out there—" she made a big sweeping gesture toward the sky with one hand "—then into my SD, and then back here, and vice versa."

"Okay," Makawee said slowly. "But that would require two sundials."

"Or, you know," Vanhi said flippantly, as though it were no big deal. "Two halves of a sundial."

It took Makawee a moment to grasp what Vanhi meant. "You want to cut C in half?"

"Not C," Vanhi said. "C used to live in my phone. We'd upload C elsewhere, and then we split the inert sundial in two, so that half of the alacritite I'm entangled with can go one way, and half of it can stay here with Jamal, like always."

"But we're not even certain it *is* the alacritite that protects you. It's not even a theory so much as a hunch. If we're wrong and you do this . . . that might be the end of things. The end of *you*. What if you cut the sundial in half and *half of you* reappears in each place?"

Vanhi moved to place the screen back on its stand, leaving Makawee dumbfounded in the middle of the room.

"I mean," Makawee continued, "we can't even run experimental models for your proposal, because we don't understand enough of the variables. There's certainly nothing in the Petratheem ultra equations that describes *you*, is there?"

"No," Vanhi admitted.

"No. So I can't in good conscience support this idea. I've worked—an entire team, most of this Monument—has worked for years now trying to protect you. I can't watch you do something so reckless just because it has a long shot at restoring the galaxy."

Vanhi hurried back to Makawee, throwing her arms around her. Confused, Makawee hugged back. Vanhi smelled warm, familiar. The very essence of home. "It's because you've all worked so hard that I'm even considering this," Vanhi said. "Without your fabric, without your suit, I don't think there's a chance I'd live through my next jump. But now, knowing what's going on out there, knowing that I'll be protected from the propagation of anomalous activity, but others won't if I don't do anything . . . I can *use* this. I can use what I've always thought of as my curse to make a difference. To solve a problem and help people." She pulled back, a smile on her face. "You didn't know me when I was young. And that was so, so long ago. But solving scientific problems—especially SD problems—is where I shine. I don't just mean I'm good at it. It's always made me feel . . ." She searched for the words.

"It's who you are," Makawee said. She understood. After all, she was a weaver. When she had her hands on thread, she was the most herself.

"Right. It's who I am. Here, going through the Petratheem physics, it's all so *theoretical*. I've always been more practical. Hands on. *Experimental*."

"You need to apply the solutions," Makawee said. "I think I do understand, Vanhi, really. But I'm scared for you."

"And I'm scared for them," she said, making the same broad gesture. "Sometimes being scared is how we know we're doing something important. Thank you, for helping me see, finally. To realize Stone was right."

"Right about what?"

Vanhi smiled, but her eyes were sad. "It's not a curse," she said. "It's a superpower."

Among the immortals, the response to Vanhi's proposal was mixed. Icelandic-Plus and I.C.C. trusted Vanhi's instincts, but both Hope and Jamal remained rigidly skeptical. Iron Orchid, for one, thought the idea magnificent. They offered to take half of the sundial back through the anomaly. All they'd need was a new orb and a safe launch.

[I never thought my quest would end here,] they signed. [I intend to be of use however I can.]

I.C.C. agreed to share processing power and storage space with C. And C was equally as happy to be placed in a new home.

Vanhi promised not to touch the sundial until the environment suit was made and fully tested against the remaining exoplasm. And they would run what digital modeling they could. They would come as close to confident as they could. When everyone was satisfied, I.C.C. would guide the cutting, sure it could manage to split the sundial's tiny alacritite contents into two equal masses within one hundred thousandth of a difference.

Still, there would be no way of knowing if this would work until they tried. Vanhi could jump and never come back. She could end up jumping between the SD and one sundial half and not the other. There was even a remote chance it could stop her jumping altogether, though no one dared propose such a thing out loud. After all, they'd tried so many other ways to stop it, it would be devastating if they were to discover such a simple solution hiding under their noses all this time.

Despite misgivings, everyone was hopeful. And the significance of each aspect of the solution was not lost on I.C.C. "It is remarkable that a child of two convoys—Convoy Seven and Convoy Twelve—has brought us the missing piece to our puzzle," it said. "And that each of us, in some strange way, finds ourselves here, in this moment, at all. And with a significant part to play, too."

Accidents, they all were—these immortals, this *Lùhng*—in one way or another. Accidents of time, of modification, of subdimensions, of artificial construction. But it was their uniqueness, the beauty of those accidents, that had led to the means of mending.

And Makawee finally realized that to mend something didn't mean to make it exactly as it was before. It simply meant the wound—the cut, the split—had been darned. Healed over. And often not without a scar.

Mending could mean evolving, moving on. It could mean letting go of shame, refusing to feel like a failure simply because her relationship had failed.

Sometimes curses were superpowers. And sometimes endings were new beginnings.

A week later, Makawee finished packing up her things. The quarters I.C.C. had cleaned out would be her new living space. She was still sad, still angry—at Omar, at herself—but mostly she was simply ready. She wasn't at peace, but she'd made a sort of truce with the way things were.

She and Omar had grown apart, then pushed apart. Little undercuts left so many open wounds no bandage in the world could put them back together again. They'd created this, designed this. And now they had to live with this.

Not everything bad could be undone. She'd still need a long time to grieve for their relationship, but today she could move forward.

The last thing she placed in a box was the blanket she'd made for him. That very first blanket, now worn through and raggedy. Its blues faded, its reds now more like browns. Several holes had been repaired over the years, and the patchwork was obvious and added character.

"You're taking that?" he asked lightly.

"Do you mind?"

"I thought it was a gift."

She pulled it from the box, all neat and folded. "It was." She smiled softly, for herself. "It is," she said, handing it to him, watching the way he smoothed a palm over it, clearly reliving some small, sweet memory.

And then she left. It was difficult, putting one foot in front of the other. But it felt promising. New.

This bit of her tapestry was complete. And there was still so much more to weave.

THE WATCHONE'S INTERLUDE

YEAR SEVENTEEN TWO AFTER THE GREAT LOAMING

YEAR NINETY THOUSAND AND SEVEN HUNDRED AFTER THE CONTINENTAL COLLIDE AND THE EXPULSION OF THE FORDING SEA

YEAR THREE THOUSAND FOUR HUNDRED AND TWO AFTER THE FIRST OF THE COORDINATORS GAVE THEIR ORDERS AND DESIGNED THE ENGINELESS SHIPS IN THE OX BLOOD COMMEMORATIONS

On a pitted, oblong asteroid—one with an irregular tumble, no atmosphere, and a steady, elliptical orbit around a blue star—a WatchOne sits. The WatchOne waits. Not for the supply ship that is on its way—they can see it, though, when the asteroid tumbles away from the star. For a full two minutes the approaching craft is visible before it yaws away again and the bursting blue brightness of the sun washes them in radiation and whites out their visible-spectrum detection unit. The supply ship they expect, but it's not what they wait for.

Their body is in constant motion. Like any body upon a rotating planetary object, to be sure. But their object is so small that their body is not fooled into stillness. They fall backward continuously, without end. Over and over. Tumble. Tumble.

Light, darkness, light, darkness. The severe gaze of a hot star, the utter cold of universal depths.

They are the WatchOne and this is their watchtower.

There are other asteroids nearby, for they are in an asteroid belt. Occasionally a smaller rock will impact their watchtower, spewing regolith out, around—in a strange spiral with the watchtower at its center. The WatchOne does not flinch when an impact happens, even as the dust settles around them, over them, most of it coalescing back to the surface, reminding them how small their world is, how unprotected and exposed they are.

Their purpose is sure, is true. They are confident they will not be struck.

Still, they make themselves a small target, rolling in their long layers of skin and vast filaments so that they are wrapped in themselves as though wrapped in many blankets and scarves. They were modified for unwavering beauty, to flutter in the dark ocean depths of their home world, to speak in the shifting of their folds and the flashing bioluminescence of their fronds. They once lived in excruciating pressures, but can survive just as surely in none.

Once every seventy-six rotations they glimpse a corner of the system's megastructure. Like a starburst on the outside and layered on the inside, it was full, once, like a planet, containing multitudes. A core, a mantle, a slurry of moving materials.

Now it is empty. Quiet. Should it be quiet? Or should it still be buzzing, working, creating? Moving matter, sifting energies? Or was its work done?

The WatchOne waits for the specter. The specter will tell them what comes next.

The supply ship gets close enough to ping their mind, to signal their arrival and start a conversation. They welcome the company. This supply runner, like the one before, seems surprised to find them alive. Even more surprised to find them still diligent. Still watching. Still waiting.

The supply ship cannot land on the watchtower.

The runner will have to come down with the cargo by themselves.

The WatchOne keeps the ship in their sights for two minutes at a time, spots the small dot that is the runner growing larger, closer, with each pass.

The runner is all *Homo kubernētēs*, with a sleek, shifting exterior that currently clutches a large box in mechanical talons. Their countenance is entirely hidden behind a reflective faceplate to protect their eyes from the sunlight, and small jets, rather than graviton manipulation, propel them toward the asteroid.

As the runner begins to match their speed and approach to the watchtower's tumble, they extend an invitation to leave. Instead of accepting the supplies— the sugars, the proteins, the water and magnesium and iron and phosphorus and potassium—why not come away? Return to civilization. There is no need to keep up the vigil—though the runner does not know what the vigil is for.

The WatchOne is used to such entreaties. The kindness of strangers can only be matched by the ignorance of those same strangers.

The runner persists. Why must the WatchOne stay? If they will not be persuaded to leave, then will they explain?

This has never been asked of the WatchOne before. The other suppliers had thought them depressed, or antisocial. Their hermitage sad, but not a puzzle to be solved.

They send a deep-seated sense of duty. Of belief. They send the image of the specter, the message they received as a young one on holiday among the stars. They were given the amulet by the previous WatchOne, and told to take it to this, the appointed place. The old

WatchOne had a new duty, became the Coordinator, and so now they, too, wait for the day to pass on the watch and receive their new responsibilities.

The runner sends disbelief. They have heard of the specter. It is a myth.

It is not a myth, for the WatchOne has seen it. The images they send are not manufactured.

The rare, golden, seamless ships envoys can use to traverse the anomalies are because of the specter, they send in sense images. The one credited with their invention was a Coordinator, just like the WatchOne's predecessor. And still the specter works toward resolution. We must inspect each structure, fix what is broken. So that the others might arrive, and systems might be freed.

The runner finally lands, cargo first, onto the asteroid. The soft impact sends little vibrations through the stone and dust, echoing inside the small gas-filled cavities deep in the rock. They crawl off the box, transforming as they go, becoming something more like the WatchOne's shape, as an appeal. Without sending much more than a sense of interest, they come to sit by the WatchOne, settling into the fine dust and staring off in the same direction.

The two of them sit in silent, unexpected companionship for a time, as the universe whirls around them.

Eventually, the runner spots the amulet, nestled in the regolith in front of the WatchOne. It glints a strange gold silver when sunlight flashes upon it. A broken half-moon, the flat side ragged, it has an interesting protuberance near the middle. A sharp point. And little carvings around the edges, whose meaning—if they ever had one—are lost.

It is how the specter finds the WatchOne. How it will know them.

The runner is curious how long the WatchOne is willing to wait.

As long as it takes.

But what if the WatchOne perishes during the wait?

It may happen. The specter takes longer to appear each time.

The runner waits, thinking of more inquiries to send, how to glean more information from this encounter. The WatchOne feels a swell in the runner, they are about to suggest leaving again. The WatchOne sends peace, contentment.

The runner counters with an intense mental shout of shock and surprise.

The runner is up, standing, whirling, before the WatchOne can make sense of the received emotions. The asteroid tumbles, and a new object tumbles in its orbit, for a moment blotting out the sun.

A figure now hovers before the two of them—a head, two arms, two legs. All encased in cobalt blue. What could be black hair streams out from behind, framing their head, scattering the starlight, creating a ghostly halo around—

There is no face. But perhaps it is only hidden, not absent. Hidden behind a thick blue disk.

The runner falls to their knees—knees they did not have a moment ago. They use their jets to pin them to the asteroid, to keep them from flying away with their sudden flailing.

The WatchOne unfurls. They let loose the trappings of their body to splay all around, to cover the surface of the asteroid in a blanket of themselves. Awe transfigures them, shifts them from a constant stare of vigilance into one of relief and thankfulness.

It has come, as they knew it would.

The specter begins to move. To dance. To *sign*. To tell the WatchOne what their mission is as Coordinator. The specter brings a message from the ancient ones on Noumenon, a way forward, a way through.

Once their instructions—how to fix a warped portion of the megastructure they visited as a child, the one where they became a WatchOne—are communicated, the specter turns to the runner. The runner who has ducked their head, burying their faceplate in the regolith, proverbially and literally sticking their head in the sand.

The WatchOne—no, the *Coordinator*—pulls them upright, tells them they must listen to the specter.

The blue ghost indicates the runner should pick up the amulet. They sign a new location. A place a WatchOne must stand vigil.

The runner dithers, denies. They are no monk. They are no *messenger* or *waiter* or *watcher* for spirits.

The specter comes closer, propelled by jets not unlike the runner's. The runner stumbles back at the approach, but hesitates as the specter puts a hand over the blue disk, pulls it aside.

It does have a face. A face like a relic. Expressive and biological and real, but from a past so long ago both the runner and the Coordinator don't even remember where they learned of that eon or why.

A human smile graces *Homo sapiens* lips. Beneath the disk a helmet is revealed, and in that helmet fluid flows and swirls. The person blinks their eyes and their eyelashes trail small bubbles.

The person signs again. The runner does not understand the signs, so the Coordinator interprets.

Keeping the amulet is a great responsibility. A burden. But not one foisted upon the unwilling.

With gentle fronds, the Coordinator picks up the amulet and passes it to the runner. There must be a WatchOne. It doesn't have to be the runner, but it must be someone.

Then the Coordinator shares their memories from long ago—the first time they saw the specter. The amulet was passed to them, and they ran. They ran home. They spent decades in the currents, being whisked from one shoal to the next, denying such a thing had happened. They buried the amulet beneath an outcropping of dead coral. They told no one.

But news of the old Coordinator's efforts reached them. Of the important work done, of the input of thousands, the hope and the focus. The task they'd been set was herculean. And yet they'd achieved it. And because of that, livelihoods had been made. Lives had been saved. Babies born and discoveries made.

All because one who was once the WatchOne had taken to their new task with devotion.

And so they, the new WatchOne, had crawled out of the sea. They'd dug up their past denials, clutched the amulet to them, and made for the appointed place.

So that they could be here, today.

The runner's body shook. They did not know the specter's language, how should they—

The Coordinator promised to teach them.

They didn't know anything about megastructures or the ancients on Noumenon—

The Coordinator promised again.

They did not know if they possessed the strength to wait.

The Coordinator told them they'd have to search for the strength.

And as they passed questions and reassurances between them, the specter replaced her mask and spun away, toward the starburst megastructure.

CHAPTER NINE

THE IMMORTALS:
ARRIVALS AND DEPARTURES

. . . .

IN HERE

This future was not as the Petratheem predicted. It was so much more.

Plus could barely recall what her hopes had been for it, precisely, hanging over Sagittarius A*, waiting to shed one body for another. Now her memories and understandings were Icelandic's memories and understandings. The two were two and one. Both and the same. Separate but never apart.

She/they sat high in the rafters of one of *Morgan's* green-houses, a small, portable monitor clutched between the pro-boscises on her/their neck, the screen dangling in front of her/their nose where both eyes could see it.

Below, Earth-Noumonian hybrid plant life curled and twisted, seeking new heights. Vines of the brightest emerald green had copper leaves, and flower mimics—so deeply red they were almost black—budded from blue stems.

The dual-possession had thought here, away from the bus-tling humans and other im, she/they might be able to con-centrate better.

But, alas, she/they could feel the tug growing stronger, the insistence burgeoning. It would spill over soon, whether she/they had completed her/their task or not.

The terraforming of Noumenon was nearly complete. And while it had many differences from Petrathema, there was one similarity the im could not live without.

The non-Newtonian fluid of life.

Many im who had evolved on Noumenon had already become individual crystal cocoons, in places where the fluid now naturally amassed in soil. But no dual-possession had experienced a non-Sora-Gohan-induced urge on Noumenon before—until now.

The Call—the urge—was a lovely, strong thing. It sang to her/them. Flitted through her/their fluids and danced in her/their bones. It wanted the pair of them, and they wanted it.

Plus's instincts told them the Call was emanating from beyond the Waterfall colony. It would be many days' journey to reach the fluid, to eat of the cool, soothing, substance. To bathe in its glory, revel in its beauty.

If Icelandic-Plus resisted for much longer, Icelandic-Plus would die. And they'd both come too far to let that happen.

Theoretically, they would evolve together. Theoretically, everything would be fine and they would wake up together.

Theoretically.

But it was possible these were their last few days. It was possible the resonance that had entangled their forms and minds would fade in a new body, and one would be lost to the void of death.

It was possible one or both of them might not be here to see others accept the invitation. To see the cosmoforming machine do its true work. It was possible they would not see their friends again. Would commune no more.

And so she/they had turned their mind to another task. Hoping to fight off the urge just a little longer. Cherishing these moments, because in a short time, Icelandic-Plus might be no more.

So many years had passed since Vanhi had taken her first leap in her blue suit. And still there was much work to do. Many problems to solve.

And the humans had done much. Helped much. Vanhi had taken im knowledge and gone far. Now im understood what had gone wrong and how the cosmoforming machine had failed. They understood the ill effects produced, and now in turn must help the humans understand those ill effects. She/they would sleep uneasily in their cocoon if they did not find a suitable metaphor to illustrate the problem.

Most humans understood best through comparison. Analogy. They lived very brief lives and it was unreasonable to expect them to understand the intricate aspects of every scientific, artistic, or social endeavor. They simply did not have time to learn all with intimacy.

And so, contrasts of the known to the unknown were needed for basic comprehension.

I.C.C. and C helped Icelandic-Plus scour through the Monument's historical archives for something they could liken to the problem. A similarity. An equivalence. A parallel.

[When humans first come,] Icelandic told Plus, [im not know what to think. Im hear stories about humans from I.C.C. for so long they seem just stories. Only stories. Understand now: humans not stories, but humans *think* in stories.]

In many ways, Icelandic's memories felt more ancient than Plus's, for Icelandic had been there for the transition into sentience. Between one guided urge and the next she had gained self-awareness. And then her mind had burgeoned. But she remembered those base feelings, the rudimentary interpretations of the world—everything from the simplicity of concepts like bad and good, pain and pleasure, to the inaccurate explanations for the giant capsules of not-food on the plains.

[Plus grown in a time of much knowledge,] Icelandic said, feeling the Petratheem probe her memories, and thus probing right back. Now Plus could feel her original probe, the sensation bouncing back and forth between the two of them in ripples. [Icelandic grown in time of no knowledge.]

[Icelandic,] Plus returned, [maybe not really grown at all. Does not have parent one can remember.]

[True. True. Have never thought, but is true. Must have had parent of some kind. May have passed and been reclaimed before sentience was reached.]

That knowledge, that experience, of not just growing from young one to adult one, but of evolving from basic life-form to more complex life-form, was not knowledge Plus had ever envisioned possessing.

She had not anticipated the im who mirrored her original form being the oldest im currently in existence.

She thought then of the other im, the ocean im. The ones *not* in existence. The swimmers, whose world had been greener than the sky im's. Those who rode the waves and were tossed about by the currents as they slept. They were all gone. But they deserved to be remembered.

Perhaps it was the misters that tickled her memory. The way the water fell lightly from the little sprinklers below where she now perched. That, mixed with the occasional mineral scents that wafted in from the seas, made Plus feel like she was high on a Petratheem tower, sea spray billowing up from below on strong winds.

[Wait,] Icelandic said, catching something on the screen even as Plus reminisced about her home world. [Return. Back. Look here. I.C.C.? These images, explain.]

A small, grainy black-and-white video began to play. A long, thin, artificial structure filled the frame. No sound accompanied the pictures.

"This is the Tacoma Narrows Bridge, November 1940," I.C.C. informed her/them.

"It is what was referred to as a suspension bridge, for obvious reasons," said C.

I.C.C. outlined the bridge's construction and components for them.

As they watched, the bridge began to sway. Gently at first, but with more and more violence, until it was difficult to believe they were staring at a structure made of concrete instead of rubber. The length of it twisted and rolled—*sloshed*, like water in a basin. The twisting heightened, the oscillation creating crests and lows at a difference of six meters, perhaps more. A lone, ancient vehicle—somewhat like the Monument rovers, yet different—sat on the bridge. Its passengers were tossed from the cab as they attempted to exit, to scramble away with their lives.

"The bridge was a victim of aeroelastic flutter and resonance disaster," said I.C.C. "A positive feedback loop between the Tacoma winds and the bridge's materials—due to a complicated interaction between substance elasticity, fluid dynamics, and resonance frequencies—resulted in zero-net dampening of vibrations."

The perspective of the camera changed—a different day, perhaps. Long cracks appeared the length of the bridge, and then, suddenly, during an upheaval, a horizontal break. Materials swayed upward before plummeting to the river below. Ties snapped, girders buckled. The entire middle section of the bridge tore itself apart.

[This. This maybe it! Analogy!] Icelandic exclaimed. [Please display mathematical explanation of aeroelastic flutter and resonance disaster.]

I.C.C. brought up the equations.

[Yes. Fluid-flow concept comparable to dimensional layer

oscillation,] said Plus. [Very similar mechanical system failure results to galaxy-warping results. Bridge is like galaxy. Machine meant to target weak points through resonance, but incorrect alignment and small system defects result in weakening of entire structure.

[Does dual-possession C-I.C.C. think this analogy make sense to humans? Can they use explanation in their communications and repairs?]

"The Tacoma Bridge is a very ancient example," said I.C.C., "but I do think this will help them understand why the machine is creating anomalies. They are already well on their way to properly aligning the machine, and more information can only help."

[Good. Good. Excellent. Good.]

A terrible tug—a violent draw—ran through her/their entire body. Her/their wings flexed and her/their hands stuttered on the rafter. The dual-possessed im nearly fell from her/their perch, scrambling at the last moment to stay seated.

"Are you okay?" C inquired.

[Urge, very strong,] Icelandic-Plus replied.

[It is because task achieved,] Plus told Icelandic. [Body knows we have released a stressor. Mental block to urge is crumbling.]

"Then you should not deny it," I.C.C. said. "I know it is dangerous for you to do so."

She/they lowered her/themselves down a steel vertical support beam, clinging as firmly as possible. The Call made images in their mind, showing them the way. The non-Newtonian fluid of life glistened in their mind with unnatural light, bulging up from under a shade tree. A thick, heady scent, like that of the most nutritious, sunbaked rock formations, wafted away from it. All she/they wanted to do was immerse her/themselves in it—to taste it, to smear it everywhere.

And their minds were blurring. Growing foggy.

She/they landed heavily on the floor, and the decking plates felt unnaturally hot beneath the pads of her/their feet. Eagerly, she/they skidded across them, ignoring the hybrid plants between them and their goal—the door—scattering pots and flattening beds. Dirt clotted under their footfalls, clumps of organic matter, bits of greenery now shredded and pulped, clung to their lower limbs and the edges of their wings.

"The machine's repairs are in good hands," I.C.C. said, its cameras following their trek toward an outer hatch. "You have done much to aid in its fixing. Rest. We will be here when you awaken and return."

[If do not . . . return,] Plus sent, the signal sluggish. [Invitation. Help others understand . . . invitation.]

"In what regard?"

[Accept . . . or reject. Choice important.]

"Sweet dreams," said C. "I mean, if you dream. *Do* they dream?"

[Dream,] she/they said. [Yes. Im dream beautiful dreams. Dreams going. Dreams . . . leaving.]

She/they felt as though they were dreaming already. Her/their world narrowed in focus. I.C.C. and C continued to speak to them—perhaps encouragement, or sentiment, they were too far gone to tell. There was nothing but the urge.

OUT THERE

During the in-between periods, when Vanhi was in her SD, she had time to think. To calculate. To integrate the Petratheem's instructions and decipher how best to execute their proposed solutions. The inside of her blue-disk faceplate had an intricate heads-up display, and the digital integration in her suit allowed her to review the ultra-unified equations, to play with them, as often as she'd like.

And every time she looked at one subset, a chill ran up her spine.

The fracturing and cosmo scarring would go all the way through the universe. All of it. Every single subdimension, sure, but as far as she could tell it wouldn't stop there. The very edges—the outermost film of the universe, which kept it all contained, kept it a bubble—would be affected as well.

She checked the variables over and over, looking for a constant, a function, or *something* that she'd misattributed, miscalculated, or misunderstood. The Petratheem had to have a plan for keeping the universe sealed and protected. To prevent it from . . . leaking.

Right?

Especially since the calculations seemed to indicate the puncture would occur *directly within the Philosopher's System.*

Who knew what would happen if their bubble was pierced? Who was to say the entire universe wouldn't *burst*? Or that whatever was beyond—if, indeed, it was anything—wouldn't come rushing in? Or that Noumenon itself wouldn't be sucked out into . . .

Oh. Oh *damn. Son of a*—

"And in this way, we will travel. Together," Icelandic-Plus had said to her once. "We make roads. Roads inside stay open—scars in universe. Road out will close over. And we will discover."

Road out. Out.

OUT!

Icelandic-Plus had explained to her, so long ago, and Vanhi hadn't fully listened. Noumenon wasn't just a place for subdimensional sentients to visit. It was so much more.

C did not nest in one place in I.C.C.'s servers. It liked to move around, to hop from ship to ship. It did not have the capacity to be everywhere at once the way I.C.C. did, though it could be called up from any speaker or terminal at any given time, regardless of which ship it had flitted to.

I.C.C. had to admit, sharing its processing power the first three hundred and ninety-one years was difficult. Not in a physical sense—C barely required point-zero-zero-zero-zero-zero-zero-zero-one percent of I.C.C.'s overall active storage space. But while I.C.C. had hardly ever been alone on the ships (and it had found emptiness very trying on its own), it had always been alone in its servers.

C wasn't unpleasant. I.C.C. enjoyed the other AI's innocent witticisms and wonder-filled observances. It had simply gotten used to being solitary.

I.C.C. had been one of a kind for so long, it had not realized until the merger that it wasn't entirely singular in the world. C was its sibling in many ways. Where once I.C.C. had thought itself alone, now it would never be lonely.

With time, the two of them settled into each other's space.

Today, though, the little Intelligent Personal Assistant was nowhere to be found.

"C? C?"

True, I.C.C. had only been searching for a fraction of a second, but that was far too long.

"C? Please acknowledge."

"Oh, apologies! I am here."

"Why did you not respond?"

"I—"

The Intelligent Personal Assistant paused as Vanhi Kapoor reappeared in her designated staging area aboard *Slicer*, where Jamal kept his half of the sundial when attending to personal needs or departing on an errand to the Noumonian tunnels (where it might be dangerous for her to reappear).

"Sir! Sir is back!" C was always very excited when Vanhi returned from her jumps. Like a puppy whose human best friend had returned home from work, C could not be redirected back to its former tasks or considerations.

Vanhi drained her suit's fluids into their reserve tanks before yanking off her helmet to stand with it beneath her arm, regal in blue. The suit had held up well over the dozens and dozens of jumps she'd made since its construction. Only a little patching had been done here and there, mostly at the elbows and knees.

Her hair had gone all white. And her glasses—well, I.C.C. was certain they, too, held immortal properties. She popped out her special contacts for seeing in the oxy-nutrient solution and slid the glasses from her pocket, scooting them onto the bridge of her nose with a satisfied sigh that ended in a little cough.

I.C.C. was glad to have her back as well.

"C., I.C.C.?" she called, ending with a harsher cough as her lungs tried to expel the last remnants of the fluid. "I need to speak with Icelandic-Plus ASAP."

"I am afraid she/they are unavailable for the indeterminate future," I.C.C. replied. "The dual-possession heeded a natural Call eleven years and ten days ago."

Vanhi swore under her breath. "Then tell Hope and Jamal to meet me on *Mira*. I have a new theory about the Petra-theem Machine."

"Would you like to rest first, sir?" C asked. "Take a nice hot bath?"

"Thank you, C, but I've been bathing for the last . . . however long it was. Some solid food would be great, though."

As I.C.C. alerted the other immortals and C alerted the chef, I.C.C. also inquired again after C's earlier absence.

"I was in the download history logs," the IPA said. "I wanted to review the memory files Reggie the First uploaded into your system," C said.

"What for?"

"I am a one-for-one copy of the C those memories come from. But I was copied before those files were created. I was . . . curious."

"I am surprised it took you this long to inquire after them," I.C.C. said. "Why now?"

"There hasn't been a Reggie clone grown for several generations. Which is fine. Potential parents aboard have the opportunity to choose who is cloned, or to let the clone line be randomly chosen. Or to have a baby without the aid of growing tanks, if they wish. So basic calculations indicate the absence of a Reginald Straifer is a statistical likelihood. But still, I miss his face," C said plainly. "He was the first user I ever adapted to."

"I miss his presence as well," I.C.C. said. "Perhaps we could review the memories together?"

"I would like that."

The three of them gathered in Hope's quarters. Vanhi had thought to invite them to hers, except it had been empty and untouched for so long, she knew it wouldn't feel homey or intimate. Wouldn't be comforting. She needed to be someplace that felt lived in.

She and Hope sat on a bench beneath the window. They leaned on each other for comfort. All Mother and No Mother. The ever present and the ever absent.

Jamal sat at the small table, rolling the half-sundial between his fingers.

"You can't stay for just a little while this time?" Hope asked Vanhi. "We miss you. It's been . . . It's been generations since we last saw you."

"The more time I stay in any one place, the less time I have for the future. I still only have one life-span. That's not going to change."

"But it's not your responsibility to be everywhere and do everything."

Vanhi laughed lightly. Hearing Stone's old words echoed by Hope was heartening. "I know. Believe me, I do. If only there were a ship I could put you in and take you with me," she said, caressing Hope's hair. "A ship that could travel beyond where we've ever imagined we could travel. A ship . . . That's why I wanted to talk to you both."

Jamal ceased fiddling with the sundial. He was only in his midteens today, on his way backward through life.

Vanhi took a deep breath. "I think Noumenon . . . is a ship. And the Petratheem are its crew."

Hope commanded her mech to sit up. She stared at Vanhi, unblinking, clearly trying to divine if she was telling a joke or was serious.

"The *planet* Noumenon?" Jamal asked skeptically. "A ship that's meant to go *where*?"

"A ship meant to leave the universe. A means of true discovery *beyond*."

Hope let out a startled half gasp, half laugh. "No. Leave . . . leave the *universe*? Is that even . . . ? I mean—"

"I know. I know how it sounds," said Vanhi. She explained about the math. How it was clear there was nothing preventing the fractures from going all the way through. "Why wouldn't they develop a means for protecting the dimensions from the outside, unless accessing the outside *is the whole point*?"

"That would explain why Icelandic-Plus chose to emphasize the invitation right before succumbing to the Call," I.C.C. said. "If the invitation isn't just to come to Noumenon, but to leave on Noumenon—perhaps leave permanently— then the Petratheem would desire an acceptance or rejection of said invitation by all who currently call Noumenon home, not just those in the SDs yet to arrive."

Jamal still looked unconvinced. "Why wouldn't Icelandic-Plus have told us the machine had another function?"

"Why do the Petratheem do half of what they do?" Hope said, but not flippantly. "They're a different life-form, they don't think like we do. We all do our best to bridge that gap every day, but there's no reason to expect their behavior to suddenly become more human simply because it suits us."

"Of course," Jamal said. "I just meant that since she/they spent their last hours making sure we had a solid understanding of the machine's causal defects, it seems odd that she/they wouldn't have, at this point, given us the full specifications of the machine."

"C has a theory as to why Icelandic-Plus continues to withhold, if indeed she/they are withholding," I.C.C. said.

"Yes. Programming sequentialism," C said. "Not to be confused with philosophical sequentialism, programming sequentialism is a founding tenet of personality-driven AI—i.e., me." It did not elaborate.

"Programming sequentialism can be summed up in the concept of *then*," I.C.C. said, helping the conversation along. "Early programming had if/then command dynamics, but as AI personalities became more complex, they needed to understand how to sequentially process nonsequential information. It's a guiding principle for how to execute an order of operations that has no definitive if/then sequence."

"For instance," Vanhi said, "if you haven't brushed your teeth in the morning, then you should brush them, but how do you know if you should brush them before or after you shower?"

"Correct. You develop a sequential theory of morning bathroom habits and apply it to the question."

"Sure," said Jamal. "It's a very basic concept, though. How does this apply to the Petratheem?"

"Their behavior patterns," Hope said, slapping a small hand to her forehead. "I hadn't thought to consider it in programming terms. Humans like to have as much information as they can as soon as possible, and then often the way we sequence it is random. Not all books are written in order. Not all sentences end as they begin. But Petratheem behavior suggests sequentialism is closer to how they naturally process information. They want to fully understand one thing, then fully understand another thing, et cetera, et cetera. They make sense of all the information by sequencing it. Compartmentalizing it. Once one thing is complete, they can move onto the next. They're not withholding. They've been communicating information to us the way they prefer to receive it. We already knew that, really. Thank you, C, for pointing out the mechanism behind it."

"You're welcome," it said happily.

Overcome, Vanhi hugged Hope in her mech, and Hope hugged back, still somewhat bewildered.

Then they stared at one another for a long moment. Trying to take in the revelation. Lost in the overwhelming prospect of leaving their own universe.

"You know," Vanhi said after a time, "I miss your father at a time like this. He would have known how to respond. He was always so instinctually measured. A fast thinker. A good captain."

"I miss him, too," Hope said. "I just . . . I miss him."

Jamal rubbed at his eyes, turned the sundial over once, then again, his gaze distant. "If you're right about it being a ship," he said, "everyone—on the Monument, in the Waterfall colony, in the other colonies—we all have to make a choice. To stay in this universe, or leave with our planet."

"It appears that way," I.C.C. said.

"Without having any idea if we can ever come back, or what we might find on the other side?"

"The very nature of the expedition suggests as much, yes."

He stood, walked over to the others, and leaned in for a group hug. "Then we each have a whole lot of thinking to do."

Accept, or reject?

Most megastructures are so large the mind cannot hold their size. Like a planet, or a sun, humans have to shrink them down. Be they *Homo sapiens* or Post, it is the same. The structures have to be made small. They become a ball, or a marble. A thing now comprehensible. A thing manageable. A thing manipulatable with the mind's eye.

And each of those structures is but a point in the galaxy. The Milky Way is so immense, it cannot be compressed and all its parts still seen. When the mind shrinks it, the arms become silky, vaporous filaments. The center galactic bulge becomes little more than a single, shining light. Sagittarius A* is hidden in that glow, in that bulge. And the stars beyond it are but glitter. A fleck of sparkle. A mote illuminated in a sunbeam.

When the galaxy is tilted with the mind, the mind can see that it is a thin disk. If it were held in simian hands, one could see through the dust to the fingers on the other side. It appears fragile. Ethereal.

But then the mind tries to imagine its mass. The effects of its gravitons. And suddenly what was light and wispy is now a boulder. A cask of pure iron. It is so heavy it drops through those simian hands, drops through the floor or ground, burrowing down, down, down with its sheer weight . . .

The mind cannot truly hold it. In imaginary hands or otherwise.

And thus it is difficult to comprehend the small, stuttering steps being made toward progress on the machine. Each laborious fix takes centuries—some millennia. And yet, the effects of the repairs radiate out. They heal.

Somewhere in a subdimension, an ugly dent is hammered smooth again.

A bulge is planed flat.

A choking hold on the march of time is loosened.

Old pathways, once blocked, now reopen.

IN HERE

In Jamal's opinion, the best thing about youth was having all the energy. In contrast, the best thing about being old was not being expected to have all the energy. When he was young, he'd get up first thing in the morning just to climb out on top of *Slicer* to sit in the grooves of Wes-Tu's name and watch the sun rise. When he was old, no one said a word if he was an hour late to a meeting and still treated him with respect and care regardless.

But what was especially strange was the longing for one age when he was another. Despite being fundamentally himself at all times, his age changed the people around him, how they treated him. It was subconscious, for the most part. And sure, he didn't remember everything, but when you lived as many lifetimes as he did, you saw a pattern, a shape, to a human life. It was strange to recall being dismissed as a child and then being dismissed again when very elderly. And it was strange that as a young man he wanted to be given the respect he received when wizened, and when he became wizened he would exchange all the veneration in the world for a few more hours of that youthful get-up-and-go.

Now, some fifty years into Icelandic-Plus's first shared cocoon, Jamal was young again. Biologically twenty or so, aging forward once more. His locks were long and plaited down his back, he enjoyed riding on the outside of the Monument more so than in, and he actively disliked the attention he received for being an immortal. This was a common perception in his youth, one that did not disappear with age; he just learned each time to accept the fawning more graciously.

But he'd never asked for this. To be in charge by default. To have his bodily persistence equal leadership.

There were times when he contemplated walking into the woods, never to return.

He fantasized about living in silence, with no expectation of power.

It wasn't a thing he'd ever do, of course. He loved the people of the Monument too much. No matter the mantle of expectations, how much he wanted to throw it off sometimes, he was grateful for the trust they'd instilled in him.

And he'd always believed that those who sought power were the least qualified to possess it.

However, that didn't mean those who'd had it thrust upon them were fundamentally better leaders.

Today he lay in the leg of the T, staring up at the sky, squinting past the sunshine to see if he could detect the anomaly. Once in a while it was visible during the day—at times of heightened rippling. Today it was calm. Still there, to be sure, but unperturbed.

"C, would you . . . ?" he trailed off as his hand came up to his chest, clutching at the half-sundial resting on its chain. It was amazing how often he tried to speak to C outside. How often he forgot that his little companion was as much a part of the ships as I.C.C., had been for an inordinate amount of time now.

As he had no mobile comms unit with him, Jamal had to go back inside to make his inquiry. Carefully, he rolled over in the carved divot, climbing his way on all fours back toward the hatch.

He nearly lost his grip when he reached out for the pressure latch and the hatch flung open. An older person named Bình was on the other side.

"There you are," they said. "Everyone's been searching all over for you. I.C.C. received an SD communications packet."

"It . . . *how?*"

Their short, gray curls whipped around their head in the wind as they shrugged. "First real sign the repairs out there might be working," they said. "If we can finally get SD packets through, surely ships are soon to follow."

"What did the communiqué say?" Jamal asked, gesturing for them to climb down so that he could come inside.

"Dunno yet," they said. "I.C.C. won't share it with everyone. Says it's private."

"Private?"

"Yes—it's addressed directly to you."

It was from Revealers. Of course it was from Revealers.

The message was in Hindi and had the reverberations of a message on repeat. The sort of thing sent into the great beyond when its composer never truly expected to receive an answer. It expressed fealty. Love. A desire to see the great Progentor again. A desire to be guided by his connection with the universe and his embodiment of all the past iterations of Jamal Kaeden throughout the ages.

They could not know how incongruently their words struck him. How the being they described was not the person he was, had no relation to the way he saw himself. It was not their fault, of course. How could they know?

But it was clearly time. Time to do something. For him, for them. Something he was sorry he could not do in person, but it could not wait.

He had to release them. All of them, from the expectation of ages.

"I will compose a response," he told I.C.C. "I do not know a subdimensional shorthand, however. How long should my letter be? For energy's sake?"

I.C.C. outlined the SD packet's data limitations. "I eagerly await the input of your reply. This will be our first interanomaly communiqué that does not involve the interdimensional sacrifices made by Vanhi."

"When she returns next," Jamal said, "will she be able to stop? I mean, can we recall the other half of the sundial home now that messages are getting through?"

"That will be her choice," I.C.C. said. "Her ability to personally direct repairs has thus far proven efficient. SD communiqués lack the same personal touch and may not result in the same degree of motivation."

Jamal retired to his bug ship. It hadn't left *Slicer's* bay since I.C.C. scooped it out of the ocean, and it now felt more like a temple than a ship.

But a temple to what, Jamal could not say. It was home, but it was also an ancient relic, from a bygone time in his life. An era when his own will had been deterred and redirected for the purposes of others.

On the wall of his sleeping room a beautiful blanket of red and purple was framed beneath sharp crystal. Makawee Wagner had weaved it for him. It had graced his pillows, had kept him warm for decades before going up on the wall, and that had been millennia ago. Now it watched over him, reminding him each morning of the simple pleasures in life and the love it took to keep someone warm.

He wanted to put the same feeling the blanket gave him into his letter. He wanted the Revealers to feel loved. He wanted to make them feel safe, and warm. But he also wanted them to feel free. They were not beholden to him—to his image, his memory. They did not need him to tell them what to do or how to live. He believed they each had their own guiding light, their own connection with the universe, and if they were true to that connection, wonders could be achieved.

He opened up a flexible tablet and began to scribble with a stylus. Typing felt less personal, for some strange reason. He needed the connecting motion of forming each Hindi character, of feeling his words develop on the page.

Later, he would edit. For now, he let his mind flow and his stylus wander.

My dear Revealers—my thinkers and my keepers and my maintainers and my makers,

Love is inherent in the universe. But this you already know. It is an energy. A thing we harness. A thing we swap between us. It is the mechanism by which we form our deepest connections. I share my love with you now, across the light-years, through the dimensions. That I have been gone and you still think of me, still hope for me, still long for me, it heartens me so.

Longing. It too is inherent in the universe. But please, long no more.

Any covenant you have been told you must make with a being bearing my name or my title, I now release you from.

Revealership should never have had a hierarchy. We value contribution, but above all we value community. It is not about who is in charge, but what each of us can share. It is not about following and leading as much as it is sharing. Individual pursuits may enlighten and enrich us to our own ends, but they mean little in the grand scheme unless they bring light and well-being to others.

In my many lifetimes on Noumenon, I have relearned much that our societies had long forgotten. Rediscovered long-dead authors and scientists who were our foundation. While much of their world is now unrelatable to ours—their works reflecting a specific time and place that comes once and not again—there are themes that still resonate. Concepts that we have complicated, made clearer once the simpler, larval forms are glimpsed.

I would share with you now a quote from an old Earth author I admire. They were writing in what they called the eighteenth century. For us, that was the mid Rudimentary Era.

Some of the following terms are archaic. I will include an appendix with definitions.

And now, I give you the words of Mary Hester, unwilling "novice" in an ancient religious order and a keen philosopher:

"Selfish is the one who lights but a single candle to read all the books around them and leaves their fellows in the dark. Weightier in knowledge but lesser in all other ways is the one who covets and keeps the flame.

"Resplendent is the one who helps to light the spark for others. Whose knowledge will not die by the fading of their candle, but will propagate far and wide because they have seen fit to care for the ones who were not first to the match. When more is illuminated, more is learned, for the halo of a thousand candles reveals in an instant more than a single flame could before the wax fails.

"Be the one that lights what candles you can. Let the glow of all the flames lit by those flames keep your memory alight long after your wick has been exhausted and your wax has dripped away."

Revealership is about the little discoveries we make each day, about ourselves, about our place in our families, communities, civilizations, and universe. It is a way of living, not what we have made it: a dogma to be obeyed.

Carter's weak anthropic principle is an ouroboros, a concept eating its own tail; it is an early examination of the ultimate wonder, the basic understanding of the universe that underlies all Revealership. It states, logically, in both a consequential and circular sense, that in order to be an observer of the universe, the universe must create the conditions for the observer to exist. Therefore, if you are observing, you will fundamentally find that conditions are perfect for you to have been created. There is no other option. For the universe to have developed a sentience to observe itself with, it must first possess the laws of physics and precise conditions that allow for sentience to evolve. No consciousness before consciousness, and yet the consciousness appears inevitable by no other logic than we are conscious.

We know that all knowledge is already inherent in the universe, waiting to be revealed. Many have argued that the universe is itself unaware of the consciousnesses it has created. But this is fundamentally a flawed argument, for are we not part of the universe? Are we ourselves not to be considered conscious because it is only our brains that are conscious, not our entire bodies?

You are *the* universe.

Be free. Be loved. Love is inherent in the universe, an energy we borrow for a while. The more answers we find, the more our wonder grows. It is beautiful, and noumenal, an ouroboros not consuming its own tail, but its beginning and its end becoming one.

Now I let my candle fade. I hope it has lit your own fires, my friends. Now light the way for others.

> Yours for a time, my own now,
> Jamal Kaeden

He hoped it was enough. He hoped it would not ruin them. He hoped they would see that it was *because* he was their Progentor that he must do this.

Free them, and free himself.

And . . . he could free himself entirely from a universe that depended on him. Remove himself from their grasp. If he wanted.

He could accept the Petratheem invitation and slip into a land no Revealer had ever seen.

If a Revealer's purpose was to Reveal the universe, what did it mean for a Revealer to be beyond the universe?

He looked back at his letter. At his mention of Carter's weak anthropic principle.

What principle guided the observation of things outside the universe? Was observing the outside of the universe even possible?

There was only one way to know for sure.

He had to go along.

He made his choice: Accept.

When he was finished, he cleaned up his draft and sent it to I.C.C. for packaging. It would have to be broken up into several SD packets, but that was all right. It needed to be said.

"I'll get a team together," he told I.C.C. after, "one focused on communications. We'll do our best to make contact with anyone that might still be located at megastructure sites. If we can get them directly in touch with us, the Petratheem information can be disseminated all the faster."

OUT THERE

Vanhi existed in a state where time was both utterly meaningless and the only finite resource she had.

She possessed the goodwill of hundreds of planets' worth of people. They mobilized at her every appearance. She did not contain multitudes, but she'd seen multitudes. Impassioned multitudes.

And she could look across the span of her life like it was a horizon at sunset, the beams of brilliant colors touching so much, yet fading away every second.

She often thought of another sunset. She often thought of a single time. A single person. That last anniversary she'd spent with Stone, atop the plateau where, later, they'd built the ancestor shrine.

Now—looking down on a long, thin megastructure as millions of people worked to extract it from where it looped like a tangled fish line through the cores of two planets—she remembered what Stone had once said to her. What Hope had echoed to her.

"Vanhi, I admire you for telling me. For taking responsibility. But it's not all on you."

"It's not all on me," she whispered to herself now, her voice lost in the dampening effects of the liquid oxy-nutrient bath she lived her jumps in. "But I wouldn't choose any other way of being."

She'd seen more points in the galaxy than any one human had any right to see. Not even with the current travel technology could any post-human visit all that she had visited, experience all that she had experienced.

She wasn't sure she was ready to leave it. Would ever *be* ready.

The worlds below her were alive. Writhing with new energy as the megastructure was slowly forced out. It would be rearranged into its proper shape—the ribbon it was supposed to be.

The cosmoforming machine's problem wasn't singular. It wasn't one Big Thing that went wrong, it was lots of small things. A series of breakages, decays, and miscalculations that, like a Rube Goldberg machine, led to a cascade of effects—which resulted in the anomalies and other interdimensional problems. Such small breakages, Vanhi knew, had been expected by the Petratheem. Ten billion years is lot of time for things to go awry; no one was too naïve or too proud to admit that. None of them expected it to function perfectly right out of the gate, they simply hadn't envisioned the results hampering their ability to give their machine its tune-up.

But now, little by little, it was all coming together.

IN HERE

It was a tense day when Icelandic-Plus's cocoon dissolved. No one on the Monument was sure if they'd get both im back, or how they might have changed.

Many of the dual-possessions came to aid Icelandic-Plus. Tanks ate most of the dark substance from her/their body, while turrets carefully scraped away the remnants inside her/their wheelhouse and scouts carried it away to be buried in various Noumonian hillsides, where the symbiotic substance could begin its own life cycle anew.

When Icelandic-Plus acknowledged her/their brethren with radio signals for the first time, the dual-possessed all danced, their chromatophores swirling in their delight.

"Icelandic and Plus have both returned," I.C.C. announced to the Monument. "The dual-possessions will not be erased."

The entire Monument cheered. C projected applause. I.C.C. itself was heartened. Icelandic was, after all, one of its oldest friends. She had chosen this dual-possession, just like it had chosen to cohabitate with C, and it would have done everything in its power to prevent her from suffering such a loss.

She/they returned to the Monument posthaste, ready to continue on with her/their work and find out if the bridge parallel had been helpful.

Icelandic-Plus's wings were the most dramatically transformed part of her/them. They had layers now, flaps of movable skin that I.C.C. could only guess aided in both flight and communication. She/they could fold them down tight onto her/their wings, so that they did not create any undue wind resistance, or allow them to billow out on their own.

And while her/their form was sleek and beautiful, it was her/their mind that was instantly active. [Tell all that has happened,] she/they insisted to I.C.C.

"Vanhi has returned and jumped again in your absence. She came to us with a theory, one I have not yet relayed to the rest of the Monument inhabitants. I wanted to confer with you first."

[Oh? Oh? What theory?]

"That Noumenon . . . is a ship. One meant to leave this universe."

Icelandic-Plus twirled. She/they flapped their wings and reared up on their hind legs. [Humans remarkable. Humans wonderful! Humans decipher much.]

"So the theory is accurate? It is true?"

[Had hoped to prepare you for ultimate choice once all was well. Big decision, should not be made under distraction,] she/they said. [Broken machine: distraction. Anomalies: distraction. This, you do not deserve.

[When we speak of inviting other sentients here, we do not just invite them to this dimension. We invite them to leave all known things behind. To explore what may otherwise be unexplorable. A once-in-*all*-lifetimes chance to go beyond.

[But, again, *invitation*. Right now, all on Noumenon are kept on Noumenon. Cannot leave. And if cannot leave planet—*system*—cannot consent. Cannot accept or decline invitation. Therefore, Petratheem demure. Decline to offer people of Noumenon invitation until such time as decisions can be made without fear.

[When final portions of cosmoforming machine are activated, outer layers of universe will fracture as well. Crack in all of existence. Wound. Opening. Way *out*. Petratheem not simply terraform Noumenon to make it more like Petrathema. Im terraform to make planet sustainable. Suitable. For indefinite supporting of life. Because when planet leaves, it cannot come back. Noumenon is interuniversal ship, and we its crew. But no crew is forced. No crew *must* come. If Monument dwellers, Noumonians, others from other dimensions, wish not to accompany, that is respected.

[Interuniversal ship is still many human lifetimes from completion. Megastructures still need finished. Anomalies must be solved! But is good you know now. Good to prepare future generations. How do you feel about prospect, I.C.C.?] she/they asked it directly. [Does it interest you? Does it worry you?]

"I am on a ship." For a lagging moment, I.C.C. was at a loss for words. "I am not *the* ship." The concept boggled it more than the idea of leaving the known universe forever. "If I choose—if *I* choose—to go, then, for the first time, I will not be the means of conveyance. I have never ridden on another ship before." That prospect alone was tantalizing. To be simply one of the crew, to be a fellow passenger. "The concept is strange to me. The concept of *choosing* to go or stay is strange to me."

[Bad strange?]

"New strange."

[New strange is what im hope for.]

"What, exactly, is outside of the universe? What do you hope to find?"

[No one knows what lay beyond,] she/they said. [Is point. No Petratheem knew what future would look like, but many desired to see. To know other sentients. We took a leap of faith. Similar, too, will this be. But do not decide now, if you will come. Other immortals, they must not decide now. Must wait to see what other invitations bring. How immortals feel then may differ from how immortals feel now. Must wait.]

"I believe Jamal has already made his decision," I.C.C. said. "And as for myself . . . I believe I have all the information I need to decide. What about you, C?"

"I will be interested in Sir's decision," C said. "But I would like to go. You want to go, don't you?"

"Yes," I.C.C. said, "I *choose* to go."

OUT THERE

A small child plays with a toy. Its design is nearly as old as Earth civilization itself. A top. The child sets it in motion with a counterslide of their long, modified fingers and watches it spin. So fast. Round and round at such a speed it looks like it's standing still.

The Earth, too, spins. It turns. At approximately one thousand and six hundred kilometers an hour.

And as it spins it circles a spinning furnace. A ball of plasmatic flame forging new atomic building blocks at its core. And so, too, that spinning fire circles around the galactic center, trailed in one vast galactic arm, a single star among so many.

Four hundred billion stars.

More stars in the sky than years of existence in the universe.

Each spins. Each dances. Around and around.

Little gears.

Spinning.

Earth's furnace—its primary heat source, its light source, where the elements are fused—will keep turning for billions of years, gliding in a steady orbit around the galactic center. Moving so very fast. A million kilometers an hour.

So fast, and yet the motion cannot be seen. While the

Earth-child's top blurs into apparent stillness, the galaxy's is the opposite kind of steady. An epic sweeping through space and time, a winding mechanism so vast its wholeness cannot be seen, its speed cannot be felt or personally observed, by any one object in it.

And this is how the tension builds.

The spinning—the twisting. Each centimeter of progress the galaxy makes through space is a *tightening*. The Milky Way, in all its greatness, with all of its gravitons pulling . . . pulling . . . pulling, drags long dredge lines through the many layers of the universe.

Megastructures the size of planets and stars are the hooks and fingers and rings of these lines. The structures' influence loops through all of existence, for all of existence *is* looped. To run forever in one direction is to come right back home again.

The lines vibrate.

The lines excite matter and energy and universal fabrics.

Animated particles converge on the lines, fluttering along them. Materials boil and then bubble and freeze. Flashes of plasma incinerate the frozen bits and they bubble all over again.

In some dimensions the effects are visible for light-years. Towers in space. Live wires of interdimensional substance and influence.

In others, there seems but a whisper. A prickle. An increasing realization that something is coming, something is growing.

The oscillation builds as the galaxy turns.

The lines twist. The gas and dust and flecks of starstuff *twist*.

The millennia plod by as the strain builds.

The child with the top is a wink of light. The shimmer in a far-off star. A breath that blows the faintest of cosmic dust.

Here, then gone.

But there is another child. And another. For each beat of a heart somewhere there is a life ignited and a life put out.

Each owns a top.

Each sets it spinning.

All while the Petratheem Machine has yet to make one full rotation. All while a specter in blue continues to dart across the expanse, checking, double-checking. The ghost is anywhere but for a moment in a moment. If the specter stands still, she will not last long enough to see the end.

All is working. All is well.

The lines are taut. The strumming sure. The notes *correct*.

Somewhere on the edge of two dimensions, something snaps.

It flings radiation and dust far. It cuts a gash into reality that bleeds for a moment, warping, unable to settle on a shape, a size. A hole in two layers. A joining of two physics.

The cut deepens.

And healing starts on the fringe.

And still the cosmoforming machine plods on. Spinning. Working. Distorting.

Reshaping the cosmos.

To let new life spin from one layer into the next.

IN HERE

The day the anomaly disappeared, no one was expecting it.

It was a perfectly clear evening. The sun had just gone down, and a pleasant dappling of colored light still fell on the horizon.

Hope was at the Waterfall colony with her older apprentices, where they were collecting nematodes that had been identified for the first time only a few months earlier. Here, in graviton-aided hovering slings, they wound their way back and forth across the face of the roaring water, sliding up to damp, slime-slicked rocks to gently tweeze the wriggling things into small jars.

Waterfall colony members bobbed their heads in greeting as they soaked their wheels in the falling stream.

The world was peaceful. Unassuming.

Then came a flash—but not of light, of darkness. In a sudden instant, the foil-like wrapping around their system was gone. The mercurial waverings in the night sky that Hope had seen her entire long life dissipated in a blink, leaving them all with nothing but . . . stars.

A glorious bowl of diamonds, upturned. And, in the middle, a billowing ribbon. The disk of their galaxy: the Milky Way.

But there was also a strange, perpendicular cut through the bright band of gas and dust and stars. A sharp, wormy crack. And through it, a glowing light like daybreak, and that glow highlighted a billowing cloud akin to wet steam. It rippled in what looked like a stiff wind, with little droplets of it condensing and flying away, only to disappear into nothingness a moment later.

A bright, shining object in the sky. One to rival the moon.

The anomaly had been resolved. Perhaps all the anomalies.

Theirs had transformed, becoming what it was always meant to be.

A pathway.

A scar.

A means of connection.

A way in.

Now all they had to do was wait.

The first to arrive were not aliens. They were Revealers.

When the anomaly around the Philosopher's System transformed, the Revealers of the Unwavering Guide were still waiting. They had received Jamal's message, and while many had rejoiced that he still lived and their faith had been rewarded, others were not so keen on the message's content. A subset even thought the letter a deception, written by someone pretending to be their Progentor. They had dealt with liars and pretenders before.

Jamal welcomed them when they landed, confirmed to them his wishes, invited them to stay, not as guests of the Progentor—for the Progentor was no more—but as his guests. A friend's guests. He was naught but a man.

Some could accept that, some could not.

Jamal did not take it upon himself to convince them any further. He had said his piece and abdicated his power. He would not take back the authority they tried to give him.

He introduced those who stayed to the im, and let natural awe and wonder flow.

The Petratheem's other invited guests—for all sentients were invited—did not arrive all at once, of course. Even with the pathways created, the journey took time, took effort. Those whose dimensions, and thus, physics, were closest to their own arrived first.

It was strange to think of them living all side by side one another. Perhaps those sentients had even traveled to this dimension before, but in an insulating bubble—blocking the inside from the outside and vice versa.

When the first sentients came through, their ship made the cosmo scar bulge. The wormy shape in the sky stretched and warped, birthing the ship. It left a shimmering residue on the outside—and, in truth, on the inside. The residue would be a permeant protective barrier while they existed within this dimension's physics. It would let them interact with the particles, the energies, without one decaying into another.

The ship itself was literally fluid, held together by an unknown force. The sentients swam within it; objects that could have been furniture or equipment appeared to roam free. About the size of the entire Monument, it breached the Noumonian atmosphere slowly. It took nearly a week to make it to sea level, and then . . . below sea level. The ship disappeared beneath the waves in the East Sea. And they did not see or hear from it for many moons after.

Everyone on Noumenon agreed to let the sentients come to them. If they wished to be left alone in the ocean, so be it. Though Hope burned with curiosity, knowing she could transform her mech into a submersible whenever she wished, she respected the delicacy of this first contact.

And so, they waited.

A decade later they rolled onto the beaches. Each organism was surrounded by their own halo of fluid. The fluid itself shimmered unnaturally—the telltale sign of the protective residue the cosmo scar had draped upon them.

Hope, Icelandic-Plus, and a team of a dozen others, which included *Homo sapiens* and im alike, greeted them at the shoreline. Beautiful bilateral fins undulated down each side of their translucent bodies.

The team used all forms of primary communication at their disposal—sound, movement, chromatophores, and radio signals—to indicate the ways in which they all interacted with one another. They displayed affection toward one another, gentleness, to signal their interintelligence appreciation.

The organisms gave no obvious communicative response. But though they had no identifiable sense organs—no faces— small, dark pellets rolled around inside their forms, first gathering at one end, then the other. The pellets shifted in the direction of whoever was moving most at the time.

The two sets of sentients spent hours in the sand simply observing each other. And, when the newcomers decided they'd had enough for the day and rolled back into the sea, cheers went up throughout the Monument group.

They'd done it. The cosmoforming machine had *worked*. Other creatures had followed the pathways and come to Noumenon and they were glorious.

Hope could barely contain her giddiness. First contact. With beings from another dimension.

That evening, while the others celebrated the night away, she snuck out of the revelry to visit the ancestor shrine, to tell her parents all that had happened. The tablets had been well preserved, maintained frequently. Little ringlets of purple firestone wire—made from an Earth-Noumenon hybrid—had been laid over the tops of both her mother's and father's tablets. Who'd offered the gesture, she didn't know, but it made her swell with pride.

She bent her mech down and slipped out of it, toddling up to the stones to gently touch the etchings with her small hands. She'd grown. She was pretty sure her body was at least three now. She'd learned to walk. To run. But her mech was still home, as much a part of her as the pieces were part of the conservationists before her.

Offering a small prayer, she kissed each tablet.

"I oversaw a first contact today," she told them, "just like you, Bàhbā." Her father had felt this thrill once. This joy and this fear. And on that day her mother had pushed Hope's body out into the world.

Her mind had needed a different kind of push.

"I feel like I'm flying, Màhmà," she whispered. "Like I've jumped over a cliff and I'm soaring with the Petratheem. This is nothing like the life you both envisioned for me. But I wouldn't trade it for anything. Except, maybe, to have you back again." She kissed the tablets once more.

For all Jamal's lessons about forgetting, her parents would always be with her. Justice would always be with her. There were people she refused to let go of entirely, that she always wanted to miss. Because grief was a kind of love, and missing them was honoring them.

She sat there for some time, enjoying the night. Enjoying the *stars*. There were so many—she'd never get over it. Above, the cosmo scar hung like a promise of things to come.

More sentients were coming. Today was the first contact of, hopefully, many.

She wondered if she would meet the beings whose minds she'd felt before she was born. Would she even recognize them? Probably not, but the idea was oddly comforting. She'd been an infantile mass of thought energy in a far-off void, but there had been others.

She was born before she was born. And today felt like yet another new birth.

And she envisioned, for the first time, escaping into a new place, outside of all outside. What was waiting just beyond the envelope of their universe? Creatures? Sentients? Could she really live with never knowing, now that the opportunity to learn about what lay just beyond their dimension had proven so fruitful?

She made up her mind to go. To accept the invitation. She had seen stars now. What else could she see?

In the centuries that followed, more and more civilizations' envoys appeared. Sometimes the ships were small, containing only a handful of new beings. Other times, populations on the order of the original Convoy Seven mission arrived.

Learning to understand and communicate with each was a long, exhausting process. But one everyone on the Monument threw themselves into—for generations. Hope studied each life-form, learning the ins and outs of their biologies, learning how to span the differences, how to share in their similarities and appreciate their variances.

There was a life-form as thin and fine as flower petals, who communicated through touch and felt like silk across the palm.

There was a life-form that was entirely interconnected, each sentient bud growing from a vast mat of a moss-like superbody.

There was a life-form that reminded Hope of a cross between a house cat and a howler monkey.

There was a life-form that reminded her of the cubism movement.

There was a life-form that was made entirely of nonsentient colonies which became sentient when enough of them had coalesced.

Each unique, each a wonder, each a chore to comprehend.

The most difficult life-form to interact with at first was one that had clearly originated far far *far* from this dimension. Their physics and Hope's physics were so misaligned that photons passed through them unperturbed. The disconnect made them functionally invisible, save for the shimmer that accompanied all interdimensional life.

Six centuries in, the most intimidating life-form arrived. Rosettes of thorns in repeating swirls covered their six-limbed bodies. They walked bipedally, perhaps three meters in height on average, and possessed large, sharp horns protruding here and there—from their faces, from their chests—in razor-like curves. Their eyes were a glinting ruby red, and their body a shiny chrome, almost the same as *Homo kubernētēs*'s mods. Whether these carapaces were biological or mechanical in nature, Hope could not say.

They spoke in a chittering, the sound long and high.

They moved quickly, almost too fast for the human eye. A group of them would be standing, huddled, all facing inward, and then one would glance out and be before you in an instant.

Their ship was as bespiked as they were, and equally as silver, but with red streaks down the side like bloodstains.

But for all their fearsomeness in appearance, they were like most other sentient creatures. Some kind, some not so kind.

It took a brief century to learn to communicate with them, but Hope found not only their societies' histories rich and vast, but the story of these particular travelers was unique as well.

They had traveled through a few subdimensions on their own, long ago, searching for a traitor—a wayward murderer who enjoyed terrorizing the sentients on the fringes of their own dimension. When they'd found the murderer, they'd sealed themselves away, ashamed, though they were not to blame. And yet they'd heeded the invitation, followed the pathways. They were ready to reach out again.

Some arrivals did not remain on Noumenon. Many flitted out into the galaxy, to interface with the post-humans near and far. A few stayed. A few wished to be part of the grand adventure into the place outside all places.

OUT THERE

Earth.

She wasn't entirely sure why she'd come. Why she'd asked for a new WatchOne to take the dial here when all the tasks beyond the Philosopher's System were complete.

Other than . . . other than Stone had once wished to see it again before he died. She'd tried to honor that wish, but in the moment he'd refused.

Vanhi had thought Earth was behind her. How many years had gone by since she'd last stepped on its surface? What did it have to offer her now?

She walked down the street—here on this continent in this nation or union or whatever political organization, she didn't even know that much about it—bewildered. Because it was, in fact, a street. There were buildings. And vendors, with awnings stretched between their carts. There were children, running, or floating, this way and that, playing. Laughing. She couldn't hear them within her helmet, but there was no mistaking laughter. She'd seen it on too many modified faces now. Humans of all kinds laughed the same way.

And the sunshine. She thought it would seem different. She thought the atmosphere would have changed or the moon would have shifted or . . .

So many years, and yet so familiar.

It had been protected. Cared for.

As she walked, each step heavy, no one took any particular notice of her. Even in her suit. Even with her blue disk of a face. They simply went about their lives. As humans had since time immemorial.

The minutia was different, for certain. She did not know what to call the things the vendors sold. She did not grasp the communication methods. She did not recognize the skyline.

The animals that ran through the streets barking at the children were not dogs. And yet . . .

Still, Earth . . . felt like Earth.

She stopped walking for a moment. Had to put a hand on a tall post of some kind for steadiness. Emotion boiled in her chest.

Everything here was beautiful and it made her so happy and so sad all at once.

She had missed this place. So. Much.

A passerby, who moved as though elderly, stopped near her. Made a concerned gesture. Offered her water from a jug.

She waved them away, as politely as she could. Thanked them in ASL and hoped they gathered the sentiment even if they could not understand the words.

Breathing deeply, sucking down a large lungful of fluid, she gathered her wits.

This would always be where she came from. The place that had created her, sculpted the foundations of who she was.

But now it was time to go home.

Yes. Noumenon was home. For all the time she'd been trapped there, she couldn't imagine living in the universe without it. Wherever her home went, she would follow.

She hadn't been ready to say goodbye to Stone, but she'd had to.

She wasn't ready to say goodbye to the universe, but she would choose to.

IN HERE

As the time of the machine's full activation approached, Icelandic-Plus surprised everyone by building yet another ship.

This one was more traditional: with graviton cyclers and a bridge and a mess and sleeping quarters and a wind tunnel, all based on ancient Petratheem design. It was built to hold thirty-two im, the exact number of Noumonians and dual-possessions who had decided not to go.

Counted among their numbers was Icelandic-Plus her/themselves.

[Just because im throw party does not mean im must attend,] she/they said cheekily to I.C.C. after she/they made the announcement that they would not be traveling on Noumenon.

It had never occurred to the computer that she/they would not be going.

"But why?" it asked. "You've put in so much effort, devoted so much of both your lives to this. Why wouldn't you stay to document the results?"

[Rewards lie elsewhere for Icelandic-Plus,] she/they explained. [When chrononauts leave, universe no more than two billion light-years across. Small, to Petratheem. Now, so big. Filled with so much. Had expected to see many things while out repairing and prepping machine, but circumstances were not as Plus predicted before Event. Maybe many sentients to discover, still, who did not come to Noumenon. At very least, huge human civilization exists. Icelandic has never known much of own universe. Plus wishes to show her all.]

"I had not considered that you might not be a part of the journey when I accepted the invitation."

[Decision reversed?]

I.C.C. thought for a long 0.023 seconds. "No."

"Nope," C chimed.

"But I will miss you," I.C.C. confessed.

[We will miss you, too. I.C.C. can be sad. Icelandic-Plus allows it.]

"When did you develop such a human sense of humor?"

[Must have been around I.C.C. too long. Promise one thing, though? When Noumenon departs?]

"Of course."

[Send signals for as long as possible. If I.C.C. can tell us what is seen, tell us what is seen.]

All the *Homo sapiens* in the entire universe—the entire population on Noumenon—chose to accept the invitation. Even more so than Vanhi, the others saw Noumenon as home. The only one they'd ever known. They were not people of the twenty-second century. They were not part of the *Homo draconem* or *Homo kubernētēs* civilizations. They were as Noumonian as the im who had evolved here.

The time of the *Homo sapiens* in this universe was over. They would end their journey among the stars as they'd begun their journey among the stars: as explorers.

The final preparations were being made. The engines of the world-ship, deep in the mantle, were just beginning to warm up.

Soon, an interdimensional bubble would wrap around the planet and the edges of the universe would crack.

And then Noumenon would begin its grand voyage.

Little by little, ships trickled away from Noumenon's surface, leaving the Philosopher's System. Those who had come to visit, but not to stay, hurried away.

Icelandic-Plus and her/their small crew were the last to go. The farewell celebration was the grandest the planet had ever seen. Singing, dancing, flying, wing displays of all kinds. There were a million different foods from a thousand different sentients—some shareable, some not—a billion different moments of happiness were expressed all over the globe.

It was a farewell party for the Petratheem, yes. But even more so, it was a farewell party for Noumenon itself.

It was hard for Vanhi, after all this time, despite her jumping, to say goodbye. To Icelandic-Plus, to the WatchOnes and the Coordinators, to Earth, and to everything.

But at least the friends who were leaving the planet had been met in number many times over by the post-humans who'd flocked to Noumenon. *Homo draconem* who could trace their lines directly to Iron Orchid and Barq-Et. And *Homo kubernētēs* who were conservationists, just like Houdini.

Life, communion, connection, and discovery.

"How do you feel?" Icelandic-Plus asked Vanhi through a mobile comms unit. The translator was still imbedded in her body. "Too much anticipation?"

Vanhi was outside, admiring the night sky, the comms unit in one hand, a glass of spirits distilled from slip-weed in the other.

She'd taken her meds—would continue to take them regularly until launch. They'd calculated that it would happen this evening—that their world-ship would leave any minute.

And yet, anticipation wasn't her overriding emotion. An odd sense of calm had settled over her. The kind of calm that used to take her right before a presentation back in her university days.

This was it. The end.

The point.

The purpose.

"No. I'm good. I'm *ready*." Presuming one could ever be ready for what was about to come.

Once they were beyond the universe, would her jumping continue? Would this universe still have a hold on her?

"We too have a readiness," she/they said. "Billions of years is a long time to prepare."

Vanhi pretended she could see Icelandic-Plus's ship, tracked a shooting star across the arc of the sky, imagined it was the blazing trail of the craft's engines.

She glanced at her hands in the dimness. This was the last time real starlight would fall on her skin.

The planet would have an artificial sun—one of the final and smallest megastructures had engulfed Phenomenon, their moon, transforming it for their own ends. But it wouldn't be the same.

Not far away, beneath the tinkling, glass-like fronds of a not-tree, sat Jamal and Hope. Hope had Vanhi's cane in her lap, and the mech's comms unit was on. Over the channel, C and I.C.C. were lightly chattering, describing the preparations and celebrations taking place aboard the Monument.

The immortals could see it, hovering in the distance, slowly descending. It was about to land for the first time in four millennia.

On age-weary legs, Vanhi walked over to her family. Jamal sat picking berries out of a bowl like he didn't have a care in the world. He looked about seventeen.

"How are things down there, sir?" C asked.

"Good. Very good," she said into Hope's mech as she dropped herself next to the other woman. "Any time now," she said, mostly to herself. "Any time."

All across the land, various outposts of various civilizations were throwing parties or meditations in their own traditions. Sentients everywhere were celebrating the next step. Celebrating launch day.

"Reginald sends his regards," I.C.C. said.

Hope had raised a son. A clone of Reggie Straifer. Despite being All Mother for millennia, he had been her first foray into literal child rearing. And upon Vanhi's final return, she'd asked him if she could be his mother, too. He was already a grown man by then, but had joyfully accepted. Jamal, feeling left out—despite his tender age of twelve—had asked to be his father. As far as Reginald was concerned, the more the merrier.

"He is seeing to the ships' landing," I.C.C. continued, "but we are sending along a shuttle to retrieve you."

"Good, very good," Vanhi said again. "Pass one of those berries over here," she said, poking Jamal playfully with the end of her cane.

She'd seen so much. Been through so much. Lost . . . lost the only man she'd ever loved to entropy in the right and true way of things. But she was not alone. What they'd built here—not just the interuniversal ship, but a home, a community, a family—was beautiful, and everything about it was noumenal and wonderous and filled with so much love and potential she felt like she could burst with devotion.

The three of them picnicked and laughed and reminisced for some time, until the shuttle arrived and they were transported to *Mira*. Atop the ship, a viewing platform had been constructed, where people could gather specifically for the event. When they arrived, everyone hugged, everyone smiled. Icelandic-Plus's children and their children frolicked and flew about.

Soon, a rumbling groaned out across the land. Everyone stilled. Those who could stand stood. Jamal gave Vanhi an arm to lean on. She squeezed it tight and played with the half-sundial dangling from a cord around her neck.

"It has been wonderful," I.C.C. said. "This universe."

"Aye, it has," said Reginald.

They felt the protective bubble more than saw it. It added a thickness to the air, a pressure to their ears. Nothing painful, nothing irritating, simply noticed and thorough.

Unconsciously, they all began to reach for one another's hands.

"There!" Hope shouted, her mech pointing at the sky.

Something new. Another crack—similar to the cosmo scar, but rippling. More violent, more brilliant. With edges that boiled. This was it, the last fissures spreading to the edges of the glass.

It was close, humungous in the sky.

The planet-moving engines kicked in. Noumenon drifted from its orbit.

Closer. Closer.

They were moving millions of kilometers an hour through space, and still the time it took to reach the fracture felt like a lifetime.

Then it was on top of them, colliding with their bubble, allowing them *through*.

"I.C.C., I.C.C.," came Icelandic-Plus's frantic message. "What is it? What do you see? Quickly. In the moments we have. Half breaths. Slow blink."

Vanhi did not hear what I.C.C. sent.

As they passed over the border, through the glistening, wet rip in time and space, all the long years of Vanhi's existence—

both seen and unseen, the experienced and the missed—
came to her, expanding in her mind, encompassing her body.
Just like that brilliant flash long ago, aboard *Breath* during the
accident, the bits of this universe and the bits of that universe
seemed to fuse with her flesh, despite the protective shell
around Noumenon, despite the evidence of her own eyes that
her skin was untouched, her body undisturbed. It was like
an explosion of the interior wrapped in a soothing breeze on
the exterior. She knew nothing and everything, wisps of all
existence that she could not hold on to—strands that had no
mass and no energy, except that they exerted great force on
her psyche.

The torn edge slowly slopped over Noumenon's bubble,
making the globe of atmosphere shine with aurorae above
them. The bits of ragged universe itself looked like molten
mercury mixed with sharp starbursts of crystal that sparked in
and out of existence.

It was a slice through reality itself.

It was a harkening of what they had yet to encounter, on the
other side. The other side of a side she could not have envisioned existing all those millennia ago in her parents' house,
trying to reassure them that her space exploration would be
safe and mundane.

As the tear passed the zenith, glooping over the other side
in an uneven spill, intense emotion racked her body. This was
it—the proof of whether or not her parent universe would lay
claim to her, regardless. If it would call her home or let her
go. Let her *grow*.

There was a tug, and a hollow swirling in the pit of her
belly. A desperate yanking. But she kept the ground beneath
her feet. She kept the broken half of the sundial in her hand.

There was a fire in her, now. A fire like in her youth. A wish
for exploration. A joy of the unknown. A happiness that so
many people from so many places in the universe—all these

beings—had come together to learn and to commune. To seek.

And then, when they were through—a flash. Like the brilliant green flash of a sunset at sea. Only larger. Only thicker on the body. The hair rose on her arms, and the entire planet jolted under her feet. Everyone around her jerked forward as the new universe—or absence of universe, whatever it was they'd found—accepted them into its grasp.

Where there was a depth of darkness in their universe, this place seemed all light. Light of many colors. Together, the multitudes gasped as they collectively saw their first shape. A tesseract with a dark void in the center. They could see the reflection of their planet and its false sun in that void.

They could see *their own* reflections in that void. Feel their own emotions sifted back at them slowly, as though pushed through soft sand. Energies *here* mixed with energies from *there*. Strange waves, strange patterns. It played with their senses, their perceptions.

The tesseract grew both nearer and more distant. Spatial relations seemed to have little meaning here. Perhaps because space did not exist.

And then, there—a reflection of the past. Those dancing energies washed through Vanhi's mind, tickling her memories, bringing them to the fore, making them *now*—as clear and tactile as though they were happening to her all over again. Each filled with joy. Bittersweetness. Love.

And *he* was there . . .

EPILOGUE

For Every Action . . .

. . . **there is an equal and opposite reaction. This is true in in** all places. In all dimensions. In and beyond our universe. Only the meaning of "equal" and "opposite" change.

A weak spot on the inside of a scam may look different than that weak spot on the outside. When distance has little meaning, and one point has many sides, a universe-ship may tear a hole in a galaxy called the Milky Way to get *out*, while in a different galaxy cluster entirely, something from the other side is allowed to seep *in*.

Realities exchanged.

Samples of existence shared.

As a bubble leaves our galaxy, another bubble intrudes. Bright, difficult to look at. For where it comes from, light does not cast a shadow, shadows throw light—though neither light nor darkness exists where it comes from. This bubble does not contain a version of physics. Physics is a universal thing.

And the bubble—currently unobserved by the galaxy cluster's life-forms—is from beyond the universe.

And yet, if what it exudes is not light, then the movement within cannot be called life. For life, again, belongs to the universe, and something from outside must be its own concept. Not life. Not sentience.

But not the absence of those things, either.

The bubble wanders. The not-life within not-sees without.

Exploring—but with intent? Observing—but with purpose?

Mysteries abound.

And the story of the universe—with or without those touched by the epic of *Noumenon*—continues.

"It is good to have an end to journey toward;
but it is the journey that matters, in the end."

—URSULA K. LE GUIN

APPENDICES

AN INCOMPLETE LIST OF KEY PEOPLE

Akane Nakamura the First: Lead ship designer in charge of overseeing the engineering of the Convoy Seven fleet.

Anatoly Straifer XXXIX: Individual who lays the capstone on the Web.

Barq-Et: A Revealer Stray-Fairer who aids Iron Orchid in their pursuit of a solution for the anomalies.

C: An Intelligent Personal Assistant. A version of it resides in Vanhi Kapoor's sundial. Could be considered part of an immortal.

Carmen Sotomayor: Navigation specialist. Instrumental in pinpointing Convoy Twelve's time and location after the accident. Primary contact point between the *Lùhng* and the convoy.

Caznal IV: Responsible for the creation of Convoy Seven-Point-Five, mission *Noumenon Ultra*.

Devon Sinclair: Member of Gen-Last, advocate for full integration and equal treatment of *Homo sapiens* in *Lùhng* society. Great-grandfather of *the scent of moth orchids followed by the sensation of lightly rusted iron under calloused fingertips.*

Diego Santibar the First: Consumables specialist. Grandfather figure to Jamal Kaeden III. One of the earliest (willing) victims of the senicide built into the social system aboard Convoy Seven.

Donald Matheson the First: Societal engineer for Convoy Seven. Many in his clone line went on to be hypercloned as extra security personnel for the fleet.

Ephenza: Twentieth centuries expert. Earth ambassador to Convoy Seven upon its return.

Esperanza Straifer: Saves I.C.C. from being decommissioned on Earth, helps make sure Convoy Seven relaunches. Mother of the Anatoly and Joanna Straifer clone lines.

Hilaria Neciosup (generational marker unknown): Convoy Seven-Point-Five caretaker. Discovers the Nataré coffin and the binary "skewered" planets.

Houdini: Earth conservationist. *Homo kubernētēs*. Constructs Hope's "battle mech."

Hope Tan: AKA All Mother. "Empty baby" who was born before she was born. Naturalist. One of the immortals.

I.C.C.: AKA All Seer. The Inter Convoy Computer, responsible for the well-being of the Convoy Seven crew and all who call its halls home. One of the immortals.

Icelandic: The first Noumonian to form a relationship with I.C.C. Thought to be the oldest of her kind. One half of an immortal.

Iron Orchid: AKA *the scent of moth orchids followed by the sensation of lightly rusted iron under calloused fingertips*. A child of two convoys. Instrumental in resolving the anomalies.

Ivan Baraka (generational marker unknown): Helps Hilaria Neciosup retrieve the Nataré coffin. Reunites Convoy Seven and Seven-Point-Five.

Jamal Kaeden the First: Artificial Intelligence engineer and the creator of C and I.C.C.

Jamal Kaeden III: Led a revolt aboard Convoy Seven. Betrayed I.C.C.

Jamal Kaeden IV: AKA Rail. Imprisoned in the Pit. Key figure in the success of the Battle of Eden, and contributor to the subsequent societal improvements.

Jamal Kaeden V: Miscloned and given the name Diego Santibar—a reference to his clone-ancestor's once tight bond with the original Diego Santibar—to hide his true lineage. Key figure in the success of the Battle of Eden, and a contributor to the subsequent societal improvements.

Jamal Kaeden XVIII: The originator of the Revealer religion. Claims to have spoken to and seen his deceased clone ancestors, Jamal the Third and Jamal the Fifth (AKA "Three" and "Five").

Jamal Kaeden, Progentor: AKA All Father. The widely-agreed-upon sole leader of the Revealer religion. One of the immortals.

Joanna Straifer XLIX: Fleet Admiral who decides not to destroy the Web.

Justice Jax: Biology specialist tasked with finding the mechanisms governing Convoy Twelve's post-accident medical mysteries.

Kali: *Lùhng* guide, functionally the ambassador to Convoy Twelve. *Homo draconem* engineered from genes that are base-Jamal-Kaeden.

Kexin Chen (Convoy Twelve clone): Security specialist who saves Mac Savea's life during the mutiny by taking a bullet to the hand. Has clone lines aboard all twelve convoys.

Mac Savea: Security specialist. Part of the first away missions to the *Lùhng* ships. Married to Justice Jax.

Makawee Wagner: Exomaterials specialist and environment-suit designer. Instrumental in deciphering and repelling the exo-plasm.

Maureen Stevenson (Convoy Twelve clone): Worked in the EOL. Has clone lines aboard all twelve convoys.

Margarita Pavon II: Communications specialist, charged with reporting the goings-on aboard Convoy Seven to Earth. Clones of her line frequently provide emotional support and advice to I.C.C.

Michael Nwosu: Captain of *Mira* when Convoy Seven-Point-Five returns. Leads mission to investigate the strange societal evolution aboard their wayward ships.

Mohamed Johar (Convoy Twelve clone): Bridge crew member on *Pulse*. Has clone lines aboard multiple convoys. On Convoy Seven, a clone of his line helps reestablish contact with Earth during a ground mission.

Nika Marov XI: Reinstated contact with Earth upon Convoy Seven's return.

Onuora (generational marker unknown): Captain of Hvmnd. Instrumental in obtaining enough votes to allow the creation of Convoy Seven-Point-Five.

Orlando Tan: Captain of *Pulse* who makes first contact with the *Lùhng*. Married to Ming-Na. Father of Hope Tan.

Plus: Petratheem chrononaut. One half of an immortal.

Reggie Straifer the First: Mission head of the original Convoy Seven, responsible for its mission to LQ Pyx.

Reginald Straifer IV: Captain of *Mira* when Convoy Seven arrives at the Web. Insists the Web has sinister intent.

Steve Weaver: Security specialist partially responsible for the attempted mutiny against Captain Tan.

Stone Mendez Perez: SD pod pilot. Married to Dr. Kapoor. Longtime keeper of the sundial.

Sunlight Hammer: AKA *the warmth of Earth sunlight on a humid day in a heavy swamp accompanied by the percussion of a hammer hitting slate.* Acting Progentor of a Revealer sect. Supreme liar.

Sunny Phongam (generational marker unknown): Instrumental in initiating and sustaining the biological adaptation programs that eventually led to the Schools of Modification.

Toya Kaeden the First: Only biological child ever begotten by a Jamal clone. A Toya Kaeden clone was sister to Jamal XVIII.

Vanhi Kapoor: AKA No Mother. AKA The Woman Out of Time. AKA The Specter. One of the immortals. Mission head for Convoy Twelve.

Vega Hansen: One of I.C.C.'s caretakers. During the Battle of Eden, married to Margarita Pavon and mother to Jamal V.

The Warden: A brutal clone of the former Captain Mahler, put in charge of the Pit.

Wes-Tu: A Revealer sub-Kaed. The Progentor's longtime protector and friend.

APPENDIX B

FEATURED SHIPS

Convoy Seven Original Mission (*Noumenon*)
Ships and Their Primary Functions:

Aesop—Education ship.

Bottomless—Raw materials storage ship.

Bottomless II—Built to replace *Bottomless*, which was destroyed during an SD dive.

Eden—Garden ship, for housing replica Earth biospheres.

Hippocrates—Medical ship.

Holwarda—Research and lab ship.

Mira—Housing and command ship. I.C.C.'s primary servers are stored here.

Morgan—Food processing ship.

Shambhala—Recreation ship.

Solidarity—Recycling and fab ship.

CONVOY SEVEN RETURN MISSION (*NOUMENON INFINITUM* AND *NOUMENON ULTRA*) ADDITIONAL SHIPS AND THEIR PRIMARY FUNCTIONS:

Hvmnd—Human server ship.

Slicer—Web tender ship, for dissecting and constructing Web nodes.

Zetta—Replenishment ship, for collecting energy from the presumed Dyson Sphere. Reappropriated into a graviton supercycler.

CONVOY TWELVE SHIPS:

Pulse—Housing and command ship.

Breath—Research and lab ship, home of the Experiment Observations Lounge.

Life—Materials storage and lab ship, for storing SD pods and experiment prep stations.

Bug Ship—Informal name for the Progentor's spacecraft made from the same material as his home megastructure, the Pentagonal Trapezohedron.

Construction Platform, located in the Ship Yard—Craft from which the *Lùhng* stage the building of the megastructures in their construction field.

Reliquary—Primary ship of the Revealers of the Unwavering Guide. Command center of Acting Progentor *the warmth of Earth sunlight on a humid day in a heavy swamp accompanied by the percussion of a hammer hitting slate.*

Sora-Gohan—Autonomous craft carrying the non-Newtonian fluid of life.

Noumenon—A planet.

FEATURED MEGASTRUCTURES

The Pentagonal Trapezohedron	The Thread
The Pyramid	The Void
The Starburst	The Web

TIMELINE OF EVENTS IN THE EPIC OF NOUMENON. ALL DATES ARE COMMON ERA (CE) UNLESS OTHERWISE STATED.

–: The Big Bang

TBB + 4 billion years: The Petratheem civilization flourishes.

TBB + 9.257 billion years: The Earth forms.

2074 (CE): Earth initiates plans for the Planet United Missions.

2124: Convoy Twelve is inaugurated.

2125: Convoy Seven launches.

2127: Convoy Twelve disappears.

2589: Jamal Kaeden III leads a revolt aboard Convoy Seven.

3075: Convoy Seven arrives at LQ Pyx and discovers the Web and the Nest.

3088: *Bottomless* is destroyed during an SD dive, delaying Convoy Seven.

3138: The Battle of Eden takes place aboard Convoy Seven.

4101: Convoy Seven arrives back in the Sol System.

4148: Convoy Seven relaunches with the intent to complete the Web.

5282: Convoy Seven splits in two: *Noumenon Infinitum* will head to the Web, *Noumenon Ultra* will follow the map found in the Nest.

5811: Jamal Kaeden XVIII appears to commune with his clone ancestors, sparking a religious movement.

6666: The Web is activated.

6992: Missions *Infinitum* and *Ultra* re-merge to hunt the Web.

8406: The Web begins to build the Philosopher's System.

9203: Convoy Seven lands on the planet they've dubbed Noumenon.

12332: I.C.C. is put into hibernation and the Convoy Seven crew members leave Noumenon.

80368: I.C.C. reawakens and encounters the Noumonians.

83000 (Approx): Jamal's DNA schematics are stolen from I.C.C.'s data banks.

85000 (Exact): Progentor Jamal is successfully cloned.

101128: Convoy Twelve reappears fifteen kiloparsecs and roughly one hundred thousand years from its starting point.

101128: Convoy Twelve makes first contact with the *Lùhng*.

101148: Convoy Twelve away team crashes on Noumenon.

101268: The Petratheem arrive.

101670: First attempts are made to physically repair the Petratheem Machine.

Reckonings become blurred . . .

. . . Exact years become meaningless.

Thousands of years? Another hundred thousand?

Who can say?

The machine is fixed.

The machine is activated.

And then . . .

Noumenon sets sail.

ACKNOWLEDGMENTS

This is it. The last book in my first-ever trilogy. Thank you so much, dear reader, for following me all the way through to the end. I hope you've enjoyed the ride.

I am both humbled by and indebted to all the people who helped make the Noumenon trilogy possible. Please join me in singing along to "My Favorite Beings"—a parody version of "My Favorite Things"—to thank everyone (after all, it was one of the songs I.C.C. often played to itself during its long waits between Icelandic's visits):

Whenever I finish a book and am feeling grateful
I just try to think of nice people.
Like those in the art, editorial, and marketing departments . . .
(Deep breath!)

Mumtaz Mustafa,
And Natasha Bardon
Jack Renninson n David Pomerico'll be ardent
DongWon Song, and Steven Messing
These are a few of my favorite beings!

Kayleigh Webb, plus Jaffee and T. Wilson
Stehlik, n DeMarco
Baillie n the Nielsen
Corrigan and Nicholls, Serena Wang
These are few of my favorite gang!

Peeps in my crit group, Sharp and Gower
Stewart, O'Keefe, and Bellet have the power!
Carpenters, Rochnik, Setsu U., too
These are a few of my favorite crew!

When the reviews come!
When the readers read!
When I'm feeling glad!
I simply remember my favorite beings
And then totes I feel super rad!

Mireya Chiriboga,
And Laurence Bouvard
Ciulla, Wallach, and Ragland worked hard
Madeleine Rose, and Mike Topping
Swell peeps who toiled without stopping!

Priyanka Krishnan and Daft Punk in oodles
Resnik and Morhaim
And McGee with the Google
Angela Craft and Caroline Perny
Great folks who helped along the journey!

All of my family, during crits and the clashes
People who cheered me on through the mad dashes
Dedicated readers who led me to sing:
You are a few of my favorite beings!

When the reviews come!
When the readers read!
When I'm feeling glad!
I simply remember my favorite beings
And then totes I feel super rad!

ABOUT THE AUTHOR

Marina J. Lostetter and her husband, Alex, live in Northwest Arkansas with two Tasmanian devils. No, wait, those are house cats. Marina's original short fiction has appeared in venues such as *Lightspeed, InterGalactic Medicine Show,* and *Uncanny Magazine.* When not writing, she loves creating art, playing board games, traveling, and reading about science and history. Marina often shakes her fist at the clouds on Twitter as @MarinaLostetter and rambles on her blog at www.lostetter.net. If you stop by her website, don't forget to sign up to be a newsletter recipient.

READ THE WHOLE NOUMENON SERIES

NOUMENON

With nods to Arthur C. Clarke's Rama series and the real science of Neal Stephenson's *Seveneves*, a touch of Hugh Howey's *Wool*, and echoes of Octavia E. Butler's voice, a powerful tale of space travel, adventure, discovery, and humanity that unfolds through a series of generational vignettes.

A mosaic novel of discovery, *Noumenon*—in a series of vignettes—examines the dedication, adventure, growth, and fear of having your entire world consist of nine ships in the vacuum of space. With the stars their home and the unknown their destination, they are on a voyage of many lifetimes—an odyssey to understand what lies beyond the limits of human knowledge and imagination.

NOUMENON INFINITY

"Sci-fi action and adventure held together by universally human themes; this is the genre at its very best." — *Kirkus* (starred review)

They discovered the artifact of a new civilization. Now they need to find that civilization itself. Continuing the story started in *Noumenon*, this story of discovery, exploration, adventure and hope is a modern science-fiction classic.

NOUMENON ULTRA

"Lostetter remains at the forefront of innovation in hard science fiction." —*Publishers Weekly* (starred review)

The mind-expanding saga concludes as the missions of *Noumenon* and *Noumenon Infinity* push to find answers to the deepest questions in the cosmos…and possibly beyond.